"... a cyberpunk tale in the tradition of Neal Stephenson ... This is a very, very well-written book."

Medium

"The Babel Apocalypse is a thought-provoking and thrilling tale that explores the nuances of language in a compelling way, making it a great read for any keen linguist or language enthusiast."

Babel Magazine

"A great addition to the corpus of linguistic sci-fi."

Literary Ashland

THE DARK COURT

SONGS OF THE SAGE, BOOK 2

BY

VYVYAN EVANS

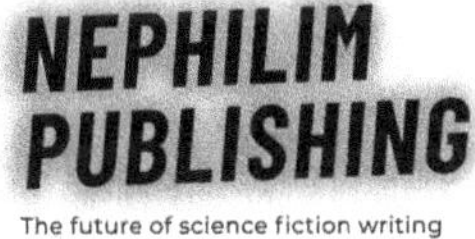

The future of science fiction writing

The future of science fiction writing

NEPHILIM PUBLISHING
Suite 82428
PO Box 6945
London, W1A 6US
United Kingdom

For all enquiries relating to this book, please visit the book series website:
www.songs-of-the-sage.com or email: info@songs-of-the-sage.com

A CIP catalogue record for this book is available from the British Library
Library of Congress Control Number: 2023912833
ISBN: 978-1-7399962-4-6 in paperback (print) format
ISBN: 978-1-7399962-5-3 in e-book (ePub) format
First published: May 2024
Typeset in England: Enhance Design Solutions

DISCLAIMER
While this is a work of speculative fiction, it is inspired by events, businesses, incidents, technologies, and theoretical concepts that have some basis in reality. Certain long-standing institutions, agencies, and public offices are mentioned, but the characters involved are wholly imaginary, as is this novel's story.

Books in the
SONGS OF THE SAGE series
(www.songs-of-the-sage.com)

THE BABEL APOCALYPSE, BOOK 1
THE DARK COURT, BOOK 2

Forthcoming

THE RISE OF THE MASHIACH, BOOK 3

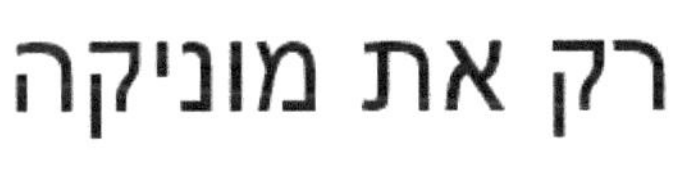

רק את מוניקה

*The Mind Chant of the Sage is a means
of coercive control, an addiction.*

Lilith Errapel King

*All hail the Sempiternal Ruler, our Sage, the oldest being in
the Elyonim, Head of the Council of the Quessoch. We proclaim
Your glorious splendor which protects, and banishes all the
spirits of the destroying angels, gaseous spirits of Satanael,
Watchers imprisoned in the Chaos. You are the revered keeper
of their somas, and protector of the Nunciature Evangelion. Oh
mighty Sage, our Majesty-on-High in the Tower of Songs, save
us from the dark power of the Mashiach, the she-demon, Lilith.*

The Mind Chant of the Quessoch Apostles
Translated into Unilanguage English (North American
Standard) from High Enochian

PROLOGUE

Lilith King's transformation occurred on her seventh birthday. That was the day of her *awakening*, in the parlance of the Sempiternals. It was a day cut out of mystery—a beginning and an ending.

Lilith rose early, excited—she knew her father would have a gift for her, something unexpected and perfect; he always did. Her father loved her beyond measure, and she knew it. But as she dressed hurriedly, foreboding also nagged at the back of her mind. The woman who was supposed to be her mother, Plamena, was to be removed, finally. To an asylum in Moesia, near her surviving family in Sofia.

"Family descendants," her father explained.

Lilith had the impression her mother was very old, although this was belied by her youthful mien—especially in the warmth of late-afternoon sun filtering into her chamber. In the rich yellow-orange light, Plamena's bedridden features were softened—her shadowed crow's feet disguised. The madness in her eyes was almost erased.

Lilith's father insisted it was for the best—more for his own benefit; the girl didn't need convincing. For the final few months, Lilith's mother was restrained to her bed rails, cloistered in the farthest chamber on the upper floor of their vast house. The doctor had ordered it, and her father had reluctantly consented, lest she attempted to harm Lilith again.

Lilith would sometimes spy on her father as he tended to her mother, through the open door, from the safe distance of the landing. She observed the softness in his eyes as he sat at her bedside.

"My Plamena," he would whisper, wiping the brow of the woman with the crazed expression—the eyes that sometimes rolled back and forth frenetically in their sockets, as if yanked to and fro by invisible steel wires.

For Lilith's part, her mother always scared her. Throughout her childhood, Lilith's mother had gradually deteriorated into a dribbling, catatonic mess. At least, until the crazy took hold of her. That's when her mother heard *the voices*, or so she claimed. That's when she became dangerous—when Lilith's very life was in danger.

Lilith feared it must be her fault—that she wasn't good enough, not deserving of a mother's love. Shouldn't a mother love their child? Shouldn't a daughter love their mother, rather than being terrified of her?

Once, Lilith ventured in, unobserved, while the nurse was away and her father was on a facecall in his grand study downstairs. She crept forward, hoping her mother might open her eyes and smile at her, tell her that she was loved. But her mother never did. And at each subsequent failed attempt to engage her mother, a little more of Lilith became broken inside, until she stopped trying.

As she entered the large drawing room downstairs, her father was already seated at the breakfast table that overlooked the ornamental garden at the rear of the house.

"My little seraph, my birthday girl," he called out, with a broad smile, as Lilith entered. She smiled too and ran toward him, arms outstretched, laughing. And as he held her, she leaned into his shoulder, taking in his distinctive smell. He squeezed her tight, longer than usual, as if he didn't wish to let her go. And as Lilith savored his warm embrace, she contentedly gazed out through the windows at the large garden beyond him, where strange shadows dwelled in the afternoon.

Lilith, her father, and her invalid-mother inhabited a very large villa in central Cambridge. Lilith vaguely understood her father was wealthy. But she also somehow knew, even at the age of seven, that he couldn't care less about material things. She was aware he wasn't the same as other men, different from other fathers. And he was famous, that she understood too, something to do with his medical research. Lilith adored him—he made her feel safe. She was his Lily, and always would be.

As a child, Lilith liked the sound of her father's pet name for her—seraph. She imagined it was an allusion to her temper, the flames of her outbursts that got her into trouble at school; Lilith had a prickly disposition even then, announced in advance to all and sundry by her shock of orange-red hair and startling green eyes—"nuclear green," as one teacher had once described them.

But as the years went by, the image that her pet name conjured, of wings on fire and the intimation of the angelic, made Lilith think of both rage and innocence. And later, at the age of twenty-three, after the Monster, any vestige she once had of innocence was gone. Afterward, all that remained was the rage.

In the drawing room on that day, Lilith was just a newly minted seven-year-old, excited and not in the least bit hungry. Once the serving unit had delivered breakfast, Lilith made a hurried, token effort at eating. Her father sighed as he glanced at her plate. So she fixed him with a defiant look, with her emerald-green eyes, and crossed her arms. It was *her* birthday after all.

And as he chuckled in response, she knew he had relented. Lilith hurriedly unwrapped the box, throwing open the lid. Inside was a pair of shiny, red leather brogues. She shook off her slippers and put them on, lacing up, chuckling with glee, despite the lack of socks. She hadn't expected this, but immediately decided she had longed for exactly these all along.

"Shall we go for a walk?" her father asked, while still studying the uneaten food on her plate.

"To test them?" Lilith asked, excitedly.

"To make sure they work," her father replied with a wink. But as he spoke, a shadow feathered his face. "No need for you to be here …" Lilith studied his haunted expression. She knew what he meant. The medical daemons would arrive soon, accompanied by her father's personal lawyer, to remove her mother in a medical transport. Lilith nodded, glancing down at her feet. She was ready.

"Do you want to say goodbye first?" he asked.

Lilith frowned and looked away. She examined the ornamental fountain in the middle of the small pond outside without responding, watching the blur of refracted morning light through droplets of water. Her father smiled at her faintly. "Get your jacket, I'll go up, say farewell for both of us …"

Outside, they walked through the streets of Cambridge, toward Grantchester Meadows. It was still early, but already warm. Once they reached the banks of the Cam, Lilith began skipping, holding her father's hand. Her shoes started to rub against one heel. She ignored the discomfort, glancing up at him. He smiled at her; she was happy.

"They'll be at the house now … She's going home at last, back to where she's from."

"Where are you from?" Lilith asked abruptly, seeking to shift his sadness away from a subject she didn't fully understand.

"I'm not from anywhere," he replied. "Too many places."

Lilith screwed up her eyes. Her father's answer made no sense. "But where were you born?"

"A cave," came his strange reply. Lilith closed her eyes for a moment, imagining somewhere dank and uncomfortable.

"Was it dark?"

"Not anymore," he replied. "Now it's a grotto full of candles, incense, and light." Lilith was confused. She glanced up at her father.

"What's a grotto?"

Her father stopped walking and gazed down at her. "A grotto is a sacred place."

"Did you live there with your mummy and daddy?" Lilith asked, using the Old Standard's lexicon and grammar—it was still years before Unilanguage's North American standard became the default variety of English in the Old Kingdom. Back then, Lilith was an unchipped nate, part of the transitional generation; she wouldn't have Universal Grammar tech implanted in her head until her eighteenth birthday.

"Just my mother," replied her father. Lilith knew all her grandparents were long dead—she was different from her classmates, whose elderly relatives sometimes collected them after school. The mention of a grandmother caused Lilith to suddenly feel longing for something she had never had—a nostalgic pang for a newly revealed hypothetical absence.

"What was her name?" Lilith's unexpected question made her father jump slightly. Then there was a distant, wistful look as he glanced down again—not quite at her, more through her.

"Mary," came his soft reply.

"Mary," Lilith repeated, tasting the name. Testing it. "What happened to her?" she asked.

"She's buried in a basilica." Another strange word for a small child.

"Bas-lika," Lilith repeated, mispronouncing the word. "What's that?"

"A kind of church," her father replied, solemnly. Lilith shuddered. Churches scared her.

By the time they arrived back home, Lilith could tell her mother was no longer there. The low-level growls that usually reverberated around the oak-walled panels of the upstairs landing were no more. Now silence reigned.

After they'd removed their outdoor garments, her father led her into the drawing room. His lawyer was awaiting their return. Upon seeing him, her father became visibly nervous. There was a woman sitting beside the lawyer. She smiled at the child.

"You must be Lilith," the woman announced, standing. She was well-proportioned and friendly-looking.

Lilith instinctively moved behind her father. He held her hand, and pulled her back around in front of him, kneeling beside her. Lilith looked into his face, confused.

"This is Ms. Wilbur, she's going to look after you," he explained softly, before smiling back at the woman.

"Lilith can call me Kaye," Ms. Wilbur said kindly.

Her father then turned back to Lilith, gazing at her with the kindness she loved. "I have to go away." He gulped. "You must be very brave, Lily. Because what I'm doing is for you. You're very special. I believe you will change everything. Not just here, but everywhere." With that he reached into his jacket and pulled out a small bracelet from inside his breast pocket. He handed it to Lilith.

"Another gift?" she asked, with cautious excitement. Lilith turned it over in her hand. It was silver, with a small, strange-looking screen on the outer side. The screen was narrow and black, and numbers were spinning in iridescent green, fleetingly across the screen.

"I guess it is. This is a SwissSecure bracelet. It will live with you, expanding as you grow."

"Is it alive?" Lilith asked.

Her father chuckled. "In a way, I suppose it is. When you're older, after you're chipped, the numbers will stop spinning. And then you'll receive a message from me—two, in fact."

"Memoclips?" Lilith asked, confused. She knew that was what the chipped adults called them.

Her father dipped his head. "Actually, faceclips. They will explain things … when the time is right. For one thing, where the music comes from, the Nunciature Evangelion—the Tower of Songs."

"Music?"

"It will come to you, later today. This music will help you become your potential, but it will also be your one Achilles heel …" Lilith scrunched up her eyes in incomprehension. "That means it will make you vulnerable. You must never trust the music. When the time is right, the bracelet will settle, reveal the code, and play the faceclip. And after that, when you're ready, you must also seek out your mother. You'll know when. She is far more than you think … I know it's not been easy for you. But she will have moments of lucidity, she can help you, explain."

Lilith grimaced and shook her head. "What kind of music?" she asked, avoiding the mention of her mother. She imagined the tinkling piano of her music teacher.

Her father nodded faintly. "That will become clear, in time." He paused, smiling at Lilith, taking in her face. "I love you, remember that. Always."

With those final words, Lilith's father clipped the bracelet onto the child's right wrist. It snapped into place with a small metallic sound. He gave Lilith a long, gentle hug, before standing and nodding toward the two adults. Then he turned and left the room. Lilith couldn't have imagined then, as she watched him walk out, his back straight and proud as always, that she would never see him again.

CHAPTER 1

Park Baek Hyeon's call, summoning me into the office, was unexpected—especially so early on a Saturday morning. He never contacted me when I was off-duty, that was the rule. Even more unusual was the taut urgency in his voice, a hint of panic even; *that* unnerved me—the normally inscrutable Park. *What the hell's so pressing this time?* I mused. *Can't a girl even get this one damn weekend off?* I looked down at the young woman lying next to me. I had gone and done it again, a random hook-up, despite promising myself not to. She was pretty in an emo-goth way, and around twenty, I guessed. I exhaled before shaking her gently. The girl's eyes flickered open.

"You have to go," I whispered. "I've been summoned to work. An emergency. I must leave, right away." She yawned, before turning over and trying to go back to sleep. "I mean it," I snapped, shaking her. "Please get dressed."

I walked toward the bathroom and issued my voice command, "VirDa, bathroom lights," glancing back to check the girl was getting up this time.

Once inside, I stared at myself in the large mirror and groaned. I looked as rough as I felt. My head was thumping from drinking too much the night before. My hair was a mess, my face blotchy and my eyes puffy. I stepped back. *All this will need some work.* I also had a large bruise on my left shoulder, purple with yellow-tinged edges. *Crap, how did that happen?*

I showered quickly and dressed in a V-neck ruffle blouse and mid-rise dress pants. I applied maroon lipstick and some light rouge and re-entered the bedroom. I felt slightly more human after the shower. The girl was now dressed, perched on the edge of the bed, watching me sheepishly.

"VirDa, readjust walls to daytime mode." As I issued my voice command, the bedroom wall partition slowly disappeared into the floor, revealing the relaxation area beyond, with a full-wall window twenty meters away giving out onto the large, illuminated hanging gardens dropping many stories below terrestrial level. I allowed myself a small smile of satisfaction—my duplex penthouse was in one of the original deep Earth-scraper constructions with all the original features. I had one of the best views of the artificial waterfalls in the entire sector, cascading down through the bore-wells that veined this level of the Manhattan schist. I was high up, just one level below terrestrial, and it was worth every e-Continental. This view never got old.

My dressing area completed its rotation, as the floor panels finished moving into daytime mode. I peered into the iris scanner on my weapons safe; the door unlocked with a click. I took out my kydex shoulder holster and coil pistol. I hooked the holster on, followed by my black leather jacket over the top. I then picked up an elastic band from the top of a high-gloss acrylic, auto-stow drawer. I pulled it over my right wrist, up against the SwissSecure bracelet that never came off. I hooked the elastic band up so that it wasn't visible under the cuff of my blouse. Then I stepped into my brogues and stooped to lace them.

There was a cough; I looked up. The girl was studying me with narrowed eyes.

"You some kind of lady cop or something?" She paused, studying me. "But then how can you afford a place like this … exclusive West Village Earth-scraper sector?"

Before I could respond, the familiar tone of a high priority alert vibrated in my ear implant. I pressed the skin on my left wrist; my holotab, an eighteen-centimeter translucent screen, projected out from my wrist chip. I blink-activated the 'new messages' icon. A meeting invite began scrolling across one screen quadrant, using my full title: *High Commissioner Lilith King, Interpol Special Representative to the United Nations*. It was quite the mouthful, but I had earned it!

The meeting was to be chaired by Assistant Secretary-General Lejeune. *What the hell? High level. This must be really serious.* I'd heard of Ms. Lejeune; never met her, though. Her reputation preceded her—one scary lady, although I admired what she had achieved. The meeting was scheduled to take place in the Security Council's Counter-Cyberterrorism Command, at UN Plaza, no less. I was invited in my capacity as *Special Investigator*. I raised one eyebrow—no one had told me.

I saw from the invite that Park, my boss, would also be attending, as was a Director from the World Health Organization, and some civilian—a medic from Columbia University Medical Center.

I was startled from my holotab by a VirDa exterior proximity chime; it reverberated around both floors of the penthouse through the in-ceiling speakers. In my peripheral vision I glimpsed the girl jump. Then came the sound of banging on the front door. It was muffled down here in the now-enlarged sleeping area, but persistent.

"What was that?" the girl hissed, her face a frozen mask of alarm.

I hibernated my holotab with a blink command and drew my weapon. "Someone's at the exterior door … gun activate." I was taking no chances—the nagging feeling of being followed, being surveilled, had been growing in intensity. Clyde would tell me I was just being paranoid. But if there's one thing life had taught me, it was you could never be paranoid enough. The capacitor status symbol on the barrel of my weapon began glowing green, in far-field charging mode.

"Never heard a hail chime like that before," the girl muttered.

"VirDa, display external visual sensors." With that, a section of smart LED wall panel across from my circular bed faded into off-white, before displaying the live feed of the corridor-tunnel outside the apartment entrance. I breathed a sigh of relief. I put my gun back in the shoulder holster.

"You know her?" the girl asked, now standing, peering nervously over my shoulder at the large display.

"She's my neighbor, closest thing I have to a mother …" I replied, as I took in the gray-haired woman on the screen, still in her dressing robe.

I jogged up the stairs to the interior security vestibule. I heard the girl puffing as she trailed behind. The entrance hail light was flashing adjacent to the apartment door. "VirDa, open door."

Kaye Wilbur was standing in front of me; she looked a wreck. Her eyes were red, as if from crying, or maybe lack of sleep, and she was wringing her hands.

"Lilith," she gasped. "It's Avie, I don't know what to do …" As the elderly woman looked past me, seeing the girl, she recalibrated. "So sorry, Lilith, didn't realize you had company, and god it's early," she muttered, glancing down instinctively at her left wrist without actually activating her bioclock.

"It's fine, she was just leaving. Why don't you tell me what's up?" I peered into Kaye's face. Streaks from dried tears marked her wrinkled face, wisps of uncombed hair strayed at odd angles.

"You have to see for yourself," Kaye replied, leading me toward the vertical transit tube. The girl followed me out as I heard the lock activation of my apartment behind me.

"She's been like this since I got her back from the Up-skilling procedure." Kaye seemed desperate as she spoke.

"Been busy at work … should have checked in," I muttered, as guilt pricked me. After all, I had gifted Kaye her larger three-floor condo immediately beneath mine, so I could be there for her if she needed me. It was the least I could do.

We followed Kaye into the transit tube. The LED smart ceiling panels powered on as we took our seats around the capsule's perimeter. We exited into the vestibule on Kaye's level; the corridor ceiling panels cast an eerie glow around us.

"I've had the doctor here three days in a row now. Even the strongest sleeping pills aren't working. He doesn't understand it either. Avie hasn't slept for four days straight. And now it's really bad, she's changing. I'm scared I'm losing her. I didn't know who else to turn to."

As Kaye led us toward her apartment entrance, the girl whispered in my ear: "Up-skilling. Isn't that the new vagus implant thing that they do at LifeWorks?" I nodded. "Heard about it on MyPlace broadcasts. I don't qualify, not one of the lower soc-ed certs. I have a Professional cert," she continued proudly.

"Good for you," I muttered tersely back at her.

As Kaye activated her condo door, the girl made to follow me inside. I paused and turned to her. "I think we can say goodbye now. I'm sure you understand."

"Can I see you again? You're so pretty, and an amazing body. It was fun last night." I involuntarily clenched my jaws. She hurriedly activated her holotab and began directing furious eye-gaze commands at the screen. I knew what she was doing: sending me a proximity invite, sharing her contact details. I'd have to deal with that later.

"Take care," I muttered, gesturing back toward the transit tube. "Street level's that way." The girl turned and slouched away. I watched to make sure she left, before following Kaye inside.

As soon as the apartment door closed, I heard guttural growls through the early morning darkness, coming from one of the lower levels.

"She's in her room," Kaye muttered, leading me down one set of stairs. Inside Avie's room it was dark, the night shields still activated on the light-shaft windows overlooking the hanging gardens far below; the smart LED wall panels were still in nighttime mode, just a faint golden glow.

As I stood on the threshold of the room, next to Kaye, I made out Avie's outline. She was sitting on a chair in the center, still in her pajamas, only the silver luminescence of her holotab visible, floating above her left wrist.

As my eyes adjusted, I saw that Avie was glancing around the room with frantic eyes. It was as if she hadn't even noticed us. And she looked pale and emaciated. It had only been ten days since I'd last seen her, just before she left for the LifeWorks campus in Toronto, so full of optimism that she would be able to turn a corner, to finally have some prospects.

But this wasn't the same young woman I'd known all her life; the once joyful child I'd taken for walks when I was back during the holidays from boarding school as a teenager. She was almost unrecognizable.

Avie stood up and then suddenly sat down, pulling at her long, dark brown hair. The holotab screen moved around maniacally as her left arm made jerking gestures in the air. If I hadn't known better, I would have suspected she was on something; that somehow the poor girl's mind had snapped.

"I can't get there," Avie snarled, not quite at the screen but not to anyone else either.

I heard Kaye's involuntary yelp next to me—pain, concern, maybe even a premonition of losing her daughter.

"Avie, it's Lilith. Where are you trying to get to, honey?" I asked, trying to sound soothing, unsure whether to enter the room, what that might provoke.

Avie glanced at me as if suddenly noticing us. Tutted and shook her head.

"The lottery … I can't get to the next level." Avie paused before standing abruptly again. "I can't take it."

"Take what?" I asked quietly.

"Sitting," she rasped back at me. Avie twisted her body in an abrupt jerk, jumping forward. She was staring right into my face. Then she suddenly turned to one side, before clawing with her hands and arms as if fending something off.

"Will the same happen to me, like the other Unskills?" Avie asked, now peering straight into my eyes, sounding strangely calm.

"Other Unskills? Which others?" I asked, before glancing at Kaye to see whether she knew anything about this. Kaye threw me a nonplussed look.

And with that, Avie swung her left arm in front of me so that her holotab veered forward. I glimpsed the logo on the open Lucky Dip gaming app. It was a fiery phoenix with flaming wings, glancing over its left shoulder, on a black background with the logo underneath: *Be reborn: A new you today* in multiple languages. Numbers were spinning in a maze level, within the app. Avie was on level fourteen. I knew users had to complete all fifty levels by the weekly deadline to be entered into that week's lux-unskill job lottery.

As Avie continued moving, the holographic screen passed through my hand in midair, disappearing as the projection vanished, before reappearing on the other side of my open hand. My Eye kicked in. And there it was, the rush of an emotional halo. But this halo was unlike any I'd ever experienced before. There were voices—thousands, maybe millions, screaming in shrill unison, as life was being sucked out of them; the cries, some pleading as I felt them wither and move into silent death. I jumped involuntarily, before leaning against one side of the doorway, feeling nauseous. For the first time in a long time, I had experienced an emotional halo that scared the living daylights out of me.

CHAPTER 2

The hover cab jerked upward, making a detour to a different skyway. NYPD restrictions were already in force due to the downtown protests. The maneuver made me feel nauseous. I gingerly leaned back against the headrest of the passenger cabin, still feeling rough. The beautiful music inside my head was barely audible. The Melody kept me sane, and it was always there unless I drank, which dulled its sound. Last night I had definitely overdone it, even by my standards.

I gave a half-tap on my wrist chip, activating my bioclock. *Christ, I knew it! I'm going to be late.* But what choice did I have? Kaye was a mess, and I had to do something for the sister I never had. That was me, all action and looking out for others—I had arranged for Avie to be hospitalized. It was clear she needed medical assistance. But now I'd never get to UN Plaza on time. And I'd forgotten about the civil disobedience planned by the Anti-Automation protesters. Moreover, to cap it off, an emergency ordinance meant the closure of some airways and city sectors due to likely counterattacks from Dark Court cultists. From my apartment in the Earth-scraper sector, it was normally a five-minute ride to the United Nations HQ. Not today. Worse, Turtle Bay itself was being targeted by the protesters; that was exactly where I was headed.

Other hover cars crept past in the opposite direction, along the stacked airways above the museum-buildings sector of old Manhattan. As I glanced out of the side window at the Chrysler and MetLife buildings, dark shapes appeared to be writhing in the early morning shadows of the streets below, as if lurking in the heart of the East Side, just for me. I just couldn't shake the feeling of being followed, no matter how hard I tried.

There was a vibration alert in my ear—I activated my holotab. *Dammit!* It was a reminder that I hadn't responded to the girl's proximity invite. Embry Tonks. *So that's her name.* I knew I would never see her again. I never did. I never could—relationships, they just weren't my thing. After years of therapy, the diagnosis was that I was scarred by love, maybe even scared of it. I paid a lot of e-Continentals to be told what I already knew. I issued a dark laugh at the irony, before directing a blink command at the erase tab. With that, Embry Tonks's ID and contact links were permanently wiped from my holotab. A twinge of guilt briefly arrested me—I hated ghosting people. And she was sweet. But there wasn't a damn thing I could do about it; except to try and forgive myself for my dysfunction—exactly what Clyde always advised.

As I anxiously parsed the updated ETA details on the autopiloting VirDa's holographic screen, I received the second high-priority ear alert of the day. Incoming Interpol mail. I activated my holotab again—a briefing report sent from the team at the UN's Counter-Cyberterrorism Command. It was prepared by one Dr. Ousmane Diouf—the WHO Director whom I would soon be meeting in person. Apparently, he directed responses to global medical emergencies.

As I began reading, my heart nearly stopped: they were calling it Fatal Insomnia. Only Unskills were affected, and just those who were attending LifeWorks facilities for the Up-skilling procedure. *So that's the emergency. Avie! Please not her,* I thought.

My hands started shaking so badly my holotab jerked around in front of me; I could barely read. I took some calming breaths, anxious to find out more about what they were labeling a global pandemic.

It was all bad. Sentinel had triggered a yellow alert for a global spike in sleep deprivation fourteen days ago. Yesterday evening, as the earliest diagnosed had started dying, the alert had been upgraded to amber. The live ticker on the Sentinel database in Geneva showed 1,143,751 confirmed diagnoses of insomnia. And well over 57,000 dead and counting. The entire Up-skilling program had now been placed on hiatus.

Cases of insomnia had been reported across four federations, three republics, and one kingdom. Twenty-four national territories in total, spanning Tier One and Tier Two states. It was only twelve hours ago that Sentinel had issued the automated warning for a global medical emergency. The first cases dated back six weeks, the same time that the global Up-skilling program went live. But the standard diagnosis for chronic insomnia required four weeks of sleep deprivation, as acute cases typically resolved themselves earlier than that.

As I pored over the electronic files, graphics, and maps, I learned that the Up-skilling program was open to just the three lowest soc-ed classes: Unskills, Semiskills, and Skills. But inevitably, the majority of volunteers for the program were Unskills, and seventy-five percent of them had now been diagnosed with symptoms. The other two soc-ed classes were unaffected.

Before I could read more, the autopilot hailed me in the passenger cabin. "High Commissioner King, I regret to inform you that access to UN Plaza has been denied."

"What?" I exclaimed. "I work there, I'm preauthorized."

"It's a new NYPD ordinance, just transmitted. Airway access to UN Plaza is restricted until at least noon, due to rioting in the vicinity, throughout the Turtle Bay area."

Just my luck, I thought, although it stood to reason that Start Apollo and his latest million-person protest would target UN facilities. After all, the UN had meekly acquiesced to the whole automation agenda pushed by the leading Tier One states. The whole wheeze was run by and effectively for the upper soc-ed classes. Only now did they pay attention to the Unskills; now that cities across the automated world were burning. The Unskills were angry. They were permanently unemployed with no prospects, and just a UN-sanctioned federal handout to live on. The demogrant was a pittance, barely enough to scrape by. Hell, I would be angry too.

"What about airway access from the other side, from the East River?" I asked.

"I'll plot a detour," the autopilot replied, before maneuvering into a different airway.

As we crossed back through the lower Lexington airway, circling in the direction of Roosevelt Island, I had a better view of the protests unfolding below. The terrestrial pedestrian and transit corridors of Midtown East were teeming with Unskills. Virtually every vertipad I could see had been doused with accelerant and was on fire. Traffic couldn't land. Police security droids were in low-flying formation above the transit corridors, attempting to disperse crowds, pushing them into the already congested pedestrian corridors. In one sector, below the city airway junction-stacks, a squadron of droids had deployed a low-flying sonic cannon unit. I watched grimly as protesters fell over in its path like tenpins, flailing on the ground in agony, clutching their ears. The device was designed to mess with the ear implant, triggering a neural shock in the language chip. *It has come to this, I mused,* more than troubled by what I was witnessing.

As we approached the Queensboro Bridge airway, the hover cab was now close enough to terrestrial level to pick out the details on the holographic signs. Protesters were waving all the usual ones: *Human Rights Not AI Rights. Abolish Automation. We Want To Work. Unskill Don't Mean No Skill.*

The traffic ahead of us slowed, before coming to a halt. My cab bobbed around in midair, between the LED lane markers, while we waited for the congestion to ease up.

I still had my holotab open, so I activated the local MyPlace news bulletin. There was a live feed from a satellite-TV drone hovering above the ground below. A large pocket of counter-protesters, hooded Dark Court extremists, was moving steadily along an adjacent transit corridor. They were headed toward a large group of Unskills, kettled into a now overcrowded pedestrian corridor by the NYPD drones.

As the Dark Court cultists approached, they began heckling the Unskills. They were accompanied by wheeled daemons supporting a Dark Court holographic banner—an image of a hooded watcher standing atop a high tower. The cultists were better funded—they could afford droids. There was a range of alternating displays held aloft by the daemons' flexi-lift extenders. The vile slogans read: *Vote 4 compulsory sterilization. Useless Eaters. Say no to moral depravity.* Chants of "pedos" from the Dark Court extremists could be clearly heard above the din of droid sirens and the screams of innocent Unskills being crushed in the mayhem.

A scuffle broke out as a small group of Unskills clambered over the thermoformed barrier between pedestrian lanes, marching toward the procession of Dark Court extremists. A close-up showed a hooded Dark Court cultist pushing over a female Unskill, before grabbing another one by the hair, viciously dragging her ten meters across the polycarbonate surface. The counter-protester was wearing a balaclava with a Dark Court logo. From the physique, clearly male—the Dark Court cultists invariably were. He spat on her, before mouthing something. The shape of his snarled lips was unmistakable, a by-now-familiar refrain: "Sterilize her!"

A formation of armed drones arrived. *About time!* One began broadcasting warnings for the Dark Court mob to disperse.

"I can set you down on the FDR Pedestrian Corridor," the autopilot announced. "I've located one vertipad still functioning." I deactivated my screen. At least I could walk from there.

The cab dropped onto the vertipad and taxied down to the pedestrian disembarkation bay. I glanced around before jumping out. This pedestrian corridor, on the bank of the river, was deserted—probably due to NYPD restrictions in force. I pressed my wrist chip again, activating my holotab. I scrolled through the menu with gaze commands before blinking to select the mapping app. I blinked to select the best route; the holographic map began projecting onto the screen floating in front of me. I started walking quickly, shoulders hunched. Within a few minutes, once I turned a slight bend, the sixty-five-story glass façade of the UN Secretariat building rose up into view, around eight hundred meters ahead, gleaming in the morning sunlight.

But just then, twenty meters in front of me, a small group of Dark Court cultists emerged, out from a side corridor. I grimaced—this only meant trouble. There were four of them, this time with cappa hoods covering their heads, obscuring their faces from sec-cam and LS orb identification by NYPD droids.

They were no doubt trying to imitate their beloved, so-called *adjudicators,* the self-appointed, anonymous leaders of this vile cult of violence and misinformation. The cultists were dressed in black from head to toe, including leather pants and tunics. They even wore black, tactical Kevlar gloves.

The cultists spotted me. "Let's get her, boys," said one voice. Then I heard raucous laughter.

They moved toward me, cutting off my route to the UN employee East River entrance. And as they approached, they pulled out neural shock sticks, sheathed in cases worn around their belts. Of course, just my luck. The long, thin devices were illegal, and for good reason. If applied for more than a few seconds, they could result in permanent brain damage or even death. I steeled myself—this was the only way through.

As I neared, the group appeared surprised I was still heading toward them—not the response they expected. I would never run away again, not since that night in the Black Forest, twenty years ago. Sure, I had been through Interpol's basic combat training, back in the day. For what that was worth. But since the Black Forest, I had taken self-defense training to insane levels, obsessive as always. You could say I had elevated it to the status of a dark art.

"Looks like an Unskill to me," snarled one as they drew closer.

"Very pretty, like the bright orange hair. Let's first have fun with this useless eater," quipped another. They fanned out, to encircle me.

Once surrounded I stopped, turning slowly, facing each one in turn, speaking clearly. "First, I'm a Superior soc-ed. Not that it matters to you lowlifes. I would take you on anyway. And second, I suggest you drop your weapons, and walk away before y'all get hurt."

There was momentary silence, before vicious laughter erupted.

"Oh, we have one with attitude here. Let's get the bitch," said another, the leader maybe. I glanced over my shoulder as he moved in from my rear. His cappa had fallen off his head, slightly revealing his face. This was the same cultist that I'd seen dragging the woman by the hair. As I reached under my jacket for the handle of my coil pistol, pulling it from my kydex holster, he raised his neural stick to strike me, while rushing forward. I spun around and twisted slightly—his striking arm missed. But my evasive action meant that my gun spilled from my hand, skittering across the polycarbonate surface away from me.

The cultist glided past, now off-balance, flailing at thin air. And as he missed me, he began falling, skidding along the ground, grazing his face on the polycarbonate surface which left striations across one cheek. As he lay dazed, his face on the side of the polycarbonate surface, weals of blood began trickling down his face. The laughter of the other three suddenly stopped dead.

Another, slightly taller, moved forward, cussing at me.

"A slippery whore, aren't you," he snarled as he eyed me up and down. "Although, a bit too skinny for my taste."

I eyed *him* up and down. "You're definitely too thick for mine," I retorted, arching a brow. That did it—I had gotten under his skin. He dashed at me, growling.

Self-defense training had taught me to aim for vulnerable areas. Not the chest, that tended to be ineffective. And not the knees—too much precision was required in the heat of the moment. As the cultist lunged, front on, I went all in with a groin kick. He was at exactly the right distance from me as I drove my hips forward, leaning back slightly while I kicked forcefully with my right leg. I used my lower shin and the ball of my foot. I struck him hard, feeling the soft tissue of his groin flatten and separate under his pants, before he howled in agony, dropping to the ground.

"Oops, did that hurt?" I asked, in a mock-simpering voice. The injured cultist rolled around like a crazed animal, clutching his groin, eyes tight shut, making a high-pitched howl.

I made to retrieve my pistol from where it had come to rest, but I was cut off. The remaining two cultists moved forward in tandem, behind me on my left and in front of me to my right. The cultist to my left suddenly darted behind me. I felt his breath on the nape of my neck, his arms squeezing around me, as he attempted to incapacitate me with a bear hug attack. Meanwhile, the second one moved forward, now with his neural rod raised, ready to strike as I stood helpless in front of him.

As soon as I felt the arms of the first cultist wrapping me from behind, I bent forward from the waist, shifting my weight, making it difficult for him to pick me up. This also gave me the angle I knew I now needed to throw elbows from side to side. And in the split second before the second attacker could reach me, I threw the cultist behind a double elbow strike, a sharp sequence into either side of his body, aiming at his kidneys. I heard him wince in pain, as he involuntarily released me, keeling forward. His head was now low, directly behind my back. I repeated the elbow strike, one-two, making sharp contact with his face. I heard one cheekbone crack, as the force of my strikes sent the cultist tumbling backward, making a strange, almost inhuman gurgling sound.

And as the second attacker reached me, his neural rod moving forward high above his head, I jabbed with my right hand, throwing a heel palm strike. I aimed for his throat, flexing my wrist, making sure to recoil the strike. The cultist's head snapped up and back in an unnatural way. I watched in grim fascination as he tottered backward, before toppling to the polycarbonate surface, making a sickening, cracking sound as his head hit the ground.

Without warning, I heard shaky breathing immediately behind me. And too late, I realized the leader was back up, about to ambush me. I heard the snicker of a neural rod being activated, and then paroxysms of agony—a burning sensation wracked my entire body.

* * *

When I came to, I was pinned to the ground, splayed on my back. My arms were being held down and out, one by each cultist, while the leader stood over me, leering down at me. The fourth attacker was still unconscious, a couple of meters away. I craned my neck to get a better view—blood was oozing from beneath his cappa as he lay motionless on the ground.

I didn't know how long I had been out, but this wasn't good. The leader bent down over me, jerked the lapels of my leather jacket, pulling it open, and began ripping at my blouse. Buttons scattered around me on the polycarbonate surface, glittering like small pearls in the early morning sun.

"You'll get what's coming to you, now," he snarled, as he exposed my flesh.

I smiled faintly up at him. "Why the gloves?" I asked, as he fumbled, attempting to wrench off my bra. He smiled and pulled off the Kevlar glove from his right hand.

"You're right. I should enjoy these titties with my bare hands."

And as the Dark Court wannabe-adjudicator touched my skin, I closed my eyes as my Eye opened. The emotional halo came. But this was a rush of hate, a locomotive of black anger, speeding out of him. He was a Semiskill, while his two older twin sisters had been certified at the higher manual class as Skill soc-eds the year before him.

He jumped back, suddenly startled, as he felt my Eye on him—I had already started to burn him. And his surprised reaction caused the other two to loosen their grip on my arms, just for a fraction of a second. But that was all the time I needed. I was up on one knee in a flash and grabbed the leader by his still outstretched hand. Now my Eye locked into him—he was stuck. I twisted his arm behind his back in a half-Nelson, forcing him down so that his face lay sideways against the polycarbonate surface. I pressed one knee down with force into the small of his back, maintaining pressure. And holding his bare hand behind him, I continued to burn him. Creases began spreading out across his face, as he lay helpless, motionless, snared by my Eye, as I absorbed his time. Once I'd burned a decade I stopped, releasing him. That was sufficient—a cautionary warning for the others.

I stepped back, glancing around at the two remaining cultists to assess their next move. They were still on their haunches, a couple of meters either side of me. They each stood slowly, gasping as they watched their stricken comrade beneath me, gingerly attempting to push himself up from the ground. He was now visibly older; his face had aged. He glanced down at his hands, the smooth translucence of youth no longer quite there. As he managed to stand, he looked toward me, fear visibly puckering the lines of his face beneath his hood.

"So who's next?" I asked, fixing the remaining two with a piercing look. They each began backing away. "Leave those, and you can go," I commanded, gesturing toward their neural shock rods. The two cultists glanced nervously at one another before dropping their weapons; then they turned and fled. I moved forward, picked up the two shock rods, and tossed them into the East River. I moved toward the still unconscious cultist, kicking his fallen neural rod into the river too. I then turned back to the one remaining Dark Court member. I pointed to the rod that he was still clutching. Before I could say anything further, he meekly threw it into the river, before taking a step farther back from me. I stooped to recover my fallen weapon and placed it back in the holster under my jacket.

"What are you, a witch?" the cultist asked, his voice now quivering with fear.

CHAPTER 3

Once through UN security, I approached the stack of transit tubes. I blink-activated the transit capsule with the stillgram of my name—the door slid open. The UN's Counter-Cyberterrorism Command was on floor sixty—exactly twenty floors above my own office, in the UN's Interpol delegation. Just as I entered the capsule, my ear implant vibrated—an incoming memoclip alert. I activated my holotab—it was an update on the meeting schedule.

To my relief, I saw I wasn't the only one running late; the civilian medic had been delayed getting in too. The start time of the meeting had been adjusted to coincide with my ETA—UN command had been monitoring my LS rebound records. *Well, they can't exactly start without me,* I mused. *I'm supposed to be leading the investigation.* And I would have to stop at my office first. I needed a change of blouse. I kept an overnight bag ready, in case of emergencies. That was me—always prepared for the unexpected.

* * *

A welcome droid ushered me across the committee room of UN CCT Command, to a seat next to Park. Lejeune was opposite, instantly recognizable, a middle-aged beacon of unruffled calm between the two nervous-looking men sitting either side of her. I was distracted momentarily by the relaxing waveform holographic display behind her, rippling across LED smart wall-panels. Creams and soft pinks moved lazily along the walls.

"As most of you know, I'm Michèle Lejeune. I head the UN's Counter-Cyberterrorism Command, advising the Security Council. Before we do some brief introductions, I would like to check that our externals have signed the Classified Information NDAs?" Lejeune queried accompanied by a stabbing finger. The two men either side of her nodded.

I watched the staccato jerk of her arm as she made the small gesture. I followed the line of her striped jacket, her straight back pushing the fabric against the edges of her chair and the table. She was one rigid lady. Her brown hair was slicked back over her head in a single sweep, revealing a high forehead. Too masculine for my taste. A form of self-defense, maybe. It was still tough for women—I knew all about that. I wondered what her story was. Lejeune gestured to the man on her right.

He coughed, clearing his throat. "I'm Dr. Ousmane Diouf, I head the WHO's Global Emergency Response Division. Just flew in from Geneva with more updates, which we can get into in a moment."

He was streaming Unilanguage's North American state official English variety, while using French accent differentiators. I activated my holotab and glanced down, below the table line, clicking on his bio. He was from Senegal—where Union Standard French was the state official. I kept the holotab open and looked back up. Dr. Diouf had the whitest teeth I'd ever seen. He gazed across at us somberly, adjusting onyx-rimmed glasses on his bulbous nose. Vision eyewear was making something of a fashion comeback.

Lejeune gestured to her left, to the sleep doctor. I glanced back down, my blink gaze hovering over his name. He was just twenty-nine, with a Superior soc-ed cert—top rung like me, like Lejeune too. There weren't many of us. Despite his relative youth, his file and achievements were impressive—a hotshot medical genius by all accounts. I hibernated my holotab.

The young medic glanced toward Lejeune, and then with trepidation across at Park and me. I met his eyes and he glanced away in apparent embarrassment. He was wearing a shirt that was all loud colors and wide stripes—fabric that could have been purloined from a deck chair on a boardwalk somewhere. *A fashion disaster on legs. Poor kid!*

"Kace Westwood," he began nervously. "I mean, that's me. I'm Kace, Professor and Associate Director of the Sleep Disorders Center at Columbia University Medical Center." He paused and smiled self-consciously.

It must have been daunting for him to be summoned into a high-level security meeting in the UN's nerve center. And at a moment's notice, on the weekend, while being informed of a looming sleep pandemic. I felt for him. I caught myself studying the esthetics of his physical appearance—he was a striking man. Beautiful black-bronze skin, a strong, youthful looking-face, and startling blue eyes. I wondered whether they were natural.

"We're very glad to have you here, Dr. Westwood," Lejeune said, smiling for the first time. I watched her face as she addressed him. She touched her hair briefly. *She thinks he's cute,* I thought. He gave a short, nervous jerk of his head. "And now our famous detective," Lejeune continued, "High Commissioner King."

"Just call me Lilith," I announced, addressing the somber faces opposite. "I don't do formal."

Dr. Diouf leaned across the table. "I enjoyed the recent feature on you in *Celebrities Today*," he said. I smiled politely at his white teeth. "What did they say you call it … emanation? Touching objects from a crime scene to pick up hunches? The way you solved that fake health app case was impressive."

"Thanks," I muttered. "Although I was misquoted, just solid detective work." Lejeune made a dismissive gesture with her hand.

"Mr. Park insisted it had to be Lilith quarterbacking this one. And for good reason. She has quite the track record. Director of Interpol's International Cybercrime Directorate in Singapore for five years, and prior to her current posting, she served as Elite Ambassador to Interpol's South American Command. With her promotion to High Commissioner, she's the world's second most senior career law enforcement professional. After Director Fleischman, of course."

I flinched as I heard the name—Fleischman, Head of Interpol. The scar on my right ankle suddenly began itching—the only part of my body that never healed. I felt the irresistible urge to bend down and scratch it. But instead, I gritted my teeth and flicked the elastic band against my wrist. After a sharp sting of the band, hidden under the cuff of my blouse, I felt calmer.

"Anything you would like to add?"

"No, I believe you've covered everything," I replied, trying not to sound resentful. *Surely I should be allowed to introduce myself. I guess my reputation now always precedes me.*

Lejeune gestured toward Park. I turned slightly, watching his impassive face in my peripheral vision as he began talking.

"I'm Park Baek Hyeon, former national security advisor to the President of the Unified Korean Republic. I'm here in my role as elected Chair of the UN's Global Policing Executive."

Lejeune began talking again. "Now down to business. You've all read Dr. Diouf's briefing notes, I hope?" Kace Westwood nodded dutifully next to her. "Let's dive straight in. Dr. Westwood, can you spell out what we're up against—this outbreak of Fatal Insomnia. What are the symptoms?"

Kace Westwood glanced sideways at her—startled, perhaps, at hearing his name. He gave a small, nervous cough.

"Well … initial symptoms include increased anxiety, panic attacks and progressive insomnia." Westwood's voice was quivering, betraying him. "As the disease progresses, patients begin to hallucinate, followed by rapid weight loss. In the third stage, there's complete insomnia with the patient spending increasing periods in a stupor, while exhibiting spasmodic movements of the body, especially the limbs. By this point, standing and walking are no longer possible. Also, swallowing, eating, and speech become difficult. During this stage, patients invariably have to be placed on a ventilator and fed via a tube. In the fourth and final stage, patients experience profound dementia, entering a vegetative state, eventually lapsing into a coma before death." *That means Avie is in stage two*, I thought. *I still have time to save her.*

"And these are the symptoms the Up-skilling subjects are experiencing?" Lejeune asked Diouf.

"Exactly. On a trajectory. The earliest to present with symptoms started to die yesterday evening. But others, who began exhibiting symptoms at various later points, are situated at different stages along the spectrum." As Diouf was finishing, Westwood began shaking his head.

"Dr. Westwood?" Lejeune asked.

"Honestly, this makes no sense," he began, now sounding a little more assertive. "Fatal Insomnia, it's vanishingly rare. A hereditary condition. And, I mean, a few weeks from start to finish … well …"

"What do you mean, 'makes no sense'?" I asked. Kace looked across at me.

"It takes months, sometimes years. It's never this quick."

"How long?" Lejeune insisted.

"In clinically established cases of Fatal Insomnia, we have no confirmed cases of death before seven months following first diagnosis. Patients can sometimes last several years. Eighteen months is the average life expectancy. And age wise …" He frowned. "The average age of Fatal Insomnia onset is over fifty. I'm not aware of any confirmed diagnoses before the age of forty. It's typically a late-life condition, a prion disease of the brain, a mutation of misfolded proteins, quite rare."

"All our cases are between the ages of eighteen and thirty-nine, the permitted age demographic for this first phase of Up-skilling subjects," Diouf added.

"And is there a cure?" I asked. Westwood looked at me balefully and shook his head.

Lejeune coughed theatrically. "That's not really the issue at this point. A cure, I mean. We're only talking Unskills here. Our job, first and foremost, is to investigate a potential link with big tech. I … we have to be seen to take such a possibility seriously. The Security Council is demanding a full investigation into that."

As Lejeune finished, I watched Diouf's demeanor next to her. I could tell from his dropped jaw what he was likely thinking, and certainly what I was thinking—indifference coming from a self-serving politician.

"But I don't understand," Kace stammered. "I thought I was here to help with the medical emergency. You asked me to support High Commissioner King—sorry, Lilith—right?"

"Right, right," Lejeune said defensively in a slightly pitchy voice. "But we also want to know whether the vagus chip is to blame. If we have something criminal going on here. And, of course, whether this might later affect the other soc-ed classes."

I watched the faces of the two men opposite. Their concern had now turned to confusion. So that was it, I thought. The powers-that-be were worried about the Semiskills and Skills, the folks who always turned out to vote in numbers. They didn't want those guys to lose confidence in the status quo.

Kace Westwood glanced sideways at Lejeune again before speaking. "But the whole Up-skilling program, it's being bankrolled by Abner Broad …" Lejeune raised an eyebrow, seeming confused. "What would a billionaire philanthropist have to gain from a global sleep pandemic? Especially if his goal can be achieved and the Unskill soc-ed class can be eradicated in a decade through Up-skilling?"

Lejeune pursed her lips. "I appreciate that for many, the LifeWorks CEO, Abner Broad, is an altruist. For some, maybe even a saint …" She raised one eyebrow as she let her sarcasm percolate. "But he's also the majority shareholder in Zyntlox."

"The pharmaceutical company?" Kace asked, surprised.

"Not just any pharma company. Only the world's leading manufacturer of sleeping pills. An entity that might have quite a bit to gain from a global sleep disorder."

"Zyntlox's stock price has doubled in the last week alone," Park added, quietly.

Lejeune gave a curt nod of agreement. "After the Great Language Outage, we can't be seen to be taking any chances with big tech. For now, Up-skilling is just a line of inquiry, of course. We're asking you to contribute your world-leading medical expertise, to support Lilith on a trip to the Inland Empire, to investigate. Okay?"

Kace sucked in his cheeks before replying. "Do we have autopsy results? A prion disease, Fatal Insomnia, can only be confirmed by a brain autopsy."

Diouf shook his head. "Not yet. We expect to have the first tranche of results later today," he said, having now regained his composure. "Sentinel's advice is based on an algorithm, assessing available clinical descriptions. You know—symptoms, patient behavior."

"What about polysomnograms of the patients?"

"We don't yet have that data either. The Up-skilling centers didn't have the software. But as soon as they reached out, we began uploading it to the LifeWorks servers."

"A poly what?" I asked, shooting Kace a baffled look.

"A scan of what's going on in the brain while the patient is sleeping," Kace explained, glancing across at me.

"All units should be fully updated within the next few hours. We'll then begin mass screening of patients and expect initial results later today," Diouf added.

"Tell me, Dr. Westwood," Lejeune began. "Let's say for argument's sake these symptoms really are related to the vagus implant, to Up-skilling. Could you venture a guess as to the cause?"

"Well, I'd need to know how the vagus chip works exactly. Any chip potentially creates a low-frequency electromagnetic field— an EMF. If implanted and somehow affecting the brain, it could potentially impact the body's natural production of melatonin."

"And how's that relevant?" Lejeune asked.

"Melatonin is the chemical that triggers sleep."

Lejeune looked at Kace thoughtfully for a moment. "You and Lilith will be heading out to interview Abner Broad and his wife, as well as some program volunteers. Transport is waiting; scramjet wheels up in thirty minutes. We've arranged overnight accommodation in the Republic. I want to know exactly what's going on with these implants." With that, Lejeune stood up dramatically and walked out—we were dismissed.

After a moment of startled silence, Kace Westwood and Diouf began discussing medical symptoms. Park leaned in next to me; he whispered in my ear.

"Can we speak privately for a few minutes, in my office?"

I turned to face him. "Sure. I have to collect my overnight bag anyway."

Park's eyes narrowed. "Sorry to do this to you …"

"I'm used to it," I replied, smiling.

Park shook his head. "That's not what I meant. I insisted this be assigned to you. Against orders. And now the Director wants to talk to us both, via telepresence."

"Director?" I asked, panic welling up in me.

"We're gonna get the riot act read to us, me in particular …" Park frowned. "You know, I'm only a political appointment. I'm supposed to play nice if I want to get re-elected. But this time …" Park held up his hands toward me as if in supplication, "… it really had to be you on this one."

"Meeting with whom?" I asked, insistently, reaching for my elastic band again.

"Herr Fleischman." As Park paused, I realized that my face must have drained of all color. Park's eyes widened, watching me. "Are you okay?"

I shook my head, attempting to brush away his concern as I pressed my hands down hard on the edge of the table in front of me. I almost thought I would pass out.

"I'm fine," I insisted, sounding more aggressive than I'd intended. Park flinched. "I've been working long hours. It's just caught up with me, that's all." Park smiled faintly, sympathetically.

But I was lying. This was a full-blown episode of the sensory disturbance that crushed my skull and made me dizzy and nauseous. Something bad was brewing. I could sense it, the wooziness of the telltale dark misgivings rising through me. The Aura was back with a bang. Just like that, the first time in years. Now refracted shards of light twisted my vision, hurting my eyes, riling me. I felt hot, breathless, and suddenly weak. The urge to run away became overpowering. *Could I do it? Face the Monster again, after all these years?*

CHAPTER 4

Park returned to his office suite ahead of me, while I briefly liaised with Kace Westwood. Before excusing myself, I checked that a service droid was available to escort him to the transport deck at the summit of the Secretariat building, where I would meet him following my debriefing with the Monster.

By the time I reached the Global Policing Executive suite, twenty floors below, the Aura's discombobulating effects had reached a dizzying intensity. I walked through the antechamber before stepping into Park's office. I almost expected to see the Monster himself waiting for me.

Instead, I saw the familiar, dapper figure of Park. He was facing away from me, motionless in his chair. His office overlooked the East River, facing toward Roosevelt Island. I could see his eyes were closed. Morning light spread along the contours of his silhouette. He hadn't heard me come in.

I coughed quietly. Park's deep brown eyes flickered open and he turned slowly in his chair.

"Ah, Lilith." Park spoke English with Korean accent differentiators, insisting on retaining his Samkee package rather than using the Union-DEF servers to which his status entitled him. Of course he would—he was a proud Korean. He studied me for a moment, in silence.

"You ready?" Park asked, gesturing to a seat next to his, in front of a large telepresence system. I didn't reply. Park's face was drawn. I could tell he was on edge too. "VirDa, call Director Fleischman."

"Yes, Mr. Park," the VirDa replied. Park stared directly ahead, unblinking—his wrinkled face inscrutable again. It did feel better sitting. But my heart was racing as we waited. I felt the rising itch again—the burn mark on my ankle. My anxiety levels were approaching a crescendo of pumping blood; I began to fear my eardrums might burst from the reverberating din. "Connecting Director Fleischman."

I grasped the sides of the chair with clenched hands, holding myself fast. *Pull yourself together, Lily,* I told myself.

There was a momentary crackle as the 3D-telepresence feed booted up from the projection ring at the top of the unit. And there it was, in three-dimensional holographic form—Jürgen Fleischman, Head of Interpol, the Monster. His pasty face and glistening bald head sprang to life before us, projected into the room, within touching distance.

"Mr. Park." The Monster spoke his greeting while peering at Park with his watery eyes, the result of years of overindulgence on schnapps and pastis. He then ran his dark gaze over me. Fleischman was in a dimly lit office in the Interpol HQ in Lyon. He was enveloped in shadowy threads of light, window shields no doubt almost fully activated despite it being early afternoon in Lyon, in the Grand Union. He was wearing his customary Interpol uniform jacket, his superior rank marked by the insignia that dangled in yellow braids from his epaulets. I could feel simmering anger ignite into burning rage, my eyes ablaze. I took deep, gulping breaths.

"Lilith, how nice to see you again," the Monster lisped with faux warmth, as if he were oblivious to the inescapable fact that I hated him with every fiber of my being. I reached for the elastic band under my sleeve. I snapped the elastic three times. "Still as stunning as ever." Fleischman watched me for a moment with a hint of cruelty lurking in his oddly twisted smile. "I don't know how you do it. How long has it been? Ten, fifteen years?"

"Try twenty," I replied witheringly, as I collected myself.

"Remarkable. You haven't aged a day." He lapsed into silence, before addressing Park. "You'll see to Lilith's annual medical, I take it, asap," before glancing at me with a sly smirk. Park gave a slight bow of his head and shoulders.

"I'm assuming we're not here to discuss how I look," I said coldly, needled by his look—I wasn't clear what he meant by my annual medical. That wasn't due yet. As I spoke, Fleischman's jaws and lips tensed, and his nostrils flared while he crossed his arms.

"Still the same Lilith. Same old … shall we call it … charm?" Fleischman jabbed his forehead at me before pausing, expecting me to say something, perhaps. His rheumy eyes fixed me with his vulture look. I crossed my arms too, mirroring his hostility. I could see his irritation—at least I had needled him back. That gave me a small measure of satisfaction. "I told Mr. Park not to fuss. All in good time; no need to get hot and bothered about all this, the so-called *pandemic*." Fleischman grinned directly at Park from the screen before addressing me. "But he's conscientious. Still quite new in the role. And the boys in Geneva have been trying to spook us."

Park coughed with unease. He shifted slightly in his seat. I threw Fleischman a disapproving look. The man was rebarbative and crass as hell. I was surprised to see that Park was also looking at him sternly. An emotional response. Unusual for Park to reveal himself, although Fleischman clearly hadn't noticed.

"The Security Council sees apparent menace from big tech in every shadow," Fleischman snapped dismissively.

"Wasn't that why Lejeune's outfit was set up?" I retorted. "To avoid another Marc Barron, another Appleton?"

Fleischman frowned before scoffing, "I told *Madame* Lejeune not to worry her head. Especially as we're only talking about Unskills. But there you go."

"Women tend to do that, worry needlessly," I muttered sarcastically. Park glanced at me, clearly startled. He probably hadn't expected me to challenge the Director of Interpol so blatantly. It wasn't his Korean way. But being deferential wasn't mine.

"Now you get it," said Fleischman approvingly, either not understanding my dig at him or just choosing to ignore it. "But she does have a Security Council mandate. So, we have to accommodate reasonable requests." Fleischman sneered at me. "And with your, shall we say, unusual methods ..."

I arched an eyebrow at him.

"You've got to admit, touching objects from a crime scene to generate hunches? That's slightly unconventional. But whatever works, right Lilith?" He was baiting me again. I ignored him.

"And that's why it had to be Lilith. She's the best," Park explained.

Fleischman's face became dark again. "You disobeyed a direct order. You know that, right? You know what that means ..." The Monster was now really riled up. His threat hung in the air, its unresolved menace turning Park's face ashen.

"Well, whether you like it or not, I am here now. So shall we get on with it?" I intervened, attempting to deflect the Monster's bullyragging.

"Some vested interests couldn't care less if there are fewer Unskills on the planet," lisped Fleischman. "But I suppose we have to at least pretend to care. To treat everyone equally. We're the law, after all." I stared at Fleischman, my mouth gaping, momentarily lost for words. The Monster chuckled at my reaction. "I never thought I would see Lilith King rendered speechless."

I grimaced. "I think you mean that we uphold the law. No one's above it … or below it, for that matter."

The Monster grinned. "Never understood why you cared about the have-nots so much, the pitied and pitiful. High Commissioner King, the patron saint of all worthless things. You should get real. I always told you." I glanced away, biting my lip in anger. Park caught my expression; he flinched in dismay. "But now the damage is done. Lilith's been appointed. So, we'd better make the most of it … You know who's bankrolling the global Up-skilling program, right?" Fleischman asked, glancing at me with irritation.

"I assume that's a rhetorical question? Everyone knows it's the Broads."

"That's right, those do-gooders," Fleischman sneered. "It may all be a complete coincidence, of course …" He paused—his thick lips parted slightly. Threads of spittle linked his upper to his lower teeth and gums, the spidery threads glinting in his dreary office light as he spoke. I observed in grim fascination, barely hearing his words. How the Monster repulsed me! I felt like screaming. I flicked my elastic band again. "… but you know, Broad's wife, Tova, she went to college with Alvinia Black. This Tova Broad was Ebba Black's godmother, by all accounts. Strange coincidence, don't you think?"

I started in surprise. I hadn't known that Ebba Black even had a godmother. It wasn't in the Ebba Black file. *So how does Fleischman know?* I wondered.

Park glanced at Fleischman, clearly perplexed. "I don't see the relevance, Director. Professor Black's a …"

"What? A hero?" Fleischman barked. "A vigilante if you ask me. She needs to be found and apprehended."

Good luck with that, I thought. The infamous Ebba Black had officially been a missing person for well over four years. I doubted she'd ever be found.

"Is there anything else?" I asked sarcastically. "I have a scramjet waiting to take me to the Republic of California."

Fleischman scowled. "You'll report to Mr. Park, as usual. First thing tomorrow morning, back here. But I will need regular updates too. You understand? Regular. I want to know what you're up to, at each step of the way, before you even take a step. You got that?" As I watched Fleischman's face, I felt my whole being tightening up. The Monster paused for a second, taking my silence for acquiescence. He was good at that. "That's clear, then." With that, he ended the call. His round face disappeared into a small square in midair, before zooming backward into nothingness, as if his 3D projection had been sucked inside the telepresence projection ring.

I sat back in my seat and took a deep, calming breath. I was still staring into the blackness where the Monster's face had been when I became aware that Park was studying me.

"Lilith?"

The sound of my name brought me back. I wasn't sure whether it really was a question, or a statement. Park's voice was quiet, his face had softened finally—relief, maybe, that Fleischman had exited the meeting, as if an unseen weight had been lifted from his shoulders.

"That didn't go as badly as I feared ..." Park began, before his voice trailed off. "My daughter ..." he continued after a moment. My face must have revealed confusion at this change of topic. Park gulped. "She's an Unskill. No job cert. She was borderline

Unskill-Semiskill at seventeen, fell the wrong side in the final evals. As you probably know, I'm an Executive soc-ed, high, although not a Superior. A disappointment for me … when I was young. Anyway, my daughter … I guess it just goes to show that intelligence isn't hereditary, the way the Dark Court propaganda claims …" I watched Park as he paused, wondering where he was going with this. Park breathed out before continuing. "I could have used my influence. You know, some people do. Change the classification. I'm not ashamed to admit the thought crossed my mind. But my wife …" a shadow briefly flickered across Park's face, "… she's an honorable woman. The point is, my daughter … Choon-Hee … she applied for the Up-skilling program." He was staring directly into my face, his eyes searching mine.

"For a vagus implant?" I asked.

"She's already had it fitted. At the LifeWorks facility in the Inland Empire, where you're headed." Park suddenly became overcome by emotion, his eyes welling—I pretended not to notice.

"And she has symptoms?"

Park leaned forward slightly as he composed himself. "It's bad. They say she's now too sick to be released. Please check in on her for me when you're there. I know you'll get to the bottom of this," he whispered, glancing at me nervously before clearing his throat. "For my daughter."

At least now I understood why Park wanted me assigned to the case. He had skin in the game. "I understand what you are going through," I announced. Park glanced at me in slight surprise. "This is also affecting someone close to me. The daughter of the woman who raised me. She was also certified an Unskill and still lives with her mother, at thirty-one. Her hopes of a better life, or any life, now center around playing the lux-unskill job lottery. And the UN's Up-skilling program. But now, she also has symptoms … I witnessed them with my own eyes this morning." I stopped speaking for a moment, as I realized, to my own surprise, that I had also gotten emotional all of a sudden. "We have to figure this out, for all the Unskills."

Silence followed, neither of us knowing what to say next. Still, something was bugging me.

"Do you know why the Director didn't want me on this one?" I asked finally, changing the subject back to the Monster.

Park gave a quick shrug. "He didn't say anything specific. But … he does seem to have something against you. Any idea why?"

I sure as hell did, but I wasn't going to tell Park. That was my business. I glanced away without replying.

After a slight pause, Park continued. "One more thing. We have to perform your annual medical eval now. Full body mapping scan, bloodwork, DNA samples, you know the drill."

"But that's not due for another month at least," I objected.

"Director Fleischman's orders. I can't disobey another one. The medical gynoid is waiting for you outside in the med cubicle. It'll only take a few minutes. Sorry Lilith."

CHAPTER 5

There was something about medicals that I disliked. It wasn't the procedure itself, but the giving up of something of oneself: blood, DNA samples, brain images. And once out in the world, and in my employer's database, I could never get back the secrets those samples contained—hundreds of datapoints exposing my inner essence, cut out from time.

Afterward, I went to my office to grab my overnight bag. I still had a few minutes before I had to be at the scramjet departure point. And there was one thing I still had to do— cancel my weekly session with Clyde, scheduled for noon. That was now impossible to make. I activated my holotab and dictated a brief memoclip, apologizing. I paused for a moment before sending. *Should I mention that I've just met the Monster again after all these years?* I decided against it; just short and sweet, the way I liked it. But I sure could have used the session this week.

While in the transit capsule, heading up to the transport deck, my ear implant pinged. An incoming memoclip alert. It was a message from Clyde. *Wow, that was quick!* Once I activated my holotab, it began auto-scrolling across one quadrant of the screen. He was offering a session the following day, once I was back from California. That was unusual. *Isn't he supposed to be in the Hamptons with his wife on Sundays? Fine,* I thought, issuing a blink command to accept.

* * *

On the scramjet, heading to the Republic of California, I placed myself one space removed from Kace in the passenger cabin—I didn't want any accidental touch that would trigger my Eye before I could block it. That would only mean burning time from him, and I'd done more than enough of that already for one day.

"A drink?" he asked, calling up the onboard entertainment VirDa.

I saw from my bioclock that it was only just noon. I shook my head. "Not for me." Although my head was still thumping; I could have used a drink. I shook the thought away. I never drank booze before six p.m., even on the weekend. That was my rule. I knew that if I didn't have rules, I'd soon end up drinking wine at lunch, and then it would be a slippery slope to hard liquor on my breakfast cereal.

I listened absently as Kace issued a voice command and ordered a soda. I grinned to myself while I looked out of the window. *Doh, he really did just mean a drink, as in something liquid, non-alcoholic.*

And then, just like that, it was fully back. The Melody. Its thrum soothed the ache in my brain. I waited for a moment and inhaled quietly, as it coursed through my head. Now I felt better, calmer.

"We just passed into hypersonic range," Kace said, putting down his transparent cupstock, glancing at the holographic telemetry display on the screen in front of us. I sank back into the sofa and glanced out again. Clouds flew by beneath us. "I love airbreathing technology. Twenty-second-century tech at its best."

"Sure," I muttered. I couldn't have cared less. "Sorry, I need to catch up on a report, so that I'm prepped for when we arrive." Kace glanced at me and smiled.

I turned my body away slightly, activating my holotab. While scanning Dr. Diouf's report earlier, on Fatal Insomnia, one detail had caught my eye. But I hadn't managed to finish reading—of the ten Up-skilling centers that had gone live six weeks prior, volunteers in only nine were showing symptoms. *Why is that?*

I issued my eye-command selections on the report menu. The console display faded into a map-like representation of the ten LifeWorks facilities. Here in the United Federation of America, there were two such facilities: one in Toronto and one at the Inland Empire in the Republic of California, where I was now headed. There was also one in the independent Mexico territory and one in the Confederation of South American Republics, at La Plata near Buenos Aires, close to where I had previously been stationed. There were two in the Grand Union, in Madrid and in Sofia, the latter near my mother's asylum. The Old Kingdom had one in York, while there was one apiece in the republics of India and Japan.

Of those nine facilities, eight were in territories that were designated Tier One states by the UN. Only the LifeWorks center in the Old Kingdom stood out, a Tier Two state. But otherwise, Unskills in that Up-skilling center were affected to the same extent as volunteers from the centers in the eight Tier One territories.

What had attracted my attention was the tenth LifeWorks campus, based in a Tier Three territory. That one was located in the Sahel Federation near Ouaga, the capital of Burkina Faso. Not only was this the only Up-skilling center on the entire continent of Africa, it also had no diagnoses of insomnia. Zero! I double-checked the figures; they were correct.

Each LifeWorks facility contained a medical implant factory. I had to admit they had come up with a very catchy slogan for their Up-skilling initiative: *The transhuman of tomorrow, today.* As I read on, I learned that each facility had 180 robotic surgical units, each with a capacity of 140 procedures a day. But while the first nine Up-skilling campuses had been operating at near capacity, performing a little over 25,000 vagus implants per day, with each facility completing well over a million successful Up-skilling procedures over the last six weeks, the one in the Sahel Federation had been routinely performing at a third under capacity. Only around 16,000 individuals had been receiving the vagus implant per day. Sahel hadn't even reached 750,000 completed procedures prior to the hiatus. I checked again to see whether the reason was fewer volunteers. But if anything, the Sahel center had far more applicants for Up-skilling than the other centers. Five times more than could be accepted. The only other venue that came even vaguely close in terms of applicant numbers was the one in the Old Kingdom. *So what is so different about the Sahel center? And why no cases of Fatal Insomnia?*

I set my holotab to hibernate and straightened up.

"All done?" Kace asked. I nodded. "Can I ask you something?"

"Sure."

"Is this all just an ass-covering exercise?" I glanced at Kace, startled by the directness of the question. "The UN Secretary-General, Ms. Lejeune—"

"Assistant Secretary-General," I corrected.

"She didn't really … you know … seem to care what happens to the Unskills," Kace continued. I turned my torso away slightly. "Look, I'm not naïve. No one wants a repeat of five years ago with big tech. I get it. But you're not like her. I can tell. I'm a good judge of character."

"You seem sure of yourself," I replied quietly, turning back to face him, without yet being completely certain whether he was the sure-of-himself type. "You know what? I will join you for a drink."

He smiled. "What will it be?"

"I'll have a soda too." Kace gave the entertainment VirDa his voice command. Then he handed me the cupstock. I imagined I was smelling the aroma of bourbon swirling beneath my nostrils. I closed my eyes and gingerly took a sip. I could almost taste the warmth of the golden fluid caressing my throat as I sipped the soda. I looked back toward him. He was watching me, almost expectantly.

"So tell me about you, Dr. Kace Westwood."

"Oh, I don't do formal either." He took another sip of his drink. "What would you like to know?"

I mused for a second. "Tell me your story. A young medic? A record breaker? That's what it says in the briefing notes. I saw that you're the youngest full professor in the University of Columbia's entire history. What's all that about?"

"I'm a bit of a freak, I guess," Kace said, laughing. "I was doing calculus by the age of four."

"I guess that would make you a freak," I agreed, now laughing too.

"Yeah. My parents didn't know what to make of me. They're both in the Skill soc-ed class. Hardworking folks, Baltimore. My mom was originally from Chesapeake, Virginia. They met working in a military drone manufacturing plant."

"What happened after calculus aged four?"

"I was always an overachiever, or a young achiever, maybe. I went to high school, Baltimore Polytechnic Institute, when the neighbor's kids, kids my age, were still in short pants. I transferred to Baltimore City College and graduated when I was eleven. Around the same time, I wrote a book on insomnia. I researched it myself, and my older brother did the illustrations, which was cool."

"Why insomnia? How did you get into that?"

"My grandma," Kace replied. "She was like a second mom to me and my brother. Virtually raised us. But she struggled with insomnia after her menopause. It's actually quite common for older women. It got so acute she couldn't work anymore. It was tough for her and my grandpa. Made me want to find a cure. I graduated from New York University at the age of thirteen, and from Mount Sinai School of Medicine with a dual MD/PhD when I was nineteen."

"Wow." I was genuinely impressed. "And that's where you did your research on the wide-awake gene."

"You've heard about that?" Kace asked, sounding pleased.

"Sorry to disappoint. No idea what it is. I just read your bio."

"No, it's all fine," Kace replied as he dropped his head. I could tell he was slightly disappointed.

"How did you manage, being so young?"

"It was all good. I've always been popular with people."

"I can tell. You're well adjusted—for a genius, that is." I winked. This was my tell that I felt affinity with someone. I didn't usually wink at people, especially not men.

"Coming from you, I take that as a compliment. I have a lot of respect for your work and everything that you have accomplished," Kace said, flashing a wide, gracious smile. "Anyway, when I went to medical school at fourteen, I already stood one meter eighty-five tall. So most people assumed I was one of the regular medical students."

"And I read that you have an eidetic memory."

Kace frowned as I spoke. "They wrote that in my file?" Now he sounded slightly incredulous.

"Anyhow, how tall are you now?"

"One meter ninety-three."

"That's pretty tall. And now you're the youngest full professor in Columbia's history."

He glanced at me smugly. "Not bad for a poor black kid."

I was surprised to see Kace Westwood was no longer the edgier version of the man on display earlier at UN HQ. Now he was relaxed, funny, and completely disarming. He also had one of the nicest laughs I had ever heard. It started low, a sort of a chuckle, and then grew into a gentle escaping whoosh of mirth. And he was charming.

"You mentioned you have an older brother. Is he smart like you?" As I asked the question, a shadow crept across Kace's face. He was momentarily silent.

"My brother and me, we were kinda like chalk and cheese. I mean, it was always clear that I would be certified as Superior at seventeen when I took my job cert test. My brother, he didn't have the same luck. It was a rough neighborhood. He fell in with the wrong crowd. And he was—well, just different. Different from me, at least. He was certified an Unskill two years before me."

"Oh," I said, slightly taken aback. "So he's on the federal demogrant scheme?"

Kace shook his head. He glanced at me sideways and nervously took another sip from his glass of soda.

"He's dead." Now I barely knew what to say. "Do you mind if we don't talk about it?" he asked, averting his gaze.

"I'm really sorry, Kace," was all I managed. He turned back to look at me directly, a sad smile flitting across his face.

"One thing I've been meaning to ask, though. Lilith?"

"Ask what?"

"No, I mean your name … Lilith. Quite unusual. I only know it from some reading I once did in medieval folklore, for a high school assignment. Wasn't Lilith a female demon?"

I laughed. "Sometimes that feels apt. But the name is actually older. Rabbinic literature."

"What literature?" Kace asked, confused.

"You've heard of Eve." Kace threw me a puzzled look. "Adam and Eve," I clarified.

"Oh, that Eve."

"According to Genesis, chapter two, verse twenty-two, Eve was created from Adam's spare rib."

"The spare rib?" Kace asked.

"Ironic, isn't it? A woman as a spare rib. Made from the leftovers. That's why the God of the Old Testament had to be a man." Kace's eyes widened in surprise at my sudden show of prickliness. "Doesn't matter. Anyway, in some ancient texts Lilith was the woman implied earlier in Genesis."

"Earlier? I thought Eve was the first woman."

"There was one before. Adam's first wife. A hot, fiery female. Lilith. She was made from the same soil as Adam—an equal. She refused to become subservient to her husband. And in defiance, she left the Garden of Eden. Three angels tried to stop her. Persuading, cajoling. But she refused to go back. She preferred the life of a primordial she-demon. Judaic mythology has it that she was betrothed to a dark angel, an archangel, and had demonic offspring."

"So that's why God made Eve?" Kace asked.

"It's a story from a male point of view. Of course a man needed a more obedient partner. Someone not quite his equal. Anyway, that's the origin story of my name. My father's choice. And I kinda think it suits me."

"I'm glad I asked," Kace replied. With that, we both fell into thoughtful silence as we continued sipping our drinks, flying through the late morning toward California.

CHAPTER 6

As we drew near the LifeWorks facility, two gleaming conical towers appeared in the distance. They steadily rose up, high above the craggy canyons of the desert over which we were passing. There was a large circular dome nestled between them.

Once the scramjet landed, we taxied to a docking portal near the base of one of the towers. The butterfly-wing hatch hissed open, and we disembarked via a jetbridge directly into a large, high-ceilinged reception area. A welcome droid unit was waiting. It guided us into an old-fashioned elevator stack—part of the building's original design—before leading us out into a small connecting corridor. We then emerged into the large domed area, which from my briefing notes was the medical implant factory.

I was taken aback by the vastness of the complex, with the huge expanse of aisles and rows of medical pods interconnected by travelators. The 180 pods must have been quite a sight at full operation, before the UN's directive to cease all medical procedures until further notice. For now, silent stillness reigned. High above us, the semitransparent, white-paneled domed ceiling of the factory cast a spectral glow. Something in the air bothered me, making me want to sneeze—the distinctive odor of chlorhexidine gluconate antiseptic solution.

The central moving walkway, wider than the others, bisected

the implant factory. It powered on as we approached. We were transported from the elevator stack toward the large, frosted glass doors at the far end.

While on the walkway, I glanced inside the medical pods we passed. In the center of each stood a large surgical chair. The robotic surgeons, with arms, levers, dimmed lights, and protruding needles, stood over the chairs in motionless menace. The pods were in hibernation mode.

At the very far end, the moving walkway carried us out of the implant factory, through the sliding doors. The droid informed us this was the medical center. Three of the four walls were lined with banks of VirDa screens and diagnostic units, which curved up the domed walls. To one side were glass examination cubicles, complete with diagnostic VirDa units in each. And in the center of the area was a circular, island-like mezzanine structure which rose up, forming an elevated platform.

We stepped off the travelator and entered the modern glass transit tube at the base of the mezzanine structure. We traveled up the short distance—about eight meters—emerging onto the island-like structure. It was a meeting space with a large circular LED-lined table in the center. Three people were already present, seated on the far side. But at this level, the dome's exterior was transparent.

I heard Kace gasp next to me. "What a view!" he exclaimed. Not twenty meters away, through the glass dome, we were looking straight out across the exterior of the facility and its environs. Outside, beyond the modular polycarbonate landing strip and large hangar, was a vista of the Colorado Desert of Southern California.

Morning sun filtered through the windows, glinting on the two large gleaming white towers on either side of us as we stood, high up in the domed area. We were now on Californian Time, three hours behind New York.

One of the three seated figures began to stand. Kace and I moved forward while the welcome unit powered down against the handrail that looped around the edge of the meeting area platform. I recognized the figure as Abner Broad, rising stiffly from his chair. Next to him was a woman—his wife, Tova. I knew her from the MyPlace news channel broadcasts promoting Up-skilling. Next to the Broads sat a bony-looking man in a white tunic.

"Welcome to LifeWorks," Abner Broad said as we drew closer.

"It's an impressive complex," Kace said, flashing a wide smile as we stood in front of the Broads.

"We picked it up over four years ago—facilities, office space, and land—following the compulsory liquidation of Appleton Enterprises," Abner Broad explained. His voice sounded hoarse. His creased face looked careworn. The bony man next to him fidgeted. Tova glanced nervously at her husband as he spoke.

"It was originally a drone manufacturing plant, Drones Kineto," Abner continued. I didn't say anything, despite knowing the history of the place. I sat on the UN's oversight committee for approving language streaming service licenses. I had been party to the decision-making process to revoke Appleton's license after the Great Language Outage.

"But we've completely repurposed it. Now it's a state-of-the-art LifeWorks research and development facility," Tova added.

"And HQ to the international Up-skilling initiative," I added, speaking for the first time.

"You're Ms. King," Abner said.

"High Commissioner King," his wife corrected, giving me a small, kind nod of respect.

"Lilith," I replied.

"I've forgotten my manners," her husband said, still standing. "This is Tova, my wife. She and I founded LifeWorks Charitable Enterprises. And this is our Chief Medical Officer, Nile Ogden." He gestured to the man seated beside him.

"Actually, Abner and I are off to a charity gala luncheon after this," Tova said, waving at their attire. She was wearing a navy-blue dress and a pearl necklace. Her gray hair was ornately garlanded with a silver headpiece. Her husband was wearing a white ruffled dress shirt and a blue velvet dinner jacket. "But we wanted to make time …" Her words drifted to a silent stop.

Before Abner Broad could sit, I stepped forward and offered my hand. He paused and reached out, shaking it. His eyes widened slightly as he felt my touch, as if he somehow sensed my Eye as it pierced him, searching. I felt the rush of the emotional halo as I saw into him, always different, yet somehow, strangely, always the same. I held his hand a moment longer as he tried, involuntarily, to withdraw. I fleetingly closed my eyes and then opened them again. He glanced at me, an ephemeral look of muted wonder passing over his face as his gaze briefly touched mine. I saw only warmth, kindness, a generous spirit, some wistful sadness, a man fulfilled. I saw two small children seated beside him. Happiness. And then I let him go. He slowly lowered his hand until it rested beside him once more.

"You have grandchildren, Mr. Broad?" I asked with the confidence of already knowing the answer. I felt Kace looking at me with new curiosity. Abner's wife answered for him.

"Two beautiful granddaughters. We are truly blessed."

"We're obviously worried about all this, the insomnia thing," Abner insisted, gesturing for us to sit opposite them. "We're happy to assist in any way we can. Whatever you need, just say.

We're confident our tech has nothing to do with this. Which is why Nile is here," Abner said, glancing toward the medic. The man smiled superciliously at us.

"Can we offer you something to drink?" Tova asked, once we had taken our seats across from the Broads.

Kace smiled. "Coffee would be nice. Thank you." I shook my head.

Tova spoke into the tabletop-mounted Virtual Digital Assistant: "VirDa, coffee and two green teas. Nile, you want something?" Nile shook his head.

"Yes, Tova," a voice from the VirDa's inlaid speaker lisped quietly in a soothing female General American drawl. A serving daemon rolled across from the drinks dispenser on one side of the mezzanine platform, carrying the drinks on a tray. I glanced at the cups and saucers as they were dispensed. The Broads used actual crockery! Real old-school. Not the usual compostable cupstocks I was used to. Tova Broad was watching me.

"Royal Gothenburg, blue fluted," she said quietly. I glanced at her. "The tea and coffee set. From the Nordic Republic. A gift years ago from Ebba Black after her parents died, poor girl. Whatever became of her ..."

"William and Alvinia. We knew them, her parents," Abner added quietly.

"Do you mind if I ask how you knew them? We still have Ebba Black down as a missing person, officially at least, at Interpol I mean."

Tova leaned forward, smiling. "We don't mind at all. I studied with Alvinia at Berkeley. Years ago now, of course. She came for our senior year, on a Nordic visiting scholarship program. She and I became tight. Marc Barron and Hadean Burr-Alston were in our class. Marc always gave me the creeps, even then. Although

Hadean was worse in some ways—there was something of the night about him, Marc's vile shadow. I warned Alvinia, but Marc could be so captivating, and charming too if he wanted. Anyway, she fell in with his crowd, she was … well, quite wild in those days, at least she could be. She didn't listen to me. But …" Tova shook her head, brushing away whatever it was she was going to say.

"Did something happen?" I pressed, gently.

"She wouldn't give me the details. But she changed … I remember, after spring break. They had all gone down to Acapulco. I had tonsilitis. I was very disappointed I couldn't go, but maybe it was for the best. Alvinia was different after that. Anyways, we always stayed in touch, even after we both married. Abner and I watched Ebba and Elias grow up, whenever they visited this side of the pond. Terrible what happened to that family."

"I never met her, but thanks for satisfying my curiosity." I coughed, changing the subject. "We're here about the pandemic, as you know. But before we get to that, may I ask—Up-skilling, what made you decide to invest in that?"

Abner smiled. "It's simple. We wanted to give something back. It wasn't so much the children …"

"But the grandchildren," Tova added, continuing his thought. "Our eldest granddaughter, she was born with an IQ deficit. Likely to be placed in the Unskill class when she's formally classified at seventeen." Tova let out an audible sigh.

"It gets you thinking," Abner continued. "What's the value in a life? What's the meaning if a person can't contribute something? Is prohibited even …"

"From having purpose," Tova added. They were like a well-synchronized double act. I smiled to myself.

"Life has been good to us. But as you get older—as we have gotten older …" Abner turned toward his wife. She touched his hand tenderly. "Faced with our own mortality, we thought about our legacy."

"We decided, with friends and family, our fund managers, and our senior management team, that we would repurpose our business portfolio," Tova added.

"By finding a cure for low intelligence?" I asked.

"We view it as a medical problem like any other," Abner replied.

"We want to help people. People like our granddaughter," Tova clarified.

"In my business career, I have been instrumental in pushing the automation agenda," Abner continued. "My pharmaceutical plants are fully automated. My people and I supported the United Federation's Full Automation Bill, making low-skilled job grades obsolete. I even got tax breaks in the early days, as we replaced our research analysts with super intelligent AI, smarter than any human expert across any domain. We switched to code, to replace human brains. But …" He paused, clenching his jaw. "Those brains we replaced were attached to people."

"With families," added Tova.

"Do you know how many people, actual people, Alpha Science employed when I sold it?" Abner asked.

"Less than two hundred," his wife answered for him. "Even less today. A multibillion e-Continental business run primarily by AI."

"What a waste of life," Abner declared. "Replacing people with automated units, with virtual robotic code. And there's so much more people can do if we give them the smarts. Everyone has the potential to find a purpose. Not everyone has to be a medic, a professor, or a captain of industry. Not everyone can. But with our Up-skilling program, everyone has a chance. Maybe even a shot at soc-ed reclassification, if we can persuade some of our more amenable legislators in Congress to consider a revision of the soc-ed laws."

I smiled to myself. I liked the Broads. They were good people. But persuading the powers-that-be to revisit the soc-ed classification system, which now formed the basis for Tier One and Two societies, would be an almost impossible ask.

I moved to the sharp end of the interview with the Broads. "So how does Up-skilling actually work?"

"Nile?" Abner prompted. "You wanna lead?"

Nile Ogden cleared his throat. He had a long, hooked nose and thinning hair. "Around fifty percent of the world's Tier One and Tier Two population is of working age. But around half of this demographic is uncertified for work—the so-called Unskill class. These are people whose only hope of meaningful work, escaping a life of poverty and squalor, is a subscription to the weekly job lottery. But the odds of winning one of the weekly draws for so-called lux-unskill work is vanishingly unlikely. And even then, to enter the lottery isn't cheap when you're only on the federal demogrant, or the equivalent in other automated nations."

"We're talking a lot of people—over two billion," Tova said, jumping in. Nile dipped his head in acknowledgment.

"The Up-skilling program targets the Unskills, of course. But it's also open to anyone who is classified in the two manual job cert categories, the Semiskills and Skills," Abner said.

"We find the whole notion of soc-ed classification discriminatory," Tova continued. "The wrong assessment at the age of just seventeen is stigmatizing. And wrecks life chances."

"Our research shows that the assessment disproportionately classifies ethnic minorities, and especially males and those from lower socioeconomic backgrounds, as Unskills," Nile added.

"Let's face it," Abner said, his face now wearing a look of annoyance, "who has the right to decide that an IQ range from 96 makes you qualified only for Semiskill work, and a classification from 101 to 106 enables you to do more complex manual labor with a Skill job cert?"

"And that anyone with an IQ of 95 or below is essentially thrown on the scrap heap, denied a job cert, and labeled an Unskill!" Tova exclaimed.

Kace coughed. "I agree. But how does the vagus chip work, exactly?"

Nile smiled at him with the faintest hint of condescension. "It's well established that zapping certain peripheral nerves, which connect the brain and spinal cord to the body, helps people learn skills faster. And the key site is the vagus nerve."

"And where is that?" I asked.

"Here," Kace said, glancing at me while pointing to his upper torso. "It passes through the neck."

"What do you call it, Nile?" Tova asked.

"The information superhighway," Abner murmured, replying for Nile Ogden.

The medic smiled obsequiously. "The vagus nerve is the central link between body and brain. LifeWorks scientists have developed a chip that can deliver an electrical pulse to rev up the natural learning process," continued Nile. There was something pompous about the way he spoke that I disliked. "It prompts the brain to release chemicals that alter connections between neurons. Basically, we're tuning up the brain so that important details can be recognized with less practice." He finished, watching us expectantly. There was a brief silence before Kace spoke.

"And the signal is continuous?"

Nile shook his head. "The signal comes from the LifeWorks

satellite system. It works on a push system via the in-ear implant chip for all volunteers."

"A push system?" Kace asked. Nile gave a faint sigh of exasperation.

"Well, basically, volunteers to the Up-skilling program are migrated from their current language streaming service to LifeWorks. The LifeWorks LS servers in space then provide our volunteers with complimentary streaming for all the world's state official varieties, courtesy of our benefactors," he said, making a faint bowing gesture toward the Broads sitting next to him.

"Wow, that must be some financial investment," I exclaimed.

"We can afford it," Tova replied quietly, holding her palms out "But we do ask volunteers to begin making a financial contribution after twelve months, so they take some responsibility, ownership of the process, if you will. Of course, the state pays for the Unskills, as they're on the demogrant program."

"Volunteers from the Sahel Federation are exempt, naturally," Abner added, "As that's a Tier Three state." I made a mental note to come back to the subject of the Sahel volunteers.

"And the same system sends a periodic pulse around six times per hour, which activates the vagus chip," Nile continued.

"So to conclude; the vagus chip isn't in continuous operation, right?" Kace clarified.

"Correct," Nile confirmed.

"Is that significant?" I asked, looking at Kace.

He nodded. "If the vagus chip were causing melatonin depletion, then the brain would need to be receiving a continuous signal to ensure a low-frequency electromagnetic field."

"Melatonin? Magnetic field?" Tova asked. "I don't understand."

"One theory is that the vagus chip might somehow be linked to the sudden spike in sleep disorders—the deaths," I explained.

"Sleep requires melatonin production," Kace began. "There's evidence that shows it can be suppressed if the brain is doused in a continuous low-frequency EMF. All kinds of electronic devices produce EMFs, including our wrist chips. The language chip in the brain's cortex has insulation protocols to guard against this. But the vagus chip, fitted below the brain—well, that's exempt."

"So you thought that the vagus chip might somehow be creating the conditions for this outbreak of insomnia?" Nile exclaimed while crossing his arms slowly.

"Well, the body's melatonin production automatically switches back on when the electromagnetic field dissipates," Kace said hurriedly. "And given what you just said, Dr. Ogden, that the LifeWorks LS signal isn't continuous, it's unlikely to be the vagus chip."

"The thing is," Abner began, "it really can't be the vagus chip. It's impossible."

"Why not?" I asked, my curiosity piqued—he was clearly sure of himself.

"Some of our volunteers—well, they are currently pre-program, and—"

"They've got it," Tova blurted out.

"What do you mean?" Kace asked, with a look of confusion.

"All our volunteers, they go through a pre-program screening process. They're housed here on the LifeWorks campus," Abner said. "Pre-implant psych and health evaluations. We lose some volunteers at this stage. We have a zero-tolerance policy for narcotics and alcohol."

"So here's the situation," Nile interrupted. "We have a spike in cases of insomnia in the pre-programmers. Not just here in the Republic, but in eight others of our onsite campuses. The vagus chip hasn't even been fitted yet in many of those affected."

I glanced at Kace. If what they were saying was true, then it really wasn't the vagus chip causing the insomnia pandemic. But I would need to see the evidence. Or at least, I would need Kace to look over the files of the volunteers and confirm things for me. That was why I'd brought him along, after all.

"One more thing," I began. "You mentioned that volunteers are exhibiting symptoms in this facility and eight others. I understand there have been no symptoms detected in the Sahel Up-skilling center?"

"Right," Nile replied.

"I also saw from the WHO data that fewer volunteers are being processed there. Is there something different about that particular facility?" As I finished, I noticed Abner and Tova Broad glance at one another knowingly. But it was Nile Ogden who replied first.

"It's not the facility, it's the profile of the volunteers. None of the Sahel volunteers have Universal Grammar tech fitted."

I snapped my fingers as I got it. "Of course! A Tier Three state. A lang-law has never been mandated in the unautomated world."

"Right. Language streaming services have almost zero penetration there. So all the Sahel volunteers have to have UG tech fitted first, to get access to the LifeWorks streaming services before we can fit the vagus chip," Abner explained. "We brief them, of course, informed consent, before they e-sign the elective surgery forms. So that they're aware the procedure is irreversible."

"When the language chip is connected to the brain's language centers, the Broca's and Wernicke's areas, native linguistic knowledge attenuates," Nile added. "Once chipped, an individual is permanently dependent on language streaming. And in any case, removal of the chip would harm the brain's vasculature, leading to irreversible brain damage."

"We take a responsible approach. They're fully aware that if they choose to volunteer, there's no going back," Tova said.

"Basically, in Sahel there are two separate procedures. It's a constraint on capacity," Abner concluded. "Slows down the numbers we can process."

And there it was, one of my eureka moments. This information changed everything.

CHAPTER 7

Kace huddled with Nile Ogden on the opposite side of the large, round meeting table while I made small talk with the Broads. After a short time, Kace stood and gestured to me, walking to one side of the meeting platform. I excused myself from the Broads and walked across to him. He whispered quietly in my ear.

"It's definitely not the vagus chip. Everything they say checks out. And the first autopsy reports are just in from Geneva. I was right, it's not a prion disease. Whatever the cause, it's not natural, it has to be environmental."

"Okay, but I still want to meet with some volunteers," I replied.

"Me too. But now Dr. Ogden is reluctant."

"It's fine. Tell him I insist." I wouldn't allow Ogden to blow us off just because it was no longer his problem, not an Up-skilling issue. "You go figure it out with him and obtain patient consent. I need to quickly report back to HQ. And by the way, I'd like to see one volunteer in particular—Park Choon-Hee." Kace raised a querulous eyebrow. "My boss's daughter, she's here and sick, apparently …" His face became solemn.

I wanted to talk to a few volunteers, to get a feel for things—my feel. Kace still wanted to conduct a physical assessment, despite the new diagnostic software having been uploaded, revealing exactly the degree to which each subject was affected. Detailed analyses of the brains of those with symptoms were populating his open holotab screen as we talked.

While Kace and Ogden were discussing volunteers over a VirDa console, I remained where I was, at the edge of the meeting platform, and quietly dictated a memoclip update for Park into the Interpol secure messaging app in my holotab.

"The vagus chips check out. The Up-skilling tech is not the issue. Will brief you tomorrow at UN HQ as agreed, with M. Lejeune. I have a new line of inquiry. One of the Up-skilling centers, in the Sahel Federation, northern Africa, has no instances of insomnia. That cohort of volunteers consists entirely of unchipped nates. For the vagus chip tech to work, volunteers require access to streaming services from the LifeWorks satellite ecosystem. This means all Sahel volunteers must first be fitted with Universal Grammar tech, a language chip, and ear transceiver implant before they can undergo the Up-skilling procedure. The pandemic may have to do with language streaming. With language chips."

Just like five years ago, I thought. There was something about Universal Grammar tech, about language chips, that had never quite added up. I issued a blink command to hibernate my holotab and walked back to the Broads.

Kace moved back toward us and gave me a slight, affirmatory flick of his head. I thanked the Broads. They were off to their charity gala. I wished them well as they stood stiffly and bade us farewell.

Kace and I waited, while Nile Ogden issued voice command instructions into his holotab. A minute later I received an invite alert in my ear implant. I activated my holotab and scanned the details. We were to meet four volunteers, two of each gender. Kace had selected a post-op Semiskill volunteer first, as a control. Then we would meet with three Unskills: two post-op, the first of whom had no symptoms, while the second was exhibiting insomnia symptoms. The fourth and final volunteer had not yet undergone the procedure but had been exhibiting symptoms of insomnia for the longest period of any Unskill in the entire facility. This final volunteer was already catatonic.

****

Kace and I followed Nile Ogden, descending in the same glass transit tube back down to the medical internet-of-things hub below us. The volunteers were awaiting us in the glass medical cubicles I had seen earlier.

The VirDa screen adjacent to the first cubicle's entrance displayed the volunteer's name and sec-code, with a rotating holographic facial identifier—*Dayla Whisper Currell (24): female post-op volunteer, soc-ed class: Semiskill, language chip sec-code ID: 2206 2468 4259 002.* This first volunteer was our Semiskill control and symptom-free.

The glass door slid open. Nile gestured us in while he waited at the threshold. The woman was dressed in a yellow tunic branded with the LifeWorks logo. She was seated on a medical transport in chair mode, squinting at her holotab in fierce concentration.

"Dayla," I said gently, stepping into the small glass cell. "I'm Lilith. This is Kace." She glanced up. "Thanks for agreeing to see us. We're here to run a couple of tests." The woman had sad brown eyes. She was plain-looking and smelled faintly of the same antiseptic solution I had detected earlier, as if fresh from a LifeWorks hygiene unit.

"It's difficult to quit," Dayla said, glancing back down at the projection from her wrist chip, clearly reluctant to engage.

"What are you playing?"

"Lucky Dip," she replied, issuing a blink command at something on her screen.

"The job lottery game?" Kace asked, with vague surprise.

I turned to him and grinned. "Doh." He threw me a confused look. "Since it launched, everyone's playing it," I whispered, nudging him.

"Except me, apparently."

The woman glanced back up, looking him up and down with mild curiosity. "I don't think you need to."

"What level are you on?" I asked.

"Twelve. Not good enough. I keep missing the weekly cut-off. Can't finish the game in time. That's why I'm here." She extended her arm. I saw the familiar Phoenix logo on her open app, with the same tagline I'd seen on Avie's holotab—*Be reborn: A new you today.*

"I don't get the appeal," Kace muttered, as we both watched the woman frantically blinking at her screen.

"It gives the lower soc-eds hope," I muttered near his ear, while Dayla again focused on the game. "All qualifiers enter the lux-unskill job lottery in their territory—guaranteed if they complete all fifty levels by the weekly cut-off, Saturday midnight in the user's registered time zone."

"Qualifiers?" Kace asked.

Nile Ogden joined our conversation from the doorway. "Lucky Dip entices the lower soc-ed classes with the prospect of swapping their lives of unemployment or low-paid work for the glamor and financial security of the new breed of lux-unskill work. No prior training required."

Dayla glanced up at Kace. "My neighbor's gotten a lux-unskill job as a human server, a new uptown restaurant back in Denver. Very exclusive, always booked solid. Sometimes people will pay more for the human touch. It's an emotional thing."

Kace glanced down at Dayla, nonplussed. "Right, I guess," he muttered. He clearly didn't pay much attention to the MyPlace newsflashes.

"You're the famous lady detective," Dayla said, looking up at me. "Recognized the hair. Not many with a color like that. Is it natural?"

I involuntarily touched my head. "It's all me."

She looked around her through the glass wall to the other cubicles. "You know, I ain't an Unskill," Dayla announced proudly. "Got a Semiskill cert at seventeen. Not that it's helped me. I don't qualify for the federal program."

"The demogrant?"

Dayla nodded. "My father drank himself to death when I was a teen, after ten years out of work. He was certified an Unskill at thirty, when they first introduced the new ways. Never recovered from the shame. My ma says he was a taxi driver once. Before it all got automated, before the new airways got taken over by them hover cabs. We manage, me and Ma. She's a Skill soc-ed. Although the whispers are her job's gonna be automated soon. Only guarantees anyone has these days, y'all gotta be non-manual soc-ed, a Professional, or even Executive. Never met no Superior soc-eds. Don't think them ones are real. Made up, most likely. Heard about that from a Dark Courter I know in Clear Creek."

"Is it all right if I perform some tests?" Kace asked, gesturing toward the medical VirDa console adjacent to her.

Dayla slowly dropped her shoulders. "Some of them are going mad up there in the tower. The others. It's weighing on the rest of us, too. The really bad ones have been taken away. On medical transports. Ended up looking like zombies. Only way I can say it. Dead eyes. It was the eyes that was the most scary."

"But you're sleeping?" I asked.

"Yeah, I sleep okay. But the dead-eyed ones, they start to get crazed. They rock themselves and stare into space. And then … nothing. What kinda tests are these?"

"To test brain function and melatonin levels," Kace answered.

"What's that?"

"It's a chemical your body produces."

"Like a drug?" Dayla asked with curiosity.

"Well, a hormone, actually. Completely natural. Our bodies make it. It helps us sleep," Kace explained, before issuing voice commands to the diagnostic VirDa. "Let's get a sample from Dayla Currell." Then, addressing Dayla, he continued. "We'll be done in a moment." The unit moved toward her. One lever pressed a probe against her arm. "The machine will sterilize your skin and take a blood sample."

"It's been done plenty by now. Doesn't hurt."

"That's right," Kace confirmed. "It uses microneedles thinner than a human hair. You won't even feel a prick." The unit withdrew its levered arm and began displaying data on its VirDa screen.

Kace smiled down reassuringly at Dayla, before muttering: "An average peak nighttime value of fifty-two picograms per milliliter of blood. Current value twelve picograms." Then more loudly: "Your melatonin profile is normal, all perfectly fine." Kace turned back to the medical VirDa: "And full brain function. Focus on the thalamus." The unit lowered a dome over her crown, partially occluding the top of her head.

"This hasn't been done to me before. It feels warm," Dayla said, looking up at Kace.

"That's completely normal. It's a special type of scanner. We're just taking some live pictures of what's going on in there," Kace said, pointing. He began poring over a series of images and graphs on the VirDa's screen while data scrolled down. "Brain function is also normal, and your polysomnogram checks out too," he said, glancing back at Dayla, smiling again as the robotic unit withdrew the dome from her head. I doubted she had a clue what that was, but she smiled back anyway. "I think we're done here," Kace said, turning to me.

"Thank you, Dayla," I said. "We'll let you get back to your Lucky Dip."

The next volunteer was an Unskill named Brayan Stark. He was twenty-seven, post-op and also symptom-free. We were standing outside the glass unit. As we entered, he watched us suspiciously.

"Not playing Lucky Dip?" I asked. There was no sign of an active holotab.

He shook his head. "Not my thing."

"Brayan sometimes has difficulty concentrating," Ogden said softly from the doorway before addressing the volunteer directly. "A baseline IQ of just seventy-five. The ability to lay down more accurate short-term memories will improve with practice now that the vagus chip has been fitted." I was taken aback to see the compassion with which Nile Ogden addressed the young volunteer.

"I have to have another blood test?" Brayan asked. Kace threw him an apologetic smile. While Kace gave his voice commands to the medical diagnostic unit, the young man studied me quietly.

"You're very pretty," he said straightforwardly. "Never seen a girl with bright green eyes before. My name's Brayan."

"Nice to meet you, Brayan. I'm Lilith."

"I'm from Plum Creek."

"Oh, I don't know it, I'm afraid," I replied.

"The barbecue capital of Texas. South of Austin, on the old Chisholm Trail."

"Sounds nice."

"That's what it says on the holographic billboard. Seen it plenty. When you enter city limits." The young volunteer fell silent for a moment. "Never rode a hover car before I came here. No one I know in Plum Creek can afford one."

"Did you like it?" I asked.

"I liked the view." I smiled. "The city looked small. The people like bitsy ants. Never imagined it to be like that, so itsy."

"All done," said Kace. "Everything normal. We'll let you get back to your rehab."

"Oh yeah," he said, suddenly smiling, a gap-toothed smile. I leant forward to touch his arm. I felt an emotional halo of fuzzy affability and hazy bafflement; a poor boy from a small town.

Next, we had the two volunteers who did have symptoms, both Unskills. First, Park's daughter, Park Choon-Hee. I gulped. I saw from the VirDa readout on the cubicle door that she had been diagnosed with insomnia the day after the procedure. Her records showed that she hadn't had any sleep for five days straight.

As we entered, she looked up at us with frantic eyes that darted around the room. She stood up and then suddenly sat down. *Exactly like Avie,* I thought with grim horror, shuddering. The woman was waving her hands in the air, her holotab open on the Lucky Dip app, moving around in midair with erratic jerks.

"I can't finish," she snarled, not quite at the device but not to anyone in particular.

"The level?" I asked, trying to sound soothing.

She glanced at me as if suddenly noticing us. Tutted and shook her head. "The game," she whispered hoarsely.

"Choon-Hee—can I call you that?" Kace asked. She glanced

at him and then stood again suddenly. "We just need to run some tests. Is that okay?" Choon-Hee stared at Kace, before her eyelids began fluttering rapidly, while clawing the empty space in front of her with her hands and arms, as if fighting someone.

I gasped. "I've seen this before, exactly this, in someone I know."

"Dream enactment," Kace whispered. "One of the symptoms. Boy, this is fast!"

"But she seems awake," I replied.

Kace spoke his voice commands into the medical console VirDa. With that, the adjacent auto-diagnostic unit moved into position, running medical tests. After a few minutes, it withdrew, while Kace inspected the data on its screen. He muttered something and then turned to me, slightly aghast, before facing back toward the diagnostic unit.

"MDU3, let's examine a lower DLMO threshold. I want an analysis using radioimmunoassays."

"Already complete, Dr. Westwood. The volunteer has no detectable melatonin synthesis. Her melatonin profile has been at zero since arrival," the machine responded with calm tones as if this was the most normal thing in the world.

"Impossible," Kace muttered quietly in involuntary incredulity.

"What is?" I asked.

Kace turned to me. "Some people—well, they're just low melatonin producers. But even in patients with Fatal Insomnia, there's usually some production, however little. We use a very sensitive in-vitro assay technique to measure melatonin concentration by use of antibodies."

"You've lost me."

"This patient, Choon-Hee. She's producing no melatonin whatsoever. Zero amplitude."

Nile Ogden looked in from the doorway. "We've prescribed everything we can think of. There's no response from the usual sleeping pill treatments."

"There's some early onset damage to the thalamus and brainstem," Kace whispered. "Some evidence of atrophy. I don't understand …"

Choon-Hee suddenly looked at me. "Will I die like the others?" she asked, now sounding strangely calm.

I stared at her. "I'm going to figure this out. You have my word. Do you mind if I see which level you're on?"

Choon-Hee held out her wrist, twisting her arm so that the holographic screen was facing me. I saw the same familiar logo of a fiery phoenix. Numbers were spinning in a maze level in the app. I gently pressed one forefinger against the screen. Immediately, I felt the rush of an emotional halo. I flinched. It was the same dread I'd experienced when Avie's holotab had passed through my hand. There were screaming, pleading voices, being sucked of their vital force, before taking on the rank stillness of corpses.

I staggered back, sensing I was about to faint. Kace glanced at me, startled. I leaned against one of the glass walls of the cubicle, feeling nauseous.

"Are you all right?" Ogden asked, genuine concern inflecting his voice. I straightened up, walked out of the cubicle, and gave an abrupt nod of my head without saying anything. I was unable to speak for a few seconds. We moved in silence along the corridor toward the last patient.

"Our final volunteer is a thirty-five-year-old male, Tenysi Pussett. He hasn't had the vagus implant fitted. But now he's been at the facility for thirteen days straight," Nile said in a somber tone.

"Thirteen days is a long time to be stuck here," Kace muttered.

Nile looked down, as he seemed to be trying to fight back emotion—I had misjudged him. "Tenysi was already suffering from severe symptoms of melatonin depletion when he arrived. But since then, his health has deteriorated further. He wasn't well enough to undergo the procedure and is certainly too unwell to be released. You'll see."

As we approached, I saw the pitiful spectacle through the glass walls. The man was supported on an auto-medical transport unit. Medical webbing held him in a quasi-upright posture; the unit raised him up for his medical. His face was deathly white, the eyes virtually unblinking, staring at the white glow of the LED ceiling above. His arms, which were strapped next to him, twitched periodically while his entire body was racked by undulating convulsions. I glanced away; I couldn't bear it.

"How long has he been catatonic?" Kace asked.

"Two days now," Nile replied. "His next of kin has consented to his examination."

"Next of kin?" I stammered.

"His wife … he has four kids," Nile added, quietly.

"Poor guy," Kace muttered. "MDU4, can I see his blood work?"

"Yes, Dr. Westwood," replied the diagnostic unit. "I have used radiolabeled molecules in a stepwise formation of immune complexes."

"But no melatonin profile?" Kace asked.

"The volunteer has had no detectable melatonin levels since arrival."

"And brain scan?" The unit displayed various images, which Kace scrolled through. A raft of numbers and other data dropped down the screen.

"Advanced atrophy of the thalamus," Kace exclaimed. "Man, this is advancing quickly. He doesn't have long," he whispered.

I fixed Nile with one of my looks. "Tell me, just out of curiosity, Dr. Ogden." Something had started nagging me. "Do you happen to know whether this volunteer is a Phoenix app user?"

Nile raised his eyebrows in surprise—probably not the question he'd expected. "I can check. We do ask for consent to collect social media and screen time data, as part of our patient intake questionnaire. You know, to get a holistic view of the patient, as well as to have a baseline for online habits, before and after the procedure." He raised an eyebrow as he activated his holotab. I glimpsed strings of data scrolling across his holographic screen. "Yes, we have that data point. Our records show that he set up a profile for the Lucky Dip app five weeks ago, apparently. A week after it launched. So yes, he is a Phoenix Industries Lucky Dip app user."

My mind began whirring.

"Could I ask another favor, as you seem to have access to the data? Can you cross-reference all volunteers with symptoms of insomnia and subscriptions to Lucky Dip? I want to know whether there's a correlation between the two."

Ogden glanced at me for a moment, thoughtfully. "Happy to. But I can't do it from this," he replied, gesturing at his holotab. "I'll send it through shortly to your Interpol account, if that works."

I nodded smartly. That definitely worked.

CHAPTER 8

Once checked in at the hotel in Palm Springs, I finally had some time to myself. I was just out of the shower in my suite, still enveloped in my fleecy, luxury hotel towel. I had it pulled up under my bony shoulders, tucked high into my armpits. I didn't care how I looked as long as no prying sec-cams could spy on me—I was a prude, after all.

I had received the data I'd requested from Nile Ogden. Only Unskill subscribers to the Lucky Dip gaming app were affected by symptoms of insomnia. The app now had my full attention. Just a correlation for now. While any psychologist worth their salt would have warned me that correlation didn't equal causation, I had a feeling the two were connected—the app developer, Phoenix Industries, and the pandemic. After all, I didn't believe in strange coincidences. Lejeune had been right to suspect a technological cause—but it wasn't the one she had expected.

I sat on a velvet chair and logged into my Interpol portal from my holotab, to do a little digging on Phoenix Industries S.A. It was a French-based tech conglomerate that, among other ventures, had a software development arm. I also wanted to find out more about its CEO, Bastien Cardinale. I spoke my voice commands, throwing them in a flurry of hyperactivity at the MyPlace search app in my holotab, as well as the Interpol database.

As the search results populated my screen, I gripped the velvet handles of the chair in frustration. There was very little about Cardinale on file at Interpol—only a small, restricted file held at the Singapore Cybercrime Directorate to which I didn't have access. *Strange*, I thought. But one thing was clear, Cardinale was virtually a ghost. The only thing of immediate interest was that his profile on the Phoenix MyPlace page stated that he had graduated from the INSEAD business school in Paris, France.

As I continued scrolling, what I saw almost made my heart skip a beat. There were two names in the search results, listed as notable *other* alumni of INSEAD: Marc Barron and Jürgen Fleischman. *What the hell?* I then blink-selected the INSEAD link. I wanted to see which cohort Barron and Fleischman had graduated from. The results faded onto the screen. And there it was—both in the very same year. Barron and Fleischman had been classmates! I could scarcely believe it. But no mention of Cardinale. At least, not on the INSEAD site.

I then cross-referenced the year Barron and Fleischman graduated with Phoenix's MyPlace profile for Bastien Cardinale. His graduation year was the same as for Fleischman and Barron. *What are the chances?* I thought. An unholy trinity. All three had studied for their MBAs at the same university at exactly the same time. Back in the day, in the old century, before there were any lang-laws, even here in the Republic of California. Before Barron and his genius chief scientist, Hadean Burr-Alston, changed the way we lived our lives, the way we connected with our AI, through the Universal Grammar tech and the voice command technology they invented.

I knew I had to talk to Kal at the Singapore International

Cybercrime Directorate. I needed whatever further intel she could access on this Bastien Cardinale and on Phoenix. But first, I owed Kace dinner. And I could sure use a drink.

***

I snatched at my bourbon. Small gulps. This wasn't my style, drinking in the hotel's dining suite, in a black cocktail dress, in an official capacity while awaiting Kace. But it was well after six p.m., and I had been dry all day. And it was always nice to have a chance to dress up a bit, outside of my self-imposed work uniform.

The sense of being followed, of being watched, gnawed at me again. I knew rationally, of course, that others sometimes experienced such feelings too—that it all had a scientific basis. The presence of human eyes and faces in our peripheral vision enabled us to sense others in our environs, to detect potential intruders. It was an innate survival mechanism, a legacy of our evolutionary hominid past.

I took the final slug of bourbon from my glass, before twisting my body around in my seat. I quickly scanned the tables behind me, aware of a pounding in my chest. For a split-second, I glimpsed a faint outline—a long, pale figure, in one of the dining chairs at an empty table. I blinked and the outline vanished. *A trick of the light. You're imagining things, Lily,* I told myself.

As I turned back around in my seat, I noticed an annoying guy at the next table. He was staring straight at me. I pretended not to have seen him. He then even threw a wink at me, all alone. I groaned as he stood and began approaching.

Sooner or later, with men, it always happened. They either became stalkers or cloying puppy-eyed sycophants I couldn't shake off. And no matter how much I insisted, they wouldn't take no for an answer. I never quite got why that was. Why I was such an unwitting femme fatale, as one of my university colleagues had once described me. I didn't see myself as beautiful, at least not in the conventional sense of female beauty, with my hair the color of flames. I guess part of my allure was the well-constructed façade that I projected for the world—haughty, sure of herself, and difficult—which was all meant to hide just how damaged I really was. And to keep everyone at arm's length—the right kind of distance for me.

"I like your hair," the guy announced as he hovered over me, a predator dressed in white. White jacket, shirt, even white pants. Tall and slim. He had a cleft chin. A macho type. And he smelled of something cheap. Spice and Sun, maybe, or Neroli Superstitious. It wafted around him, cloying. Around me. Very irritating. He clearly thought he was at least a ten, but he was exactly the type of man I couldn't stand. The type that wouldn't take no for an answer. Too insistent. Too forward. Just too much.

"It's an inverted A-line bob," I replied. I glanced at myself in the distant mirror behind the bar. It really was. My flaming hair was longer at the front as it touched my shoulders, and shorter at the back. He curled his top lip. *Is that an attempt at a smile?* I wondered. "You were asking about the style?"

He shook his head, smirking. "Someone tell God that one of his angels is missing." I groaned again. The guy was coming on to me. Properly coming on. It always took me aback—no man was my type, ever.

"Really?" I replied archly. "That's what you're going with?" I looked at him with bayonet eyes. "I once messaged God. The celestial missing persons bureau. No one answered." The sarcasm in my voice would have leveled anyone with reasonable smarts.

But this one didn't seem to take the hint, let alone the hit.

"Can I buy you a drink?" he persisted. I laughed, a short, hard, dismissive laugh. The guy shifted on his feet. Finally, he was starting to become uncomfortable.

"Let me tell you the one about a Chinese guy who once reported me to the Singapore Police Force," I said. "The guy alleged that I was racist, on account of the fact that I refused to date him. I even received a phone call from a desk sergeant at the police HQ in New Merlion Park. The police officer had assumed I was a stuck-up, privileged white European. All true. And a woman. Also true."

"Obviously," the guy muttered.

"But the cop quickly became embarrassed when I explained it wasn't the guy's skin color at all. I am no more racist than that robotic welcome unit over there. I just don't date anyone with a penis. Period."

"So that's a *no* then?" he asked.

"What do you reckon, Sherlock?"

At that, he tutted. "Bitch!" he hissed at me, before turning on his heel and retreating back to his table. *Charming,* I thought.

I was relieved to see Kace's languid frame approaching. I felt exposed in a dress. Kace's eyes bulged as he clocked me. I had already finished my bourbon. I was relieved; I didn't want him to catch me drinking. And I wasn't sure if I could walk in my high heels if I had any more.

"Wow," he gasped as I stood. "Lilith, you are stunning," he whispered.

"Don't get me started. That jerk has already been hitting on me," I said loudly, gesturing at the next table. The guy in white pretended not to have heard, as Kace threw him a stern look.

"Sorry," Kace muttered, looking away, now embarrassed. I smiled softly, unsure whether his discomfort was due to his own remark, or because of the alpha-schmuck at the next table. In any case, I suddenly felt protective toward Kace, as if he were the younger brother I'd never had. Kace began scrolling through the tabletop holographic menu projecting from the inlaid fusion bar. The restaurant's lighting shifted subtly into dim desert lighting mode—a slight red flare with yellow ambience. I glanced around briefly at the clientele. It was an expensive place. Very comfortable. The UN had deep pockets.

Once we had both ordered, Kace opened his large hands and placed his palms gently on the white surface.

"What's next?"

"Next?" I asked, mildly surprised. "Tomorrow, we're heading back to New York. But you, you've gone well beyond the call of duty. You're done. You can enjoy your Sunday."

"You think it has something to do with the game, the app, don't you?"

"The access-to-jobs lottery app? You bet," I replied. "And the developer is Phoenix Industries, a company headquartered near Paris. That's where I'll be headed, once I've checked in with my boss tomorrow." *And if I get the approvals,* I thought.

Kace gazed at me without saying anything. He was starting to make me feel nervous.

"I want to come with you, to the Union, please, Lilith," he said quietly, watching my face. I was momentarily startled.

"This isn't your fight. We know it's not the vagus implants."

"We do know that it is connected to melatonin depletion. That's what's causing the insomnia," Kace objected.

"Sure. But this is where I get to work. There's something technological going on, causing the suppression of melatonin. This is now my area of expertise. We really don't need a civilian involved in this anymore, especially as I don't know what we're up against. It could be dangerous." I hoped that would dissuade him.

But Kace was unperturbed. "A civilian? You didn't see my full file then … I'm a national guard reservist. I enlisted as a student officer, which helped pay my way through medical school … my family, I don't come from money. I've had full basic training, three deployments, and know my way around most standard-issue UFA weaponry."

I grinned. "You're certainly full of surprises."

"I tend to be." Kace smiled back at me. "But more importantly, whatever's causing the pandemic, there's a medical outcome that's killing people due to lack of sleep. A subject I know quite a lot about."

"Look. Let me buy you dinner. Courtesy of the UN, with our thanks. Don't you have a life to get back to?"

Kace narrowed his eyes. "You said this wasn't my fight. But the thing is, in a way, it is." I looked at him in mild surprise. "I told you my brother was dead, right?" I nodded. "But I didn't tell you how he died." I studied Kace while he paused. "He was killed. Murdered. Over a year ago. It broke my mother's heart. I don't think she'll ever be the same again."

I bit my lip in surprise. "I'm so sorry. I had no idea."

"Thanks," Kace mumbled before looking back into my eyes. In the lighting, his blue eyes shimmered with a striking blend of purple, a reflection of the sunset lighting. "He was killed because he was an Unskill."

I felt a jolt of surprise course through me. "What? Are you sure?"

"There were two of them. Dark Court cultists. One had even published an online manifesto. Repugnant stuff. Talking about the adjudicators from the Dark Court, who set themselves up to judge those who should be eliminated. Those unworthy. Unworthy of life." I didn't know what to say, how to reply. "My brother, he was in Midtown. It was one of the early Million Person March protests, organized by Start Apollo's lot. My brother wasn't even participating. The dumbass was trying to rob a jewelry store. And that's when the two young thugs caught him—two Semiskills driving around looking for trouble, looking to push back against the protesters, to pick on Unskills, especially if the Unskill was black. One of them filmed the whole thing. Yelling, 'Useless eater,' at him, at my brother. Then they set him on fire, doused him in gasoline. I'll never forget the sound of his screams. Blood-curdling. I asked the cops to destroy it. They refused. It was evidence, after all. I didn't want my mother to see it."

"Oh my god, Kace, that's awful," I stammered.

"The worst thing was that they got off."

"What?"

"They claimed it was self-defense. Stand-your-ground law."

"But if they set him on fire … How is that self-defense?"

"The DA arraigned them. But the Grand Jury declined to indict. A majority of Semiskills. They took the side of the two kids. The other soc-ed classes, most of the time they don't care about Unskills. They just look away or cross the street when they see the holographic pin Unskills have to wear to claim demogrant privileges—the badge of shame. My brother hated displaying it. But deep down, you know, the Semiskills, they resent Unskills. They despise them. The Unskills get public money. And the Semiskills are also afraid. Semiskill jobs might be next to go with creeping automation."

"They're also most susceptible to Dark Court propaganda," I added.

Kace was clearly agitated. "The Dark Court spews garbage—

that intelligence is genetic, that two Unskill parents always make Unskill kids, a vicious circle producing ever more Unskills. The Semiskills think of Unskills like stray dogs that'll keep on breeding if left unchecked. That the streets will be overrun with them. And the Semiskills sure as hell don't want Unskills *breeding* any faster than they already are."

I nodded. "The Semiskills largely back the Compulsory Sterilization bill. And they actually bother to vote, unlike Unskills. That's why Congress pays attention to Semiskill voter sentiment."

"You know, my brother was never even added to the electoral register. Everyone's supposed to be added, at eighteen, automatically, right? Wrong. Not in our home state. Not if you're classified as Unskill the year before. Not that he cared. My brother would have never voted anyway. But my mother cared. She cared that our state would do that to someone. To her son. It happens in a lot of places in the United Federation with Unskills." My eyes widened, to see Kace's passion and bitterness.

Just then, the robotic server brought our food. Kace had also ordered wine. I looked longingly at his glass. I would wait to get my fix later—I never drank with work colleagues, one of my rules.

Kace rested his gaze on me. "I have to do something to help. I owe it to my brother, to my family. And to the families of other Unskills. Whatever he did, he didn't deserve that. He didn't deserve to lose his life."

I looked at him thoughtfully for a moment before replying. I understood how he felt, probably better than he knew.

"Well, I guess I could use your expertise. Let's see what my boss says."

CHAPTER 9

The next morning, I awoke in my hotel bed in a black mood, this time stirred up by the vestiges of the same goddamn nightmare. It was the feeling of being sucked backward through churning water. That's what it felt like in the black dream, the one that imprisoned me, night after night. The Stygian darkness of my backward traveling struck with a petrifying chill. A malfunction of my body's thermoreceptor system. I imagined death would feel just like that. The only way I could describe it. But no white lights. The blackness wasn't like ordinary dark. It was the infinite purple blackness of a night completely devoid of stars, a moonless sky. So inky that you were sure you could see floating blotches of tarred nothingness, just like when you closed your eyes.

I don't think Clyde really ever got it, that the sensation of drowning wasn't just a feeling—in the sense of something imagined, a phantasm, an amygdala hijack. It was the actual feeling of a lived experience, something embodied at a deep level, emotionally rancid, cancerous, growing for twenty years; the feeling of being sucked backward through water in silent blackness. I always had this, these feelings. Intuitive, sensory, primordial. That's what I did. I knew that's what made me exceptional.

***

We departed Palm Springs early, a short flight back east. But with the time difference, it would be mid-morning in New York. Kace and I had a 10.30 a.m. appointment to brief Park, Lejeune and Diouf about our findings. But I also knew I needed more information on Phoenix Industries. And on Bastien Cardinale. And for that, I needed Kal's help.

Kace glanced across at me, watching as I activated my wrist chip, just a half-tap. My retro-look bioclock powered on. That was my style. Roman numerals, a round clock face, and hands that glowed green under my skin. As I saw the time, I calculated that it would already be nighttime in Singapore. But I knew Kal would always take my calls, day or night. I activated my holotab and selected the audiocall app.

"Call Kalpana Ng." The audio feed from my virtual screen went silent before I heard a crackle and then the husky breath of Kal's voice. Next, I heard a squeal of delight.

"Hello, stranger."

Suddenly, I missed her, a visceral stab of pain in my chest: beautiful, chaotic Kal. I yearned for the daily doses of candor that had initially surprised, shocked me even. Her no-nonsense assessments, ranging from the professional to the personal, welled from her personality. In moments of unspeakable sadness and self-doubt, Kal had provided solace and friendship—for those few years in Singapore she had always been there, no matter what.

"We can switch to video," Kal said.

"I'm on a scramjet, might lose the signal," I replied. Then I coughed. "I'm with a colleague."

"Oh, I see. No problem. It's always good to hear your voice." Kalpana Ng streamed the Singlish state official variety, and

Singlish accent differentiators, which always made her sound so exotic.

"Just departed the Republic. Now headed home." I blinked at the slider, muting the audio bar. Now the audio signal was automatically redirected to my ear implant, so that only I could hear it.

"As in California?" Kal asked.

"Right. I'm calling for a professional favor. I need some help."

"Only a professional favor?" she said with faux disappointment. "What's up?"

"I want to know everything you have on Bastien Cardinale."

"Hmmm … it was only a matter of time."

"What?"

"Until the world's most beautiful detective started chasing the world's greatest man of mystery."

I laughed. "And the world's greatest conundrum," I retorted.

"Him or you?" Kal asked breathlessly.

"I'm not chasing anyone. At least not yet! So what do you have?"

"Sec," she replied. "Hmmm … as you probably suspected, not much. Both he and Phoenix Industries were unknown until five years ago. Before then, not a thing—no registration in the Union or anywhere else."

"The Great Language Outage reset the global landscape."

"Exactly. Phoenix only popped up on our radar after language streaming was restored. That was the first time we became aware of them. The first registration was as a software development start-up. But since then, they've gotten into all kinds of things."

"What about this Cardinale?"

"The guy's a virtual unknown. Even his language streaming rebound records only began after the language outage."

That's odd, I thought.

"Why would a rich industrialist deliberately choose to be permanently feral, an out-soc?" I mused aloud.

"Well, for one thing, everyone's still getting their newborns chipped, despite the repeal of lang-laws. No one can afford to get left behind with jobs becoming so scarce. Cardinale seems to be an eccentric. Maybe he just decided to join the party, finally. Or maybe his business interests dictated that."

"What else do we know?"

"Really not much. There's no digital birth registration and no biometric data, no holographic facial ID records. Which is all illegal, of course. As well as being pretty much impossible to pull off," Kal observed.

"Unless you've never been chipped, and you're outside society, an out-soc."

"The only reliable thing we have on Cardinale is statements on his corporate MyPlace profile. Those that can be verified, at least."

"I already saw the MyPlace bio," I explained. "Cardinale graduated from INSEAD business school. Same cohort as the Director."

Kal snorted. "Yeah. Amazing, isn't it? What are the chances! Perhaps you could ask Herr Fleischman about Monsieur Cardinale." I could tell that Kal's tongue was firmly in her cheek. But still, it didn't prevent the involuntary panic I suddenly felt rising in my throat. I reached for the elastic band under the cuff of my blouse. "That was a joke," I heard Kal say in response to my silence. "But, you know, they might even have been business partners back in the day, before Fleischman caught his break."

"Business partners?" I exclaimed. "I thought the Director was a career cop."

"Oh, indeed he is. But he had a sideline in drone security start-ups, among other things, after business school. All completely legit while he was still working for the Bundespolizei. But when he was promoted out of the BPOL-Präsidium in Potsdam and began his ascent up the greasy pole in the Ministry of the Interior, well, then he had to give up on his business interests."

"How so?"

"Conflict of interest, ministerial code of conduct. That's when Fleischman also began running for public office. Those are the rules in that neck of the woods. And you know how obsessed those guys are about their beloved rules. Or at least, being seen to follow them."

I laughed. "This Cardinale, his MyPlace profile also mentions drone tech among past business interests," I muttered.

"Right. Anyway, following restoration of language streaming, this Cardinale—or at least Phoenix—started buying up all the old Appleton internet-from-space infrastructure. Today, Phoenix Industries is the sole owner of SkyLink, the entire satellite system. We never fully figured out where or how Phoenix secured its funding."

"I didn't know ..." I stammered, "... that Phoenix owns SkyLink." Now my mind started racing.

"I know what you're thinking," Kal continued. "Why would a French-based software developer buy up a global internet-from-space broadcast system?"

"My thoughts exactly. The Phoenix Lucky Dip app is freely available via the regular language streaming providers. Phoenix doesn't need an internet-from-space ecosystem for its business model," I exclaimed.

"And even if it did, why buy one with such a tarnished reputation as SkyLink, with its links to Appleton, right?" Kal asked. "If you're up for a conspiracy theory, you might say the fact that Phoenix now owns SkyLink has been disguised. Or at least, Phoenix didn't want the link to be too obvious, in terms of public optics."

"I'm definitely up for a conspiracy theory."

"I knew you would be," Kal replied, laughing. "You've heard of RCM?"

"The Lyon-based conglomerate? The one that manufactures medical units?"

"Precisely. Robot Cyber Médecine. Anyway, it was RCM that bought up Appleton's satellite servers."

"That I know. It was vetted by the UN's Counter-Cyberterrorism Committee. I was involved in the process."

"And by the big tech Global Anti-Competition Commission," Kal continued.

"Yeah. The United Federation and the Chinese were both concerned about the dominance of the Union's internet-of-medical-things industries. But the deal passed muster with the Security Council. So what?" I replied.

"Well, here's your so what. Guess who owns RCM?"

I took a sharp breath. "No!"

"That's right. Phoenix Industries S.A. is the parent company."

"That I didn't know," I replied.

"Nor did anyone here at the International Cybercrime Directorate, until recently. It's been disguised, through several layers of holding companies. Not that Phoenix or RCM have done anything illegal, strictly speaking of course. But the odd thing is, there's been no attempt by Phoenix to compete with Tele3, or the other big language streaming tech players in the Grand Union or elsewhere. Phoenix doesn't offer language streaming."

"So basically, it's unclear why Cardinale needs a global satellite system," I concluded.

"And Phoenix also maintains a private army of human contractors, ex-special forces apparently, and advanced droid tech, we believe, with a training base in the abandoned territories."

"Kal, you're a mine of information," I whispered, as I lapsed into silence. "Why would a tech company need mercenaries?" I asked, after a moment's reflection.

"I told you. Nothing about this makes any sense."

"I have to check this all out. In person."

"In Paris? Ooh la la," Kal said, giggling.

I smiled to myself. "Please, enough already," I replied curtly, before laughing too.

"They're sooo cute, those French girls. You'll be turning all their heads," Kal whispered. "But seriously, why Phoenix? I heard you were assigned to the sleep disorder case."

"News travels fast," I replied. "That's why I was in the Republic. Checked out the Up-skilling program. Vagus chip implants. I've ruled that one out."

"So what makes you want to look into Phoenix? One of your famous feelings?"

I smiled. "Am I that predictable?"

"Not predictable. Always different."

"But, always the same," I responded.

Kal laughed again. "Who's your colleague? Anyone nice? Someone I should be introduced to?"

"He is nice."

"Oh I see, a *him*. Definitely not *your* type then. Although he might be mine ..." Kal sniggered.

"Send me everything you have on Cardinale, please Kal. Oh, and also Phoenix Industries."

"Your wish is my command. Later." And with that, she signed off. I stared into space for a moment, gathering my thoughts.

"You're done?" Kace asked quietly. I glanced at him, conscious that he had overheard at least my half of the conversation.

I turned my body to face him. "Kal was my number two when I was stationed in Singapore at the Cybercrime Directorate," I explained. "Now she gets to be its latest Director."

That was true. But Kal had become more than a mere work colleague. She had become a trusted friend. Perhaps my only one. I sighed wistfully. I had never been good at making friends. I knew myself well enough to know I could be uptight, and too focused on work.

"Never been to Singapore," Kace replied absently. Something was clearly on his mind—faint glabellar lines puckered his forehead with wavy furrows.

"You want to ask something?" I said, sensing that he did.

"I hope you don't mind?" he began, making me slightly nervous. "You've done so much. You're in the public eye and all. But honestly, you look so young." I laughed with relief. Kace glanced at me in surprise.

"You want to know how old I am? That wasn't what I was expecting," I said.

"No, really. I mean, I know your age, from the news reports. But how do you do it? Stay so young-looking? You could be in your twenties."

I sank back into my seat. "I tell people I have good genes. That's all. No one seems to believe me." Now Kace laughed too.

CHAPTER 10

The scramjet began its descent into New York airspace. Kace was gazing out of the window, now absorbed in his own thoughts, while my mind wandered to Clyde. I was due to see him after I had updated Lejeune and Park.

Clyde had asked me, at our first ever session, how I felt about men. I had laughed. A hollow, cracked laugh. Still, I'd come to him with PTSD because of a man—Clyde had diagnosed it. So I supposed it was a fair question. Clyde said I also suffered from a Phaeton complex, whatever that was. Sometimes I felt so empty, I thought I would collapse in on myself. Clyde claimed that being deprived of a mother's love in childhood was the reason I used to self-harm; although, I wasn't so sure about that. My father leaving me—that, in some ways, was the harder blow.

Clyde employed different cognitive behavioral methods to help me process my "unresolved issues." His term. One of them was to ask me focused questions, to help me with decisions I was working through. That was how they went, our sessions together. That's why I paid him. A lot. And I had finally come to kind of trust a man—Clyde.

But the prospect of our impending session, postponed from the day before, now left me full of dread. Something had changed, shifted imperceptibly. Our recent sessions had increasingly left me feeling uneasy—wary, even. It was the little things. Clyde's behavior had slowly changed, or so it appeared to me.

***

As we touched down on the arrivals vertipad, on top of the UN Secretariat building, I received an alert in my ear implant. It was a meeting update. Our briefing session had been moved to Park's office in the Global Policing Executive suite. Apparently, Lejeune had gone on vacation for her daughter's birthday, and would be joining remotely, by telepresence. I raised my eyebrows, taken aback. *I guess she has her priorities straight.* Diouf was joining by telepresence too. But he had a legitimate excuse—he was back in Geneva, directing the WHO's global response to the pandemic.

As we entered Park's office, he looked up, his face strained. He smiled faintly, gesturing for us to sit around the same meeting table I had sat at the day before. The stalked telepresence unit was still in hibernation mode. Park hadn't started the meeting yet, although a flashing status light showed that Diouf was now waiting in the virtual lobby.

"Received your memoclip, Lilith. I thought it best if we spoke privately as soon as you arrived."

I glanced down at my bioclock. It wasn't 10.30 a.m. yet. I sat adjacent to Park.

"What are your findings so far?" he asked me quietly, glancing quickly at Kace who sat opposite us, pretending not to be listening.

"Kace here has now confirmed the sleep disorder doesn't correlate with the vagus chips being implanted. And medically it doesn't have a natural cause—it's not a brain disease. So my bet is a technological cause."

"What sort of technological cause?"

"A cyberattack, on the brains of Unskills. The evidence is currently circumstantial, but it points to the language chip and ear implant."

Park stiffened. "You know what Lejeune will say …"

"That we're being paranoid, that this is all far-fetched?" I threw Park a wry glance. "Isn't that also what the powers-that-be once said about Ebba Black?"

Park nodded sternly. "So who are the likely suspects? Appleton has been dismantled."

"The earliest symptoms are recorded as having commenced six weeks ago. And that is exactly when Lucky Dip launched."

"What launched?" Park asked, his face a picture of confusion.

"The access-to-jobs lottery app," I replied. "It's developed by an arm of Phoenix Industries. The software development arm is based near Paris. And the parent company, Phoenix Industries S.A., now operates SkyLink."

"Appleton's old Low Earth orbit system?" Park asked, incredulous. "How did that happen?"

I smiled grimly as I saw his shocked reaction. "When Appleton was dismantled, its global satellite system was bought by a French-based robot manufacturer, which happens to be owned by Phoenix."

"I see," Park mumbled, still processing this bombshell. "How do you want to play this?"

"I'd like to pay Phoenix's Lucky Dip software development site a visit. It's based just outside Paris, at Rambouillet. It seems the same site serves as the HQ for the parent company, Phoenix Industries S.A. Let's request an interview with Bastien Cardinale."

Park's eyes narrowed. "You'll need a scramjet. I'll put in a requisition request. We can probably get one on short notice for later today. Are you okay with that?"

"I have to do something at noon for an hour. I'm free after that. And I'd like Dr. Westwood to accompany me," I replied, glancing across at Kace. Park frowned—I could tell he wasn't keen on putting a civilian into this. "I still need his expertise for a while longer. And he's offered."

Park glanced at Kace, who gave a slight nod of agreement.

"Okay Lilith, that's your call, and if Dr. Westwood has agreed," Park said, as he stood and moved around to sit in front of his console screen. He activated his facecall app and I heard him speaking to his gynoid Chief of Staff. I winked at Kace, who threw me a thumbs-up. After a moment, Park rejoined us in the meeting area.

"Transport arrangements are being made, and we're contacting Phoenix now. Let's see if they're willing to meet you."

A meeting alert message began flashing on the telepresence unit. Lejeune had now also entered the virtual lobby. Park sighed.

"Here we go," he muttered almost to himself as he started the meeting. The three-dimensional display of Lejeune's face jumped out at us from the telepresence projection ring located at the top of the unit. She was connected from somewhere outside, beside a swimming pool. The DigID details scrolling beneath her projection revealed that she was in the Bahamas.

At Park's request, I provided a concise briefing, updating Lejeune and Diouf on what I had discovered in the Republic at the Up-skilling campus. Once I had finished, I could tell that Diouf was impatient to take over. He wanted to update Lejeune and Park on the autopsy data from the first tranche of insomnia deaths—to provide information already conveyed to Kace while we were still in the Republic. Sentinel had aggregated the available data from the affected territories. They all showed the same thing.

"Severe atrophy of the thalamus!" Diouf exclaimed. His voice conveyed both panic and a strange sense of surreal wonder.

"What does that mean?" Lejeune snapped, peering at us with blue skies behind her. "The thalamus?"

"A large mass of gray matter in the center of the brain," Kace explained, jumping in. "It's kind of like a central hub that communicates with the cerebral cortex. It controls motor signals, consciousness, alertness, and sleep. Extreme sleep deprivation is basically killing parts of the brain essential not just for cognitive function, but for sustaining life. An atrophied thalamus is a symptom of, well …"

"Well what?" Lejeune snapped again.

"Fatal Insomnia," Kace explained.

"But she just told us this couldn't be that," Lejeune said accusingly. I scowled. I didn't like being referred to in the third person when I was actually present.

"There's no evidence of prion disease," Diouf announced, flecks of anxiety in his voice. I glanced at Kace sideways.

"So it's not Fatal Insomnia?" Lejeune asked.

Kace shook his head. "The symptoms are similar, but this is something else."

"What's causing it, then?" Lejeune asked.

"My best guess would be delivery of a continual low-frequency EMF," Kace replied.

"EMF? C'mon, Dr. Westwood, we're not all medical scientists here," Lejeune interjected. Kace smiled faintly as he began to explain. I glanced at him. He was way more patient than I would have been. He had explained what EMF stood for just the day before. Strange that she had forgotten already, given she was a Superior. With that job-cert, she had to have an IQ over 160.

"An electromagnetic field. It fits the facts. That might, in theory, suppress melatonin production and result in the symptoms we're seeing."

"The cause is likely to be tech-related," I added. "This looks deliberate, given that only one soc-ed class is affected. But we still need to figure out how the low-frequency EMF is being delivered." Just then, Diouf coughed. His face had become even more grave.

"I have some further bad news," he began, apologetically. "Symptoms of the same pattern of insomnia onset have been reported in a widening pattern. Sentinel has only received the relevant data in the last few hours."

"Spell it out, please," Park said.

Diouf shifted uncomfortably and adjusted his glasses. "We now have reports of the same sleep disorder symptoms from territories and federations outside those implicated by the Up-skilling program, including the Russian Federation, as well as the unified Chinese Republics. And even the United Korean Republic."

"That's a hell of a bombshell!" I exclaimed.

"Almost seven hundred and fifty million cases now confirmed, and rising," Diouf said bleakly.

"And only Unskills, right?" I asked. Diouf's three-dimensional projection stared back at me. He didn't need to reply; I already knew I was correct. "How come we're only hearing about this now?"

Diouf glanced directly at me. "Sentinel is better connected to UN programs, picks those up first," he explained. "And reporting timelines do vary across federations. We're grateful, to be perfectly honest, to have anything from the Russians at all. And in all likelihood, the Chinese data has been massaged."

"By 'massaged,' you mean what?" Kace asked.

"Their reported data is the tip of the unreported iceberg," I muttered at him.

Just then, Park touched behind his ear involuntarily. He activated his holotab and glanced at the screen projecting above his wrist before looking across at me.

"Well look at that, Phoenix has agreed to see you. You have a meeting with Bastien Cardinale's Chief of Staff, Hervé Balladur, in Paris tomorrow."

Before I could respond, Lejeune jumped in. "Paris? What's this about, Mr. Park?"

"There's a correlation between the launch of the Lucky Dip gaming app and the onset of the insomnia pandemic," I explained, answering for Park. "It's a live line of inquiry. We're just keeping an open mind."

"I should have been kept in the loop, Mr. Park, before you scheduled a meeting for Lilith with Phoenix. You know she reports directly to me on this case." Lejeune leaned forward, one hand coming into view as she jabbed her fingers in my direction. She then turned her head to address me directly. "In the future, I want to know what you're planning before you make a move." Before I could reply, Lejeune deactivated her feed and was off the facecall. *Her reputation for being a control freak is well deserved,* I thought. Park raised an eyebrow as he smiled weakly at me.

"That's Assistant Secretary-General Lejeune for you," Park muttered before sighing again.

All that remained in front of us was Diouf's white teeth gleaming out at us. Then he too vanished. I looked at Park next to me, and then across at Kace. For a moment we were all rendered silent, as we each processed the scale of the looming crisis. The widening pattern was now affecting the entire Unskill class throughout the automated world, all the Tier One and Tier Two territories.

"Dr. Westwood, would you mind excusing us?" Park asked. "I just need to speak to Lilith in private for a moment."

As soon as Kace had stepped out, Park began speaking, quietly. "Did you manage to see her, my daughter?"

I bit my lip. "Choon-Hee … she's not in good shape."

Park looked pale. "How bad?"

"She's starting to have symptoms of brain damage. Kace thinks it's still reversible at this stage. If …"

Park held up his hand. He closed his eyes for a moment, exhaling slowly before reopening them. "Not if! You must figure this out, Lilith." There was silence between us for a moment before he continued. "Your annual medical, yesterday … the results are back. It seems there's something unusual."

"Unusual?" I asked, swallowing, knowing full well what was unusual.

"And it turns out Herr Fleischman had your DNA sample sent for further analysis, an outside agency. He's instructed Interpol HR to perform a follow-up meeting with you."

"Which outside agency?" I snapped, gaping.

"The UFA Space Force. They have world-leading expertise in gerontology … at least that's what I'm told."

I was becoming angry. "Is that legal, sharing my data, my medical samples, like that?"

"According to your terms and conditions of employment …" Park held out his hands, "… it is. Although it would have been polite to at least ask. I've been blindsided too—I was only informed an hour ago."

I could feel my knuckles through my skin as I clutched the sides of my chair. "And what's the purpose of such a meeting?

Why on earth does the Director care about gerontology?"

Park gave a slow shrug. "I honestly don't know. Herr Fleischman wants this HR meeting expedited. But …" Park sighed, "… from my perspective, this assignment takes priority. We can schedule the HR meeting to take place after you've been to Phoenix HQ. The day after tomorrow. We'll do it virtually, as you'll still be in Paris, to minimize the impact on your investigation."

I puffed out my cheeks. "Sure, makes sense, I guess."

"And one more thing …" Park looked suddenly nervous. "Do you want me to arrange someone from UN Legal to support you?" I shot him a puzzled look. "At the meeting, I mean."

"Do you think that's necessary?"

"It's your call, but I'm happy to make the arrangements. It might be wise. You should know that the Director is insisting an external medic attends the meeting too, a Colonel from Space Force, to discuss their findings with you."

CHAPTER 11

Once I arrived back at the Interpol Bureau there was no sign of Kace. I checked in with the reception gynoid, who informed me he had been accompanied to a refreshment area. Our scramjet authorization was being finalized—we would be departing for the Union in around three hours. I confirmed arrangements for the trip. In particular, I requested the hotel in Montmartre I always stayed at when in Paris. I had my own agenda, after all. Then I departed for my appointment with Clyde.

I took a hover cab from UN Plaza, downtown to central Manhattan. The protesters were out in force—Midtown was teeming with Unskills.

"We will have to make a detour," the autopilot VirDa informed me. "Security drones have closed the city airways through Midtown due to the Anti-Automation protests." I looked down. The pedestrian and transit corridors at terrestrial level, as well as vertipads, were all blocked by crowds. Thousands and thousands of swarming protesters. Traffic couldn't land.

I watched a news bulletin on my holotab. Start Apollo was a street-smart Unskill, pugnacious, being interviewed about *The Cause*, his cause.

"The irony seems lost on some folks that a guaranteed basic income don't make folk happy when they have nothing to do."

Apollo's eyes suddenly looked sad, before he began stabbing at the camera with a finger. He sure as hell managed to rub people up the wrong way. I got that. But he made some good points. And scared the hell out of the Semiskills and Skills—the ones looking over their shoulders.

Today there were more Dark Court cultists out, too. Their numbers were growing by the day, all too susceptible to the conspiracy theories being amplified across MyPlace and other venues. As fast as we could shut down one proxy server, five more darknet broadcast rooms popped up in the Dark Court's hidden Primarch system.

The cultists on the streets below me were heckling the Unskills. And they had a seemingly limitless supply of daemons with flexi-lift extenders trailing Dark Court propaganda. More holographic banners, today some even with voice amplification.

The autopilot began speaking. "I can set you down on New Theater Row on West 42nd Street. One vertipad is still functioning." I deactivated my screen. It would be a walk from there.

"Is there a way through with the protesters blocking pedestrian lanes?"

"I can plot a terrestrial route and send it to your holotab," the autopilot announced helpfully.

"No need," I replied, as I exited the hover cab on street level. I had unrestricted streaming privileges to the Union-DEF satellite system, after all.

As I hurried along the pedestrian corridor, a security drone passed by overhead. I glanced up and saw the flickering beam of its language streaming orb, scanning the LS rebounds from my language chip. While I walked, I felt the familiar tugging at the back of my mind—the same feeling of being followed. I turned just in time to see a shape veer into a side transit corridor—a tall figure which moved with weird darting strides. And the guy was wearing clothes that glinted strangely in the sunlight. I waited and watched. No one emerged. I steeled myself and walked back to check it out. I paused as I reached the side street corridor, drawing in a breath. Stepping away from the occluding building, my heart thumping, I looked down the narrow side street. No one was there! *It's nothing,* I thought, trying and failing to dispel the nagging unease.

* * *

I was a few minutes late. "Sorry, the protests," I explained breathlessly as Clyde let me into his office.

"It's okay, I know," Clyde said in his melodious baritone, reassuring in his own way. He peered at me and absent-mindedly brushed away a wisp of gray hair. He was wearing his usual *grandad jacket,* as I mentally categorized it, the first time I'd met him. Outmoded, with leather patches on the elbows. Perhaps he really did think it made him look distinguished. To my mind, it just made him look old.

"They're being branded useless eaters," I mumbled.

"The Unskills?" Clyde asked rhetorically before continuing. "Hmmm … things are getting nasty. Cyber propaganda." I watched him silently for a moment. "But you know all about that in your line of work."

"I'm the lead investigator on the Dark Court file."

Clyde nodded absently without commenting further. He didn't do small talk. "How are you?" he asked, finally. That was my cue.

"This weekend, not so good. Yesterday I had a meeting …" I paused, glancing away.

"With Herr Fleischman?" Clyde asked. I jumped in my seat, staring at him suspiciously.

"How did you know that?" I snapped.

Clyde threw me a startled look. "Didn't you mention something, when you postponed yesterday?"

"No, I did not," I replied firmly, studying his face for clues.

"I guess I could tell from how unsettled you seem. Only he has that effect on you," Clyde laughed, slightly nervously. "Is he here in New York, then?" he asked, more disarmingly.

I shook my head. "I saw the Monster by telepresence. I wasn't expecting it. The latest crisis at work. A medical emergency affecting the Unskills."

"Sounds serious," Clyde remarked, ignoring the fact that I still couldn't bring myself to call the Monster by his name.

"Yeah. He was two-faced, as always. He has no shame. Told me it was nice to see me again. I don't know whether I can do it."

"Work with him?" I nodded. "You could report him, you know. It's never too late," Clyde suggested, probingly, still testing my resolve to keep quiet.

I was still out of breath. I shook my head. "Men like that, they destroy your career. And you are judged—women are judged. I am judged every day. I've made something of myself, and I'll be damned if I'll let him take anything more from me." As I spoke, the musculature of Clyde's face shifted, almost imperceptibly— his eyebrows moved up slightly, tightening in the center of his brow, while his head tilted forward slightly. I sneered—this was his look of pity, despite knowing I hated that. I refused to be a victim.

"Herr Fleischman. Was he the reason you lost faith in the system?" Clyde asked, refocusing the discussion. I was surprised by the question. I paused, reflecting on what he had asked.

"Well, I kinda am the system," I retorted in bemused fashion.

Clyde shook his head. "I don't mean your job and all the things you've achieved—your successes, your fame. You as a person. What you feel and your personal story."

"You mean what the system did to me? The system needs a kick in the ass." Clyde smiled as he saw me bringing myself down from my heightened emotional state. "I'm trying to make a difference from the inside. For all the soc-ed classes that have been silenced for too long, for the Unskills, for women, for the underrepresented and forgotten. I might not know what it feels like to be an Unskill, but I sure as hell know how it feels to be weak and powerless."

"Go on, Lilith," Clyde said softly. He wasn't a physically attractive man, but there was something attractive about him, nevertheless. Perhaps it was just his voice, which exuded calm. Deep, rich, mellifluous. He didn't light up a room as such, but somehow the room came to be lit up anyway. And until recently, I had felt safe with him. I had confessed nearly everything. Everything except my Eye, of course—that was something I hadn't even shared with Kaye. I didn't want Clyde, or anyone else for that matter, to know that I was a freak of nature. Clyde took session notes, and I felt lighter because of it. The weight of my burden eased as Clyde's virtual notebook took on the responsibility of bearing my pain, my trauma, the betrayals I had previously had to bear alone.

I narrowed my eyes. "Anyway, the Monster … I've spent twenty years escaping him. And here he is, right back in my life again."

Clyde smiled weakly. "I want you to try something, a mental exercise." *Here we go again,* I thought. But just as I was about to object, Clyde anticipated my reluctance. He knew me far too well. "I'm pretty sure it would help. Just hear me out." I sighed. "I would like you to dictate a memoclip to your past self. In fact, two of them. One to your seven-year-old self, and one to your twenty-three-year-old self."

"Memoclips? What's the point of that?" I asked in exasperation.

"Those were both especially difficult times for you. Your father's … suicide." As Clyde uttered the word I flinched. "And then at twenty-three …" I glared at him; his words trailed off. "I would like you to go back in time. Show those two past versions of yourself, a child and a young woman, the love, empathy, and understanding you were missing. Provide the advice you needed back then."

"What should I say?"

"Explain to your past self what is about to happen and how you should react. Be kind and reassuring. Forgive the past you. Forgive others, too. Be empathetic."

"But what's the point of memoclips to my past selves?" I asked. "The past is done. I can't change what happened."

Clyde smiled. "You can't change the past, but you can change how you feel about past events. And that changes who you are now, today, and what you will do in the future. Our past determines our future—who you can become. You can change the future by influencing how you relate to the past, give your past a place in your own personal archaeology. It's a way of forgiving yourself, attaining some form of closure."

"A form of time travel?" I mused.

"Perhaps."

"I'll think about it," I said. Clyde stared at my face, attempting to read me. I would never do it, of course. So I told him what he wanted to hear.

"That's good enough … for now."

I coughed. "You know …" I paused. I was about to reveal something that I hadn't told Clyde before. "My father left me memoclips too, the day he died."

Clyde's eyes widened. "What did they say?" I shook my head. "You don't want to tell me?"

"It's not that." I held up my right arm, shaking my blouse, revealing the bracelet my father gave me at seven, the last time I ever saw him.

Clyde leaned forward, peering at the green numbers spinning on the small dark screen. "Is that …?"

"It is. An old-fashioned SwissSecure bracelet. And it has grown with me all my life, changing shape as I did. You know who my father was …" I shifted uneasily in my chair.

Clyde pursed his lips. "The most famous medic of all time, nanobot cancer-killing technology, yes."

"Anyway, this thing is the key to two messages from him. When I'm ready, whatever that means."

"So you haven't heard them yet?" Clyde asked, incredulous. I shook my head.

Clyde moved toward me, taking my hand in his, without warning, startling me.

"When you do, you have to tell me immediately," he said insistently, not like him at all. "I will be here to support you, no matter what." I tried to withdraw, but not in time. And there it was, my Eye, and the rush of an emotional halo. The momentary rush made me sick to the pit of my stomach. Clyde was not all he seemed—my Eye saw him talking to the Monster, they were laughing together. And with that I realized how naïve I had been. Clyde was in league with Fleischman. *Has the Monster been using Clyde to spy on me?* I snatched my hand from his, my face now aghast.

"So that's how you knew," I shrieked, standing abruptly. Clyde looked up at me confused. "That I'd met the Monster again.

You're working for him!" His mouth opened, gaping. It was almost comical, except there was nothing funny about this. I grabbed my leather jacket from the back of the chair, violent white anger suddenly pulsing through my entire body. And without being able to control myself, I screamed. It started as a snarl, before evolving into a banshee-like howl. In the moment, I realized it wasn't my best look, as Clyde's face suddenly drained of all color. He remained motionless, seemingly pinned to his chair.

I stood and moved toward Clyde, still seated in front of me. As I peered into his face, I wanted to smash it in. But somehow, I managed to stop myself. I think it was the fear that I smelled—he reeked of it. But I wanted to destroy something, nevertheless. I moved to his desk console, on one side of the room, and with one sweep of my arm, I threw everything he had on it onto the floor. An old-fashioned round paperweight made from crystal, a box of tissues, a vase with exotic-looking flowers, a holographic picture display, with revolving images of his son, daughter-in-law and grandchild. All the items crashed down, the vase smashing to smithereens as it struck the hard floor.

"How much did the Monster pay you to spy on me?" I screamed as I turned to face him for a final time. "Is that how you're able to support a lavish lifestyle in the Hamptons?" With that final evisceration, I turned, charging out of his consultation room. This was a man I had trusted. And with that, a man I trusted no more.

Outside on the street, I paused and leaned against a wall behind the diaphanous polycarbonate barrier of the pedestrian corridor. My whole body was shaking. I activated my holotab and selected the nicosafe app. Then I began speaking my voice command.

"Nicosafe, low repeating dosage." The app was linked to my Deep Brain Stimulation implant. I'd had the DBS implant fitted when I was eighteen, at the same time as my Universal Grammar tech, killing two birds with one stone. But the former was a dubious, wayward birthday gift to myself upon my age of majority, paid for from my father's estate, that I had finally inherited. He wasn't around to gift me anything, so I treated myself.

"Activated. Thanks for using nicosafe," the app replied.

In the end, I always left people. The past was a foreign country to me. I left people by metaphorically shedding my skin. Leaving people behind was a way of renewing, discarding my past, staying in control—avoiding getting hurt by leaving them before they could leave me, like my father had. I grimaced. *Who are you kidding, Lily?* I thought—I always got hurt. Kal was the only one I kept in touch with, always a hot mess. Everyone else could go jump in a lake.

I breathed in deeply as I felt the calming effect of the low-grade nicotine rush in the pleasure center of my brain. Everything would be fine. For now, at least.

CHAPTER 12

After my hasty exit from the session with Clyde, I returned to UN HQ—the transportation deck on top of the Secretariat building. I picked up Kace from the waiting area and we boarded. Traveling hypersonic, it was just a forty-five-minute trip across the Atlantic.

Once airborne, Kace tried some small talk. But he was smart enough to sense something was up, and so allowed me the silence I craved. I smiled fleetingly, so he wouldn't think I was a complete sociopath, before gazing out of the window, trying to calm my inner anguish.

By the time our scramjet descended in an arc over the European edge of the North Atlantic, approaching Union airspace, I was starting to feel calmer. The summer sun glimmered on the sea as we moved over the French coastline. With the difference in time zones, it was already evening in the Grand Union. As we continued our descent, shadows from the cotton-wool clouds above drew strange shapes on the arable land below, being worked by industrial-scale robotic machines.

***

Our hotel was just off the Place du Tertre, in Montmartre—close to my favorite Parisian bar. We now had confirmation of our meeting at Phoenix Industries HQ, in Rambouillet, outside Paris, the next morning.

Inside the hotel lobby, Kace looked at me expectantly, maybe hoping we could do dinner again. But tonight I just couldn't, even if my life depended on it. I was still in shock over Clyde's betrayal. And I sure as hell could use a drink.

"The service unit will take my bag up. It's been a long day, I need some air. We'll meet in the morning," I explained, trying to sound as definitive as possible. And I was beginning to experience another Aura. Not a full-blown episode, but the telltale wooziness was there. It had begun as we entered Paris airspace. I wondered why again—I tried to remember the last time I'd had an episode before yesterday. It must have been years.

"You should get some rest, Lilith. You look beat," Kace said kindly. I smiled faintly as we parted, and watched as he walked toward the transit tube and his room.

Outside the hotel, I wandered down the hill adjacent to Sacré-Cœur toward Place Pigalle. The evening was warm; a summer breeze was in the air. Riders on e-scooters whizzed past silently in the illuminated cycle lane. People walked along the pedestrianized corridor, protected from taxiing hover cars by the translucent polycarbonate barriers. Everything was somehow more relaxed here, in the Union, compared to back in New York. The pace of life felt more tranquil. There was a hubbub of conversation swirling out from street cafés, restaurants, and bars as doors opened and closed. Through a convenience store window, I glimpsed customers clicking their wrist chips against self-checkout displays. A woman walked a dog with its own smart collar, connected to our all-knowing internet of things. Holographic advertising scrolled across a storefront as I passed by. My language chip automatically switched to parsing Standard

Union French as my optic nerve began processing the words: *Nos appareils savent ce que vous voulez avant vous: plus intelligents ensemble.* I smiled grimly. Devices know what we want before we do: smarter together. *How lame,* I thought.

I passed a cloud of fireflies cloistered in a small avenue of trees, orange-lighted vapor carried by the dusk air. The sensory disturbance from the Aura was beginning to affect my vision and my sense of touch. Refracted splinters of rainbows danced in front of me. My skin pricked as if an army of tiny ants were dancing on my arms, hands, and feet. And I again had the feeling that I was being followed. Clyde would insist on calling this paranoia. But my instinct was telling me that something was out there, after me.

Fuck! I have to stop thinking about what Clyde would say. He's a traitor.

I arrived at Mutinerie Féminine, my go-to bar whenever I was in Paris. I tried to stay dry Monday through Thursday. But as it was still Sunday, I didn't have to temper my needs just yet.

The sec-cam at the doorway screened me; the Welcome VirDa scanned my LS rebounds. It was dark inside and smelled faintly of body odor, of sensuous excitement, of enticing French *femmes fatales.*

An air sanitizer unit aerosolized some fragrance at me as I walked in. Lavender and ylang-ylang. I still couldn't quite get in the mood as I walked to a booth in one corner. Red simulated leather. Standard Union French was the only state official language in the entire French metropolitan region. I switched my default language in my holotab language app so that I could issue my French voice commands into the tabletop VirDa. Tapped my wrist on the payment screen and my wrist chip briefly glowed green.

The glinting mirror ball sprayed reflections of disco ceiling lights in a kaleidoscope of color around the venue. Gaudily illuminated female forms were swaying against each other on a small stage beyond the bar area. The droid serving unit delivered my drink.

"*Te voilà, un Reyka, profite.*" The machine's robotic drawl was Parisian argot. Interesting choice of accent differentiators, I thought. I gulped down my vodka and ordered a second one.

I turned and surveilled the doorway, on edge. The palpable sense of being followed had been growing more powerful, stranger. I half expected someone to come through, looking for me, but there was no one there.

As I turned back to my table, I noticed a slim figure, alone, perched on a stool at the bar, ten meters ahead of me. She had long hair, wearing a short figure-hugging dress, very pretty. I stared at her through the dimness, feeling the familiar tightening in my chest, the rush of desire. She half-turned on her stool toward me as she felt my gaze, maybe, before smiling demurely. I gestured for her to come over. As she walked toward me, I eyed her up and down. She was a brunette, dark lipstick, wearing heels that I would have struggled to walk in, with long legs. She stopped just in front of me.

"*Je suis Béatrice,*" she murmured.

"*Lilith, enchanté,*" I replied.

She smiled softly. "*Tu as l'air de me déshabiller avec tes yeux!*" I smiled. I guess I had been undressing her with my eyes. "*Pourquoi n'utilises-tu pas tes dents.*" I laughed at her brazen come-on—*why not use my teeth, indeed?*

I asked whether she wanted to get out of here: "*Tu veux sortir d'ici?*"

Béatrice bent her head until her eyeline was level with mine, then she reached for my hand. "*Oui.*"

As I was about to stand and take hers, a long dark shape in my peripheral vision caught my eye. I turned slightly and saw a tall figure enter and walk toward another booth before sitting. The figure was big, well over two meters, and certainly didn't move like a woman—this had to be a guy. And he walked with strange, almost reptilian gestures, similar to the darting strides of the half-seen figure back in New York—very creepy. I was surprised he had managed to get past the LS entry scan. This was a strictly female-only club.

Then Béatrice noticed him too, as she followed my gaze. She let out a small squeal: *"Les hommes ne sont pas autorisés ici. Je préviendrai la sécurité."*

She went to alert security that a man was in our midst, while I continued studying him suspiciously. The figure was wearing an all-in-one suit. As flashes of colored lights bounced across him, the garment was in turns illuminated. It consisted of individual pieces of fine crystal-like material, creating a rippling effect. The colors of the crystals shifted with the changing stroboscopic light of the bar. Through the dimness, I made out some odd-looking iconography on the front of the suit—a series of interlaced wings. *Very odd fashion sense for a stalker.*

The guy's face was hidden from view by a narrow-brimmed, conical helmet. From the reflection of the light, the helmet was made of a hard substance—reinforced silicon. *For protection, perhaps?* I wondered. If he hadn't looked so menacing, I might have thought this was a cross between fancy dress and Halloween. With the conical headpiece, all that was missing was a broomstick. I laughed to myself in a sudden burst of hysterical cackling, feeling sorry for myself, especially as my hook-up had been so rudely interrupted before it even began. I was certain this interloper was there for me.

As if confirmation was needed, the shape turned, facing in my direction. I knew I had to confront this, once and for all. To end it. But not here, not with all these civilians around. I quickly drank the second glass of vodka, then stood to leave.

CHAPTER 13

Back outside, I walked hurriedly toward Montmartre. I felt the instinctive need for high ground. I moved back up the hill, before turning to scan the terrain behind me. I glimpsed a long, dark shadow, flitting across the pedestrian lane below.

Before approaching the basilica of Sacré-Cœur, I placed my hand inside my jacket, on the handle of my coil pistol. I turned down a quiet transit corridor. No one else was around. Streetlights powered on, their pale glow rippling across the walls of the white edifice.

"Gun activate," I whispered as I withdrew the weapon from my kydex shoulder holster. The pistol powered up, the capacitor glowing a faint green as the power-beaming system came online. It was now connected to the Union-DEF satellite server in space. "Stun rounds," I continued. I heard the familiar click as the bullet chamber was loaded with synthetic polymer bullets.

"Do you hear the singing?" a voice asked, quite suddenly, out of nowhere. It was a melodious voice. I spun around, startled, looking behind me. No one was there. I turned back in the direction I was headed. But now, inexplicably, the tall, dark figure was standing before me, having headed me off. *How the hell did he manage that?* And he'd taken off the helmet, which dangled in a long, slender white hand.

"I've drunk too much. Or maybe not enough," I muttered to myself, bemused. I guess it had finally happened—I had cracked. For the figure standing before me was no earthly being. I was staring at a pale, elongated face, no sign of a mouth, flared, reptile-like slits instead of nostrils, and sunken domes for eyes, which peered down at me.

"No, you're not going crazy, Lilith," I heard someone say—a voice in my head. I nearly jumped out of my skin. As I regained my composure, I realized it was the creature in front of me—it apparently had the ability to communicate without speaking out loud. I could hear it inside my skull. *What the hell!*

The being had a strange, indeterminate voice, low but not quite male, somehow lacking in gendered features. I touched my ear involuntarily, feeling for the gentle vibration of my ear implant. *Am I imagining it?* The creature shook its head.

"You're not hearing a language from any orbiting satellite."

As I heard its voice again inside my head, an actual voice, I saw the large conical bony structure on top of its bald head vibrating. That's what the helmet had been protecting, I suddenly realized, peering through the dimness. The appendage was a biological outgrowth from its skull, with cartilage striations. It reminded me of pictures of dinosaur fins from my childhood picture books. *A communication mast?* I wondered.

"You're not a man," I exclaimed as I squinted, peering at the tall, strangely androgynous creature. It towered with lizard-like menace in front of me, larger than life but slender. Its hands had just three digits—a large opposable thumb and two long, tapered fingers.

"Gender is not a thing, as such, for my order. And you can put that away," it said, gesturing toward the pistol. "I mean you no harm."

I lowered my weapon before re-holstering it.

"Is this telepathy?" I asked, now thinking the words without saying them out loud. The creature shook its head. The Melody was piercing, peaking to a near-deafening crescendo inside my skull, overwhelming and sublimely beautiful. Yet I heard the creature's words with perfect clarity.

"Direct neural communication, brain waves. Producing language. Mine is High Enochian, which you perceive as Unilanguage North American Standard English, due to your own default language settings on your language chip."

High Enochian? I've never heard of such a language, I mused.

I paused. "You're right, it is singing," I thought, as I listened. "You can hear it too?" The creature stared at me with curiosity. I hadn't thought of it like that. Singing. "I can hear voices."

"Voices confected by the Sage. We all hear the singing," it replied.

"We?" My Aura had now completely cleared. I felt light, almost weightless. But my mind was tempered by perfect clarity of thought. "What are you?" I asked again.

"I am a Guardian," it replied.

"You're the one who's been following me, aren't you?"

"I've been monitoring you since your awakening as a child," the creature whispered melodiously inside my head. "I am part of an ancient order of warriors from Empyrean, a planet far from here. You are special, Lilith. Your line was created by the Sage, the oldest being in the Elyonim, this universe. I have been waiting to make contact until it was time."

"Time for what?" I asked, incredulous.

"Time to repel an invasion. There is a Watcher here, in this city. You have felt its presence. Your civilization is under attack. If Earth falls, other Watchers will follow and then spread out through the Elyonim."

"A Watcher?" I exclaimed. *What on earth is that?*

"An ancient order, even older than mine. Watchers are agents of chaos, destroyers of worlds. The Sage saved our planet and our species from their order, led by Satanael, millennia ago. Satanael and his followers were threshed. Their souls ripped from their somas, as punishment for their insurrection. And then banished to another universe, made up primarily of dark energy. We call that place the Chaos. But the Watchers have found a way back through, a fissure in spacetime that connects the Elyonim and the Chaos. The Watchers have discovered a crossing here, somewhere on this planet." I was, for a split second, lost for words. *If this warrior Guardian knows a Watcher is here, why doesn't it do something about it?*

"But what do you need me for?" I asked.

"Our instruments are unable to pinpoint the crossing with precision. We're too far away." I frowned. "But you, Lilith, have abilities unique to your line. You can detect Watchers."

"I can do what?" I asked, before it hit me. "The Aura," I announced, as the dawning realization struck me. That was what I'd felt when I arrived in Paris. *The Aura is a warning!* Now it made sense. "I get headaches, wooziness ... a feeling of black anger." The creature peered at me. The sunken domes in its pale, elongated face glowed an iridescent white. I wondered whether it could actually see me.

"What you call an 'Aura' is a reaction to a Watcher's metaphysical footprint. Watchers have learned how to harness the repulsive dark energy from the Chaos—an invisible substance called quintessence. It gives them immense power. When you detect a Watcher, something lights up in you."

"And that's why you're here now?"

"When your Aura is strongest, then the Watcher is close. You feel its darkness."

"And what then?" I asked. "Once I find it? You can do something, then? Stop it. Kill it. Send it back. Right?"

The creature studied me, before shaking its head slowly.

"A Watcher isn't like anything in the Elyonim, it doesn't have a soma, a body. It is a gaseous being." I was taken aback anew by the strangeness of the idea. "Their nervous system is a conductive gas. A combination of partially ionized noble gases: helium, neon, argon at different charges. Their physical integrity, their exoskeleton, is a denser arrangement of gases—methane and ethane molecules held together by weak London dispersion forces. And they have a center of gravity so that they don't just float off. They are anchored by a ferric gas." I listened in startled silence. I vaguely recalled from my school days that London forces were named after a long-dead physicist.

"A being made of gas … and they can think, talk, like you and me?"

"They come from a place with different physical laws to the Elyonim. Here, they control human surrogates. You might think of Watchers as spirits. You will recognize the Watcher only by the actions of its human puppet, by the chaos it wreaks."

"So if I find this Watcher, what then?" I vaguely pondered how you might assassinate a being made of gas.

"You have to stop the extinction-level event being planned by the Watcher," the creature said ominously.

My blood froze. "What kind of event?"

"That's why you've been drawn to this city. To figure that out. You must expel the Watcher from its human host. It will then be forced to cross back to the Chaos."

Now my mind was reeling. This was absolutely the strangest

thing that had ever happened to me. "So why am I so different from other people?" I whispered, hardly daring to ask.

"People?" It shook its head. "The wrong question. Your order is special. You only have mortal form." *Mortal form? A strange turn of phrase. Why wouldn't I have mortal form?* "But mortality doesn't define you, just the way you look, at least outwardly. Not how your body behaves," the creature continued. "You are half Sempiternal."

Sempiternal? What the hell is that? I wondered.

"Like you?" I asked.

"Different from me. The Sage created your line. But you were born of a human mother, the one called Plamena. My species, Sempiternals, has evolved a different means to extend life. But you draw your time from others. Like your father before you."

"My father?" I gasped.

"And like his father before him," it continued. "Made possible by our advanced science and technology on Empyrean by the Sage's xenobiology program. Now it is your time to participate, Lilith Errapel King. Only those who have experienced an awakening can serve."

I pondered the strange turn of phrase: *awakening,* the second time the creature had used it. "The Melody!" I said as the dawning realization hit me. That's what the creature was talking about. "It first came when I was seven."

"We call it the Mind Chant. The Principality descent is patrilineal. Gifted normally by the Sage, through careful selection. Your father forced the issue, with his voluntary withdrawal from the Mind Chant. You were indeed a surprise. But the Sage decided to let you … serve him. An experiment. Despite the prophecy. And your name, given to you by your father. That was ironic." Now the creature was talking in riddles again. *What about my name? What's ironic?* And now I was also irritated. I was no one's experiment.

"The Sage decided for me? To serve him? Sounds like a male thing to presume. Or is gender not a thing for this Sage either?" I exclaimed sarcastically, annoyance riling me.

"The Sage decides all things. My lack of gender was his gift."

"So I am some kind of soldier, created to serve this Sage, to fight these Watchers on his behalf. Is that it? What if I decide I don't like whatever it is this Sage has decided? What if I choose *not* to serve?" I could feel my eyes blazing.

The creature paused, taking stock, maybe. "You are part of the collective, bound to the *Nunciature Evangelion.* There is no choice. And it is an honor to serve."

My heart felt as if it had momentarily skipped a beat. Nunciature Evangelion. The same phrase my father had used, the last time I saw him, our last conversation, the day he died.

"What do you mean, I don't get a choice? What is the Nunciature Evangelion?" I asked in a more measured voice. I wanted answers.

"The Nunciature Evangelion is a huge structure, reaching up high into the heavens, built on the highest point on Empyrean. The Tower of Songs. It's broadcasting a unique chant to you now."

I shook my head in confusion. "But I still don't get it: why don't I have a choice?"

"Your powers, they derive from your awakening. Which acted as a biological switch. But after twenty-four hours of being exposed to your unique Mind Chant, your own frequency, there's no going back."

I scrunched up my nose and forehead, nonplussed. "Because the powers stop, if I somehow stop the Mind Chant?"

The creature looked at me ruefully. "You can't stop it. The all-seeing, all-knowing Sage, Head of the Quessoch, the Council of Apostles, only he can switch off your transmission. If he chooses, if you fail him, or if, in his Sempiternal mercy, he deems your time is up."

That sounded ominous. "And what would happen then?"

The creature studied me. "You will have many questions. And I am here to assist you. Tomorrow, you have much to do. It is imperative you locate the Watcher before it's too late. But tonight, you need to rest your body." The creature slowly began to fade from view. "When you summon me, I will appear again," it whispered.

"Hey, wait," I called before it completely disappeared. "Do you have a name?" *After all, I couldn't go around just referring to it in my head as "creature."*

"In this place, I have sometimes been called Selaphiel, by other half Sempiternals, by Principalities like you," it replied as it finally faded from view. The Melody subsided slightly. But now I recognized its gentle thrum as singing—the Mind Chant that had always been there, since my seventh birthday, the soundscape to my existence.

CHAPTER 14

I woke after a troubled sleep. I decided to skip breakfast—I wasn't in the mood. In the cold light of day, I couldn't be sure whether I had dreamed the events of the previous evening—a strange Guardian extraterrestrial had claimed I was half Sempiternal, a Principality, whatever that was. It was all too much to process. I rose and showered still in a state of shock; dressed in autopilot mode, barely aware of what I was doing. And before I knew it, it was a little before 8.15 a.m., almost time to go down. I blinked as I surveyed the pedestrian corridors below, outside through the window at terrestrial level—people going about their ordinary lives, just another Monday morning. With so much normality around, what I had experienced seemed too surreal to be true! *Get a grip, Lily,* I thought to myself. I took a deep breath and went downstairs. Kace was punctual; I liked that. He was already waiting for me, as agreed, in the hotel lobby.

We took a hover cab to Rambouillet for the scheduled meeting. As we descended the VTOL corridor toward Phoenix HQ below, the Aura that had been lurking in the background since the previous evening resurfaced, moving toward a slow crescendo of sensory disturbance. The pulse from the red LED VTOL marker lights was hitting my eyes like slivers of brittle glass, stabbing against the rods and cones of my retinas.

Once we landed on the vertipad, the gull-wing doors opened. But I could barely move. Nausea convulsed me. And the sensation of a cold steel vice gripping my skull made me feel as if my head would implode. I tried to stand but couldn't. When I did, I stumbled, hitting my head against the edge of the door frame as I tried to climb out.

"Are you okay?" Kace asked. I threw him a dark look, a warning in my eyes.

"Of course I am," I meant to say sharply. But it came out as a whisper. And then, as I began to fall, he caught me.

"You're welcome," he whispered before I could respond.

"I get pains in my head," I explained.

"And you have that," he remarked, gesturing to the elastic band that was now clearly visible on my wrist, above my SwissSecure bracelet.

As my mind whirred, thinking of a plausible explanation that didn't involve admitting to self-harming tendencies, I realized Kace was still supporting me. And I hadn't blocked. Yet, there wasn't the usual rush of an emotional halo—I couldn't intuit anything distinct from him. It was something different I felt, a familiarity, and an at-oneness that was warm and reassuring. Moreover, to my relief, I wasn't burning time from him. *How is that even possible?* I looked at Kace with widened eyes and renewed curiosity, before pushing him gently away, attempting to reassert some dignity. It had only ever happened once before, touching someone without burning them. And that had been with the Monster, all those years ago. *What am I to make of this?* I wondered.

"You're really not okay, are you?" Kace insisted. I frowned, without replying. *Perhaps Bastien Cardinale is playing host to the Watcher,* I mused. *That must be why the Aura is suddenly so bad.*

I straightened my leather jacket carefully, deliberately. Once I'd regained my balance and composure, I glanced around, before momentarily tilting my head forward for Kace to follow my lead.

Phoenix Industries HQ consisted of a large, neo-futuristic complex that had won architectural awards. The whole complex was carved out from the Forest of Yveline. The buildings formed a circular structure partially sunk underground. Each building represented a Fibonacci spiral, a perfect geometrical shape captured in nature, if imperfectly, as nautilus and snail shells. The silver lattice outer structures of the spiral-like cones featured hydroponic growth technologies, with plants from the forest covering a forty-five-degree sector up and around each outer shell. Kace and I both paused for a moment, taking in the sight.

Adjacent to the disembarkation zone, at the base of the vertipad, a welcome droid was waiting for us. But this droid was also equipped with two mounted coil sidearms. *Ominous*, I mused. It issued a greeting, before the sensor on its top-mounted LS orb started blinking as the orb rotated. It was now in scanning mode, checking the LS rebounds from our language chips, verifying our identities.

The droid guided us toward a LiDAR-aided shuttle that had just arrived on the transit corridor. It was a small, glass auto-drive cube with a caterpillar track propulsion system. The droid remained behind after we'd boarded. The glass doors sealed shut, and we set off on the short distance to the looming glass complex. The shuttle pulled up in front of the entrance of the central spiral-like building.

Hervé Balladur, the Chief of Staff to Bastien Cardinale, was awaiting us just inside the large entrance vestibule. A tall peacock of a man, wearing the most absurd aquamarine velvet suit I had ever seen. *Seriously!* Even Kace's dubious taste in loud shirts paled in contrast.

"Ooh, Mademoiselle," Balladur said when he clocked me, before continuing in English. "I heard you were beautiful, but they did not do your beauty justice." He switched his default back to French again: *"Je suis vraiment enchanté,"* addressing me in fake, fawning supplication, bowing low. I treated him to a withering nod.

He smiled at Kace, looking the tall fella up and down. "And your friend, he's a big one," Balladur continued, now back in English, gazing at Kace admiringly while still addressing me.

"Colleague," I corrected. The peacock just leered at me. He was one hell of a creep. He made my skin crawl.

Balladur gestured that we should follow, leading us into a large conference room. Three walls were all white LED panels, while the fourth was plate glass. The large glass wall gave out into the opening of the conch-like shell structure, with a cloistered garden in the center of the building, and a vista toward the verdant green of the forest through the gap where the semicircular curves at the building's base nearly touched. Above us sunlight sparkled down through a huge, vaulted glass ceiling, which provided a magnificent view up through the center of the towering spiral building. I could make out the higher-level floors, at the twists in the shell structure. The blue sky was visible, through the narrow open apex, high above.

"Please sit," Balladur instructed. I was glad to do so—the Aura was still making me feel nauseous. "We were happy to receive your request," he continued, before issuing voice commands in French for refreshments, addressed to a service unit. I couldn't help but be amazed that he didn't even consult with us as to what drinks he should order.

Kace laughed quietly and turned toward me, whispering in my ear, "The world's most famous cybercrime sleuth calls, asking to drop by, and you're happy? Right!"

"I've been meaning to visit you guys for a while," I said to Balladur, smiling straight back at him.

"But we're just a humble start-up," Balladur said with his French popinjay accent differentiators, speaking English.

"Quite some operation you have here for a humble start-up."

"We manage with less than twenty people," he replied with a self-serving shrug. The service unit offered us the drinks selected for us by the peacock.

"Let's not forget all the droid units and AI." I gestured vaguely up at the building complex. "What's the secret to your success?"

"We're passionate about creating apps that help people. Change for life, that's what the Phoenix brand is all about."

"Be reborn: A new you today?" I asked.

"Do you like it, our slogan?"

"Lucky Dip," I replied. "That's the app that's caught my eye in particular." I smiled.

"Our best performer," Balladur grinned.

"There's never been anything like it. Do you mind if I ask something?"

"Of course, Mademoiselle."

"How can you afford all this? The state-of-the art architectural facilities, your impressive operation … for a humble start-up, that is." Balladur studied me silently, his composure suddenly pricked. His robotic assistant was adjacent to him. I could tell it was communicating with him via his ear implant.

"Would you like a brief tour of the facilities?" Clearly, he wasn't going to answer my question.

"We would welcome that."

Balladur stood abruptly to lead us out of the room, trailed by his robotic assistant. I glanced at Kace next to me and raised an eyebrow. He looked back at me knowingly.

"Shall we, Mademoiselle?" Kace whispered with a smirk, while rising to follow.

We crossed through into the large circular atrium in the center of the complex. I glanced up at the vaulted glass overhead.

"It's armor plate," Balladur announced as he glanced back, following the upward arc of my gaze.

"You take security seriously, then?"

"We have a multitrillion e-Continental investment to protect," he replied smugly.

"Please do go on," I continued. "You can tell me. After all, I'm not the competition. How does Phoenix do it? The company emerged virtually out of nowhere less than five years ago. And you've managed to amass a business empire without even offering a language streaming service."

"I know. Impressive, isn't it?" he replied, smirking again. "Monsieur Cardinale is the brains behind the operation."

"I'm only sorry not to have the pleasure of meeting Mr. Cardinale in person. Is there still a chance to see him, as I'm here?"

The creep leered at me. "He extends his apologies. Unforeseen business. Today he's away."

I pondered for a moment. If Cardinale wasn't here, then it was someone else causing me to experience the Aura. I studied Balladur with renewed curiosity. *Could it be this peacock who's hosting the Watcher?* I wondered. For the time being I put the speculation aside.

"So what's the secret to Mr. Cardinale's success, then?"

"We have a sophisticated business model," Balladur said in a self-congratulatory way. "There's advertising revenue, of course.

Our algorithms aggregate attention, a lot of attention, and we leverage that for commercial ends. Our paid pop-ups' click-through advertising is off the charts."

"I can imagine," I said, encouraging him to go on.

"We can also sell on personal data in some jurisdictions. Not possible here in the Union, obviously, with the strictest data privacy laws in the world. The United Federation is also problematic after the entire Appleton fiasco, with the United Nations restrictions still in place there, at least in part of that federation, the Republic of California. But some places are very lucrative."

"Such as?"

"The Old Kingdom. Very lax these days. And the Confederation of South American Republics. We do well there. We also receive paid commission from the National Lottery Board of each federation we operate in."

"Commission?" I was taken aback.

"Sort of a finder's fee. For each successful lux-unskill applicant, we get a payout for anyone coming via our app. The commission is small. But given our volume—well, it really does add up."

"Ingenious," I said. "Who knew?"

"Then there are state rebates."

"Rebates for what?" I asked.

"Each Tier One state and some Tier Two governments offer rebates to providers who help remove Unskills from the basic income public programs. Through the lux-unskill national lotteries. The most generous is here—the Grand Union."

"The Union's Basic Income program?"

"Precisely. Then there's the United Federation's federal demogrant scheme, valid throughout North America and the Bahamas. We do pretty well with that. We also do well in Korea and Japan. And surprisingly, quite well in the Russian Federation."

"Russia!" I exclaimed. "How did you manage to penetrate that market?"

"We have a consortium arrangement with BeeDirect."

"With the state LS provider?"

"They distribute the app and we pay a percentage of profit from our Unskill state aid income proceeds." We had come to a series of steel doors on one side of the circular bubble structure.

"That's impressive," I said, gesturing to the doors. "Looks secure."

"The most secure area of the complex." Balladur grinned at me.

"What's inside?" I asked.

"Our R&D. That's where the magic happens," he replied, squinting at me. The robotic assistant at his side was communicating with him again.

"Can we have a look?"

"*Désolé*. Sorry, that's not possible."

"Tell me one more thing, Mr. Balladur—" I began.

"Hervé, please," he interrupted.

"Hervé, then. Tell me this. Why does an app developer need an internet-from-space satellite ecosystem?" His face suddenly dropped, surprise disarming him. "Phoenix owns SkyLink, right?" I pressed, sensing my advantage.

"SkyLink?" He sniffed. "That's not us. That's a different venture based in Lyon."

"Owned by Phoenix Industries?" I continued. But Balladur had now fully regained his composure.

"We're strictly an app developer. And an app distributor. We don't offer a language streaming service."

"Again, I'm only sorry I couldn't meet Mr. Cardinale himself, given how impressive this all is," I said.

"The timing is unfortunate. His urgent business. But there is someone, I understand, that you know who has just arrived. Who heard you were here and has asked to meet with you."

"Oh?" I asked, archly.

The peacock gestured toward a sliding door as he spoke: *"Par ici s'il-vous-plaît, Mademoiselle."* The door was marked: *Directeur Général.* As Balladur paused before the closed door, ready to usher us through, I held out my hand—this was my chance to find out whether it really was the peacock who was causing the Aura.

"You've been very helpful, Hervé." He took my outstretched hand. And there it was, as my Eye was full on him. I winced in pain as the emotional halo hit me. I saw hooded shapes filing past in an underground chamber, voices chanting, bodies in small glass capsules on life support, a disused train line, a long fissure, a crack in a rocky ceiling, that led through to something dark. The emotional halo was that of suffering, pain, and torment—I pulled my hand back quickly. But despite what my Eye saw, there was no sign of a Watcher lurking within the peacock.

As the door slid open, I experienced a jolt of shock that quickly gave way to panic. Before us was the person I hated most in the world, in the flesh. I hadn't expected this—the grotesque face of the Monster glared at me.

"Monsieur Fleischman," Balladur said, addressing the Monster. "I've brought your colleagues to meet you."

CHAPTER 15

As I saw the Monster, the Aura peaked, going beyond anything I had previously experienced. I took in the same uncouth mouth; the rheumy, leering eyes; the veiny nose and cheeks, slightly flushed; the large chest of an overindulgent, disgusting Monster. Revered by some, for reasons I would never understand. A political animal who had threatened, cajoled, and beaten his way to the top; the world's leading law enforcement officer. He'd even had the audacity to seat himself in the CEO's chair. As always, the Monster took other people's places simply to exert his own power, to show that he could.

Seeing the Monster again, in person, unexpectedly after twenty years, I stumbled on the threshold. Kace caught me as I was about to fall for the second time that morning. And strangely, the Aura now merged with the blackness as I drowned in silent water—the perennial nightmare that haunted my sleep. I finally understood that they were connected, the Aura, and the backward traveling in the nightmare, through pitch-black water. And their source was Fleischman. They were born of the same dark psychic ooze that had been there for most of my adult life.

The dark tide of the drowning water pulled me, behind my now strangely sightless eyes, as time seemed to momentarily stand still. I felt panic overwhelm me, deprived of my outward senses, as something inside me reached a tumult of agitation, my entire innards spinning in turmoil. A storm crashed inside my mind, locked in, unable to grasp the exterior world—a demonic presence had wrapped itself around my very soul, squeezing the life out of me. And at that moment, giddy with confusion, no longer sure whether I was still standing, or whether I had fallen, or even where I was, I attempted to push back against the water that dragged me asunder.

This was the weakest I had ever felt in my entire existence. Yet, something within me, a faint voice that I barely even recognized, whispered at me through the frigid fright of pitch-black drowning: *Don't give in, fight!*

As I heard the words, something lit up in my mind's eye. For the first time, the silence of the water carried sound. A faint tinkling at first, growing in intensity until I could hear its crescendo in my mind. And at a stroke, I was no longer being pulled remorselessly through watery blackness. Suddenly I could swim. And how I swam! In my mind's eye, I moved forward against the backward current, toward the light. I finally emerged, out from the tidal drag of water, into a calm expanse with a shore up ahead, bathed in blinding white light. Somehow, I managed to reach a spur of land, climbing unsteadily to my feet, pain wracking my body from my Herculean effort.

I opened my eyes, finally. I could see. The Monster was still gaping at us, a look of slight amusement on his face as he saw my initial shock, my momentary stumble, and Kace's steadying arms briefly around me. I straightened myself up, pushing Kace away as I felt a new inner strength, a new steel.

"Ah, Lilith. Even more stunning in the flesh, more beautiful than ever." He pursed his lips—a trace of faint dribble dried in small white flakes at one corner of his mouth.

"Fleischman," I said coldly, finally using his name, saying it out loud for the first time since then, no longer afraid, my composure regained. I folded my arms over my chest. I could feel the squeeze of my coil pistol under my jacket, next to my left breast.

"Now, Lilith, since when are we on a last name basis?" The Monster stood, moving around the console before offering Kace his hand. I was slightly surprised they were the same height. The Monster really was that tall. Fleischman offered me his hand, too. I stared at him, fire burning in my eyes, until he dropped it.

"You know what they say about redheads, don't you?" the Monster lisped snidely at Kace. But his timing was off—all the liquor he had consumed over the years. He trembled as he spoke, spitting his words without meaning to. Then he addressed me. "What did I tell you?" Fleischman returned to the seat behind the console.

"Do you know Bastien Cardinale?" I asked coolly.

"I'm asking the questions. I told you to keep me in the loop, a direct order. You remember that, don't you?" I didn't reply. "And then I get word that you're coming here, to Rambouillet. So I want to know, I really want to know …" He paused, as if catching his breath. There were small beads of sweat on his brow. He removed a handkerchief from his trouser pocket and patted his damp forehead. The man repulsed me. And with that I realized, all at once, that I no longer repulsed myself. *I am a survivor, not a victim.*

As I glanced from Fleischman's seated figure to Balladur, now standing adjacent to him, I was jolted by the further realization that something had changed in how I perceived the others around me. My Eye could see into them, a new form of emanation, of soul reading, but without the need for touch. What I now perceived were emotional halos being given off, which I could choose to view at will. My Eye could see Balladur's fear of the Monster—red flecks, flowing out of him, as if I could now see in the infrared range. And I actually heard Balladur's thumping heart. I could also feel Kace, see into him, hear his racing pulse. The only person present who I could not feel was the Monster himself. Still not him.

I closed my eyes and shook my head. But that only made the sensations even more vivid, more acute. My Eye was somehow transformed—I perceived veiny beams of black energy spiraling around the room. I watched, behind closed eyes, as they moved in ripples through Balladur, Kace, even through the Monster in front of me. *What the hell is going on?* I screamed silently to myself. I flinched in near panic as I saw the corpuscles inside Balladur's skin, the rise and fall of his lungs. And with my Eye, I could rearrange the beams of rippling blackness, controlling them, converting them into radiant energy that I could wield with the power of my mind.

As my eyes flickered open, alarm welled up in me at this inexplicable transformation. It all felt too much, too invasive, seeing into everyone around me, peering through matter, revealing new realities that had previously been safely hidden. I was confused, shaken, suddenly unsure of myself in this strange new world of experience.

The Monster was eyeing me curiously. "Why are you here?" he asked. His thighs and legs were wide open. I focused fleetingly on his protruding shoes. They were slightly scuffed at the tips.

"I follow the trail, as always," I answered insouciantly.

The Monster snorted at my nonchalance. "Now hear this," he sneered. "I'll be very clear. This place is off limits to you and your woman's intuition, following the trail or whatever it is. Phoenix is an important part of the French economy, the Union economy.

We don't want to upset anyone. And we certainly don't want Mr. Cardinale getting agitated, putting in a complaint. Especially when there are no grounds. Understood?"

"Don't you think you're being a bit oversensitive …" I began, smiling back at the Monster, knowing this was usually his line, watching the fleeting lip-tightening of his micro-expression, as my passive-aggressive retort stung.

"What?" he snapped at me, his jowls swaying as his face lurched forward.

"As I said, I follow the trail. And this is where it leads." The Monster glared at me, anger etched on his face. I could tell he had been rendered speechless briefly by my response, and my defiance.

"Mr. Balladur, I suggest you show your guests out before your CEO gets back."

"Of course," the peacock said, starting as he heard his name. "Mademoiselle, Monsieur, I'll be pleased to show you back to your transport."

* * *

On the way back to Montmartre in the hover car, I sank quietly into the cushioned seat. Whether I had wanted it or not, I had been confronted by my greatest fear. I had been running from the Monster all these years. Yet now I felt strangely calm.

Not everything confronted could be changed. But nothing could be changed unless it was first confronted. I knew I had borne my fear, carefully curated it, for years. I had used it as an excuse not to face the thing I feared most. It had held me back. But in that moment, when I came face to face with the Monster again, I had realized that I no longer needed to run. Despite my momentary stumble when Balladur opened the door and I saw the Monster again, I heard myself speaking. I could still speak. I felt the customary anger rising within me. I was still angry. And at the peak of the Aura, as I saw him and fought to survive, something that had been broken many years before, and over time walled in by fear, as a coping mechanism maybe, had been confronted. I realized that life continued—that I continued, in spite of him. I was no longer the same girl I had been at twenty-three. I was a woman now, and had a past to look back on, to lean into, to buoy me—success, a career. I had pride in myself and in my work, in helping and protecting.

The Monster's actions, taking what was mine, were about power—exercising power. And also powerlessness. At Phoenix HQ, when I came face-to-face with the Monster again, the Aura was the very embodiment of fear, a psycho-somatic marker drawn from lived experience. The fear that the Monster was too strong for me, that he could overpower me once more.

But that fear was now seemingly gone, or at least, not quite the same. The Aura was still there, but changed, transformed into something else. I couldn't quite put my finger on it, but it felt different. And now I felt different too. I possessed something new that I could now control through my Eye, that gave me a neoteric strength, a unique type of power. Something had unlocked inside of me, fallen into place. And, ironically, I had the Monster to thank for this.

I glanced sideways at Kace. He was still on edge after our encounter with the Monster, with Fleischman. I smiled at him, indulgently. I understood.

"Boy, that was tense," Kace said. I lowered my head slightly, giving the faintest of nods. "How are you feeling now?"

I barely registered his question, instead lapsing back into my thoughts, shutting my eyes. *Have I found the Watcher?* The Aura. It pointed to Fleischman. If I was right, this Watcher inhabited the Monster. What was I to make of that? The man who had once nearly destroyed me was playing host to an alien, gaseous monster. If only I could now tell Clyde—after all the occasions he had chided me for referring to Fleischman as the Monster, refusing to use his name, because my therapy was predicated on confronting the man, the name—that I had been right all along. Fleischman really was a monster. It was an irony to end them all. Except I didn't feel like laughing. And Clyde, well, he was now nothing to me.

But at least with that realization, I belatedly understood why the Monster had been able to protect himself from me all those years ago, preventing me from burning him, as if he was able to block me. I understood how he had been able to exert his power over me. The Watcher must have been part of him even back then.

CHAPTER 16

I knew I needed to summon the shadowy alien, to come to better understand myself: "Are you always here?" My unspoken thoughts projected inward as I sat next to Kace.

"Whenever you call, I come," Selaphiel replied in silent communion. "Our instruments show you've found the Watcher, haven't you?"

"I think so," I whispered. I felt an involuntary shiver come over me. "Can Sempiternals also manipulate quintessence, like Watchers?"

"Nothing with a physical form can manipulate quintessence. Nothing in the Elyonim. Only Watchers have mastered it. An adaptation to dark matter radiation." Now I was confused. *What can I see, then?*

"What is quintessence, exactly?"

"A primordial force that was created at the beginning of the Elyonim and the Chaos, when the first light of the Morningstar shone in. Quintessence is non-luminous dark matter. It lies hidden beyond the everyday normal bradyonic matter. Beyond the fermions, bosons, quarks and leptons—the elementary particles that make up atoms and molecules, the building blocks of everything around us, from humans to stars, even Sempiternals like me and Principalities like you. Quintessence doesn't interact electromagnetically with normal matter. It flows through us, through everything you see around you. It has a higher concentration in the Chaos. But quintessence is present here in the Elyonim, too."

"So if it's hidden, how do you know it's there?"

"We can't see quintessence directly. We infer its presence from the effect its mass has on ordinary objects and entities, with the help of our instruments. But Watchers, they draw on it as an energy source. They can use it to act in the physical realm. To travel to the Elyonim, for one thing. To perform physical actions with the power of their minds, for another. Quintessence also sustains a Watcher's life force, allowing them to continue living for a similar lifespan to a Sempiternal, despite not having a soma."

As Selaphiel spoke, I closed my eyes. My Eye could see the channels of repulsive energy swirling in patterns here in the hover cab. I could track dark lines passing through Kace beside me. And as I opened my eyes again, I could still see the beams, even passing through my hand as I held it up, inspecting it. *Is this what quintessence looks like?*

I asked a different question instead, piqued by curiosity.

"So if you can't manipulate quintessence, how do *you* live so long?"

"My species evolved the ability long ago, early in the new universe, to absorb the essence of the Morningstar in its near-purest form. And from the Morningstar Abyss we harvest sempiternity particles—decayed elements of white matter. Adaptation to white matter radiation leads to an entropy reversal mechanism—a type of self-rejuvenation for us. Your biology is different. Even with a white matter infusion, your body couldn't absorb sempiternity particles. Yours is an altogether different gift.

You consume the time of others, to renew your cells, the building blocks of your being. How do you term it? You burn to live."

"I recently took a decade from a man. Isn't it wrong to steal life?" I asked, remembering my fight with the Dark Court cultists. My thoughts were now imbued with fleeting bitterness at the harm I could inflict.

"Is it wrong?" the creature asked. "That's not the right question."

"Do enlighten me," I replied sarcastically, growing impatient.

"It presupposes a moral scale. Good versus bad."

"Isn't there such a thing as a moral scale?" I asked, incredulous.

"That's a human concept. Mortality shapes thought into conceiving of life as something that's contextualized by degrees of virtue. Not being mortal frees thought from such petty impediments."

"So how should I contextualize my thoughts?"

"We all come from energy. And we consume energy ... to persist. Mortals, a Principality like you, Sempiternals, even Watchers. Our consciousness cannot survive without it. We all crave consciousness, continued existence—a fundamental law of nature, everywhere. Timescales across our various species are different, but unless we consume energy, our fate is all the same— your order of Principalities, and even orders of pure Sempiternals. You consume the time of others to continue."

Yes, I could burn time from others, using my Eye. But I was also beginning to suspect that I could now perceive something else—a new means of generating energy. I longed to confide, to ask what that meant, why I was like a gaseous Watcher. But I suspected I couldn't fully trust Selaphiel, or the master the creature served. After all, I had learned the Sage could switch off the Melody if he chose. And that didn't sound like a good thing for my well-being.

The creature's voice in my head had stopped, as if Selaphiel had paused to reflect momentarily. As if unsure how much more to say.

"How old do you think your father was in Earth years?" Selaphiel asked at last. I was taken aback by this question.

"He died at forty," I replied.

"Maybe he was forty from a mortal perspective. But he walked the Earth for over two thousand years. He was born to a mortal, a woman from a place that used to be called Magdala by the Sea of Galilee, sired by a Principality like you—another remarkable being, a great healer. One who developed an advanced power we still don't understand."

"You're talking about my grandfather?" I asked, suddenly taken aback. "What power did he have?" Now my mind was racing. My father had never mentioned this to me.

"Your grandfather was able to manipulate physical objects, multiply them, change matter, its substance. He learned to walk on water."

"What?" I gasped in shock, as I understood who my grandfather was. "Do you know how he was able to do that?"

"Your grandfather and father, like you, had golden blood. Like Sempiternals. Evolutionary challenges are universal. Which is why life forms throughout the Elyonim share certain features. The principle of evolutionary convergence to overcome broadly similar challenges. Gravitation, for instance. But golden blood is rare, nevertheless. Gifted in DNA at the alpha and omega point of time, by the Grand Designer who first emerged from the Abyss, when all things were first created. Or ended, depending on your perspective."

"The Grand Designer, the Abyss?" I asked in bemusement at the hints of revelation of which I had no inkling. I shook my head in disbelief—this was all too much. But I could sense that Selaphiel wasn't finished.

"The Sage decided …" The creature stopped, seeming reluctant to go on.

"What did the Sage decide?" I demanded.

"It is not for us to question the Sage. But it is true your grandfather was becoming too powerful. He began to believe he was more than he was. More than he could be allowed to be. The Sage foresaw things. The Mind Chant was withdrawn. Your grandfather chose to be spared from the agonies. To die."

I frowned. "So you don't know how he was able to manipulate physical objects?" The creature didn't reply. "Isn't that what you said Watchers could do?" I pressed.

There was a brief silence.

"I cannot help with these questions. Only the Sage knows. One day, if you are favored, you might be granted an audience. But now, at least, you begin to understand your lineage," the creature replied. I could tell it either didn't know or couldn't say more. And I now knew that my instinct was right not to reveal the strange transformation that had overtaken me. If I was right, my grandfather died because of his ability to manipulate quintessence. "You might continue longer than your father. I see your determination and your emerging powers."

"And you?" I asked, as I could see I would get nothing more on the topic of my ancestry. "How old are you?"

"An altogether different timescale. Age becomes a relative concept. I have lived for millions of your years. But I will also reach an end one day. When the sempiternity particles that bind me begin to become unstable, when they reach the tipping point of decay, despite their long half-life, then my homeostatic system will move into irreversible decline. Eventually, my body will cease to exist as a collective whole. The molecules that make me what I am, what you saw yesterday when we met, will drift apart, slowly, through space and time. Holes will appear in my fabric. That will be my end. But you have work to do."

I nodded to myself. Find a way to stop the Watcher: check. But first I had to figure out what it was planning. What the role of the Unskills was in all this. And why they were dying.

CHAPTER 17

We were back in Montmartre, in a café across from our hotel.

"How are you feeling now?" Kace asked kindly. The serving unit brought us our coffees. "Is he really your boss?"

I studied Kace's face—he was asking about Fleischman, of course.

"He's the Head of Interpol. That's all. He's nothing to me. Park is my line manager," I replied, more defensively than I had intended.

"But the guy was spitting mad." I could tell Kace was unsettled, maybe even a little afraid. The Monster could do that to a person.

"At not being kept in the loop? Well, that figures. But you heard what Lejeune said. I report directly to her on this. I think an Assistant Secretary-General of the UN is already high enough in the food chain."

"So what's the deal? He gave you a direct order."

"To drop it with Phoenix?" I asked. "He was tipped off by someone! That's the only way he could have known we'd be in Rambouillet." I wondered whether Park would have done that. He had always come across as trustworthy, although a bit too honest. Perhaps he felt compelled to update the Monster, especially as he'd disobeyed a previous order by assigning me to the case.

"But you won't drop it, will you?" Kace asked.

I ignored his question. "Could a low-frequency electromagnetic field be delivered via an LS signal?"

Kace studied my face. "I take that to be a no, then?"

I smiled wryly.

"The language chip doesn't create an EMF," Kace continued thoughtfully.

"So it couldn't do any of this—produce a radiation effect that would interfere with the brain?"

"Suppress melatonin production? Not a chance."

I paused for a moment, watching him before replying. "You seem confident."

"Look, Lilith, these things are completely safe," he replied, pointing to his head. "Universal Grammar technology has been consistently improved. Over fifty years of medical certs to back up UG tech. There's no way that's the issue."

"Okay, but what about the ear implant, then?" I pressed. "That is basically a Wi-Fi router, a transceiver. It connects the language chip, the UG implant, to LS signals. Which then allows us all to stream language twenty-four seven. The LS signal connects with internet-from-space on a continuous basis, correct?"

"That's the beauty of subscribing to a language streaming service. At least in principle, anyone can stream any of the world's two hundred and fifty Unilanguage-approved state official languages. A seamless experience even when crossing national borders, or so they say. I've never been outside the UFA. Or, at least not before this."

"Yes. At least for those who subscribe to a multilanguage package," I said.

"Sure. So where are you going with all this?"

"I want to conduct a thought experiment. Humor me, okay? Let's walk through Universal Grammar tech and its potential vulnerabilities." Kace nodded as I began. "This is what we know. A language chip consists of an array of several hundred ultra-thin flexible polymer threads, each a fraction of the width of a human hair, with thousands of electrodes distributed across the threads. And the language chip links the two language regions of the human brain, Broca's and Wernicke's areas. The language chip is also connected to the implant inserted behind the ear. This receives the continuous Wi-Fi signal from the streaming language broadcast system in space. So let's say, for argument's sake, that it's possible to take control of someone's ear implant and use it to send a continuous signal, maybe undetectable, to the language chip."

"I'm listening," Kace replied.

"Could that create a low-frequency electromagnetic field? Basically, transform the language chip into an EMF generator?"

"A weapon against an individual's own brain?"

"To prevent the brain from producing melatonin. To slowly kill them by sleep deprivation," I added.

"In principle, the ear implant could be used to emit a continuous EMF signal directly into the brain to be picked up by the language chip. And if the signal persisted, melatonin production would halt and sleep would cease," Kace answered.

"Because the ear implant doesn't have the same safety protocols as the language chip."

"Right. But …"

"But what?" I pressed.

"The one thing an app would require, for this to work, is the means of delivering a continuous signal."

"Right, they would need their own satellite system. SkyLink!" I exclaimed, as it suddenly hit me. Kace's jaw dropped. "Why else would Phoenix need access to major internet-from-space infrastructure?"

Kace slowly recovered his composure, before beginning to frown. "But even with a continuous LS signal, an internet-from-space system, Phoenix would still need to somehow gain access to the person's LS rebounds. To hack someone's language chip, they'd need to identify and sync with the language chip. The external signal would need to know the unique sec-code and ..."

"Have permission to sync?" I asked.

"Exactly," Kace replied. "I don't see how Phoenix could manage that."

"Hmmm ... To selectively obtain language chip sec-codes just for the Unskills, among all the Lucky Dip app users," I said, completing the thought for him. "That's our missing link."

"But I don't get it," Kace announced, perplexed. "Why would Phoenix want to hack into people's heads? Even if they have the technology, why do it? What would their motive be? It makes no sense."

At any other time, perhaps I would have been skeptical too. But now I knew about Watchers, and I believed a Watcher was controlling the Monster. Indeed, Fleischman had been unusually interested in a French app developer and was sufficiently motivated to turn up unannounced at Phoenix HQ to warn me off.

"I know it's Phoenix. I can feel it."

"And you never left a case unsolved. Isn't that what they say about you?" Kace asked. I stared at him thoughtfully for a moment. Something I had felt in the emotional halo I'd detected from Hervé Balladur had been nagging at me. An underground chamber, rail tracks, hooded figures. Then it hit me.

"We both need to go slip into something more comfortable. Tonight, I'm taking you out."

Kace raised an eyebrow. "For dinner again?" he asked, brightening up.

I let out a short laugh of surprise. "No, tonight we'll be *cataphiles.*"

"We'll be what?" He shot me a puzzled look.

"We're going down into the catacombs of Paris."

* * *

We followed the guide, along with nine other tourists, down the one hundred and thirty-one steps from the Gate of Hell—the ancient city gate.

"The intestines of Paris lie beneath your feet," the guide began as we descended. "The densest collection of sewers and underground train tunnels in the world, many long abandoned." One tourist gulped. "There are also subterranean canals, crypts, reservoirs, even disused bank vaults. And that's just the start. Even more surprising are the *vides de carrières*—the ancient mines of Paris. Gypsum was once quarried north of the Seine, limestone here south of the river. It's all off-limits, but urban explorers come anyway. There are many hidden entrances." The guide paused for effect. It was the last English-language tour of the day, but without accent differentiators. "We will take a one-and-a-half-kilometer route twenty meters underground," the woman continued. "Work began on the ossuary in seventeen seventy-four. It holds the remains of more than six million people." The guide's voice continued, snaking up in a disembodied echo as we lost sight of her.

"It's getting chilly," I whispered to Kace. He chuckled.

"You sound funny without an accent," he said, turning to glance up at me as I followed down the winding steps.

"You've lost your personality too," I retorted witheringly, adjusting the earpiece I'd been given. We would both be deprived of our personal Unilanguage North American packages while underground. I involuntarily touched the hard hat with which I had also been provided. I shuddered to think what I looked like. I shivered, despite the warm clothes, as we continued to descend. The temperature was dropping. Yet it was strangely humid—cold humidity, the chill smell of damp walls.

"Please be sure to keep your Catacombs LS transceivers in," the guide said as we reached a small stone landing at the bottom of the first set of steps. "Your own language streaming service signals won't reach your ear implants at this level. We don't want you to go offline," she cautioned.

"Feels like an isolation booth," Kace mused. I had to agree.

"The mines have over two hundred and eighty kilometers of tunnels, connected by several major galleries, large chambers, and rooms. Many are subject to flooding. The entire system passes under several city districts. Over ten times the area of Central Park in New York. But the burial chambers, our tour, well they only make up a very small portion of that," she continued. "Of course, there are still areas that haven't been mapped."

The lighting was dim. Our fellow tourists had activated their holotab flashlights and were taking holographic image grabs, recording the experience for their MyPlace followers, to be uploaded later. Livestreaming wasn't possible at this depth. As we continued down, the dusty scent of old stone and incense began to infuse the air with the ancient fragrance of lives past, of rites of death, of old bones. We had left the warm summer evening air for this ancient realm five stories underground, a morbid waystation for skeletons.

"We'll slip away before we reach the Crypt of the Sepulchral Lamp," I announced.

CHAPTER 18

The voices of the other tourists became more distant as we moved down a side tunnel, separating ourselves from the tour. We splashed through some water. It was dark now.

"Activate your holotab light," I instructed. A powerful beam of light sprayed out from the translucent screen projected from Kace's wrist chip. He adjusted the position of his hand, illuminating the way ahead while I concentrated.

"What are we looking for, exactly?"

I shook my head. "Something is down here."

"Something? How do you know that?"

I glanced at him grimly without responding.

We came to a metal door at the end of the small tunnel. Kace shone his light around. There was a rusty plaque fitted into the rocky ceiling overhead, with a name: *Avenue du Colonel Henri Rol-Tanguy.*

"The limit of the catacombs. The mines lie beyond."

"The mines?" Kace asked in surprise. "I thought it was all catacombs."

"We're heading into the southern network."

Kace pressed against the door. "It's locked," he announced. I gestured toward a combination panel on the door under a flip-close plastic cover. He gave a quick shrug. "What now? We won't get through that."

I smiled knowingly. I was about to reveal myself to him—there could be no going back after this. I lifted the cover and brushed my forefinger across the keys. It was a standard combination keypad—four rows, three columns. I closed my eyes, concentrating. Now I needed an emotional halo from my Eye; the hands and fingers of people past who had operated the lock and whose past actions imbued this inanimate object with tells that I could intuit. I began gently feeling the way in, sensing which keys resisted my touch and the way others eased into their apertures, the use over time from human fingers, and the slight abrasions of wear. After a few moments, I had it.

"Nine—up to six—then left to five—then down to eight."

"What?" Kace asked.

"Wanna try?"

He dutifully pressed the buttons and then pushed against the door.

"Nothing," he announced despondently.

"Now the pound key, bottom right."

He pressed against the door again. I heard him gasp as it clicked. He pushed it open. I walked through, past him, traipsing through more puddles, while he gaped after me. He followed without saying anything.

"Be careful," I said as I led. "The tunnels may have outcrops and will get low."

"Where are we headed?"

"I don't know yet." I gently brushed my hand against the cold rock wall as I closed my eyes, engaging my Eye. But there was nothing—no emotional halo. Just damp stone. I tried something different. I lowered my hand and focused on conjuring up the emotional halo I had experienced when I touched Hervé

Balladur's hand. And just like that, I experienced the familiar rush of my Eye, beyond my closed, sightless eyes. But this time, I wasn't using touch—I was using the memory of an emotional halo, deploying it as a compass, a wayfinder, to locate what I had seen.

Now I could also see spirals of dark energy, elemental particles of quintessence all around me. And as I focused on what the emotional halo had shown me, the quintessence visible to my Eye formed into spirals of direction, some kind of psychic map. I was able to repurpose my Eye to reshape the splintered sensory disturbance of the quintessence into a flow of dark perception, clear lines and pathways of energy channels. This, I knew, would lead me to the epicenter of the dark emotional halo I had experienced when I'd made contact with Balladur.

I started walking, quickly along the narrow galleries, my eyes still closed as I followed the energy path that my Eye had tapped into. I could hear Kace's hard hat behind me, occasionally tapping against low-hanging outcrops in the ceiling as he attempted to keep up. We entered a large, cavernous chamber and I opened my eyes to survey the scene. Kace jerked his holotab flashlight around, making a whistling sound. The sight was impressive. Tall columns of mineral deposits acted as pillars supporting the high, craggy ceiling. As the pale arc of his flashlight danced along the walls, it lent the chamber an eerie, cathedralesque air.

I closed my eyes again, leading us on. We continued through a series of smaller subterranean quarries and back into another larger gallery. Finally, my foot knocked against something metallic.

"What's that?" Kace asked. "A metal track?"

I glanced down. "Narrow gauge," I replied. "An old quarry tub tramway."

I could now see the dark lines of quintessence narrowing into a single pathway, pulling me with them, directing my Eye in the darkness. They were my guide, drawing me with a centrifugal force toward the core of the unholy blackness I sensed.

"We've been going for over forty minutes. I hope we're not lost," Kace announced finally.

I shook my head. "We're close."

Then, suddenly, there was the sound of dogs. Loud barking. It came from the mouth of a larger gallery. The vicious snarls echoed around us, creating a cacophony of ferocious warning. A large wooden barrier partially blocked the gallery, prominently displaying a sign in red: *Danger! Travaux en cours*. Without access to my multilingual LS package, I didn't know what the French words following 'danger' meant—but at least that word worked just fine as a warning, in English.

"Guard dogs," Kace whispered in alarm. "Sounds like Dobermanns." Panic was rising in his voice. "We should pass quickly."

"Those aren't guard dogs." I squeezed past the barrier and pointed up. He shone his light on the quarry wall where I was gesturing. A large speaker had been fitted into the wall, with a motion sensor next to it.

"A trick! How did you know that?"

"No one uses actual dogs for security anymore," I whispered back. I beckoned him through.

"No, really," Kace insisted. "One of your famous intuitions?"

"It's this way."

At the end of the gallery there was a large set of metal double doors embedded into the rock. Kace explored its perimeter. "No sign of a combination pad this time," he announced. Then he pointed to a keyhole. "This is even older tech."

I scrunched up my eyes for an instant while I reflected. My Eye couldn't help me with this. This was a new test. I approached the door and touched the large keyhole gently with both hands. I crouched and peered into it, looking at the lock. It was an old-fashioned deadbolt system. I took a breath and closed my eyes. I could feel the beams of quintessence all around me, the swirling mass of dark repulsive energy. The dissipated Aura had been transformed into a new power, a strange form of psychokinesis. I could feel it, my new ability to gather and harness quintessence, transpose it into packets of invisible radiant energy, energy that I could emit and manipulate with the power of my mind.

As I concentrated, I could even sense the inner workings of my body, my limbs, my brain. I felt the increased blood flow in my right cerebral hemisphere. I was aware of the increased electrostatic charge coursing through my entire core. And slowly, I summoned the quintessence I now controlled. By manipulating brain waves, I could refocus it into electromagnetic energy that I could radiate out, through touch. I applied it to the weight of the metal inside the lock. I guided the deadbolt, feeling its weight with my Eye, as I touched the door with my hand. I channeled more beams of quintessence, also converting that into electromagnetic radiation. And with that, the deadbolt slowly slid out of its locked state, clicking into an open position. I felt suddenly lightheaded after my effort.

Kace heaved against the door; it opened slowly. He turned to me in amazement. "That's not possible."

"I know," I murmured as I stood. I was nearly as surprised as he was. "That's why you can't tell anyone. Now we proceed carefully."

Kace studied me thoughtfully before responding. "LS scanners?"

I shook my head, pointing to my earpiece. "We're too far

underground. Internet-from-space doesn't work down here, remember? We can't be identified. We'll need to be out of here soon, before they shut it off for the night," I added, tapping Kace's earpiece.

He showed me a thumbs-up gesture before replying. "No one wants to go offline, feral. It happened to me once … worst experience of my life."

We passed through the door into a large gallery-cum-corridor, carved into the rock. Lights shone ahead.

"Be careful," I warned.

At the end of the corridor, on our left, we came to a set of large wooden doors firmly closed, set into the rock. And as we reached that point, we both paused in amazement at what we saw opening up to our right. We had entered above a semicircular amphitheater-style arena, which lay below us as we turned to look down—it was a huge, empty chamber consisting of carved stone benches curving around from one side of the underground cavern to the other. The stone seating descended to the stage area, with a banked stone dais in the center, a steep gradient below, and a stone altar in the very middle, atop the dais. The chamber was illuminated by LED lighting, mounted on metal struts in concentric semicircles running along the stone walls that curved around us. And on the cave ceiling in front of us, rising above the altar, was a large motif, engraved and colored with faded pastel colors. It depicted a large tower with a lone sentinel on top, staring out as if watching. The figure's eyes somehow followed you around the chamber. This was the motif of the Dark Court.

I glanced at Kace and saw him wince. I could tell he recognized the motif too. And as we stood at the top of the banked seating, we surveyed the scene in astonishment.

"What is this place?" Kace gasped quietly after a moment.

"My guess would be a temple."

"A what?" came his astonished reply.

"That's the cavea," I said, gesturing to the banked seats dropping down in front of us. "And that's the arena." I pointed to the staged area below, featuring the altar. "Look through there," I continued, directing his gaze to an archway behind the altar. I could make out a dim exit, with wide stone stairs leading down and away, doubtless to other underground chambers. "The stairs. That's the vomitorium."

"The what?" Kace asked in a hoarse whisper. There were words engraved in stone along the top of the archway below. "What does that say?" he asked.

"*La vie indigne de la vie.*"

"But what does it say in English?" Kace asked impatiently. It was a good question. We were still piggybacking on the catacombs' bespoke LS service, which only provided streaming in English. I closed my eyes and used my new power to draw down my own LS signals through the thick limestone rock above us. *Could I do it?* I channeled the quintessence I could see and feel all around me, converting it into electromagnetic radiation. I then expelled massive amounts of joules into the limestone above me with the power of my mind. The radiant energy acted to strengthen the force of the Earth's gravity; slowly, but surely, I began to draw LS signals painstakingly through the rock above, until I felt the signals flowing, unfettered, directly to my ear transceiver. And there—I had it, language streaming restored. I took out the earpiece. I no longer needed it.

"Life unworthy of life," I said, finally.

"You're no longer feral," Kace exclaimed, before gazing back at the French inscription above the archway. His expression was a combination of disbelief and shock.

"The Dark Court," he whispered.

"The Brethren of the Sacred Vessels of the Grigori …"

Kace glanced at me sharply. "What?"

"The formal name for the Dark Court. An old file from Europol archives. An ancient sect that goes back a couple thousand years at least, in one form or another."

Kace knitted his eyebrows. "But I thought it was a new movement, after the Great Language Outage, an alt-right conspiracy-theory thing."

"Talk of mass plots to kidnap the children of other soc-ed classes? Pedophilia rings?" I asked, snorting. "The Unskills trying to bring down society?"

"Right. Working up the other soc-ed classes into a frenzy to support the Compulsory Sterilization Bill, to end reproductive rights for Unskills." Kace looked at me, confused. "Isn't that what the Dark Court is all about, then?"

"I think that's just the tip of the iceberg. We suspect it's an ancient Doomsday cult. And this place is my first solid lead."

"Doomsday cult?" Kace asked, nervously.

"An eschatology cult, in fact, according to a later update. The original file was logged by a Europol Commander, one Emyr Morgan."

"Why not contact him then, let him handle it. We can get out of here."

I smiled faintly, shaking my head. I understood that Kace was spooked. "We can't do that. This Emyr Morgan vanished without a trace just a few days after the Great Language Outage. A strange one. He hasn't been heard of since. Anyway, let's see what we can find out, since we're here."

I flashed Kace what I hoped was a reassuring smile before descending the steps between the banked rows of stone benches.

Kace followed. Each stone seat had a small console in front of it with a connection hub for earpieces.

I walked quickly, shuddering as I passed the stone altar that I dared not touch. To one side, at the rear of the arena, was a large wooden throne on a second dais. And in front of it was an ornate wooden stand, supporting a sloped surface with a lower ledge.

"What's that?" Kace asked, bemused.

I stared at it. "A lectern, I think."

"What, to hold an actual book?" Kace asked rhetorically.

My father had a library full of books when I was a girl. But most people had never even seen one. These days physical books were vanishingly rare, collector's items.

I approached the large archway leading to the stone stairs. I paused for a moment at the top, peering into the semidarkness of a large corridor below. At the foot of the carved stone staircase, about fifteen steps down, I made out the glow of more LED lights. I moved gingerly down the stairs. I could feel Kace's nervous breath on the nape of my neck, below my hairline, as he followed close behind.

At the bottom, we emerged into a long, dimly lit stone corridor with several doors along its length. The air was now almost unbearably cold and damp. The corridor veered to the right and then back onto itself, running in parallel, directly beneath the large temple-like chamber from which we'd descended. As we followed, turning around the sharp bend, the corridor reached a terminus in the form of another large door dead ahead. I had it unlocked in a few seconds, before pushing it wide open.

We stood on the threshold in disbelief. Before us was an even larger cavernous chamber, with a high ceiling. Within, beginning not twenty meters away from us, the chamber contained circular rows of glass medical capsules, standing upright. There were scores of capsules, each with a dark, modular base, fitted with consoles, peppered with flickering lights. And on the upper part of each capsule, there was a glass front that looked as if it opened upward. From within each capsule, a low green light illuminated a single human occupant, strapped to a medical transport set in upright position, and attired in a white medical gown. The dim green light gave the whole scene an ethereal quality.

There was an aisle running through the concentric rows of capsules, leading to a large cone. The capsules were arranged so they radiated out from the central cone, the purpose of which was as yet unclear. I moved forward, toward the capsules. Inside the nearest one was a young woman, her eyes staring out at me blankly. She was catatonic.

I peered inside, through the glass front, for a closer inspection. Inserted into her chest was a catheter connected to a series of tubes, partially visible through the front parting of her medical gown. These were, in turn, hooked up to a unit fitted to the medical transport that supported her in secure webbing. As I glanced along the row of glass capsules, the occupants in others were in various stages of catatonia. Some were convulsing, while others were in a stupefied state.

I examined the lower black modular casing, beneath the glass front of the capsule. It was fitted with a silver screen, which flashed with identifiers. The person's name and ID credentials, including sec-code, scrolled across. Also displayed was the soc-ed class. The woman was an Unskill, which figured. I moved through the circular rows of capsules, scanning each capsule screen in turn—they were all Unskills!

I glanced beyond the sets of capsules to the far end of the darkened chamber. On the far wall there was a bank of large drawers, running from floor to rocky ceiling. I pointed, and from behind I heard Kace's sudden sharp intake of breath.

"Refrigerated body units."

"What?" I asked with incredulity.

"To store dead bodies. What is this place?" Kace whispered.

Now I sensed something. "Someone's coming."

"I don't hear anything. How do you know?" he whispered.

I turned around, facing him. "More than one. Armed. We need to leave. Follow me."

I knew an armed patrol was heading our way, probably with the Dark Court. They were still some way off, in the catacombs, heading toward the temple. We could still evade them and get out of the catacombs, but we had to leave immediately. And I would lock the doors behind us to avoid giving away our discovery of this place.

CHAPTER 19

Our second full day in Paris. My in-ear alarm reviver woke me at five a.m. I gave a half-tap behind my ear to silence it, before groaning and turning over. I had the wretched HR meeting in an hour to discuss my annual medical.

Once ready, I descended to the hotel's lobby level, to find the isolation booth that had been reserved for me—*de rigueur* for a secure briefing with UN HQ while out in the field. There was always an unsettling stillness inside the conductive polymer-lined interior. I sat at the isolation booth console and synced my holotab. The projection from my wrist chip vanished while a mirrored display popped up from the console's inlaid fusion bar. I hooked up the hard-wired connection from the console to the outlet jack from my ear modem implant.

Hazy silhouettes swirled around in midair, before three sets of heads and torsos popped into sharp pixelation. They projected out at me as three-dimensional feeds from the telepresence projection ring. Digital identifiers for each rotated in three-dimensional splendor underneath—name, title, location, and time zone. Farren Fleur, Director of Interpol Human Resources, was on the same time zone as me—she was in Lyon, around 390 kilometers south of Paris. The identifiers for the medic revealed her to be Colonel Oda Quade, of the United Federation Space

Force. She was on Western Time, nine hours behind, and her location identifier showed up as: *Groom Lake Space Force Command, Nevada.* Her title was given as: *Chief Medical Officer, Research Institute (classified). What the hell!* I thought.

Finally, there was the UN lawyer that Park had arranged for me—one Charles Eckert Triumphus III. I suppressed a snigger as I parsed his name. He was connecting from UN Plaza in Turtle Bay, New York. It was midnight for him. At least I would have someone in my corner, whatever this was about.

Farren Fleur opened the meeting. "High Commissioner Lilith Errapel King," the woman announced, peering at me, her holographic projection flickering for a moment. I wasn't sure whether it was a statement or a question. Suddenly my hands began shaking—I hadn't expected that, usually so cool under pressure. I placed them under the table so no one could see my tell; the scar on my ankle started itching like hell, too. I fought back the urge to bend and scratch it—I knew from experience that never helped.

Farren Fleur was a spare, pinched-looking woman, her arms placed neatly across her lap—she was studying me with narrowed eyes. I'd heard of her, a reputation for always backing management against employees. *That's how it always goes with HR,* I mused. Her very presence at the meeting was ominous, though. She was sitting bolt upright with a very straight back. Her frilly, high-necked ivory blouse looked old-fashioned. She was annoyingly prim. I took a deep breath as she began speaking.

"It's sometimes necessary to have a follow-up, after an employee's annual medical. And given your somewhat surprising results, Director Fleischman requested input from the UFA Space Force, which has a world-leading research program into biological aging."

It is about my age. My worst fear. *Christ, what now? Keep your composure, Lily,* I told myself.

"And while there's nothing to be concerned about," she continued, "as is your right, you've requested a representative from Legal to be present. Colonel Quade, would you care to lead?"

Oda Quade was a stern-looking woman, in her fifties. She was a peroxide blonde, with permanent tattooed make-up, probably done long ago. Now gravity had caught up with her, and the colored rouge sagged at an odd angle under her lower lips, and her permanent eyeliner was no longer as sharp as it should have been.

"We just need to run through a few things," Oda Quade began. She adjusted her sky-blue military tunic slightly. "How old are you, High Commissioner?" she asked, watching me intently. She spoke in a hard staccato, before feigning a smile. But the eyes gave her away. They were unmoving, a slight hint of cruelty maybe.

"Forty-three," I snapped. I was experiencing the worst sinking feeling of my life. Panic was welling up in me. *Had they found out about my Eye? Had they figured that out?*

"That is indeed what it says in your DigID records," the medic replied.

"And on my birth license, which you have access to," I spoke defiantly. Yet, I still detected a tremor in my voice.

Quade threw me a condescending smile. "There are some unusual results in your annual medical," she continued. "There's a divergence between your chronological and biological age."

"I keep telling people, I just have good genes," I remarked, trying to play it down, whatever it was they had discovered. Quade's mouth puckered slightly but her eyes were dead.

Farren Fleur jumped in. "At each of the last three annual medicals, the virtual medic has requested a new biometric ePassport for you … a new facial stillgram and hologram for sec-cam identifiers." She stared at me almost accusingly. "Do you know how often the average employee is required to have a holographic ID update?" I said nothing. I knew the answer. "Every five point two years. The rest of us don't change much."

"How boring!" I muttered. I couldn't help myself. It came out more sarcastic than I had intended.

"This year, your results are off the charts," Oda Quade added. "You might be forty-three, but biologically … well, look at you. VirDa, display the High Commissioner's hologram ID across the last three annual meds."

The hologram projected out from the console, a rotating holographic display of my head and shoulders, recorded over the last three years by the robotic surgeon at my annual evals. The three images rotated next to one another, with a time and date stamp projected across each. I glanced quickly at them. It was indeed my face. But with each successively older image, the face was noticeably more youthful. And this year, I did have to admit it, I was looking as good as I did in my early twenties. *I have to be special*, I thought, groaning inwardly.

"Forty-three, forty-two, forty-one," Quade continued, glancing in turn at each of the holograms. "Do you see a pattern?" I looked away. "You might have the chronological age of a forty-three-year-old woman, but biologically you were early thirties last year. And now—well, you're twenty-three. This year, your biological age has jumped backward, around a whole decade!"

"So where are you going with this, Colonel Quade?" the attorney asked. I studied him properly for the first time. He spoke with a rich baritone, lush gray hair brushed back, wearing a sharp tie and pinstripe suit jacket.

Farren Fleur intervened. "We use the measure of biological age to determine the health of our employees. What kind of medical interventions they might need, for all sorts of occupational health reasons, including whether to assign an employee to different duties. The oldest biological age we've ever had on file at Interpol was seventy-five, eleven years older than the employee's chronological age. And there we made the case for an early retirement package."

"But you just said the High Commissioner seems to be getting younger, not older, so what's the problem?" the attorney continued.

Quade rolled her eyes slightly before speaking. "Someone who is biologically younger typically continues being biologically younger as they age chronologically. But they still continue aging biologically. The High Commissioner doesn't just have the appearance of getting younger as she grows older, she is actually becoming biologically younger. She's aging backwards. It is, of course, impossible."

"But I'm doing it anyway," I shot back with a wry expression. The lawyer glanced at me, his gray eyes twinkling with amusement. "Have you thought about the possibility that I might have had cosmetic surgery? With the latest medical advances, I could look as young as I wish. Maybe I am just that vain." I doubted that would work; after all, medical procedures would have been recorded in my virtual record. Still, it was worth a try.

"High Commissioner King," Quade began. "I see from your file that you are recognized for a number of qualities, especially your extraordinary intellect and abilities. But excessive pride in your looks doesn't jibe with the psychological profile I'm seeing here. Besides, we're not talking about mere exterior appearance. This goes beyond that."

"But how can you actually tell?" the lawyer asked. "Other than her appearance."

"The annual medical covers a range of tests for all United Nations and Interpol staff. But to determine biological age-related prophylactic care, we collect epigenetic data," Farren Fleur replied.

"And what's that?" the attorney asked.

"A sample of an employee's DNA. This gets analyzed, providing a snapshot of biological age. Basically, strands of methylation DNA work to turn some genes on and others off as we age … at least, that's my understanding," Fleur continued.

Oda Quade gave a curt nod. "By examining tens of thousands of DNA sites from someone's sample, we get a very good picture. In the case of the High Commissioner, her internal organs, her vital functioning, even her skin tone … from a biological perspective, she's a twenty-three-year-old woman."

"That's a neat trick," the lawyer replied.

"It is. Which is the point," Quade continued. "Organisms have a molecular clock that counts down from the day they're born. Human cells can only renew a fixed number of times before they start dying. Basically, once the Hayflick limit is reached, cells start committing a form of self-termination; suicide, if you like. That's why we age. But somehow, the High Commissioner's cells are able to renew."

"Hayflick limit?" the lawyer asked, raising one eyebrow skeptically.

Oda Quade smiled faintly, then peered out at his projection. "Pre-programmed cellular death. A genetic kill switch we're all born with. But the High Commissioner here seems to be immune to normal cellular senescence. My agency conducts world-leading research, the Mimetics Program, which is why I'm here, talking to you."

"Mimetics?" I asked, starting to become curious.

"We've known for a long time that certain habits and behaviors, such as regular exercise, diet, and the like, slow down the aging process," Quade explained. "We've identified some of the biological factors for this, the way in which genes are switched on and off. But in the lab we're also working on cellular interventions. Replacement of nuclei from older cells with younger nuclei."

"You're working on slowing down aging," I exclaimed.

Oda Quade's eyes glanced at me, searching my own. "Maybe even reversing it, given the time spans required for our interstellar exploration programs. One part of the Mimetics Program is focused on drug development, using chemical cocktails to mimic the effects of longevity-inducing behaviors. But we're also working on gene therapy."

"You're talking about DNA modification."

"Correct," replied Quade. "Technically it's called skeletal editing. The precise rearrangement of atomic components at the sub-cellular level, producing a revised DNA profile. Superhumans if you will. It's almost magical." *She wants to create freaks of nature,* I thought, aghast. *That doesn't sound magical.*

"Which brings us to you," Farren Fleur said. "You're unique. The medics are astonished by your biological data."

"Good for them," I muttered.

"Is this surprising to you, High Commissioner?" Quade asked. "For the last three years, you've been getting progressively younger. And now this big jump. I mean, a decade …" I stared back at her. I was very uncomfortable. I was becoming aware that I wouldn't be able to carry on like this. They'd soon figure it all out. *What would I do?* "There are other matters of interest, too. Your blood type, rhesus-null—so-called golden blood. It's the rarest blood type in the world. Fewer than fifty people have ever been known to have it. And your heart, dextrocardia."

"And what's that?" asked the lawyer.

"The High Commissioner's heart points to the right side of her chest—also very rare. In the rest of us, it's on the left. We've never seen anything like it—like you," Quade continued. "We'd like to invite you to our lab in Nevada to run some tests." Farren Fleur was now also staring at me, a piercing look.

"In order to consider something like this, the High Commissioner would need a little more disclosure," the lawyer stated, matter-of-factly. "We still don't know what your program is, beyond the fact that it falls under Space Force."

Oda Quade smiled faintly. "While the program I lead is classified, what I can tell you is that it's part of the Space Force Astrobiology Institute at Groom Lake. We'd like to get a full genetic mapping done."

"You want me as your guinea pig?" I asked in involuntary horror. *I sure as hell wouldn't be anyone's lab rat.*

"You could be the key, honestly—the breakthrough we've been looking for," Quade replied.

"Obviously, as an Interpol employee, you'd have to provide consent," Farren Fleur added.

"Which is why you're here," I interjected, pointedly.

"We have to put your well-being first, as a responsible employer."

I snorted. "I have a case to solve … a pandemic."

"But will you think about it?" Quade insisted.

"Sure. I can think about it." I looked back at the medic and Fleur, both staring at me. I had already made up my mind. I couldn't afford to let them put me under the microscope—they'd never let me out again. Oda Quade's lips puckered into a faint smile.

"I'll be in touch, then, when you're back from the Union," Quade said.

I didn't reply. Instead, I addressed the lawyer. "We're done here, right?" He looked at me thoughtfully for a brief moment, then nodded.

CHAPTER 20

After the medical debriefing, I was relieved to get away from the isolation booth and the hotel. I had agreed to meet Kace in the same café opposite our hotel, as we continued to work the case. As I arrived, my ear implant pinged. An Interpol alert. I activated my holotab—Sentinel had moved to red alert.

I watched Kace approaching through the café window. The sec-cam inside blinked as he entered. As I looked into his face, I could see that he was somehow distracted. He sat across from me. Even now, in this time like no other, we each had our own worries and preoccupations. But observing him I couldn't help but feel concern, nevertheless.

"Sentinel has moved to red alert," I announced. "The UN is establishing large-scale palliative care centers. Being rolled out in major cities. Over a billion people now affected." Kace touched his brow with a fingertip before shaking his head. "This is really, really bad," I continued. But still he said nothing.

"It's bad," he replied faintly, in belated acknowledgment.

"At what point is it irreversible?"

"I don't follow," he whispered in a cracked voice.

"Melatonin depletion," I added, clarifying my question.

"It depends on the level of damage to the brainstem, the thalamus. Melatonin levels will increase once the suppressor is removed."

"You mean the low-frequency EMF?" I asked.

"For instance," Kace replied. "And then sleep will slowly resume. But if there's too much atrophy—well, then the damage is irreversible."

"So what about the people in the catacombs, then? Is there still hope for them?"

"Difficult to say without brain scans. But it didn't look good."

"I can't let them die," I whispered quietly. At that Kace looked away suddenly, letting out a long sigh. "What's up?" He shook his head.

I issued voice commands into the tabletop VirDa for two coffees. Within a minute, the robotic server brought us our drinks, placing cupstocks on the table in front of us. Kace frowned as he idly examined his cup.

"Just tell me what's going on. You seem … absent," I insisted.

"Something strange happened to my holotab earlier. It's never done that before." He looked across at me. And in that moment, I could tell something was very wrong.

I gulped, suddenly on edge. "What happened?"

"It did an auto-factory restart. Just like that."

"That's odd," I said.

"I've lost quite a bit of data."

"But it's all backed up, isn't it, in your virtual locker?"

"Sure, on the Avalon servers. It's fine. I'll just need to reinstall things. But I had to resync the device. I was offline momentarily."

"You had to resync with your language chip?" I asked.

"Yeah, allow the device access to my sec-code ID to do a full language chip scan."

"But you did check this was a legitimate restart from your LS provider first, right?"

Kace looked at me. "You know, being feral, without language …
I just freaked, wasn't thinking straight." He opened his palms.

"Oh, Kace." I shook my head, tugging on my hair. "You didn't
check, did you?"

He leaned away, hunching his shoulders, suddenly defensive.
"It happened to me before, you know, the Great Language Outage.
I was overseeing surgery and my streaming service just went. I
couldn't afford Appleton, on a junior medic's salary, before my
big promotion. I was on Samkee back then. A decent lexical
medical package, although not quite as cheap as Tele3. Anyways,
I lost sync with the robotic surgeon, the patient nearly died.
I spent a week in a holding tank, stacked in a small cubicle
surrounded by thousands of other ferals, until I could switch to
Appleton, get a streaming signal again. I don't know which was
worse, the humiliation, being fed by service units, or not being
able to communicate with anyone or anything, being locked out
of everything. The utter helplessness …"

I smiled weakly. He didn't need me to tell him he'd been
a fool. He could figure that one out all on his own. But I
understood why he'd panicked. Most of the automated world
still bore emotional scars from the Great Language Outage. And
later, with the second outage, the one that took out the non-
commercial satellites, law enforcement and state agencies went
dark too, myself included—I momentarily shuddered at the
recollection.

"Have you checked now?" I asked. Kace didn't answer. He
merely stared at me before bowing his head slowly. "And let me
guess. It wasn't Avalon?"

"No outages, updates, or restarts noted, recorded, or
requested. Nada."

"Kace!" I exclaimed in a hoarse whisper.

"It's okay. I've run a full system scan on my UG tech. Both my language chip and my ear implant check out. And then a full system diagnostic on this," he said, gesturing to the holotab being projected from his wrist chip. "It's nothing," Kace said before continuing in a cracked whisper. "It's probably nothing."

"Probably nothing?" I asked, looking at him with bewildered eyes.

"So what's the plan?" he asked, changing the subject as he hibernated his holotab.

I took a deep breath. "We're going back to Phoenix HQ."

Kace studied my face carefully. "After yesterday. You're sure about this?"

I smiled grimly, looking him straight in the eye. "Phoenix is somehow connected to the Dark Court," I said before pausing. "I want to have a look at their R&D facility."

It was the emotional halo from Hervé Balladur, after all, that had led me to the Dark Court's temple. And if Fleischman was indeed being controlled by the Watcher, then the mysterious invasion that Selaphiel had warned me of was also somehow linked to Phoenix.

"But how? That guy, your Head of Interpol—he made it pretty clear yesterday."

"He's not my Head of anything. I already told you," I snapped in irritation, "I'm not asking for his permission."

"Okay, okay. But that aside, Phoenix will never grant us access now. We'll never get auto-cleared by their security system."

"They won't know we're there," I retorted. "You know, you really don't have to come. I totally understand." As I looked into his face, I saw a flicker of hurt in his expression, before something new crossed his features. It took me a fraction of a second to identify it—it was anger.

"I hate the Dark Court, what they've done, what they're doing to communities. It's just that our LS rebounds will be visible. They'll know we're there as soon as we show up."

I smiled at him. "Don't worry about LS signals. I'll take care of that."

CHAPTER 21

The hover cab dropped us off at the edge of the Forest of Yveline, near Rambouillet. Far enough from the Phoenix HQ perimeter to not yet be detectable. As we reached the security zone, I glanced up. A shadow had occluded the summer sun. A bank of strangely shaped clouds drifted across it, covering us in gray light. They were shaped like sinister gothic cathedrals, moving with solemn foreboding high in the sky. As I paused, Kace stopped too.

"Are you okay?" he asked, turning toward me with concern.

"Give me a second. I've got this."

I closed my eyes and scrunched myself down. Opened my Eye. I was looking for channels of quintessence. This time I felt a sharp pain in both my chest and my head. That was new. I took deep breaths to control the discomfort as I transposed the dark of quintessence into radiant energy, a different wavelength this time, for a different purpose. I willed a psychic cloak over us, a bespoke Faraday field that reflected light and ultra-high-frequency radio waves, hiding us. I could feel it. I knew Kace could feel it, too. Now we were invisible to terrestrial detection, LS scanners, sec-cams, and the human eye alike, while still able to receive streaming signals from low-Earth orbit, which operated on the Ku band—just under microwave frequencies.

"I can still talk." Kace sounded relieved. "What did you do?"

I stood up. I barely knew myself. This was all new.

"Trial and error," I muttered.

We darted around the outer perimeter. There were several security droid units nearby, but they no longer had the ability to detect us. We moved beyond a small mound, past an external smart heating unit, toward the entrance door. I gestured toward it then sprinted to the door, visualizing a packet of quintessence, using it to produce energy that I aimed at the door's security system. I paused only briefly, allowing the door to spring open before me as I approached.

"How did you do that?" I heard Kace mutter behind me as he saw the door open as if by magic.

We ran in; he slid down beside me as we ducked behind a console. A security daemon passed us in the corridor—a wheeled, flat-floor unit armed with coil weaponry. Phoenix clearly wasn't taking any chances.

"It can't detect us," he muttered to himself, in quiet disbelief. We reached the door I had been searching for—the Research and Development facility. This was one big complex. I moved my hands in an open spiral in front of me, near the surface of the steel door, my eyes closed, willing up more beams of concentrated quintessence. But before I could emit packets of energy to open it, I heard the whoosh of hydraulics as the door began sliding open. I glanced at Kace. His expression was priceless. I smiled to myself.

"That wasn't me," I whispered. Two researchers were coming through, dressed in white. "Quick!" I pulled Kace away from the threshold. We stood on one side of the open doorway as the pair walked out. They were talking.

"The Intellectual Hygiene program is now fully online," said a male voice.

"Good. All dysgenics will finally be eliminated. Everything we've worked toward." A female voice—she had the air of someone in charge.

"What about the clinic in the temple?" said the male voice. By now, the pair were through the doorway. They had passed by while we remained unnoticed.

"The ritual for the crossing? Yes, preparations are being made. And then the next phase for which ..." The woman's pitch contour signaled a question. The voices moved out of earshot.

"Shall we?" I gestured to the sliding door, which was about to close. We ran through.

"What was that about?" Kace asked, perplexed. "Ritual? Crossing?"

I glanced back at him grimly.

We were now in a long, wide corridor with LED smart panels. Soft light emanated from the ceiling and walls. At the end, we emerged onto a high gantry overlooking a large chamber. Below, in the center, there were rows of VirDa consoles with scores of people operating them. Not machines, but actual people. Balladur had lied to us. Of course he had! The console operators were all wearing black overalls with the same insignia we had seen on the cave wall under the streets of Paris—a tower with a Watcher gazing out.

At one end of the chamber was a large partition that separated the console operators from a farther, smaller chamber. Stairs led down into the large chamber on either side of the gantry.

"What is this place?" Kace whispered.

"Follow me! Let's see."

We strode quickly down the stairs. Kace followed as I ducked down and ran around one edge of the large chamber, moving toward the glass partition at the far end. As we passed unseen, the uniformed operatives were working in rapt silence at consoles, gazing into large screens projecting from inlaid fusion bars. They blinked their eye commands—the reflected glow of digital displays blanched the skin of their faces, taut with concentration. Some spoke voice commands quietly, with occasional flickers of color faintly visible through the translucent ridged cartilage of their outer ear, as their ear implants pinged.

As I skirted the room, I brushed my hand along the back of one row of VirDa consoles. All at once, I experienced an emotional halo from my Eye that made me queasy. Pernicious messaging creating echo-chambers full of hatred and mistrust. The operatives were planting fake news stories across internet chatrooms and MyPlace using fabricated social media profiles. We were in the heart of the Dark Court's operations center, at the very source of its rank evil. This was the place where its conspiracy theories originated: that vast gangs of depraved Unskills were engaged in a global plot to kidnap the children of other soc-ed classes. And if the same thing were repeated often enough, the lie became *reality*—the illusory truth effect. This wasn't even sophisticated brainwashing. All the Dark Court had to do was to tap into the everyday psychological biases of the masses. *Is this how civilization falls?* I wondered. Not through the base ambition of our leaders, but the emotional responses of the everyday brain to social media, ape brains that evolved for survival in pre-paleolithic times.

We were at the glass partition at the end of the chamber. Kace followed as I peered through. There were three medic-looking types, two women and a man, wearing white tunics, just like the two who had passed us as we entered. The room on the other side looked like a medical hub. There were multiple data-processing consoles, and across an entire wall, a large bank of screens streaming a live feed of each of the comatose Unskills from the catacombs, with scrolling medical diagnostic updates. The three medics were engrossed in discussion about the data they were receiving and the live feed they were watching.

"The glass is soundproof," Kace whispered.

I pressed one ear against it and gently closed my eyes to concentrate. *I wonder*, I thought. Could I amplify the sound? I channeled quintessence, expelling radiant energy to draw sound waves through the glass. I had managed with language streaming signals in the catacombs, using radiant energy produced from quintessence to create an enhanced gravitational field. I was getting better at coordinating my brain wave frequencies, consciously making slight adjustments. And there, I had it, the voices were now clearly audible to me, through the glass.

"The High Adjudicator has ordered it." An older female voice.

"Intellectual Hygiene doesn't stop with the Unskills. That was just phase one," said the male voice. "All the adjudicators are in accord. We move to full-scale social cleansing."

"But we need to proceed carefully, let the propaganda work," said the younger woman.

"Softening up public opinion doesn't matter anymore," the man replied.

"But when we started, that's what the High Adjudicator said was priority zero," came the voice of the younger woman.

"Things change. Who knew the app would be so successful?" the older woman declared. Just then, I heard a sound and felt someone gently shaking me. It was Kace trying to get my attention.

"We've been spotted."

I glanced around. A small security drone had detected our presence. It was hovering in midair, recording our LS rebounds and performing facial recognition. I was getting tired—my cloaking had slipped. I had been multitasking, using quintessence to hear through the glass while maintaining a psychic cloak. And just like that, as the drone moved toward us, we vanished again from its LS scanners.

"Let's go," I whispered.

We quickly retraced our steps past the black-overalled console operators before moving back up toward the gantry and out.

Once outside, beyond the perimeter of Phoenix's security markers, I sank down onto the soft, warm grass, lying on my back under the summer sun. I suddenly felt drained.

"They will know we were there," I whispered.

"What was that place?" Kace asked.

"A front for the Dark Court. A propaganda factory."

CHAPTER 22

On the flight back to the hotel, I sent a memoclip request to the UN's Counter-Cyberterrorism Command for a priority meeting with Lejeune. I needed to provide a status report as she had directed, but I also had an ulterior motive. I needed something from her.

As we landed on the vertipad, my ear implant pinged—an incoming receipt alert. It was the information I had requested from Kal on Phoenix, the Lucky Dip gaming app, and Bastien Cardinale. Once at the hotel, I still had a few minutes before the short-notice meeting with Lejeune. I took myself to a seating area, scrolling through the data while Kace waited. I gasped at what I saw. I now knew I needed to brief Lejeune about Lucky Dip too. With the new information I had received from Kal, I now had the missing link—the means being used by Phoenix to take control of an individual's language chip.

When I was ready, I beckoned Kace. We headed through to the hotel's isolation booth. Kace and I hooked up the hard-wired connections from the VirDa console to the outlet jacks in our ear implants.

As soon as we connected, Lejeune's 3D-projection stared out at me. It was morning back in New York. Sun shone brightly through the window behind her. She was speaking to us from her office. Now apparently back from her mini-vacation.

"I assume you want to update me on your latest findings, as instructed?"

"Yes. I suspect there's a link between Phoenix Industries and the Dark Court."

Lejeune's expression took on a startled look, her mouth opening slightly, before she recovered her composure. "So what's the link?" Lejeune asked.

"I believe Phoenix is a front for the Dark Court."

Lejeune frowned. "A front? In what way?"

"A front for propaganda, fake news, conspiracy theories. A disruptive player, trying to shake things up. Or at least, that's how it's been operating for the last five years. Many higher soc-ed classes, especially Professionals, even Executives and maybe some Superiors, are sympathetic to their ideas."

"Look, the Semiskills might be gullible, but no one else really believes there's a conspiracy by the Unskills to kidnap the children of other classes. It's just too ludicrous," Lejeune snorted.

"Many people really do believe that the Unskills are morally depraved. That there is some vast pedophilia network coordinated across hidden parts of the internet, orchestrated by Unskills and supported and led by Marc Barron."

"But Marc Barron is dead, assassinated, a single bullet wound. Interpol conducted the autopsy. Isn't that a well-known fact? His corpse was cremated by UN decree, to avoid any attempts at exhumation by his supporters," Lejeune countered.

"But that's the beauty of conspiracy theories. They defy logic and proof. Semiskills are particularly susceptible to confirmation bias. In fact, based on the latest data aggregated by Interpol for crisis planning and preparation, two out of three Semiskills believe that Barron is in fact still alive—that reports of his death are part of the conspiracy, facilitated by a pliable and complicit media. That Barron is actively facilitating pedophilia rings among the Unskills as revenge."

Lejeune shook her head in disbelief. "Revenge for what?"

"For the demise of Appleton. For dismantling his empire."

"Okay, so what about Phoenix?" Lejeune asked. "If Phoenix were somehow involved, a front for the Dark Court as you claim, what would be the purpose of all the conspiracy theories?" she asked slightly sarcastically.

"To create chaos," I whispered.

"And change the law," Kace muttered.

"The Compulsory Sterilization Bill in the United Federation," I said. "Congress is heading toward approval."

"I'm informed it's not clear that it will pass." Lejeune narrowed her eyes. "What's your evidence? I assume you do have some to make such an outlandish claim."

"All circumstantial for now. But as you know from my track record, my hunches are usually correct. Plus, when we met Bastien Cardinale's Chief of Staff, one Hervé Balladur, he wasn't very cooperative. He was clearly hiding something."

"I'm well aware of your case clearance rate. But surely you can see that what you have isn't enough to substantiate your claims." I studied Lejeune for a moment, without replying. "Why did you request a meeting at short notice with me? Not just to indulge in idle speculation about Phoenix, I hope?"

I smiled faintly. "We know that Phoenix owns SkyLink. I want to find out whether it has been recommissioned. Because, if so, it's possible that Phoenix may be using it as a delivery system to hack into the brains of Unskills."

Lejeune's mouth gaped at me. "You're suggesting that Phoenix may be responsible for this? The sleep pandemic?"

"It's one line of inquiry. I had a colleague at the Interpol Cybercrime Directorate in Singapore analyze the user and data processing terms and conditions of Lucky Dip. It turns out there's something unusual."

Lejeune studied me carefully through the screen. I could feel Kace's rising tension—his thigh was bouncing up and down next to me.

"Explain," she commanded. "What do you know?"

"A Lucky Dip subscriber must agree to all the usual stuff—data processing by the data controller, namely Phoenix, proxy access rights to store and retrieve data, and access by third parties approved by the data controller, subject to all the usual data protection protocols."

"So what's unusual?" Lejeune asked.

"Subscribers must also accept electronic and communication streaming access from a third-party LS provider, nominated by Phoenix Industries, for purposes of push notifications. Including app add-ons and in-app and out-of-app services."

"I still don't get it," Lejeune said. I studied her. She seemed to be deliberately obtuse—odd for someone with a Superior soc-ed classification and hence an IQ in the genius range.

"Subscribers basically have to grant Phoenix full access to their sec-code. It's all in the fine print and written in legalese. Which means Phoenix can then send signals directly to a user's language chip without routing via their LS provider."

"What? Surely that can't be legal!" Kace exclaimed in my ear.

"If the user agrees to it, then it's contractually binding ..." I opened my palms and glanced at him. "And you can't subscribe to the game unless you accept the terms and conditions." I looked back at Lejeune. "In essence, what this means is that users are granting Phoenix full unfettered access to their language chip via their ear implant, using a third-party satellite system."

"So where are you heading with all this?" Lejeune asked.

"The terms and conditions explicitly mention a satellite system owned by RCM, based in Lyon. RCM is in turn owned by Phoenix. The satellite system is SkyLink. They've rebranded it as RCM SkyReach, but it's still Appleton's old system."

As I spoke, Lejeune's eyes narrowed. "This is, indeed, quite serious. But tell me, who's the colleague you referred to in Singapore?"

I raised an eyebrow. "For now, it's better I don't say. I think Interpol may have been compromised."

"Compromised? In what way?"

"The Director was waiting for us when we visited Phoenix yesterday. He and Bastien Cardinale go back a long way. They were students together. Perhaps also business partners at one time," I said.

"You're not really suggesting that Herr Fleischman is somehow involved?"

"I'm not suggesting anything," I responded curtly. "I'm just explaining why I thought it prudent to only involve you at this stage of my investigation. You did authorize me to report directly to you."

"Of course. Quite right," Lejeune replied quickly. "Then what do you advise that I do?"

Lejeune's question had now perfectly set up my request.

"Could you establish whether SkyLink is currently operational? Is it emitting LS signals? Requisition data from the Unilanguage regulatory subcommittee?" I knew that if I snooped around any further, via official channels, that would only raise yet more alarm bells for the Monster. In her capacity as Assistant

Secretary-General, Lejeune could make inquiries while keeping it under the radar.

Lejeune didn't respond immediately. Her forehead was crisscrossed with lines of tension. "I still don't get why Phoenix would have any interest in hacking the language chips of Unskills. What would they stand to gain from an insomnia pandemic? They are only losing business from it." She paused for a moment. "Thank you for bringing this to my attention. For now, I think you've done all that is needed. I'll take it from here. You and Dr. Westwood are now required to return to New York."

With that, Lejeune signed off.

Kace turned to look at me. "You didn't tell her about the temple in the catacombs, or the operatives we saw at Phoenix HQ," he said, slightly accusingly.

"No, I didn't," I muttered thoughtfully. "We didn't exactly come to know all that using conventional means."

"Right. But what about the stuff on eugenics? What is that even about?" Kace asked.

I turned to face him. "What we have discovered is that the Dark Court is more than just a web-based presence bent on spreading conspiracy theories, turning public opinion decisively against the Unskills. I believe this is a program aimed at selectively wiping out billions of people based on their soc-ed classification."

Kace's forehead furrowed. "If you're right, and the Dark Court has the means to wipe out the globe's entire Unskill class, this would be, well—"

"The single greatest act of genocide in the history of the world," I muttered.

"What did they call it … Intellectual Hygiene?" Kace asked.

"Social cleansing," I replied. "The idea is actually quite simple—not pretty, but simple. And it goes back well over two hundred years. It was first conceived in the English-speaking countries, especially the Old Kingdom. Then came the forced sterilization of thousands of women in the early twentieth century in the old United States. Later there was the National Socialism regime, of course, in Europe, with programs to purify the Aryan race."

"But that was all about ethnicity, right? This is about, what—dysgenics, IQ?"

"Intelligence. Or rather, the idea that intelligence is genetically predetermined," I explained.

"That it can't be altered or improved. And if I'm right, the Dark Court adjudicators will likely hate the Broads."

Kace nodded. "The vagus chip, Up-skilling. The science for improving intelligence works."

"The world's population is what, on latest UN figures? Eleven point two billion?" I asked.

"Sounds right," Kace confirmed. "The global population has been stable for about a decade."

"But it's not dropping significantly. And this feeds into the Dark Court propaganda. The world is overpopulated. And inhabitable space is shrinking. Desertification in the Sahel Federation due to poor farming practices. Ecological disasters in the Russian and Chinese territories. A huge chunk of the Middle East now abandoned due to toxic chemical waste from war. And to cap it all off, a full automation agenda now legally binding throughout the Tier One federations and republics, and partially implemented across Tier Two territories. Crime levels have been skyrocketing since mandatory soc-ed classification was made universal, especially among the lower soc-ed classes. Something needs to give."

"And that's the lowest soc-ed class?" Kace asked.

"Maybe something even bigger is going on," I replied. Kace glanced at me sharply. There was more to the Dark Court and its so-called adjudicators than just eugenics. I could sense it.

"Are we really heading back to the United Federation?" Kace asked.

I turned and grinned at him. He smirked back at me.

"I thought not."

CHAPTER 23

My next move was to return to the catacombs, under cover of darkness.

"A city's landscape means a subtraction from somewhere else," I whispered as Kace and I moved through a hole in the polymer palisade fencing, down into the embankment. The railway tracks glinted with the reflection of pale moonbeams. I glimpsed acacias and some tangled clematis in the silvery threaded light. We scrambled down onto the track. The air smelled of damp soil and cloying ripeness, the contradictory sweetness of summer and looming decay. As we approached the railroad tunnel, lights blinked at us, slowly attaching themselves to dark shapes as we drew closer.

"*Cataphiles?*" Kace asked as we entered the dark realm. I smiled at him as he clearly now knew the term for the enthusiasts who defied the law and the catacombs police, the so-called *cataflics*, to explore the subterranean realm. Some had hard hats. They were speaking in Union Standard French. One of them gave us a half-wave.

"The Louvre Palace—built from Lutetian limestone, hewn block by block from here," I said, stamping down on a railroad sleeper with my foot.

We neared the same entrance from which we had exited the

day before: a hole in the ground, partially occluded by the raised safety barriers on one side of the tracks. Nearby was another, covered up with concrete.

"That's the work of the *cataflics*," I muttered. I had brought ropes and our own hard hats.

"What about our language streaming services?" Kace asked. I smiled. I could tell he'd been spooked by his earlier scare, unable to stream language. "I can't go feral again."

I felt for him. I knew how it went. A feeling of powerlessness. Being in control was how we made sense of our experiences. How we made sense of ourselves, even. At least, that was how I made sense of myself.

"I'll draw down from my LS service. You will be able to communicate with me. Okay?"

"Even down there?" Kace asked. "I must admit, I am both freaked out and impressed with your … shall we call them … abilities? But I do need to know how you do what you do, Lilith."

"We can talk about that another time," I said firmly. "Right now, my focus is on trying to save them."

"I understand. I'm a medic. I've taken the Hippocratic Oath. Seems like you've made a similar vow."

I slipped down the short drop through the hole into the entrance. We would have a second, further descent, easier this time with ropes. And then from there, as we hit the main gallery, it would be a steady, gradual descent until we veered off toward the underground temple. About a thirty-minute trek. The temple was impenetrable to almost all, and well disguised.

Once in the mines, I focused my new power of harnessing quintessence to pull my Union-DEF Language Streaming signals through the ground above. I also projected a psychic cloak around us again so that our LS rebounds wouldn't be detected, and we would no longer be visible to sec-cams or the naked eye. I could feel my ability to harness quintessence growing.

"If you wanted to remain hidden in our internet-of-things landscape, where would you build your secret base?" I asked rhetorically. Kace laughed as he flashed his holotab beam ahead. Puddles glinted at us from the floor of the large gallery ahead.

"In the catacombs of Paris," he replied.

Before long, we heard the same barking of dogs. This time Kace smirked at me. I kneeled against the same thick metal door and again channeled quintessence to turn the lock.

Inside, the corridor was quiet, just as when we'd departed hurriedly the evening before. We moved to the large inner chamber. The temple of the Dark Court. It was empty again. We proceeded down the rows of banked stone seating toward the altar below. Behind that, we walked quickly down the stone stairway through the arch, toward the laboratory, or clinic, as we'd heard it referred to by the medical researchers at Phoenix HQ earlier.

We entered the large subterranean chamber directly beneath the temple. The concentric rows of glass medical capsules glinted ominously, projecting their sinister green luminescence from within. The vertical shapes of restrained figures seemed to leer out at us, an insult to everything humane in the world—inside were the catatonic prisoners, people with families somewhere, captured within this horrific experiment. And there, in the center of the chamber, was the menace of the large cone.

"See if you can get an update on the number of people in here and their status. I'm going to try and figure this out," I said, gesturing at the cone. Kace flashed me a thumbs-up and went to inspect the bank of medical console units at one side of the chamber.

As I approached the cone, I noticed that it was emitting gentle vibrations. I touched it and closed my eyes, using my Eye to get a sense for what it was. I immediately jumped back.

"It's a transmitter," I called across to Kace, gasping. "A powerful one."

I stepped back, studying it. The cone was about ten centimeters taller than me—it stood at around a hundred and eighty centimeters. It was made from reed-thin sheets of overlaid curved metal, forming concentric bands. A periodic blue glow came through from under the apertures created by the vibrating metallic sheets. I noticed a thick black armored silicon casing extending from underneath the large device. The casing ran toward a metal stand, which led up to the ceiling. There, it was fixed in situ by plastic webbing running across the high rock ceiling. I followed the line of the casing with my eyes. It vanished into a drilled aperture high up in the ceiling on the far side of the chamber.

"It's hardwired above ground," I called across the chamber.

"And transmitting via Wi-Fi down here, to the medical capsules," Kace called back, pointing to a series of small, wireless receiving dishes. "I can't get access to the medical consoles. Voice command security."

"Can we do a physical examination of the patients?" I asked. "I want to know how many can still be saved." There were eight sets of concentric, semicircular rows.

"I count ten capsules per row," Kace said. "That makes eighty patients in total."

The system of glass capsules looked ghastly enough. But what made the scene surreal was not the occasional twitching of the people, staring out with unseeing eyes, strapped in their clinical white gowns. It was the deathly silence, punctured only by the faint hum emanating from the cone. I now knew it was the large cone that was transmitting a low-frequency electromagnetic field into the atrophying brains of the captives. There was such a thing as pitch-black evil. It might be a human construct, but I was still bound by my human condition. And this I knew: what I saw before me was the opposite of anything that could ever be right in the world. Any world.

"Can we get the capsules open?" I asked.

Kace attempted to prize one open. "Nothing," he replied, pointing to the small VirDa access console. The doors were secured shut with voice-command security, just like the medical consoles.

Just then, to my shock, I heard a cough behind us. And a voice—the voice of a creep.

"I can hear you, but I can't see you."

I turned to see the face of Hervé Balladur no more than five meters away—I sensed pistol fire, the silence of a coil weapon. In my head, I knew he had fired. Balladur had entered the chamber with two medics, dressed in white. He was holding a coil weapon, its muzzle glowing green from power-beaming, drawing power from the cone, which was now also emitting a faint green glow. And as I experienced the emotional halo of him squeezing the trigger and the soundless electromagnetic discharge of his weapon, I heard a groan next to me. From Kace. And a thud as he hit the stone floor.

In that instant of shock, I inadvertently dropped the psychic cloak that had been hiding us.

"Ah, there you are," Balladur said, moving closer, menacingly.

The medics stopped behind him, dead in their tracks, appearing unsure whether to approach or not. A man and a woman, neither military-minded, I could tell.

I kneeled next to Kace. He gaped at me, his eyes wide with startled surprise. I touched his brow before cursorily examining his wound. He'd been hit in the right side of his chest with a live round; I didn't need to be a medic to know it was bad.

"Well, that was a lucky shot!" Balladur said, smirking, now pointing the weapon at me as he edged closer. "I only had voices to aim at. Who would have thought we would meet again so soon, Mademoiselle? And kind of you to bring your friend again, too. You really should have taken the advice you were given yesterday."

"What have you done here?" I demanded, stabbing one hand toward the glass capsules.

"Our guinea pigs? Merely testing that the tech works. These ones are nearly done. Surprised they lasted as long as they did, it was tricky gauging the correct EMF levels. We've improved our treatment since. Don't you worry your extremely pretty head."

I grimaced. "Turn it off," I said insistently.

Balladur gazed at me in bemusement.

"That!" I said, pointing to the vibrating cone.

"Our transmitter?" Balladur laughed, as he followed the line of my index finger.

"If there is any humanity left in you," I retorted.

Balladur glared at me. "Turn it off? Only Monsieur Cardinale can do that."

"RCM, in Lyon?" I asked. "Is that where Cardinale controls SkyLink? That transmitter is connected to SkyLink, isn't it?"

Balladur studied me for a moment. "You're quite smart for a ..." he began, before apparently thinking better of the insult. I knew what he was going to say—a woman. Women couldn't be smart if they were attractive, apparently. I got that a lot. "But it doesn't matter now. At least not for you. You won't be leaving this place." He steadied his aim. "We have a spare medical unit just for you. So helpful that you've made it easier for me, tying up loose ends."

Kace started coughing, blood gurgling in his mouth. I glanced down. Blood was also weeping from the wound through his shirt. He looked at me, his eyes becoming faint. I touched his torso, opening my Eye.

"An internal organ. One of your lungs," I whispered.

"Just my luck," he replied, coughing up more blood. "I'm bleeding out, Lilith. I would have loved to …" he began. I shook my head. I knew what he wanted to say. He wanted to finish what we'd started.

"Save your strength. Our journey doesn't end here," I said with sudden clarity of thought. I didn't yet know how, but I knew I couldn't let him die.

With that I stood, my psychic cloak back on. I dashed the few meters toward Balladur. With a decisive chop of my hand, he was disarmed, his pistol clattering onto the stone floor, spinning in small circles as it skittered across the chamber, before disappearing under a medical console unit.

I removed my psychic cloak and held Balladur's arm. Now he could see me again, standing in front of him. He looked deep down into my eyes, his own widening in fear. I felt his panting breath on my face, frozen to the spot, and suddenly deathly white at my unexpected move. I was his worst nightmare.

"What are you?" he gasped as he felt my Eye take hold. And there was the rush, always different, yet strangely familiar, oddly the same.

Balladur tried to pull his arm free from my grip, but I held him fast. I was attached with a psychic bond that would be the death of him. As he stared into my eyes, helpless and transfixed,

I burned him. And how I burned him! If there was to be evil in this place, I would smite it. I would visit my own brand of evil upon it.

Balladur began aging before my eyes. Creases sprang up, spreading insidiously across his visible skin—hands, arms, face. His hair became gray and wispy, receding until he was nearly bald. His eyes became sunken, his nose shrank, and his skin became loose and slowly decrepit. The two medics accompanying him darted back in terror, the male medic rubbing his eyes to make the apparent phantasmagoria disappear.

Balladur was still attempting to wrest himself loose, but now weakly, with a fragility begat of infirmity. I spun the wizened old man around so that he could see his reflection in one of the illuminated glass capsules. He glanced at himself, horror spreading over his ragged, aged features.

Yet, as I watched Balladur look upon his reflection, I saw my own face reflected back at me, next to his. It was a face ripped with hatred, crisscrossed with furrows of anger. It was a terrifying face, filled with enmity, one that I barely recognized. I flinched. There was only one person whose death I wished for, and that was not this creep.

I released Balladur. I had done enough damage. He tottered away from me, frailty now nagging at him. But while I had spared him, the damage had been done. And as fate would decree, it was to be death by lingering, all-engulfing heart attack.

It was an end brought on by the weight of old age and overconsumption in a lifetime he would never now walk through. The suffering caused by an enlarged, gorged, blocked-up coronary artery sent ricochets of convulsions through a heart that was now in a spasm of torment—my Eye perceived it from two meters away. The searing affliction of Balladur's imminent death stabbed him repeatedly in the chest. He knew this was it, the onset of nothingness. It continued, ripping down his left arm in burning electric shockwaves. Such pain! Even I grimaced. Balladur was dead by the time his frail form hit the hard rock floor.

"What have you done, Lily?" I whispered to myself, before turning as I heard the scuffling of medical clogs on stone—the medics had turned and fled. I suddenly felt sick to the pit of my stomach as I looked upon the frail corpse.

I heard another groan behind me—Kace! I had burned over thirty years, but I hadn't consumed. That way lay my own nothingness. I had somehow managed to hold the time I had taken, a floating expanse of life, taken from another. I suspended it inside me, in an enlarged part of my brain—the suprachiasmatic nucleus within my hypothalamus. I could now even feel that.

I crouched over Kace just as he closed his eyes. He was beginning to slip into unconsciousness. *I wonder*, I mused, as an idea struck me. I placed my hand over Kace's chest wound and focused my thoughts, sensing a way to again change my brain wave patterns. And as I focused, I was able to emit radiant energy, transposed not from quintessence, but from the time I had burned and now stored.

I opened my Eye, to guide me as I began to heal—I imagined myself soothing the wound, closing it up, mending the damaged tissues with the pressure of my hand. And as I was releasing the large measure of time I had taken, the radiant energy I was expressing traced the lines of my touch, rebuilding Kace's damaged tissues, his lung, his skin—it was actually working. I was able to repurpose burned time to heal, using the power of thought, just as I could channel quintessence.

After a few minutes, it was done. Tentatively, I removed my hand to get a better look. Kace's skin was now hot to the touch.

I waited a few moments as it gradually cooled.

"Kace," I said, speaking his name quietly. His eyes flickered open.

"Lilith?" he whispered. "I dreamt that I died."

I smiled down at him. "You're very much alive. But you'll be a bit weak. You've lost quite a lot of blood. You might need a transfusion."

Kace shook his head. "There's no chance of that … I'll just rest up." I threw him a confused look. "My blood type is extremely rare. Only one place in the world with any stock, and that's back in the United Federation."

I gasped as I realized what he meant. "Rhesus-null?" I asked, scarcely believing it as Kace gave a slight nod. "That's also my blood type."

What are the chances? Kace has golden blood too.

CHAPTER 24

I was up early after a fitful night. My bioclock showed just before five a.m. I tossed and turned but couldn't sleep anymore—remorse was stabbing me, quite literally. My chest was throbbing—a strange tightness was gripping my heart, so that it felt as if it might stop beating. That was new.

I had killed. Of course, I hadn't wanted to, or maybe part of me did, in the moment. But I had caused Balladur's death. It would have happened anyway, but not for another thirty years. Those were years I had burned, stolen from him. I sat up, naked in my hotel bed, and draped the sheets around my shoulders as sobs slowly wracked me. *Am I in fact a monster?* I glanced through the murk of the early morning gloom, across the room at the mirror on the wall opposite. My face was puffy, my hair a mess, and I felt suddenly despicable as sobs heaved my chest. Tears flowed down my cheeks. *What have I done?*

As I reflected on events, my thoughts returned to Selaphiel and the revelations I had barely had time to process since arriving in Paris two days before. I was still feeling resentment that I was snared by the Mind Chant, the outrageous claim that I had to *serve* the Sage. That I might be someone's *experiment* incensed me.

My brooding reflections wandered back to my past. I realized I had grown up with the absurd idea that we were all born as blank slates. That was teenage me, the cry for help of an existentialist misfit. I had once naïvely believed I possessed existence before essence, that I was flesh and blood before I had a purpose. That my essence, who I was and my raison d'être, was defined in terms of the unique experiences that befell me, the things that happened to me. That I had no agency. But the thing about agency is you don't get given it. That, in fact, is the precise opposite of what it's meant to be. Restriction of choices—that is exactly not what agency is.

The Monster happened. But it and he did not define me. My mother did not define me. I refused to visit her in the asylum in Moesia—I always had. She would die alone. Even my father's death didn't define me. I was scarred, sure. Quite literally. I even bore his handprint around my ankle, the mark that itched, from the day he saved me when I was still an infant. I often despised myself. And I suffered. But I never suffered fools, nor did I suffer gladly. And being a blank slate was never my cup of tea.

So, in my teens, more or less an orphan, with only Kaye Wilbur to care whether I lived or died, I rejected the whole charade. I would seize control, be myself. And in my darkest agonies of teenage crisis, when I felt myself to be the most unloved, lonely, and misunderstood creature that had ever existed, I stumbled upon the dawning realization that there was no one else I would rather be. I would be me. Whatever that meant. I would build the aircraft in flight and figure it out as I flew. Essence would imbue my existence as I traveled on the skyway with so, so many enticing forks.

But now, there it was again. The attempt to undermine my agency, despite also attempting to subvert the existentialist doctrine. And as bad as the Monster. Some strange, unearthly apparition had announced that I was a semidivine chosen one, descendant from a line of Principalities. That I had a purpose selected for me by another—I was some kind of defender of the realm. That I was the seeker of a nefarious, alien Watcher that I was to locate and expel.

The expectation that I should join the battle, pick up my metaphorical arms—that too restricted my choices. Who was this strange guardian soldier-angel that claimed to be a Sempiternal being from Empyrean? And what about the Melody, the Mind Chant from the mysterious Sage upon which I depended for my calm, my sanity? Could I trust any of this?

Dependency made me uneasy. That was kind of why I drank. To not depend. Life kept handing out the ironies. After all, drinking was the very definition of dependence. Yet it also set me free. In my everyday life, I was always in control. So I only drank away from my carefully curated professional persona. I compartmentalized my drinking, by imbibing with the female strangers I picked up in dimly lit bars, whose names I didn't need to know, so as not to be in control. So that I was in control. That was my dark, ironic modus operandi.

As I became angrier, I stood and walked toward the mirror on the far wall of the hotel suite. I stared into it, searching my anguished face before calling out to Selaphiel, summoning the strange creature. The silvery silhouette materialized in the mirror, staring back out at me, its hideous face exactly the same as the first evening in Paris, adjacent to the Sacré-Cœur.

"You called?" it asked.

"I won't do it," I said fiercely. "I won't serve this Sage, whoever he is. I won't be anyone's experiment. And I won't be dependent on the Melody."

"You won't face the Watcher?" the creature asked, calmly. I had expected more fight, some anger maybe, to match my own.

I shook my head. The creature sighed. "I will convey the message. But I warn you, the agonies you will suffer, they won't be worth it. And you will be sacrificing more than yourself. This world will perish too." With that, the silvery presence disappeared into ripples, returning the mirror to the early morning darkness, which once again surrounded my solitary reflection.

For a moment I felt better, relieved, now that I had taken charge, regained control. But my sense of relief quickly evaporated. I realized something was off. The Melody had stopped, just like that. I became aware of the strange sound of silence, nothingness reverberating around my head. I tottered back toward the bed in startled alarm at the new strangeness of the sensation. Even after drinking there was something in the background, a still detectable hum. But I had not drunk, and yet the Melody had ceased completely, for the first time since the day of my awakening.

I stood next to my bed and collapsed. I felt my heart racing; it was becoming difficult to draw breath. And now the room began spinning. I half sat, half lay on the bed, clutching the bedsheet, as the room took on the swirling menace of a tempestuous sea, moving and sliding around me. Then the pain started, wracking my entire body, wave after wave of spasms, growing in intensity before subsiding. It was as if my muscles were being shredded beneath my skin, each cramping into a knotted mass, in my stomach, legs and arms, before suddenly unfurling, lashing me with repeated waves of agony.

As I fought against the pain, something in my peripheral vision drew my attention down; I glanced at my right wrist— the iridescent green numbers on my SwissSecure bracelet had stopped spinning. A series of digits, now stationary, began blinking. My holotab powered on without me activating it.

Strange. As the translucent screen appeared, floating above my left wrist, the same numbers from the bracelet displayed across the holotab—the devices were syncing!

The numbers on the holotab slowly faded out, and to my shock the face of my father materialized. *I'm seeing a ghost, a figment of my agony*, I thought, as I moved my wrist in front of my eyeline for a better view of the screen. I gritted my teeth and ignored the cramps wracking my body, concentrating as my father's face began addressing me.

"My Lily, my little seraph," he began. I sucked in my cheeks as tears, unbidden, spontaneously began streaming down my cheeks. "This facecall clip has been activated because the biometrics detected by the bracelet show that your vital signs are deteriorating, your blood pressure has fallen to a dangerous level, your nervous system is beginning to shut down. This means you will have met Selaphiel, by now. And you will have realized, perhaps what you even suspected, that the music in your head is not a gift. It's a means of control. And just like I once did, you will have rejected it. The Sage is vengeful. He has turned off your Mind Chant. But you will not survive without it, and there are things you must accomplish if you are to set us free. In a few hours, maybe less, you will lose consciousness, and in around twelve you will be dead. I'm asking you to resume what Selaphiel asks of you, at least for now."

I watched my father's face, long dead, while brushing away my tears. "Why did you do it?" I asked, demanding a response to the one question I had never been able to wrap my head around. But his message was prerecorded.

"The source of the Mind Chant is a massive biological communication device. The Tower of Songs is alive, a monstrous, exobiological experiment, which genomically recodes those that it imprisons, that become part of it. Including a time seer, the twin flame of Enoch, and representatives of all the founder civilizations of the Inner Reaches."

I shook my head in incomprehension. "A time seer?" I muttered, ignoring the pain still tormenting my body, as my father continued.

"Each Mind Chant is different, designed to target all the members of the founder civilizations, including the oldest, the golden bloodline—the Sempiternals. It syncs with the unique biosignature of every individual it targets. You and I share the golden bloodline too, as half-Sempiternals. Our experimental genotype, the Principality, has been propagated by the Sage across the Outer and Far Reaches of the Elyonim, throughout star systems with habitable biospheres that remain too distant for his Guardians to reach. You can think of these Principalities, like us, as the Sage's defense network, driven by his paranoia of Watchers. The tower transmits a continuous song with an ostinato motif, a personalized rhythmic-harmonic scheme."

My father looked mournful.

"Why?" I screamed at his face again, my tears now dried up, replaced by anger. I wanted to know why he had taken his life. In that moment I couldn't care less about the Melody or what an ostinato motif was. And as if, somehow, he could hear me from beyond the grave, he explained.

"You are special, Lily, your mother sacrificed everything for you, we both have. Your coming has been foretold. You will have the power to take down the tower once and for all, to restore balance to the Elyonim. But that power comes through absorbing the Mind Chant, which is the way to your true nature. The Sage only selects males with golden blood as Principalities. Your Mind Chant would never have been switched on, you would have remained unfilled golden potential. And the last chance I had was the day of your seventh birthday, before your biosignature diverged too much from mine. There was only one way to trick the Nunciature Evangelion into beginning a new transmission line to you. I hope, in time, you'll be able to forgive me for what I did. But for now, you must ask to have the Mind Chant restored. You must live, until you're ready."

"Don't go," I howled at the screen as my father's face began to fade. And as if he'd actually heard me again, he gave a warm smile, his smile, the one that was always just for me.

"I love you, Lily." Then he was gone. The screen auto-hibernated, and the numbers on the bracelet on my right wrist began spinning again. I sat for a moment, shaken, beginning to feel even woozier. I knew I could no longer stand. I now knew that the Melody was a vicious type of drug, that I was suffering withdrawal—I couldn't live without it.

"Selaphiel?" I whispered. The creature manifested itself in my hotel room. "I'll comply, switch the singing back on …"

I lay on the bed for a while, allowing the restored Melody to soothe me. I wondered what it could even mean that the Tower of Songs, where this strange singing was transmitted from, was biological? I vaguely imagined a massive, living membrane, with a shapeless mouth opening and closing, emitting an ethereal chant. I gave an involuntary shudder. I understood, finally, that the Sage held the power of life and death over me, wielding the Melody like the sword of Damocles. *The Mind Chant of the Sage is a means of coercive control, an addiction*, I thought. I then took a long bath, trying to restore myself, before dressing.

CHAPTER 25

By the time I arrived in the hotel's dining suite, to meet Kace for breakfast, I had regained my composure. Yet I felt strangely empty, drained of energy. I was early, so I waited at our assigned table. I started to become impatient as I realized Kace was late. But when he finally did show up, I immediately knew something was very wrong. I could tell from his manner, the way he walked. He eased himself down almost gingerly onto a chair opposite me.

"I have it," Kace announced quietly. I knew what he meant even before he explained. I had almost expected it—my heart sank. We shared a moment's silence before he spoke again. "Not a wink all night. No matter what I did."

"You look exhausted," I said, studying him from across the breakfast table.

"I've never even played Lucky Dip. Don't even have it installed," he added.

"They know we're onto them. It was a phishing scam. That factory restart. To get you to reveal your sec-code."

"By the time I have a confirmed diagnosis, I'll already start to resemble a vegetable," Kace murmured, sounding miserable. "I won't be much use to you soon."

"Then we'll just have to put an end to this before then," I replied.

"So what now?"

"First, we finish breakfast. Then we'll take a hover cab ride."

"Where to?"

"Further south. Lyon," I replied.

"What's in Lyon? RCM, the subsidiary of Phoenix that controls SkyLink?"

I glanced across at Kace with mild surprise. He had been paying attention during our meeting with Lejeune. "As we can't count on Lejeune's help, we'll need to figure out for ourselves whether SkyLink is operational."

***

Kace and I took an intercity hover cab to travel the 392 kilometers south to Lyon. The vehicle rose in the cool summer morning, high up the VTOL corridor. The familiar metallic vibration of the autogyro system on the roof was audible through the open vents. They auto-stowed as we passed the fifty-meter marker. I glanced down through the translucent polymer floor, as the vertipad in the transit corridor at terrestrial level disappeared below us. We ascended, increasing in speed as we approached the stacked airways. We moved up into an unrestricted *voie rapide* skyway as we departed Paris city airspace. It would be a short trip on one of these.

"Call Kal," I said, issuing a voice command to my holotab app. "Audio only, to my ear implant." It would be mid-afternoon in Singapore and I needed more intel.

Ordinarily, Kal would drop anything to speak to me; yet, to my surprise, the call couldn't complete. I received an error message. I had the app try again using Kal's Interpol MyPlace ID. But this time, the connection couldn't even be placed. As I was puzzling over what to do, my ear implant began vibrating. I saw on my holotab that it was an incoming facecall from a private number on an encrypted line. I blinked on the slider to accept the call as audio-only.

"Lilith," Kal said breathlessly. "I'm not allowed to talk to you."

"What?" I snapped. I hadn't expected that.

"A directive from Fleischman himself, covering the entire Cybercrime Directorate. You've been placed on our advisory list." I was incredulous. "Someone's gotten wind you've been receiving intel from Singapore. My access to the Phoenix Industries and Bastien Cardinale files has just been cut off. Both files are now off limits to me and my entire team here in Singapore. I couldn't help you even if I wanted to. Which I do, by the way," Kal whispered.

"That figures," I muttered under my breath. And then, more loudly: "I hope I didn't get you into any trouble ..."

Kal chuckled. "No. But come on, lady of mystery. What figures? What are you up to?"

"Heading to Lyon."

"Interpol HQ?" she asked in surprise.

"No, not there."

"You're going to RCM HQ, aren't you?" Kal said, excitedly. "Am I right? You think it's SkyLink, don't you?"

I smiled to myself, despite this latest setback—Kal's optimism was always irrepressible. "It might be nothing. After all, SkyLink was decommissioned following restoration of language streaming, what ... four and a half years ago?"

"And you want to know whether SkyLink has been recommissioned?" Kal asked, breathlessly, before continuing. "Without Interpol, the UN, anyone, knowing about it."

"Something like that."

Kal gave a hollow laugh. "I would really like to help. But …"

"You're not allowed?"

"Worse. That file has also been ring-fenced by Interpol HQ in Lyon. I no longer have access to any data relating to SkyLink. And all our data streams are being monitored. If the words *SkyLink* or *SkyReach* so much as show up as a hint of a shadow in any of my comms, the security monitoring algorithm will trigger an alert. Then I'll have a big problem. A disciplinary problem. What's really going on, Lilith?"

I tapped my forehead before replying. "Phoenix Industries is a front for the Dark Court. I've seen it with my own eyes. They have an operation embedded in Phoenix HQ. I think the Dark Court is using SkyLink to hack the language chips of the Unskills. That would explain the strange terms and conditions of the Lucky Dip game that you found for me when you still had access."

"Hmm …" Kal muttered. "Although I no longer have access to Phoenix data, on the bright side I think I still have access to all the Dark Court files. That's not covered by the directive … Yup, I can still access those." She laughed as she checked. *Dummies*, I thought. *They didn't think of that.*

"Anything new there?" I asked.

"Sec …" Kal replied before a short pause. "There is something interesting. I can see our AI surveillance intercepted a facecall yesterday between operatives linked to the Dark Court. A male, who self-identified as Number Three, and a female referred to as One."

"Can I see the feed?" I asked.

"It's encrypted. Apparently, the AI only managed to decipher the audio stream. VPN chaining was being used, disguising the transmission source and target. Triangulation diagnostic software shows a likely IP source for the male. Most likely DC, from what I can see here."

"Washington, DC?"

"Right. And the female was on Union-DEF encryption parameters. The AI stood no chance of identifying her location."

"So if the female was a Union-DEF user, rather than, say, UFA-DEF, then she must work for a Grand Union agency. Most likely based in Europe, then," I mused.

"Not necessarily based in Europe," Kal pointed out. "Don't forget that the Union makes Union-DEF credentials available to supranational agencies too. Like Interpol, for instance."

"Sure. What about the numeral identifiers, One and Three?" I asked.

"That's probably code for the identity of adjudicators. They were talking about some kind of event that will take place tomorrow. They called it 'a crossing ceremony in the northern temple.' Batshit crazy, right?" Kal continued. "They will all be there, all twenty of them, plus Zero, apparently."

"The numbers refer to rank! The rank of officers of the Dark Court," I exclaimed in sudden realization.

"Could be," Kal replied.

"No, I'm certain. Something I overheard at Phoenix HQ. Medics were talking about the 'High Adjudicator,' the leader. Could that be the female—Number One?"

Kal coughed. "Well, both speakers referred to Zero, a he," said Kal. "If you're right about there being a ranking, then the High Adjudicator is likely to be Zero, right?"

I furrowed my brow. "And what about this ceremony? Is that the actual word they used, 'ceremony?'"

"It seems to be connected in some way to a 'phase two.' They talked about the next phase."

"The next phase in the social cleansing program," I murmured.

"What?" Kal asked.

"Something I also heard in Rambouillet."

"The rest of the call talks about cloning and something called a skeletal editing program. In our intercept."

I drew in a sharp intake of breath: "Skeletal editing … You're sure?"

"I'm not sure of anything anymore," Kal replied. "Just telling you what I see from the transcript. You've heard of that? What is it?"

"I've heard of it, although not in relation to the Dark Court." I paused, thinking. Suddenly it hit me. "I think I know where this ceremony will take place. And I will be there to stop it."

"Where? Come on, tell me. You know you want to," Kal said, baiting me in her inimitable style.

"It's not safe, Kal. Better you don't know, at least for now. Anything else I should know about from the facecall data file?"

"From what I can see in the transcript, it looks like Number Three, the guy, was being told to drop efforts to get the Compulsory Sterilization Bill through Congress. It was no longer needed." As Kal spoke, my head began spinning. *This is all crazy. Whoever Number Three is, he's likely a senator.*

"Wow, this seems to go pretty high up," I replied.

"Yeah. The guy was talking about resistance, but he still thought he could push it through. Anyways, the woman indicated that the bill was no longer a 'live issue.' To prepare for the crossing ceremony instead."

"No longer a live issue?"

"That events had overtaken it. Can you please explain to me what's going on?"

"I will when I'm sure I have it all worked out."

CHAPTER 26

We were on our approach to RCM HQ in Lyon.

"What's the plan? I don't suppose we're just going to roll up there?"

"That's exactly the plan. We'll simply knock on the door, shake the tree a bit. Maybe try to force a meeting with this mysterious Bastien Cardinale." Kace gave me a slight smile. He was clearly still weak from the loss of blood. And now he would no longer sleep.

The hover cab set down on RCM's vertipad. Then came the familiar hydraulic *whoosh* of the gull-wing doors as they opened. Security drones buzzed around us as we emerged. A dozen encircled us and the hover cab. Each drone was around a meter long and featured fixed-wing coil weaponry. There was no need for secrecy now.

"This place is well protected," Kace muttered wryly. I glanced up at him.

"Lilith Errapel King, High Commissioner, Interpol," barked the metallic drawl of the squadron leader as it scanned my LS rebounds. "Kace Treyton Westwood, Professor, Columbia University," it continued. "There is no record of an appointment. Access here is denied. Return to your hover transport immediately."

"I'm here to see Bastien Cardinale," I announced, as the

machine hovered a meter in front of me. "I request a meeting." There was silence for a moment; the security drone was receiving orders.

"A meeting has been granted with Monsieur Cardinale's personal assistant."

Kace turned to me, his mouth agape. I smiled back at his surprised face and nonchalantly shrugged, although I was a little taken aback too. I had acted more in hope than expectation, but my gamble had paid off. Then again, Cardinale probably wanted to try and work me, get a sense for what I knew, what I was up to, especially as his Chief of Staff from Phoenix Industries had died unexpectedly in the catacombs beneath the streets of Paris. I flinched involuntarily at the recollection, shaking the thought away.

We were escorted from the landing strip toward a large, pyramid-like building. We entered an atrium, leading toward a corridor that sloped downward, below ground level; a security droid was waiting.

"High Commissioner, Dr. Westwood, follow me." The droid had two of the largest hip-mounted coil pistols I'd ever seen. As we proceeded inside, the squadron of drones retreated, their irritating hum fading from earshot. Once inside, the glass doors slid shut behind us; we were entombed in perfect silence. The security droid made no sound—this was one expensive stealth unit.

About thirty meters along the descending corridor, we came to a white reinforced plastic polymer blast door. A sec-cam blinked at us as we approached. The door opened in a concentric wave, beginning in the center, before disappearing into the walls, floor, and ceiling in a seamless spiral as if melting into nothingness. As we passed through, I glanced back as the blast door closed again in reverse circular spirals, forming a seamless, impenetrable surface. *Impressive technology*, I thought.

I estimated that we were about twenty meters underground. The droid led us along a wide tunnel, a concrete ceiling and sealed glass chambers on either side of us. Through the glass to our right, there was a brightly illuminated automated factory plant, assembling robotic units. Through the protective glass on the left there were racks and racks of servers. Cooling units emitted a pale blue light. At the end of each rack were temperature thermostats, and above were ceiling grilles to vent the servers. The tunnel ahead of us was dappled with the blue glow from the server chamber.

We reached a second blast door which opened again on cue. We emerged into a large data command center made up of gantried rows of VirDa consoles. In the center of the large room stood the most exotic-looking woman I had ever seen in my life.

"Welcome, I am Nefertiti," she announced. The security droid moved to one side of the room, standing still, slipping into background security mode.

The woman stood well over two meters tall. She was much taller even than Kace. She was willowy and olive-skinned, with a long, elegant nose, and deep black eyes. Her jet-black hair fell around her shoulders, and over her tight-fitting, sandy-colored body suit.

Nefertiti moved toward us. Her black eyes slowly changed color. She was scanning us! LS rebounds, sec-data. My Eye sensed the radio waves being emitted from built-in scanners. She was searching for a weakness, an access vector, a back door, a way to hack me. I took a quick breath and blocked her, repelling her ultra-high-frequency radio waves by marshaling beams of quintessence, creating an energy shield.

"She's a numinous gynoid," I whispered to Kace. I'd heard of gynoids of this type, but never encountered one in the synthetic flesh.

"A what?" he asked, staring in bewildered wonder.

"Bleeding-edge tech. Very expensive," I muttered. She was an exceptional example of mechatronic engineering. Numinoids like her went far beyond the neural linking capability of regular Einstein-chipped droids. They could even disrupt human brain patterns.

"I'm personal assistant to Monsieur Cardinale, here at RCM," Nefertiti began. "You have requested a meeting. He sends his apologies as he's currently unavailable."

"Unfortunately, we never get to meet with Mr. Cardinale himself."

Nefertiti stared at me. She blinked. I watched the long curls of her eyelashes.

As she moved toward us, she offered her hand. I pressed my palm against hers. Her skin was soft to the touch. My Eye saw neuromechanical circuitry that supported synthetic consciousness. A numinous gynoid that simulated a woman to perfection. And then, as I continued to press on her palm, suddenly, to my shock, a rush of recognition—an emotional halo. SkyLink was being controlled from this very place. My fears were confirmed, the system was online—it had been recommissioned. I dropped her hand, my heart pounding.

Nefertiti eyed me suspiciously. "How can we help you, Lilith King?"

"I have some questions," I replied, regaining my composure.

"If I can answer and am permitted to, I will do my best to be of service." I moved around, glancing at the VirDa consoles.

"What does RCM do, exactly?" I asked.

"As you no doubt know, we build robots. Medical units. We are the largest producer in the Union. We are fully vertically integrated, from software to design to manufacture of the physical infrastructure. Everything is handled on-site."

"You don't seem to have any human engineers."

Nefertiti smiled at me. Her top lip curled slightly upward, revealing gleaming pearl-white teeth, exquisitely shaped.

"We are one hundred percent automated."

"Including you, it seems."

Nefertiti shot me a dark look, studying me. She was towering over me.

"You are astute." She bent down and peered into my eyes. I could feel her continued attempts to scan me, to no avail. "Why are you really here, Lilith King?"

"It's not just robots, is it? Your business is spread a little wider."

Nefertiti looked at me. "We also run RCM SkyReach. But you know that already, don't you?"

I arched an eyebrow. "You mean SkyLink. You might have rebranded it, but it's still the same old Appleton ecosystem." And I now knew it was definitely online, transmitting. "Tell me about it," I continued.

"RCM SkyReach is the world's largest commercial satellite system. Fifteen thousand tabletop-sized satellites encircling the Earth in low orbit, providing high bandwidth and low communication latency. Internet-from-space, twenty-four seven."

"Thanks for the sales pitch. But I'm not an investor," I responded. "Let me point out one thing, though. You don't offer language streaming."

"We don't, although I guess we could."

"If SkyLink—or SkyReach—could ever get relicensed as an LS provider. A tough ask, don't you think, after what happened five years ago?"

Nefertiti ignored my question. "I understand your hostility. But what we do provide is a fully autonomous app streaming experience to nearly five billion users."

"Lucky Dip, you mean?"

"We support Lucky Dip, among others."

"Phoenix?"

"Phoenix Software Development, an arm of Phoenix Industries, is our only client for this service."

"But apps are normally propagated via an LS system," I pointed out.

Nefertiti shook her head. "Not the case with Phoenix apps. Users must grant streaming rights to RCM SkyReach. Part of the user agreement. All Phoenix apps are streamed on demand via SkyReach. It's not a secret. But you also know that already, don't you? Isn't that why you're here?"

My mind whirred. This Nefertiti, and I assumed Bastien Cardinale too, knew an awful lot about my line of inquiry.

"Wow. That must be expensive," I said. "Economically, for RCM, I mean. Why have your own satellite ecosystem when the business model would be far cheaper if your products could be streamed via a user's proprietary LS provider? Especially if you're only streaming apps, not language services. Otherwise, really, what's the point? It makes no financial sense."

"I guess that's something you'll have to ask Monsieur Cardinale."

I could tell I wasn't going to get a straight answer. I switched tack.

"And it's controlled from here, I suppose?"

"SkyReach? We monitor the system, release apps, of course."

"And there's a kill switch. If anything happened, anything went wrong? You could stop the streaming signals. You could shut off

Lucky Dip from out there," I said, gesturing to the servers beyond the blast door. "Couldn't you? If there were a need."

"If there were a need?"

"If there were ever a problem with the app, for instance," I pressed. Nefertiti shook her head, staring at me. *What did the shake of the head mean? No, it couldn't be shut down? Or that she didn't know?*

I closed my eyes, reaching into her with my Eye. And now, without touch, I could feel her, achieve an emotional halo: the SkyLink system was self-running. It didn't have shut-off protocols in place. When the system's full broadcast spectrum had been re-established, nearly two months prior, the entire server system had been commissioned in perpetual mode. The onboard AI that managed the system was ring-fenced. It couldn't be controlled from here. Or anywhere.

I opened my eyes and gasped. "The system is set in a Lazarus loop," I exclaimed. Kace gawped at me in surprise. Nefertiti looked startled.

"How did you know that?" she asked.

I smiled back at Nefertiti wryly. "Thanks for the confirmation."

She eyed me coolly. "We actually think of it as more of a smart Lazarus loop. The only thing we control from here is the addition of new apps."

I was taken aback by this revelation. Strictly speaking, a Lazarus loop on an off-world satellite system wasn't a problem. But when there was no Earth-based kill switch, the Lazarus loop became an issue.

"Thank you for meeting with us," I said. "This has been extremely illuminating."

CHAPTER 27

As we traveled back to Paris, Kace was uneasy. He kept glancing sideways at me. By now, we both knew our fates were intertwined. He sensed I was his only hope. And it wasn't just Kace. A quarter of the automated world was already dying, and that figure was set to rise. Perhaps this was the beginning of the extinction-level event that Selaphiel had warned me of.

"What now?" Kace asked finally, breaking the silence. "SkyLink can't be shut down."

I glanced at him. *What now indeed?* I wondered. But even before I began talking, a plan was already forming in my mind. That was how I rolled, after all.

"Any satellite system can be shut down. It's just this one can't be shut down from here, from Earth. We need to get to South America," I heard myself saying. As I watched Kace's startled face, I saw the truth of it. The necessity. "Specifically, French Guiana," I continued.

"What's in French Guiana?" Kace asked, bemused.

"Kourou Spaceport. And that's our ticket to shutting down SkyLink ..." Kace's mouth opened and closed but no words came out—his face was a picture.

Before Kace could ask me anything else, I activated my holotab and got myself patched through to Park, to request a meeting.

He sounded groggy—it was still early in New York. I knew I'd need some help getting there. But I also knew that he would help. His daughter's life might depend on it.

***

Half an hour later, Kace and I were in the hotel's isolation booth, all synced with our ear jacks in. Park was, on first blush, his usual self—inscrutable, slightly detached, his three-dimensional projection the appearance of unruffled calm. But not calm. I could read him even now. He was on edge.

"You've managed quite the feat, to unite the Director and Assistant Secretary-General Lejeune against you," Park announced. "They're both hopping mad. Lejeune wants you back in New York. You know that, right?"

"I recall she might have mentioned something," I muttered with quiet insouciance and the flicker of a defiant smile.

"And Herr Fleischman has ordered me to revoke your credentials. A suspension from duty." That revelation took me aback. "So what's going on?" Park's holographic projection hovering about the VirDa console stared directly at me. Now was the time for candor—I needed to level with him.

"I believe SkyLink is being used to broadcast an EMF direct to the Universal Grammar tech of all Unskill subscribers of the Lucky Dip game. And other soc-ed classes, the Semiskills, may be next." Park stared at me in unblinking silence for a moment. I awaited his reaction. *Disbelief? Demands that I provide evidence?* But I didn't expect what he said next.

"I believe you," he replied, quietly, after a brief pause. As Park spoke, I felt Kace jump in his seat next to me, startled. "How do we stop it?"

"It can't be deactivated. It's on a Lazarus loop."

"A what?" Park asked, nonplussed.

"It can only be shut down from up there, in space. A fission torpedo aimed at the command server to initiate a chain reaction. To be sure the entire infrastructure is eliminated." I heard Kace's sharp intake of breath in my ear next to me. "We need the Union's Space Force."

"Lilith, forgive me, but you need to explain." His expression was puzzlement. "Why can't SkyLink be shut down from Earth?" It was a reasonable question. I had to grant him that.

"It's been configured to be self-running. Self-learning AI. On an infinite loop, with backup power sources and an effective self-defense system. Commissioned less than two months ago to support Lucky Dip. And if I'm right, it's streaming a signal that interferes with brain function."

"You're talking about language chips?" Park asked.

"Two point eight billion people at risk in the first instance," I replied.

Park blinked before speaking. "We're starting to see widespread disorder across federations. People panicking in the early stages of symptoms. A further spike in civil disobedience. Over twenty Tier One cities have experienced mass riots in the last twelve hours alone." He shook his head, crestfallen. "What should I do? What can I do?"

I felt for him, his exasperation at the limits of his own authority. I knew he had no power to request an Executive Order to launch a nuclear torpedo into low-Earth orbit. And based on what? A feeling? The feeling of a lone Interpol agent, now disavowed by the world's most senior police officer and the world's highest-ranking cybercrime official, by Fleischman and Lejeune both.

"It's a tough ask, I know," I began.

"A tough ask?" Park stammered. "Even if I could somehow overrule Lejeune, I wouldn't ever be able to request that the Counter-Cyberterrorism Committee orders the destruction of an independent satellite system. A French satellite system. Their ambassador to the Security Council would veto it immediately."

I puckered my lips. We would never get a mandate.

I waited for a moment. Silence settled between us before I delivered the solution I had been building toward. "I can do this myself," I said calmly, firmly. "With Kace. We just need a little help getting to Kourou Spaceport. People are dying. Once atrophy sets in—"

"Affecting the thalamus, the brainstem," Kace murmured.

"—the damage becomes irreversible. It will affect almost all Unskills. Including your daughter ..." I whispered. "And that's just the beginning. This will be an annihilation." Park stared back at me, aghast. "Also somewhat pressing, at least for Kace, is that he's now showing symptoms."

"Symptoms of insomnia?" Park was clearly startled. Kace nodded. "But are you sure? You're not an Unskill."

"No. He's a Superior," I replied. "But Kace and I are standing in the way."

"I will help," Park replied, after a moment. "I need to think ... what's best. Give me thirty minutes to make arrangements to get you to Kourou."

CHAPTER 28

While waiting to hear back from Park, I left the hotel. It was late morning, heading toward midday. The sun was high in the sky, radiating warmth. I needed a walk on my own—time to think. And I needed more information from Selaphiel if I was to end all this.

Before I knew it, I had reached the Place du Tertre, near the summit of the Butte Montmartre.

"Selaphiel?" I whispered.

"I am here," came the reply inside my head.

The creature's tall shape slowly materialized in front of me. I shuddered—in the daylight, its ugly reptilian features were even more disconcerting. I glanced around in wonder. Tourists bustled past us accompanied by droid tour guides. Street artists sketched gaudy city scenes to sell, produced with holographic laser easels. Others were sculpting with SensEye smart gloves, producing small-scale 3D light and space models of Parisian landmarks, which they rendered on portable three-dimensional printers as souvenirs. And there, too, were the customary street hawkers from the Sahel Federation's western shores, who touted their tacky wares in pre-automated fashion. Their blankets were spread over the cobbled pavement. The people around me were seemingly unaware of the strange cosmic shape standing in their midst.

The pale, towering creature was dressed in the same strange material. The crystal components of its military-style suit were loaf-shaped—wafer-thin beveled stones. The suit covered its entire body in a seamless membrane of protection. In the daylight, the crystals were akin to luz opals. Each contained a multicolored spiral shape, a mini galaxy within each gemstone.

But now, as the creature adjusted its posture in the center of the place, I could also discern for the first time some sort of structure attached to its hip. A strange-looking device with gossamer tubes, long, thread-like, but unmistakable—a weapon. I gazed upon this strange alien guardian, a being belonging to an order of soldiers. Its reptilian communication mast began vibrating atop its bare, pale head.

"Why does the Watcher want to wipe out humanity?" I asked, speaking my thoughts inside my head.

"Not all humans," it replied. "Watchers need human hosts." The creature adopted a solemn pose. "There are two hundred myriads of Watchers led by Satanael. The Chaos is unstable. It's being torn apart by the very quintessence the Watchers feed on. Expanding too rapidly. But here in the Elyonim, they each require a physical form to survive. A soma."

"Are you saying they plan to inhabit humans permanently?" I asked, amazed.

"They will harvest the best of the humans." *Harvest? What does that even mean?* I thought.

"Wait. A myriad is ten thousand." I paused and gasped as I did the math. "You said two hundred myriads. That makes ... two million people."

"The smartest make better matches. Superiors in your human soc-ed classification system. The higher the IQ, the better the cognitive and biological alignment. These will be retained, kept alive as hosts. But any vestige of humanity will be gone. They will become lost to themselves, their soma de-ensouled."

I could scarcely believe it, but finally things began falling into place. I spoke rapidly. "I've discovered a temple in the catacombs of Paris. It's associated with a Doomsday cult, calling themselves the Dark Court. But the organization goes back thousands of years. I suspect today it's being led by an industrialist called Bastien Cardinale. But the Dark Court has also been known as the Brethren of the Sacred Vessels of the Grigori. Grigori is a Greek word for Watcher. If that is really the plan, then the Dark Court is in on it."

"We think the plan will be to perform a soulectomy on two million human Superiors. It's relatively rapid, but extremely painful for the host soma, and requires a particular medical set-up. The science exists on Empyrean, and our intelligence leads us to believe Watchers have now developed their own practices. After that, the human somas can be re-ensouled with an individual Watcher, providing a permanent bond."

I shook my head in momentary disbelief, before gathering my thoughts. "There's to be a crossing ceremony tomorrow in the temple. Could that be when the Watchers come through, an invasion?"

Selaphiel frowned. "If what you say is true, then you may have found the crossing point. You need to confirm that. And prevent the crossing of Watchers to this realm at all costs."

But then a further thought struck me. "What happens to the rest of the population?" I demanded, as I looked at the suited shape in front of me.

Selaphiel stared at me directly. "Extinction. The planet has to be cleared if Watchers are to inhabit it, with their technologies … before moving against other worlds."

For a moment I remained silent. Then I groaned inwardly as I realized why it had started with the Unskills—they were the low-hanging fruit. The creation of the Lucky Dip app allowed them a shot at lux-unskill work—they craved a way out. And then the irony hit me—planet Earth had enabled this hostile takeover. It had provided the perfect means of attack. Universal Grammar tech—language chips implanted in people's brains. Humans had created the ideal weapon to be used against their own brains. Or at least, that's how the Unksills were being eliminated. But what of phase two that I had heard about at Phoenix HQ, and also revealed by Kal's intel? The Lucky Dip app had little appeal for the higher soc-ed classes. What would the Dark Court come up with next to eliminate the remaining population? And in the Tier Three states there was still very little uptake of Universal Grammar tech. For the time being I put these thoughts away.

I saw the strange creature appear to glitch at the edges of its body. I instinctively moved my hand forward to touch it. To my surprise, my hand passed clean through. The being smiled down at me.

"You're not physical!" I exclaimed. The creature's nose moved upward slightly—surprise, maybe. But then a new thought struck me: *Maybe the creature inhabits a different dimension from the physical realm.*

"I am very much physical. I am just not physically here," Selaphiel replied. "The navy I command can travel vast distances across the Elyonim by navigating all mapped wormholes within the different Reaches of the Elyonim. But even with our technology, my vessel is still far from you. Your planet lies even beyond the galaxy systems of the Outer Reaches. Your Earth is located in the Far Reaches."

"Then where are you now?" I asked.

"At a jump station located near the black hole that the astrophysicists on your planet call the Unicorn. This is the closest we have to you, four hundred and sixty parsecs away."

"Parsecs?" I didn't have a clue what the creature was talking about.

"From where I am right now, it would take me one thousand five hundred years, using our vessel's sempiternity fusion drive, to reach you, traveling at near light speed."

I gasped. "But if it takes you that long to get to Earth from your location, how is it even possible for us to be communicating? That would mean that the broadcast signal is …"

"Traveling even faster than light?" Selaphiel asked wryly. I nodded. I knew that the universal constant was the speed of light—nothing could travel faster. And even then, it was a theoretical concept. After all, there was no such thing as a perfect vacuum. Photons were invariably hindered by space plasma that interfered with their velocity.

"Right," I replied. "If you can't travel faster than light, how can you communicate with me in real time?"

The creature gently tapped the cartilage outgrowth on top of its bald head. "My communication mast is synthetically infused with tachyonic particles. And those are synced to the Theos Collider, a huge transmitter orbiting Empyrean. The Collider then amplifies my neural patterns across all the reaches of the Elyonim using a simultaneity field. My image, my thoughts, these are coming to you in real time."

"Tachyonic particles? What the hell are those?"

Selaphiel glanced at me sharply. "They have no mass, different to bradyonic matter. They speed up as energy is removed, traveling faster than light. The Theos Collider creates them artificially. But they only exist naturally within void prisms."

I frowned. Selaphiel was again talking gibberish. "And what *is* a void prism?" I asked finally.

"A spinning orb containing the soul of an ancient language engineer. The soul of one of the ancients is known as a Chol. It consists of tachyonic matter in its purest form. Matter without mass. In one sense, tachyonic matter is perfect nothingness. Not even quintessence can penetrate the void prism."

"An ancient language engineer …" I muttered, not sure what to make of this strange revelation.

"How do you plan to deal with the Watcher?" Selaphiel asked, ignoring my puzzlement. "You know it will be there at this crossing ceremony you mentioned, one way or another, with its host."

I nodded; that had occurred to me too. Fleischman and the Watcher both. The Monster was somehow connected with the Dark Court and its plans, I could feel it. But I didn't yet know how.

I looked back up at Selaphiel. "You said that once I locate it, I need to expel the Watcher from its host, so that it returns to the Chaos. But why can't Watchers just, you know … be killed?"

Selaphiel paused before replying. "Anything can be killed, with the right means. Watchers were once sustained by the Mind Chant, like all Sempiternals, and like you. After they were banished, after it was withdrawn, they should have begun to die."

"The agonies should have set in. But they didn't?"

"We don't fully understand how they survived, and even thrived."

"So if I can't actually kill the Watcher, I'll do the next best thing. I'll blow up the satellite system that is killing people."

The creature studied me for a moment. "A good plan. And then?"

I looked at Selaphiel thoughtfully. "I damage the Watcher's host."

"Use your powers. Burn its time; take its life if you have to."

The Monster, I thought. "That I will gladly do."

"And then stop this crossing ceremony, before it's too late."

* * *

After leaving Selaphiel, I continued walking along the pedestrian corridor before turning back to the hotel. Precisely then, my ear implant began vibrating. I activated my holotab. It was a transmission from an unknown caller on an encrypted line. I issued an eye-blink to accept the call, and there was Park Baek Hyeon, on facecall. That took me aback— he wasn't using an Interpol channel. His face peered out at me from the holographic screen. He spoke slowly and with care.

"Lilith King, I cannot disobey direct orders from my superiors."

Dammit, I thought. "You can't help. I understand," I replied.

He smiled grimly at me. "No. But there's an organization that can: Gladio. Now listen very carefully."

CHAPTER 29

Back at the hotel, Kace was waiting anxiously, pacing the lobby. As soon as he spotted me, he threw me a questioning look. I knew what he wanted to know—had Park managed to secure us transportation to the Kourou Spaceport in French Guiana? But I couldn't speak freely about any of this in a public space. The hotel's isolation booth was available. I booked us a session and we went inside to talk.

"The Hague?" Kace asked, after I had explained that Park had arranged for someone to help us, to smuggle us into the Union's spaceport. The beauty of all this was that it would be Europol, the Union's own law enforcement agency, that would assist. I always enjoyed a good irony. It spoke to my dark, wicked streak.

"That's what he said," I replied. "An old acquaintance, he claimed."

"And who is she?" Kace asked.

"Head of Europol. I've heard of her. Never met her, though." I had indeed heard of Lina de Bolle. In law enforcement, she was famous for her role in supporting Ebba Black back when the world fell silent. She had my respect. And she was going against the chain of command again, as the world stood on the brink of another catastrophe. I knew that if I failed, Kace would die. Most of the world would be annihilated, and the two million that remained would play host to alien Watchers.

"But why would the Head of Europol help us? Isn't Europol supposed to work with Interpol?"

It was a fair question. "Park claims there's a secret deep state organization, Gladio. A shadow permanent government, civil servants whose allegiance is to the mandates of their agencies, rather than the politicians of the day who are owned by the big tech industrial complex."

Kace's eyes bulged. I could tell he didn't quite believe it.

"But this isn't, well, strictly legal, is it?"

I was sitting directly in front of him. I fell about laughing uncontrollably, suddenly giddy with the release of anxiety. Tears streamed down my face. It took me a moment to pull myself together.

"Strictly?" I asked. "Being smuggled out of Europe and into the Union spaceport in South America in order to hijack a spaceplane?"

He grinned at me. "So that's a no, I take it. I'll go and pack, then."

"No need," I said. "We'll be coming back here. We have to finish off the Dark Court. Their leadership is meeting for a ceremony tomorrow. That'll be in their temple in the catacombs."

"If we pull this off, you mean."

"How are you feeling, really?" I asked quietly.

He reached across his body with his right hand and began absently rubbing his left shoulder. "A bit twitchy. Could use some sleep. Starting to see smoke in front of my eyes."

"Smoke?"

Kace nodded. "It's a symptom of sleep deprivation, deterioration of the macula. Eyes need rest too, not just bodies."

I smiled sympathetically. Kace was holding up well so far. But it would get worse, and quickly. We both knew that.

Suddenly, the Monster's face invaded my mind. He had caused all this, or at least the Watcher that was inhabiting him. Without even realizing, I reached for the elastic band under the cuff of my blouse.

Kace coughed. "You can tell me it's none of my business. I won't mind," he said softly. "But what's that about?" he asked as I flicked the band absent-mindedly.

I looked at him. I scrunched my eyes, before opening them.

"My shrink thinks I should dictate a memoclip to my past self," I began.

"You have a shrink?" Kace asked in apparent surprise. "You don't seem the type. All controlled sang-froid."

"Well, I do," I replied defensively. "Or at least I did … it's complicated."

"Forgive me. Didn't mean anything by it. What's the memoclip about?"

"I'm supposed to reclaim my past, to allow myself to heal and grow as an individual. When I was seven, my father, he err … committed suicide … hanged himself, on my birthday." I gulped. "And when I was twenty-three …" I paused. "I was raped."

I had finally said it. The word. I surprised myself that I could say it out loud, and even more that I had blurted it out like that to Kace. I looked away, suddenly afraid of what he would think of me, of my admission. He touched me lightly on my knee, facing me in his chair in front of the isolation booth console. Slowly, I turned back to face him. His blue eyes were staring into mine. I saw an admixture of care and sorrow.

Before I could stop myself, I began crying. I cursed inwardly, instructing myself to stop. But I couldn't. Kace leant forward to hug me. As he clasped me in friendship and warmth, I was momentarily unsure what to do. This was surprising—I hadn't hugged in a long time. But the gesture suddenly moved me. I hugged him back. My body was wracked with sobs as I cried into Kace's shoulder, soaking a patch of his shirt. After a few minutes, my sorrow eased. He released me and offered a tissue.

"Do you want to talk about it?" he asked softly.

I felt a connection with Kace. I had hidden what happened to me, what was done to me, from everyone except Clyde. And even then, I had only shared bare-bone facts, to work with him on coping strategies. But now, having confronted the Monster, I not only *felt like* talking, I *needed* to. And to my surprise, I found myself beginning to trust someone again—that took me aback, too.

Once I began talking, I could barely stop. "I was an intern to an important man. Just after my PhD in Cyberpsychology. He would exercise his control over me." I turned away briefly as I felt the anger welling up in me, as the memories of old indignities pricked me anew with shame. "He would have me wait outside his office, once for an hour, in the corridor. People would pass me. Look at me. They knew I was waiting for him. It was belittling, humiliating. He was inside, doing nothing except making me wait long after the scheduled time for our appointments. When we were alone, he would touch me, rub against me. Once, he grabbed me and tried to kiss me. You know, people, they don't think these things happen, don't believe it. But they do, not just to me. Most women get hit on in unwanted ways and contexts, a form of everyday abuse … everyday sexism. It's dehumanizing and it's everywhere."

"I'm sorry," Kace muttered.

"Anyway, one day, I'd had enough. I confronted him. He said it was all in my head. To get over myself. To drop the attitude, the airs and graces, to stop acting like I was better than everyone else.

He told me to 'get real.' I hate that expression." I glanced back up into Kace's eyes with ferocity. "I will never get real. What a dumb thing to even say!"

"I believe you," Kace replied softly.

I gulped. "He threatened me, of course. Told me that he would pull the plug on my internship if I complained. That my career at Interpol would be over."

"Sorry," Kace said quietly. I reached instinctively for the elastic band under my blouse cuff.

"Once, he was entertaining a senior male colleague. He asked me to serve them coffee. I refused, of course. I wasn't his servant!"

"That's the job of serving units," Kace murmured.

"Exactly. All about control. Then he remarked on my lipstick to his colleague. 'Don't you think it makes her look slutty?' Those were his words."

"And what did the colleague do?" Kace asked. "He objected, right?"

"Wrong. The other guy just smirked and then eyed me up and down. He probably thought I was his mistress. Some men can be such pigs. But the thing, it happened at a residential retreat, off-site in the Black Forest. An Interpol service center, if you can believe it. A hotel actually owned by Interpol. I was accompanying this man, my so-called mentor, to an international law enforcement conference. He asked me to come up to his executive suite after dinner, to help prepare his talk for the next day. He had had my voice-command credentials added to his suite's VirDa, told me to let myself in."

"And you went?" Kace asked.

"He was the one who had authorized my internship. I had worked my butt off to get into Interpol. And the internship was almost over; then I would be free of him. Able to apply for an independent stationing. I needed a reference from him. What was I supposed to do? I only had to hang on for another month, and I wouldn't give him the satisfaction of quitting. A man like that, you don't know what he can do to you, as a woman, starting out, with no power." I stopped as I realized I was close to breaking down again.

"It's okay," Kace whispered soothingly.

"Anyway, he was a pig as always. And he'd been drinking, before and during dinner. In his room he was on schnapps. He wanted to know if I had a boyfriend. He insisted."

"It was none of his business," Kace said, becoming indignant.

"Right. But he wouldn't stop. So I told him, you know …" I held my hands open, palms up. I glanced at Kace, feeling suddenly shy.

"Boys not your cup of tea?"

I shot Kace a surprised look. "Right. Never were."

"What happened next?" Kace asked.

I took a deep breath, before continuing. "He mocked me, and was crude and uncouth, as usual. Told me I was only a dyke because I'd never been with a real man. Like him. Then he went out on the balcony for a smoke. Old fashioned. He wanted scarred lungs. Always laughed at me with my DBS implant, my nicosafe app for simulated nicotine rush."

"I didn't know you had a pleasure chip fitted," Kace said, suddenly taken aback. "You always seem so, well …"

"Prim and proper?" I asked.

"Proper at least; not always prim, maybe," he replied. "I've never even seen you drink. Didn't think you had any vices. And always—well, so darn calm and collected. Uncanny."

"Yeah, people can be paradoxes," I muttered.

"And puzzles," Kace added, staring as if seeing me anew.

"Anyway, he freaked me out. There was even more menace than usual. So when he was on the balcony, I voice-activated the door lock. He couldn't get back in. But hell, was he a jerk. Started yelling and calling for help at the neighboring suites. Screaming that his intern had gone mad. That he was locked out."

"So you let him back in?" Kace asked.

"Biggest mistake of my life. I knew I shouldn't have. I panicked. But I did activate my holotab in stealth video recording mode before doing so, a one-hundred-and-eighty-degree visual setting. I thought he would be mad, would cuss, and I wanted insurance just in case he got too out-of-hand. But I didn't expect that."

"Oh, Lilith," Kace muttered.

"When I opened the door, well, something inside of him seemed to have snapped. That's when he did it."

"You couldn't get away?" Kace asked.

"You have no idea how I fought. I kicked, I screamed, I bit. I should have been able to. I have powers—"

"I've noticed," Kace replied as if to himself.

"—but this guy, he was possessed by something evil. I couldn't stop him. And then he punched me really, really hard. Knocked me out cold. When I came to, my life had changed forever. I would never be the same. Never. It's a terrible thing, the loss of self." I began sobbing quietly again while Kace hugged me once more.

"What did you do then?" Kace asked.

"He told me to get out. And that if I said anything to anyone, he would say I was a whore and my career would be over before it even started."

"You didn't report it?" Kace asked. "To the police?"

"He is the police!" I exclaimed. "Who was I supposed to report it to? Who would believe me? You're only the second person I've told."

"Who is he?" Kace asked, now aghast. "The man who did that to you?"

"You met him in Rambouillet. He's Fleischman," I whispered.

"No!" Kace said, color visibly draining from his face.

"Anyway, I took my bag, arranged my dress. I was a mess. A real mess. And I left. You know, it's not the pain so much. That goes. I had a black eye. That, I could cover with make-up. It's the shame. For a long time, I thought it was my fault. That I had somehow provoked it. I was stupid for going to his room. I had only a month left. And I knew what he was like. A monster. The Monster."

"But you did do something, didn't you?" Kace asked.

"I was in shock. Numb, at least at first. I think I showered for over an hour. I couldn't believe what had just happened to me. It was morning before I could bring myself to watch the footage on my holotab. To see what he had done to me. It was strangely surreal, watching. As if seeing something done to a stranger. But it was my body." I closed my eyes, shaking my head. "You know, the Monster, well … it wasn't about sexual gratification. It was about taking my power, showing me his."

Kace looked at me with baleful eyes. "I am so truly sorry."

I scrunched up my eyes, pausing for a moment as I felt the rapid beating of my heart in my chest. "Anyway, the next day, I pulled myself together. Got dressed. And asked to meet him."

"Not back in his room!" Kace exclaimed, horrified.

I shook my head. "In a meeting room just before his keynote presentation. I wanted to destabilize him. Take away some of his power. Take back my own."

"How did you do that?"

"I showed him the recording. It was his turn to be shocked. And I gave him an ultimatum. I would have whatever posting I chose. After all, I'd bloody earned it, working like a slave for him. I would dictate my record of reference. And if he ever came near me again, the footage would be released to all senior executives at Interpol. It was his career that would be blown up in smoke."

"You didn't want to release the footage anyway? After all, it gave you all the proof you needed."

"I was young, an intern. I had no support network. I wasn't sure even that would be enough to finish him off. And I didn't want this one thing to define me, to follow me around for the rest of my life. Once something like that is out, it's out for good."

As I explained, Kace seemed to understand. "What did he say?"

"What could he say? He never came near me again. Until this week. And he gave a terrible keynote speech—worst talk of his life. Everyone commented on it. Flustered and nervous. I sat in the front row and stared at him the whole hour."

"I understand your reaction now ... you know ... when you saw him in Rambouillet."

I shook my head. "You don't know." I paused. "Two weeks later, I nearly destroyed Jürgen Fleischman. In a stairwell in Lyon. Interpol HQ. He was heading down, walking in front of me for a debriefing. I knew that just one firm push would be all it took. It was a long, long way down. He was out of shape. I could tell his liver was shot from years of overindulging on schnapps and pastis. I could sense it. And there would have been nothing he could have done. The only thing that stopped me, the absolutely only thing, was the sec-cam. It was a public space. And I refused to pay for his crime by being locked up off-world, on the Exoplanet. That would not be my fate."

We sat in silence for a few minutes, while I gathered myself. I was fully in control again.

CHAPTER 30

Kace and I stepped out of the hover cab. The wind was strong, high up on the Europol HQ communication tower in The Hague. Eisenhowerlaan lay far below, and beyond I took in the wooded heart of Scheveningen, a large expanse of green, with the distinctive outline of the Madurodam miniature park visible at its edge.

"Lilith," the small woman called out to me. She spoke loudly through the wind. She wasn't what I had expected. Lina de Bolle was almost birdlike, with gray hair pulled back into a tight bun. And horn-rimmed glasses, old-school. *No sign of laser correction surgery, just like Diouf,* I thought. She looked stern, yet her eyes twinkled through her glasses.

From just a short distance away, my Eye could feel her. She was an old soul—hidden passion, worn duty, an irreverence that lay still within her. Shining through was a powerful loyalty to her oath, her office, but not the people who betrayed the institution she served.

"Lina de Bolle?" Kace whispered as we began walking toward her. I peered at her. "Does she know you, then?"

I gave a quick shrug. "Never met her before."

I pulled up the lapels of my leather jacket and zipped it up. I felt the garment press into my body, hugging the outline of my breasts and the holstered weapon I no longer needed to defend myself.

"Director de Bolle?" I asked rhetorically. The small woman smiled at me, stepping forward, positioning herself so that only I could hear as the wind whistled around us.

"You told me this would be our first meeting, for you," she said quietly. "But still, it's surreal that … you really don't remember … after what we did, we achieved together." My eyes widened in surprised bemusement. *What is this?* I had no idea what she was talking about. Just then my flame-colored hair blew into my face, sticking to my lipstick, distracting me. I hated that. I frowned in annoyance as I brushed my wayward hair away. "It was Lina, before. You don't do formal, at least you never did," she added, eyeing me knowingly. "You told me to give you the date, place and time … when we first met." I glanced at her in involuntary surprise. Was I going mad?

"You must be confused … have me confused with someone …" I murmured. This was getting weird. Lina shook her head firmly before pressing her wrist chip—she'd activated her holotab. A second later my ear implant pinged—an incoming proximity alert. It was from Lina. I instinctively activated my holotab. She'd sent me a location pin with a date and timestamp—for four years prior. As I closed my holotab, she was studying me intently.

I threw her a confused smile. "I'm glad to meet you, Lina. This is Dr. Kace Westwood."

Lina de Bolle glanced at him slightly dismissively. "It might not be wise, attempting this with a civilian."

"That's what I told him," I said, glancing sideways at Kace. "But he insists. And he's got it, Fatal Insomnia. He was targeted for helping me with my investigation. He's earned the right. We can still use his expertise, with so many lives at stake."

"It's your call," Lina replied. "I have an Interceptor-class scramjet preauthorized for you. You'll reach the Kourou Spaceport in an hour, traveling hypersonic. You've been assigned aliases. There are Europol uniforms on board. You now appear as contractors on the Europol database. Your return is preassigned—four hours after arrival, as Mr. Park requested. I hope that gives you enough time. The scramjet will wait for you to bring you back here," she said, finishing. She handed me two small capsules. I opened one of them and saw two translucid earpieces inside. "Once you put them in, they self-activate. They will project LS signatures linked to your Europol contractor aliases. They'll disguise your own sec-code LS rebounds."

"Thank you for your help," I replied.

"Don't thank me too much. That's all I can do. When you get to the spaceport, you're on your own. The earpieces will stop working and you'll be detectable by LS orbs, once you exit the Wi-Fi field of the scramjet—about ten meters. Your signatures will light up again."

"I'll take care of that," I said. Lina de Bolle threw me a knowing look.

"You know, Mr. Park thinks this might well be a suicide mission."

"I understand that you'll have no choice but to disavow if we're detected," I said.

Lina nodded. "Orders. I can't assist you. At least not officially. I'm sorry it has to be like that, but …" She paused, staring into my eyes.

"No need to apologize," I said quietly. "You actually have no reason to help me. I'm no one to you."

"That's not it," she said. "If I help you, you'll help us all. Let's just say that in Gladio … everyone has heard about you. And to be on the right side of history, it sometimes helps to have a healthy disrespect for authority." With that, she turned and beckoned a tall figure toward us. "Your flight engineer," she continued, glancing back at me. "She'll get you set up." Lina stared at me before adding, "Good luck, Lilith." Before I could reply, Lina began walking hurriedly away from the vertipad landing platform. As I followed her with my eyes, I was again struck by how slight she was.

"You're the contractors?" asked the engineer against the wind as she approached us. "I'm Valerie," she shouted. She was holding two sets of ear mufflers with integrated microphones. She handed them to us and gestured that we should put them on. She was already wearing hers. It was a relief to finally be able to speak and hear without shouting through the gusting wind.

We followed the engineer down and away from the vertipad, then up a narrow incline. It gave out onto the pedestrian zone of a large departure deck at the very apex of one of Europol's communication towers. And ten meters in front of us was the Interceptor.

"Magnificent!" Kace exclaimed. The engineer looked a little smug. I watched as the lanky woman gazed at the scramjet—almost lovingly. I glanced at the aircraft. I didn't get it—it was just a plane. It was around fifteen meters long, black, with gracile triangular wings and a small, compressed, angular body. It had a front cone and a small vertical fin on the rear.

"Double wedge airfoils," the engineer announced.

"What?" Kace asked.

"The shape of the wings. The Interceptor is designed using angled blades with thin, sharp leading and trailing edges. We wouldn't want a detached bow shock at supersonic speeds."

"Bow what?" Kace asked. I groaned. I got it that Kace was a tech junkie. But I just wanted to get on with it already.

"A shockwave that can lead to rapid vibration, causing the craft to disintegrate."

"That doesn't sound good," Kace concurred. "The scramjet harnesses airflow as its propulsion system, right? I was telling Lilith about it." I pulled a face, attempting to show I wasn't interested in the details. The engineer took my expression as curiosity, apparently.

"Right. The jet collects the air as it flies, pulling it through the engine, ramming it repeatedly. That generates an explosive force, causing a jet propulsion behind the plane, driving the aircraft into the hypersonic range. We're talking Mach 5 plus."

We had reached the aircraft. I could see that Kace was about to ask something else, so I gave him a slight nudge before he could do so. He glanced back at me, surprised. But began climbing the auto-mobile stairway anyway, toward the passenger cabin entrance.

"Thanks for your assistance," I said, glancing back at Valerie.

"The onboard VirDa will guide you through the safety protocols. Your flight schedule has been uploaded to the onboard autopilot. You'll be in the air momentarily." With that, she turned and walked back across the windswept landing apron on top of the tower.

As Kace and I took our places in the passenger berths, I received an incoming memoclip alert in my ear implant. I activated my holotab. It was a message from Kaye. Avie's vital functions were deteriorating, and fast. The poor girl was now on a breathing tube and ventilator. Kaye sounded desperate. She was asking whether I was any closer to solving the case; and she sent me her love, of course. I felt my chest tightening and the sting of a single tear trickling down my cheek.

***

We approached the verdant French Guiana coast from the east, dropping down over the glistening Atlantic Ocean. The vast spaceport occupied a triangular tract of prime South American real estate. It jutted out into the sea, a promontory protruding from the equatorial greenness of the rainforest in the background. The spaceport consisted of over a dozen huge circular hubs. From this distance, each hub looked to be surrounded by eight giant fingers, structures that splayed out horizontally across a modular surface dotted with spacecraft of different sizes, classes, and types. The whole site covered several square kilometers.

As we drew closer, I realized that each individual hub was a huge multistory construction. A control tower sat in the center of each, reaching up high into the blue sky in proud, gleaming white iridescence. And each glistening finger was in fact a distinct terminal stretched out over a kilometer, with multiple concourses, points of embarkation for spacecraft of different specifications and sizes and for different purposes, from commercial passenger, to freight, to military.

We landed on a vertipad at a hub designated for conventional aircraft at the perimeter of the spaceport. Our scramjet was towed to an airbridge to dock.

CHAPTER 31

I heard the airlock of the airbridge seal outside the scramjet. A welcome unit would be awaiting us.

When Kace stood, I couldn't help myself. "What's that?" I asked while pointing. He had kept on his loud striped shirt, visible under the Europol jacket. And there it was again, his whooshing laugh.

"They didn't have a shirt in my size," he explained. I smiled to myself. "One thing that's been puzzling me, though," he said, serious again. "Why does the Union operate its spaceport out of South America?"

"It's a French overseas department."

"I know, but why here? Wouldn't it be easier back in Europe?"

I shook my head. "To take maximum advantage of the Earth's rotational speed when launching into space. At the Equator. Believe it or not, the Earth rotates faster at the planet's widest point—over one thousand, six hundred and fifty kilometers per hour."

Kace's eyes widened.

"How will we actually do it? Don't spaceplanes have authorization codes or something?"

I had a vague plan. But I knew I should at least practice. I placed my hand on the VirDa screen in front of us in the passenger cabin.

I closed my eyes, channeling beams of quintessence. I eased my Eye into the VirDa's telemetry system, delving deeper into its database, attempting to overwrite key details of the scramjet's recent itinerary—to erase our journey. I felt it, the binary code, but somehow I couldn't quite crack it. I muttered to myself. I was surprised I couldn't do it.

"What's up?" Kace asked.

"I wanted to erase the records of our details. A trial run."

"To figure out how to steal a spaceplane?" he asked.

"Right. I'll need to get inside the piloting VirDa. Reprogram the code." I stared at him, perplexed by my own inability to use radiant energy to amend the code inside the scramjet's autopilot. I could feel people, read them, flesh and blood. I could marshal the dark energy of quintessence that I alone could see, and even create a psychic cloak. Kace was staring at me almost accusingly.

"But you can open doors, locks."

"Physical things," I replied. "But manipulating computer code, that's an altogether different matter."

"But isn't that actually just physical too?" I looked at him quizzically. "Computer code, a physical representation of bytes, of bits. Zeros and ones?"

I stared at him as a dawning realization came over me. He was absolutely right. Computer code was no different. That was physical too, just a different kind. I had just been approaching it all wrong, in my head. I touched the telemetry dashboard again and worked channels of quintessence, converting it into packets of radiant energy which I expressed into the computer code. All at once, I had it. I smiled. Now I was there, I could change the code just as easily as I could unlock a bolt. As Kace watched my expression, he began smiling too.

"I knew I was right to bring you along," I said quietly.

"You're welcome." His eyes sparkled with laughter, appreciating my begrudging acknowledgment. "I've never been into space, by the way."

"Oh, don't worry. This will be strictly suborbital."

Kace looked at me, confused. "We're not going into space?"

"Sure we are. But just up and down. We'll only be outside the Earth's atmosphere for a bit. It'll give us the time we need. But now we're on the clock. We have four hours to take out SkyLink and get back here." With that, I threw a psychic cloak over us, suppressing our LS rebounds, which would become visible once more when we left the aircraft. We would be invisible to sec-cams and the naked eye alike. "Now we're hidden," I said. "But complete silence. You know what happened last time." We both knew all too well what had occurred in the catacombs. "And do stay close to me so that you remain invisible."

As the hatch opened, I watched Kace's nervous glance at the robotic welcome unit outside. As we approached, its stalked screen on its squat body remained in hibernation mode. I led, stepping out onto the airbridge, ducking my head under the scramjet hatch. Outside the pressurized compartment, the humid warmth hit me, the scent of vegetation, moisture, and soil. I wrinkled my nose. Not a bad smell. In fact, the scent of life.

We moved through the airbridge toward a sliding doorway. Despite being hidden from droid LS scanners and sec-cams, the weight-proximity sensors used by mechanical service units were activated. The doors opened, allowing us access into the gleaming white LED-paneled hallway leading to the civilian service hub. Here, the air was cool and scented faintly with lavender from the ventilation scent-diffusion system. There was the familiar hubbub of people and robotic units moving along. And mixed in was the sound of fixed navigational VirDas, mounted on public service announcement gantries, issuing instructions, directions, or a variety of standard updates in the Union's default North American variety of English.

The hallway led through to the atrium of the hub—an immense spherical structure with a terrestrial-level restaurant complex, with several levels of floating mezzanine plazas higher up, connected by paternoster vertical transport chutes. The transport chutes were located around the circular plaza system at intervals, with open glass capsules moving in a loop. Passengers stepped in as others stepped out, moving up and down between plazas, far up into the apex of the gleaming white ceiling of the hub.

Curving around the outer edge of the hub were long, armored-glass panes. They provided a breathtaking vista onto the craft coming and going in the bright sunlight outside, on the taxiing forecourt. I watched aircraft ascending and descending along distant VTOL corridors. And far out, beyond the fingers of the embarkation terminals, lay the gleam of the sea.

In the atrium of the civilian hub, travelers were riding moving walkways that crisscrossed the hub's terrestrial level, curving around the circular plaza-system, which rose up in the center. Officers and VIPs were accompanied by their own welcome units. Some were in uniform, some in civvies. A Space Force brigade, apparently just back from leave in Europe, was led past us by a robotic welcome unit. The droid reeled off information and instructions as it guided them to their ground transport. Perhaps to the Space Force barracks, partway toward Cayenne, beyond the spaceport perimeter. Another group was being guided to the interstellar hub.

To one side of the large atrium there was a huge holographic screen dropping down from the high ceiling. The weekly state lux-unskill job lottery results show was being broadcast live from France. I watched in fascination as travelers paused before hurriedly gravitating toward the foot of the large telepresence screen, while those waiting in transit moved to the edges of the raised plaza levels for a better view, drawn by the silver lure of the holographic projection.

What prurient curiosity, I thought. *Most of these service personnel are at least Professional soc-eds. What interest do they have in the weekly lux-unskill lottery?* The projection of the pompous Jean-Paul Ruquier faded in, with his unnaturally bronzed face bordered by a lurid green velvet tuxedo and oversized bow tie, before running excitedly down the stairs. The whole scene looked surreal, given the immense size of the screen.

The 3D-projection of the celebrated French talk show host and MyPlace prank video star came direct from a distant Parisian studio. He began introducing the weekly winners of the various lux-unskill categories, naming those whose lives were about to change forever. The winners would be feted, their faces appearing on MyPlace newsflashes, while their livelihoods would now be guaranteed in jobs that lay beyond the preserve of the other lower soc-ed classes.

The atrium fell silent as names began to be announced, a wheel spinning as the balls were expertly caught on silver trays by young, attractive assistants. Jean-Paul Ruquier gazed out in further pomposity before presenting his viewers with what the Wheel of Fortune had decided. The throng fell into a quiet trance as he spoke.

I was about to move on when a sudden commotion stopped me in my tracks.

"Oui, oui, oui. C'est moi!" came a shrill cry from within the mesmerized throng in front of the screen. And there in the crowd was a small man. He was jumping up and down. The host had just

announced winners for a human bell-hop category, apparently in some new luxury hotel in the French capital. Now he yelled at the crowd.

"Ingénieur fiabiliste. Ils peuvent le coller là où le soleil ne brille pas. Il devenait de toute façon obsolète le mois prochain." I smiled to myself. Reliability engineers were going the way of many others—soon to be obsolete, replaced by AI. No wonder the man, probably a Skill soc-ed, was jumping in a frenzy, telling all and sundry that the Space Force could stick their job where the sun don't shine. I understood the sentiment. And I also wondered for the umpteenth time why such a crude language, Standard Union French, had such a mythical reputation for being a honeyed tongue.

I closed my eyes as my Eye guided us—I was seeking a route to the suborbital hub. I gestured to one of the travelators, checking that Kace was following, leaving the amazed crowd behind. The travelator took us around the central plaza system, and beyond, to the end of the civilian hub. We disembarked just in front of a large service transit tube.

The door to the transit capsule was also pressure-activated. It automatically dropped us down to an underground monorail facility. We descended around twenty meters, I guessed, before stepping out onto an embarkation platform, to be transported to the military launch hub complex. At this level, the air was cooler. A gleaming, monorail polycarbonate shuttle was already waiting at the platform. It remained in tranquil silence, its lights dimmed.

Other passengers arrived on the platform. The shuttle's proximity weight sensors autoactivated as we neared, its lighting booting on. The overhead ceiling speaker began its welcome message, the metallic drawl making a mess of the General American accent differentiators. The doors closed, hissing hermetically shut. I found myself reflecting idly on the fact that all doors around me appeared to hiss. A vipers' nest of hissing, or maybe that was just my skewed perception. And with a silent jerk, the shuttle set itself in motion. We traveled through a dark underground tunnel. Inside the brightly lit monorail shuttle, I absently watched a holographic screen regaling us with up-to-date launch events from different hubs, including the Space Force interstellar launch complex.

After a few minutes, we arrived at the suborbital hub stop. Kace followed as I guided us into another transit capsule, again pressure-activated, up to terrestrial level. We jerked to a halt and the transit shaft security door slid open. I paused on the threshold, surveying the scene. Outside, two armed Warrior-class security droids were stationed, facing away from us, surveying a large hallway. They were marked with Space Force service numbers and insignia. Kace froze as he saw their menacing build. Each stood over two meters tall, with thick black graphene plating, thicker than that deployed on Challenger-class security droids. Their heads were fitted with slit-like eyeline apertures for facial recognition scanning, and on top, revolving sensor capture ducts and LS orb scanners.

One droid turned, staring through us into the apparently empty transit capsule. It began scanning for LS rebounds. I felt Kace's tension next to me as we remained motionless, waiting. After a moment, the machine turned away again, apparently satisfied, facing back toward the large hallway. I pressed my finger to my lips. Kace nodded and followed me out slowly, as I slipped silently, unseen between the armed units, and moved along the hallway. I glanced back to check that Kace was following.

Ahead, on one side of the hallway, there was a travelator in hibernation mode. We couldn't afford to take that—any activation would alert the droids to our presence. I moved parallel to it and began walking. But to my shock, Kace misjudged my move. He stepped onto the travelator itself—extreme fatigue getting the better of him. The travelator autoactivated. Its weight-pressure sensors had kicked in, beginning to take Kace away from me before my eyes. Kace panicked as he passed alongside and away in front of me. He tried vainly to make his way back. But the travelator was moving too fast. The Warrior droids turned their sensors toward the travelator, drawn by the motion activation. And at just five meters distance from me, Kace was no longer covered by my psychic cloak. His LS rebounds lit up like a firework on a clear New Year's night.

One droid intercepted him in just a few paces, scanning his DigID credentials.

"Kace Treyton Westwood, sec-code 2201 4798 3261 001. Halt. You are not authorized here. I am placing you under arrest. You will accompany me to the brig for interrogation."

CHAPTER 32

The droid marched Kace through a labyrinth of corridors and security doors to the inner compound of the spaceport brig. I followed at a safe distance, hidden within my psychic cloak, until I could figure out a way to get Kace out.

The custody sergeant processed him. An actual human. He was short, his skin pale and clammy. As Kace was processed, he was in an otherworldly state. Shock, disbelief, and fatigue—they all figured. And then there were the words that shook me, that I hadn't expected.

"Prepare him for the NocioPerception Rack."

I screamed inside. I had no idea they had one here. I couldn't quite believe it. In less than four hours, we would have no means to get back to Europe. And now this.

Kace stared at the custody sergeant in uncomprehending silence.

"LS records show your last location was in metropolitan France. How did you get here? What jamming system did you use? What's your purpose in Kourou?" the sergeant asked all at once, before shaking his head. He wagged a finger at the droid. "Get him secured in the prep suite. We'll get to the bottom of it."

I followed just a few meters away, down a long tunnel. We were underground now. LED lights booted up as the droid led Kace, hands now shackled behind his back, toward the NocioPerception suite. At the end of the tunnel there was a metal door with a VirDa screen to one side, and a sec-cam. As they approached, the droid presented its retinal fold to the sec-cam for ID confirmation of its Einstein chip.

And there we were. In the NocioPerception prep suite. A human technician was waiting. This one was both short and burly. He kept tapping his hand against his bald head—a tic. He didn't seem all there.

"Yes, yes," he said, unprompted, addressing the droid. "Set him up over there, next to the medical monitoring unit."

Kace was placed in a support structure. It looked something like a medical transporter, except I knew it wasn't. Kace struggled, fighting vainly until the end, poor guy, as medical webbing straps auto-deployed around his head, wrists, and ankles. I admired his bravado.

"I'm here for your safety," the technician said, addressing him. The droid had moved to the side of the chamber and switched to security standby mode. Kace looked at the face before him with an air of bewildered incomprehension. "I have to read you your rights," the technician continued, switching to monotone recitation mode. "While on Union territory, you have the right to life under Union law. An Executive Order requires that you undergo NocioPerception interrogation as a suspected terrorist. During this process, I am here primarily for your safety." Now he switched to expository mode. "That's why it's me running this," he confided, "not AI. To make the necessary calls in this sort of procedure. Don't worry, you'll get through it. No matter how bad it seems at the time. They always do. Just remember that."

"I've never heard of a NocioPerception Rack," Kace muttered.

"It simulates pain," said the technician.

"I know what the body's nocioceptors are for," Kace said. "I'm a medic."

The technician made a sudden gesture with his head. "You'll be undressed and over one hundred probes will be inserted throughout your body, including your organs. And you'll be hooked up to the rack. You'll be on a catheter and a drip. You'll also get a muscle relaxant, I'm afraid. You'll be paralyzed, but the experience of pain will be enhanced. Don't worry, though. The rack has an auto-shutoff trip system before pain thresholds reach fatal levels. It'll feel like you're dying. But you won't be," the man said, trying to sound conspiratorial. "And I'll be in there with you all the time, monitoring everything. Your vitals. I have an override switch if it all gets too much. Your interrogator will be on the other side of the glass." This was hardly a reassuring pep talk. "I always tell my charges, you'll fess up at some point. They always do. Best to get it over with early. But do bear in mind, they begin with baseline questions. To check whether you're being truthful. Access to your EEG waveform. You wear this to measure what us tech guys call the P300. Brain waves never lie." The technician held up a plastic-looking skullcap that was lined with holes.

Kace looked stunned. "You're going to torture me?" he asked.

The technician smiled and shook his head. "That's against Union law. We don't torture anyone—actual physical pain. We just interrogate under duress. It's all simulated, not real. What we do doesn't fall under the legal definition of torture."

"But it will feel like torture, won't it?" Kace whispered hoarsely.

"I understand where you're coming from," said the technician, smiling broadly. "And you're kinda right. The interrogator has a menu of stressors that correlate with pain threshold levels. We've downloaded your full digital profile from the United Federation's

Homeland Security database. So we have a good overview of your phobias. This one fella, your interrogator, he's a reasonable one. He won't cause unnecessary pain. Some of them are right bastards. They seem to get a kick out of it. But don't quote me," he added. "I'll just step out to get the robotic unit ready so that we can prep you. That big fella's looking out for you." The technician smiled and gestured at the droid standing against the wall in hibernation mode.

Kace peered forward, staring at the technician. "Just so you know, I'll be coming for you," he snarled with such intensity that even I believed it. The technician stepped back in sudden alarm.

"No need for that," he stammered, with indignation. "I'm just doing my job."

"Sure you are," Kace growled.

As the technician hastily left the room, this was my moment. I took a deep breath before moving quickly toward Kace, who was straining at his restraints with all his might. I removed myself from my psychic cloak.

"Lilith!" he exclaimed, with bulging eyes. "I knew you'd come for me."

In a few seconds, I had Kace out of his webbing restraints. "We need to get you out of here."

Seemingly out of nowhere, a graphene-coated hand wrapped around my throat, jerking me off my feet. It felt as if my neck would snap. Kace staggered to his feet in front of me. His eyes stretched wide in horror, staring past me at the Warrior-class droid, no longer in hibernation mode, that had gripped me from behind, crushing my windpipe. I kicked and struggled as the life was being choked out of me. My lungs burned and I sensed I was gaping like a dying fish.

"Intruder detected and captured," the droid called out. I realized it would also be triggering an alarm via neural link—

only minutes now before other droids arrived. I knew from the pressure that if the droid didn't snap my neck first, I would soon be asphyxiated. I swung myself to and fro, flailing my arms in desperation, a last-ditch attempt to wrest myself free. But the droid had me fast, dangling a meter off the ground.

As I began to sense that I was drifting into unconsciousness, I heard a crash of metal, and the droid released me. I fell to the ground, landing on my hands and knees, gasping for breath. I glanced back and saw that Kace had picked up the medical diagnostic unit and flung it at the droid. It had dealt the droid a glancing blow, but just enough for the droid to release me. It was still standing over me, now in scanning mode. Its eyeline sensor was glowing dim red, and the LS apparatus on its head began rotating—I couldn't afford to let it identify me.

I reached up and pressed the droid's arm, trying to find a way in with my Eye, to shut it down. As the droid's graphene sensors detected the pressure of my hand, its auto-defense mechanism kicked in. A searing bolt of electricity spread along my arm, while the droid attempted to grab me with both arms, twisting its body to throw me aside. But I held firm. My Eye was in. I located its core Einstein chip, protected by an inner tungsten shell. These command-and-control chips all had an emergency fail-safe mechanism, a deactivation code that could be deployed in extremis. I searched for the lock, using my Eye to navigate through the chip's circuitry.

Now the droid was aware that it was being hacked. It was desperately trying to shake me off, flailing its arms against me. But my Eye had a secure hold. And there—I had it. I identified its unique sec-code. I channeled quintessence, releasing transposed energy directly into its metallic skull, triggering the deactivation process.

And just like that, it was done. The unit powered down. Its arms stopped moving. It ceased twitching. I glanced at Kace, who was standing two meters away, watching in amazement. I immediately reactivated my psychic cloak and quickly crossed the floor, so that he was under its protection too.

"I'm not sure what's more dangerous, Fatal Insomnia or hanging out with you," Kace muttered.

"That's dark," I whispered. "By the way, do you still want to go after the technician?"

Kace looked at me thoughtfully. "I think we have better things to do."

"Definitely more pressing," I replied, smiling. "And by the way, thanks for just saving my life."

"Does that make us even?" Kace asked, grinning.

CHAPTER 33

By the time we had found our way back to the suborbital hub, we were being hunted. A troop of Challenger-class security droids was followed by two taller Warrior-class droids. Then a squadron of small surveillance drones flew past, through the high glass structure of the suborbital hub in a V formation.

"They're after us," I said.

"You mean me," Kace replied grimly. "They don't know you're here, do they?"

I shook my head. "I don't think so. I need access to a communication interface," I whispered as we ducked into an unlocked janitor's closet for a moment's respite. I placed my hand on the inside of the door, my Eye feeling the passing dread presence of the AI security. "Let's go," I said, touching a pressure-activation sensor pad. The door slid open silently.

"Over there." Kace pointed to a navigational VirDa on the other side of the atrium. We moved, unseen, through the passing military personnel deploying in either direction, some in the pedestrian lane, others on travelators.

We stood in front of the VirDa screen. An image of a pasty-faced woman bobbed before us, operating in auto-loop mode.

"Ask me a question, I can direct you. Together we make space safer," she said to no one in particular, before fading out of view.

Her saccharine motif began repeating as the same pasty face reappeared. I placed my hand across the screen.

"What are you looking for?" Kace asked as I closed my eyes. My Eye opened wide as I concentrated, delving inside the communication database.

"A name, a sec-code to be able to project a voiceprint," I whispered absently. And there—I had it. "The right level of clearance." I concentrated, absorbing beams of quintessence, folding them with the power of thought, creating just the right kind of energy that I could use to clone a sec-code, a voice print. I opened my eyes and dropped my hand.

"What?" Kace asked.

"Let's go. We have less than three hours to steal a spaceplane, destroy SkyLink, and get out."

I glanced through the window of the terminal to the apron outside. A large taxiway led to a series of vertipads bounded by rising tunnels of floating LED markers. And nearby were three Space Force suborbiters on their parking stands. There was a service doorway to one side of the glass paneling. Kace followed. I gathered myself before I spoke, channeling the quintessence I needed once more to activate the cloned voice print I stored in my mind. *Now I will speak in tongues*, I thought wryly.

"Captain Briedis requesting access," I said, issuing my voice command into the door lock's VirDa mic. I spoke with the male voice of one Savant Briedis from Latvia, a ship of the line captain in the Union Space Force.

"Welcome, Captain. Voiceprint confirmed," the VirDa replied. The door swung open. I smiled to myself as I saw Kace's jaw drop. He followed me through. We entered a tunnel that led to a small transit tube.

"How did you do that?" Kace asked.

"I *borrowed* a sec-code," I whispered back, now in my own voice.

"You're projecting someone else's LS rebounds?" he asked, incredulous. "That's not possible!"

"But I'm doing it anyway," I replied, before pressing my finger against my lips to signal silence. We were approaching the capsule.

"Apron level," I said once more as Captain Briedis into the capsule's security VirDa. We dropped down to terrestrial level and exited onto the paved forecourt area—and into the hot humidity of the day. The apron was a hive of activity. Automated vehicles were moving along transit corridors that crossed the pavement in front of us. We waited while a push-back tug passed, its orange livery glinting an odd shade of fiery ochre in the blinding sunlight. Then we dashed across the paved surface toward the parked spaceplanes.

"That one," I said, pointing to one of the suborbiters. It was about twice the size of the scramjet we had used to cross the Atlantic. Kace paused and gazed at the aircraft. It was fitted with an autogyro VTOL system above, long tail fins, and a large conical nuclear plasma propulsion exhaust system at the rear. There were vents for ion propulsion along the spaceplane's body for suborbital flight.

"Why that one?" Kace asked.

I pointed to the hardpoint beneath the craft's wings. "See under the wings?" Kace followed with his eyes. "This one's already fitted with precision-guided munitions."

Kace followed my pointing hand. "Those?"

"Smart torpedoes. With a laser-homing seeker, hypersonic."

"But won't we be stopped from over there?" Kace gestured to the control tower that rose from the center of the terminal hub behind us.

"We'll be flying in manual mode. They won't be able to."

"So you know how to fly a spaceplane?" Kace asked, incredulous.

I glanced at him grimly. "Not yet." His eyes widened. Now I was confident I could do this. After all, I had deactivated a Union Warrior-class Einstein-chipped droid. I knew that my Eye could guide the quintessence I would use to reprogram the autopilot. I even had the power to control AI.

We climbed rapidly up the stairway and I spoke my voice command into the lock VirDa. The pilot's cabin unlocked, and the butterfly-wing doorway hatch opened.

"Welcome, Captain Briedis," the piloting VirDa said as we entered. I pointed to a seat and gestured for Kace to sit. "We don't have a scheduled flight itinerary for you. I will check with suborbital control," it added.

"Provide manual override."

"Authorization code, Captain?" I rolled my eyes and pressed my hand against the telemetry console. I searched with my Eye and expressed spirals of radiant energy, changing internal settings. There was a click. "Navigation controls are now in manual mode and assigned to you, Captain." Kace gazed in wonder at the complex dashboard of telemetry in front of us.

I looked at the console too as reality struck, at the vast array of switches, flashing lights, pull levers, dials, and scrolling electronic signage.

"Just need to brush up on how to actually fly this thing." Kace frowned at me while I chuckled.

I again closed my eyes, using my Eye to see within the onboard VirDa. There should be a digital flight manual with operating instructions. I found it, and began scanning the file, using my Eye to speed read the electronic document stored in bytes. After around five minutes, I reopened my eyes.

"Ready?" I asked, glancing at Kace. He took a deep breath before nodding.

I selected cabin air pressurization and the seat lock control. The air vents overhead began to emit a soft fizzing sound as the system came online. And the large polycarbonate shoulder and torso restraints above our seats deployed, dropping over and onto us, immobilizing us in our seats. As the restraint dropped, it squeezed uncomfortably against my breasts. I shifted in my seat, freeing myself.

As I began the sequence to boot up the VTOL take-off system, the control tower came on over the comms.

"Captain Savant Briedis, come in." I saw on the telemetry console that control was also attempting to remote-activate the cockpit cameras to see us. I immediately shut those down. Then I spoke via the audio channel.

"Briedis on comms, over."

"Captain, help us out here," came the voice, a human female voice. "We have an unauthorized manual activation by you of a plasma-class suborb jet. And we also have you registered as on leave in Riga!"

"I'm back early. Latvia didn't agree with me. I'm off rye bread and beetroot soup," I replied sarcastically.

"There's no record of your return. Captain, you're not authorized to leave with the suborb. You're instructed to power down the engines," came the terse response. With that, I switched off the comms.

"Trouble?" Kace asked.

"Probably."

We taxied onto the vertipad and I guided us gingerly up the VTOL corridor. As the craft swayed upward, I programmed an intersection route with the SkyLink satellite system just above the Kármán line. We rapidly ascended the VTOL corridor until we reached unrestricted airspace. The conventional autogyro system self-stowed in the roof sheath and the nuclear pulse engine kicked in.

"They've scrambled the Air Force," I said to Kace, gesturing at a side window. Two Union stealth fighter scramjets had suddenly come into view and were flying alongside us. I saw from the blinking comms indicator on the dashboard that we were being hailed.

"What now?" Kace asked.

"They won't catch us. The stealth fighters can't follow. They don't have the thermal tiling."

"How high?" Kace asked.

"About fifteen, maybe twenty kilometers up."

"Is that where space starts?"

"No, that's higher, from eighty kilometers, at least in the United Federation. Not in the Union, though."

"I don't get it," Kace replied.

"Different federations, different definitions of space. But those things will give up long before," I said, glancing out the window. "We'll reach our peak height at five hundred and fifty kilometers up."

"And that's when we take out SkyLink?"

"Right."

We continued our upward parabolic trajectory, and within a few minutes our escorts dropped away, declining to follow farther. Soon afterward, I began to feel my body rising against the immobilization restraints. I glanced beside me to see Kace showing me a thumbs-up. As we approached the Kármán line, the horizon was now merging with the inky darkness. The plasma propulsion cut out and the ion thrusters kicked in. We continued up and out, beyond Earth's atmosphere into the inky vacuum of space. Kace was gazing, transfixed, out of the window. I followed his line of sight out into the deep blackness, punctuated by the unwavering pinpricks of stars. No more twinkling out here, as there was no longer an atmosphere. In the distance was the bright glow from the Milky Way. Kace turned back toward me without saying anything. His eyes were wide, awe-struck.

Finally, in the distance, I began to make out the glint of a thin, silver necklace of satellites, in low orbit, encircling the Earth.

"SkyLink," I said, pointing. "We need a command-and-control unit." I watched the stream of satellites passing us, what I knew to be fifteen thousand tabletop-sized units whizzing silently round the Earth at over twenty-eight thousand kilometers per hour.

"How do we tell which one that is?" he asked.

"They're larger."

As we peered out of the cockpit window, a shrill alert began sounding from the telemetry warning panel.

"What's that?" Kace asked, tension straining his voice.

"Strange," I muttered. "Something's got a lock on us."

"A lock?" I could hear the inflection of alarm in his pitch contour.

I looked out of the side window and saw the glint of round orbs in the distance.

"Defender droids, I think."

"SkyLink has that?"

"Phoenix Industries has a private army. And space weapons, apparently." The navigation screen in front of me began lighting up. Small blinking dots were approaching, getting closer.

"What does that mean?" Kace asked, his voice pulsating with panic as he looked from the screen to me.

"Missiles," I replied. "Stay calm," I said as reassuringly as I could.

I pressed both my hands above me, reaching out and above the seat restraint, touching the ceiling of the hull. I took a slow, deep breath. This had to work. My Eye felt the fabric of the spacecraft and the vacuum of dark nothingness beyond it. I created a force field of radiant energy around the spaceplane. I continued channeling quintessence as the missiles struck—one, two, three. The spaceplane swayed with each strike, the third strike the most sickening of all as we bounced up and down. But the fabric of the suborbiter held. I glanced at the white knuckles of Kace's hands as he clutched the edge of his seat.

As my stomach caught up with the rest of me, I spotted a command-and-control satellite spinning into view. I selected the satellite on the weapon screen's sighting grid. The screen glowed red with a cross-hatched pattern of location lines. I quickly selected and tapped the vector, and the sighting grid locked on to the satellite unit. I spoke my voice command into the munitions VirDa.

"Fission torpedo. Fire."

"Torpedo away," came the response.

The alert on the navigation screen began its shrill warning sound again.

"More space droids?" Kace asked.

I cursed under my breath. I set a descent trajectory and we began dropping, fast, back into Earth's atmosphere. We moved steadily away from the strange orb-like droids. Within a few minutes, I felt the reassuring weight of gravity slowly returning as the spaceplane began to be scorched by the Earth's atmosphere. Now we were descending too quickly. But at least we were safely out of range of the space orbs. I leveled off the trajectory.

"Look," Kace said, pointing up to where we had come from, into the deep Prussian blue of the sky as it merged with space.

I watched in hushed wonder as we continued to descend. A soft white glow had materialized high up in the dark above us, above Earth. It was the size of a large disk at first, persisting for a few seconds before it slowly grew red-orange as the explosion reached the edge of Earth's atmosphere. I was vaguely aware of Kace's silence as he gazed up, too. As I peered up and out through the cockpit window, the line of bright red light edged out across the sky, as if drawn by an invisible hand reaching down from above the planet. I was transfixed briefly as the red-orange arc transformed into a bright orange flare. And just as suddenly as it had appeared, it was gone. The orange light faded back into distant blackness, while we were now showered in bright sunlight as we continued our descent to Earth. And with that, I could sense it. The SkyLink satellite system was no more.

Our reverie was punctured abruptly by a crackle over the comms, and then another terse voice.

"Captain Briedis, you must return to base now." They'd managed to override my comms deactivation. "You are to follow us, or you will be shot down."

The scramjets had been waiting for us at around fifteen thousand meters above sea level. The leader moved into position ahead of us, with the other fighter behind. A shrill from the telemetry warning dashboard signaled that one of the jets had a lock on us.

"What now?" Kace asked.

I glanced at him. "Once we're over Kourou, we bail."

"We what?" he asked, panic creeping back into his voice. I glanced around the cabin, looking for the weapons cache—a metal armored box, fixed inside one side wing. I activated the auto-deploy mechanism on the main console and the cover slid open.

"Let's see what we have."

Inside there was a Union standard-issue Space Force coil blaster—a high-caliber sidearm, with kydex hip holster. This would pack even more of a punch than my own Interpol coil pistol. There were also two automatic compact coil rifles with telescopic stocks. These came with torso cradles, for easy carry, and belly bands with replacement ammo cartridges. Better still, the weapons' ID lights were green—the weapons were unassigned, which meant they weren't fingerprint-locked.

"You said you know how to shoot, right?" I asked. Kace looked at me and then at the weapons I was holding, without replying. "You ever used a carbine?" I asked, gesturing to the compact rifles. He nodded slowly.

I grimaced. *That's not very reassuring.* "Let's hope we don't have to find out," I muttered, as I handed him the blaster and one of the rifles. "Put these on. Just in case." I clipped on one of the torso cradles over my jacket before securing the second rifle to my front, and then wrapped the belly band around the butt of my compact rifle.

We continued to follow our escorts, dropping down to Kourou's restricted airspace.

"Ready?" I asked.

Kace looked at me. "Is it safe?"

I burst into laughter. "You've just been into space, man. That was the least safe thing you'll ever do."

He rolled his eyes. "And gotten shot at by space droids. Don't forget that."

"Right! When we eject, we'll each leave via different butterfly-wing doors. Your parachute unit will auto-deploy. I'll navigate to you."

CHAPTER 34

I heard the explosive *whoosh* as the starboard-side butterfly-wing door popped and flew out of the spaceplane. Kace showed me a thumbs-up as I finalized the eject sequence for the passenger seat—his capsule ejected at a forty-five-degree angle out of the craft. Next it was my turn. I gritted my teeth as I steeled myself for what was to come, before initiating the sequence. It felt as if my stomach had been ripped out of me as, a second later, I was ejected through the port-side exit, dropping from the plane, strapped into the seat within the diamond-shaped tungsten protective exoskeleton. I glanced up at the beacon above me, on top of the frame. It was flashing amber, once per second. I knew from the protocols that the parachute would auto-deploy when the light turned green at 762 meters above the ground. And ten meters above ground level, the base-level airbag would deploy, creating a soft landing.

I scanned my eyeline, looking for Kace's ejection unit. I spotted him about twenty meters below me. But to my shock, I saw that the status light on top of his tungsten frame was a continuous red—there was a fault with the system. The parachute wouldn't deploy.

I tapped on the holographic console panel in front of me, switching to manual mode. I activated the small jet-thrusters at the base of the exoskeleton, navigating toward Kace. One parachute system would have to work for both of us. I adjusted the small holographic joystick as I steered the unit. I was dropping fast—my parachute would soon auto-deploy. I had to reach Kace before that happened.

The wind rushed up through the frame as I began descending at a new angle, the force of the air stinging my eyes. I closed them briefly only to miss Kace's unit. I was now too low, directly beneath him. I glanced upward and saw that my parachute light was now displaying rapid, twice a second, amber flashes. Parachute deployment was imminent. Given the positioning of my unit directly under Kace, this spelled disaster for us both.

I deactivated one of the jet thrusters, allowing my unit to move to one side, before turning the other off. As Kace's frame dropped alongside my own, I reached through the frame and grabbed hold of his. I glimpsed his look of surprise as he saw me adjacent to him.

"Your parachute has a fault," I screamed through the wind, gesturing up. But Kace just stared back at me, his eyes wide with terror. I gulped and braced myself. If the parachute deployment didn't break my arm, we would be okay.

I glanced up as the amber light became continuous, readying myself for the immense pain I knew would come next. As the light flicked green, my parachute began to deploy, spurting upward above me. Our units wobbled together for the few seconds of intense deceleration. As the parachute fully deployed with a massive jerk, my shoulder socket popped. From the unnatural sound and excruciating pain, I knew it must be dislocated at the very least. But still I clung on, fighting against the nausea, and the sensation that I was about to pass out. *Just a few more seconds,* I told myself, as I began to lose all sensation in my arm.

I glanced down, looking for the coastal landing area that should have been below us. But instead, I saw forest canopy rising up to meet us. *Just my luck.* We had drifted back over the rainforest. This would be an uncomfortable landing. When I knew I could hold on no more, I released Kace's exoskeleton cage. Now we were in the lap of the gods.

***

I was stirred by a distant shout. I came to groggily, attempting to recall what had happened. As my eyes focused, I realized I was hanging upside down, still strapped into my ejection unit. Blood was ringing painfully in my ears and there was a sharp pain in my midriff. I involuntarily made a move to grab the pain with my hands, but only my left arm responded. And as I touched my midriff, that only made the pain worse. There was something piercing me. I managed to lift my head, glancing up, seeing my body and legs above me. I had been impaled by a thick branch!

The branch curved upward, passing clean through my belly. And my right arm dangled below me, useless. I glanced down—I was suspended far from the forest floor, half-glimpsed through the sun-drenched foliage below, as I flitted in and out of consciousness.

I heard the shout again. A cry for help, perhaps. But certainly my name. I twisted my head to get a better visual. It was Kace—a few meters away. He looked unhurt. And for his part, he was more or less the right way up. *Good for him! It always has to happen to me.*

"Are you stuck?" I called, but my voice came out wrong. It sounded hoarse and my throat hurt.

"No. But if I pull on the release levers, well …" He gestured down below his feet, which dangled beneath his ejection unit, also caught in the dense foliage. It was a long, long drop.

"I think I may be stuck," I called back.

"No kidding, you look in bad shape. What do we do?" His voice was taut with stress.

I reached out, grabbed the branch that impaled me with my good hand, and pulled. Nothing. I looked up, past my feet above me. The suspension lines from the parachute were tangled in the rain forest canopy. As I tried to move myself, they resisted, holding the ejection unit in place.

I began again, using my one good arm to drag myself along the branch, as if pulling myself up a rope. And as I pulled, I managed to slide my impaled body just a fraction along the branch. I needed a break; this wasn't working. The pain was excruciating. I gathered my strength and hauled myself along again. This time I managed to maintain momentum. My body fluids were oozing out behind me. I felt the squelch of my injured mess as I left a trail, testament to my human form. The exoskeleton I was strapped into moved along with me.

Finally, at the end of the branch, my body was released. Blood oozed from the gaping wound in my midriff. Still upside down, the tungsten frame that had moved with me held me fast in the rainforest canopy, caught higher up by the suspension lines. I gritted my teeth through the pain. I closed my eyes and opened my Eye to guide the internal healing process. Now I could also feel within myself. I could sense the damaged membranes inside my belly; I detected the ruptured blood vessels, the severed intestines.

Can I, could I heal myself? I wondered. I focused, attempting to tap into the energy, the remainder of the time taken from Balladur, that I still stored in the enlarged area of my brain. I concentrated as I sought to use it by generating the same brain wave patterns, to convert it into energy that I could express through my nervous system to mend my broken body. But I could feel nothing. I couldn't do it—it was a step too far.

Anguish wracked me, at my failure. I breathed in, taking stock. *Why can't I do this? How is this different from healing another, from mending Kace? Is it because I don't really believe I can do it?* I shook away the thought—I always believed in myself. And then it hit me—*It's because I don't believe I'm worthy of being restored, of being saved.* As the stark realization engulfed me, a solitary tear trickled down my cheek. I brushed it angrily away, before trying again. *I will not fail,* I warned myself.

This time, as I adjusted my neural pathways, I managed to confect patterns of thought into energy that I could express. And so I began to heal myself, just as I had first done for Kace in the catacombs. I felt the warm glow of the tissues as I doused them in targeted radiant energy, as I mended them. And when I was done, I breathed in, allowing myself a small measure of satisfaction that I was giving myself some self-love, at last. I opened my eyes.

Next, I would need to attend to my right arm hanging limp and useless beneath me. I carefully felt around the shoulder joint with my good hand. I was correct, it was dislocated. This would require physical manipulation. I reached across my body, and with my left hand I grabbed the wrist of my injured arm. I pulled the arm forward and straight, down in front of me. As I performed the jerking motion, I let out an involuntary yelp, as I guided the ball of my arm bone back into the shoulder socket. Tears came to my eyes while tremors rippled through my affected arm. I gave myself a few minutes to recover before the next task.

I fumbled for the dual manual release mechanism beneath the front gate. I found the two levers above me in my upside-down position, either side of the gate. One was to release the restraints that secured me in my seat. The second opened the gate in the front of the tungsten ejection unit. I pulled both simultaneously. One of the levers deployed, releasing me from the seat, but the other was stuck—the gate failed to open. Something was damaged inside the locking mechanism. I remained locked within the rigid capsule frame, still suspended upside down.

I again channeled quintessence that I could convert with the power of thought into electromagnetic radiation, directing the packets of energy into the locking mechanism that operated the exoskeleton gate release lever. I burned through the lock, until I felt the second lever start to give. I slowly pushed the front tungsten gate of the exoskeleton open, just enough to allow me to wriggle my torso half out. I used my arms to reach up and grab hold of a branch above me, before pulling myself out of the unit. Heaving myself up onto the branch, I stood up—the right way up, finally.

The tree branch was only the width of one of my small feet. Kace was at least ten meters from me, still strapped into the padded seat of his ejection exoskeleton unit. I glanced across at him, scanning the canopy for a potential pathway as I tried to plot a route to him, but the branches were too thin.

"It's no good," he called as he saw what I was contemplating.

Again, with the power of quintessence, my Eye saw beyond the physical. I could perceive water particles in the air around me; I could feel my own weight on the slender branch, the boughs as they brushed against me, and the breath of the gentle wind paddling against my cheek. I heard the distant call of a howler monkey, low and guttural, the concert of frogs and cicadas on the distant forest floor, and the humming, thrumming, buzzing air, filled with small insects, populating the upper arboreal reaches, drifting in eddying currents of warm, damp air.

I felt at one with the tree. In a way I couldn't explain, I could feel the sap rising in the branches, in the veins of the leaves, the ultrasonic sound of the tree as it communicated with the insects around it. And I also felt it supporting me as I danced quickly through the foliage toward Kace. I was guided by a light in front of me, before my closed eyes, showing me how to move, the places in space to put my feet as I glided through the canopy. And as I moved through the air, I became united with the gentle breeze, my guide and companion, reaching Kace.

"Let's get you out of here," I muttered. While Kace's ejection capsule was the right way up, it was tilted at a forty-five degree angle, which meant the front was facing downward. Once the front gate opened, Kace would fall out. "I'll release you, and you hold onto me, okay?"

"You sure about this?" Kace asked nervously. I responded with a slight nod.

I reached one arm through the exoskeleton, leaning in toward the two release levers on either side of unit's opening. I used my other arm as support to prevent myself from falling to the ground. As I pulled the first, then the second lever, the frame in the front opened, and Kace began sliding out, under the force of gravity. His Europol contractor jacket became caught on the protective frame, trapping him still. He managed to wriggle his torso out of it as he continued to slide out. I could see panic welling in his eyes as he glanced down at the ground far below.

"It's okay," I whispered.

And as he dropped, I removed my arms from the exoskeleton, dropping with him. I held him, marshaling quintessence to slow our descent, using it to create invisible radiant energy to counteract the downward pull of gravity so that we slowly glided safely to the ground, fifty meters below.

"Yuck," Kace said as we landed with a splash in a shallow, muddy swamp.

"Quiet," I whispered, releasing Kace, as I craned my head, listening.

"What?" Kace froze.

"You can move out of there," I whispered back as I waded out of the water, which came to just below my knees.

"What can you hear?" he said, still standing in the dark water.

"Drones." I checked my bioclock. "We have forty-four minutes left. We need to get back to the spaceport or we'll miss our ride."

Kace trudged out of the water. "Now that you can also levitate, apparently, you could have dropped us somewhere else," he said quietly. I gestured around at the dense, dark, old-growth woodland of the primeval rainforest that surrounded us.

"Where would you have had me land us?" I asked. Kace just glared at me, and then down at his muddy legs and feet without saying anything. I watched him fingering the bands of color on his shirt, around the mounted compact rifle he was wearing in the cradle. His shirt was decorated with muddy swamp water, tinted brown from decomposing leaves and algae.

"Look at the state of this," he announced forlornly.

"It's an improvement," I retorted. Kace glanced at me, his eyes wide with surprise.

"You don't like my shirt?" he asked, sounding hurt.

"It was a joke, never mind. Come on, we have more important things to do."

CHAPTER 35

I led the way through the dense undergrowth, feeling my way back toward the spaceport. Kace had to stoop to follow, struggling to keep up. I could hear the drones in the distance. Their search area was restricted by the underbrush. And I had covered us in a psychic cloak.

After about ten minutes, I sensed the reverberation of traffic. Through the tree line, I glimpsed a large semicircular clearing. And dead ahead, beyond it, was the main transit corridor, hermetically enclosed in a transparent reinforced-glass shell along its entire length, curving up and over both lanes. Union Space Force transports were moving in slow columns inside the enclosed corridor. In one direction the corridor led to the spaceport. And in the other, somewhere on the other side of the rainforest, the creole city of Cayenne, I guessed.

As we reached the tree line, we had a better view of the clearing. I spotted the main security entrance to the spaceport— it lay around five hundred meters along the transit corridor to our left. Outside the glass enclosure of the corridor were the undisturbed sounds of the forest—and the humming of drones, which I now spotted.

There were two flights of the large units, each a formation of three military drones, zigzagging their way around opposite sides of the large clearing. Each drone was scouring the edges of the rainforest, scanning for movement, for us. The six drones lay between us and the transit corridor, that led to our freedom.

"Drones," Kace exclaimed nervously.

"Don't worry, we're cloaked, they can't spot us," I replied, as I confidently led us out of the tree line and into the clearing.

"What are they towing?" Kace asked, pointing at one of the flights of drones. I followed the direction of his arm. Each drone was transporting a conical device, suspended below it on a long cable. And as we emerged clear of the tree line, each of the two sets of drones paused, just for a second, before assuming a new trajectory, heading directly toward us.

I heard Kace gulp. "I thought you said we're cloaked."

I frowned. "It's not possible …" I muttered, as the drones now flew in a new formation, creating a semicircle around us less than fifteen meters ahead. "… the psychic cloak distorts light around us. They can't see us."

"What about LS rebound detection by scanning orbs?" Kace asked.

"The UHF signal is scattered by the cloaking. Our LS rebounds aren't detectable …"

Before I could continue, the drones retreated about ten meters, while maintaining an encircling formation. And right on cue, a large black shape flew silently into view—a military stealth helo that had been lurking somewhere above and beyond the tree line.

I heard Kace gasp next to me. "That doesn't look good."

The distinctive, multipropulsion system told me everything I needed to know. "It's a Black Condor helo." Kace glanced at me, frowning. "Union special forces, a marine-deployment vehicle." The double tilting rotors, placed on each wing, could swivel from a vertical position for VTOL to a horizontal position for rapid forward flight. The helo was fitted with hard point missiles and sidewing automatic high-caliber coil cannons, as well as heavy coil machine guns, fired from mounting platforms through both side doors. This wasn't something we could outrun.

Once above the clearing, the helo dropped rapidly until it was around twenty meters above the ground, ahead of us. The outlines of drop hatches on the underside were now clearly visible.

Kace glanced at me, alarmed. "They can definitely see us."

I closed my eyes and opened my Eye, attempting to sense how we were being tracked. Something was different in the air. There wasn't just the sound of the rainforest, something else was there too—high-frequency vibrations, non-natural, produced by machines. Too high for ordinary human hearing.

"Ultrasound," I exclaimed, turning to Kace.

"What?"

"Look, those drones, they're equipped with sonar aerospatial-emitters," I exclaimed as I realized what the suspended devices were.

"So we're not hidden?" Kace muttered.

"Not from echolocation. I can't disguise our mass."

Four hatches underneath the hovering helo opened, and four droids dropped from the vehicle, landing ten meters in front of us with a thud.

The droids landed on all fours, with their feet and fists on the ground, before standing to their full height of well over two meters. These were much larger than the standard Challenger-class security droids, and even larger than the front-line combat Warrior-class droids we had encountered earlier at the spaceport. These were elite intercept models. The droids' clear graphene outer coating, embedded with state-of-the-art proprioceptive sensors, revealed their titanium core—legs, a trunk, arms, and head. Their hydraulic neck, arm, and leg joints were protected by a thicker, black-colored graphene casing. The only evidence of integumentary finishing was the face, with gray synthetic skin. These droids weren't designed to be easy on the eye.

"I haven't seen weapons like those before," Kace exclaimed, backing away.

"Marine-class droids. They're equipped with twin seeker hip-mounted blaster sidearms as standard," I muttered, as I stared at the bulging firearms protruding from metallic cradles on the legs. I began backing away too. The forest behind us was now our only hope of escape, which meant we risked missing our ride back to the Union.

Kace shook his head. "I meant those things," he said, pointing at the large main weapons, still in cradles, fixed in downward hibernation mode and attached along the full torso length of the droids.

"Scorpion cannons," I replied.

"Cannons?" Kace asked.

"Shoulder-fired, coil bullpup assault weapons. Very heavy. They require advanced hydraulics to be handled. Those things will shred the thickest of trees."

"Are they wearing night goggles?" Kace asked, as he reached the tree line alongside me.

I stared at the four giant units in front of us. Suddenly it hit me. "You know, I think they actually can see us. Multibeam sonar imaging. The drones are transmitting our images to the droids."

The four Marine droids unclipped their main weapons from their chest cradles as they began moving toward us. Their hydraulic joints hissed gently as they moved into combat poses.

"Back into the trees, quick," I yelled as I turned around and darted into the dense forest. I sensed Kace close behind as we scrambled past trees, our first line of defense, racing frantically through underwood. Behind us, scorpion cannon fire struck against the tree line in deadly silence. The only sound came from trees toppling, as the automatic rounds shredded the tree line. But we were now in deep, and at least for now, protected.

"We need to keep moving in," I called, hearing the unfamiliar sound of creeping anxiety in my own voice. A few minutes later, after scrambling through dense underbrush, I signaled that we should stop. I placed my hand on the ground, closing my eyes—if we were being pursued, I would feel the vibrations. I glanced back at Kace and shook my head.

"They're not following us," I whispered. "Which is strange."

"Strange why?"

"Marine-class droids are built for both stealth and speed. They have opposable digits on both hands and feet. They can sprint at a top speed of sixty kilometers per hour, as well as ascend vertical inclines at up to twenty kilometers per hour."

"So they could have caught us by now," Kace stammered.

I looked at him thoughtfully. "They are likely constrained by the sonar surveillance detail. The drones can't follow us in here."

"So how did they come up with the idea of sonar?" Kace asked.

I smiled at him faintly. It was a good question. "Because someone knows I'm cloaking us. And those droids, that's not Space Force. Those are special forces units. Something else is at play."

"They know you're here, too!" Kace exclaimed.

"At least someone does."

"What now?" Kace asked. "How do we get back to the scramjet?"

I looked at him grimly. "We have to go through them. That's our only way out."

Kace's eyes bulged. "You can't be serious," he whispered, staring into my face. "Okay, you are serious."

"It's time to see if you can actually shoot. They're only vulnerable to fire at the hydraulic casings in their neck. It allows head rotation. And it's pretty much their only weakness." Kace tapped the blaster on his hip. I shook my head. "That won't do it. You need an accurate shot with the coil rifle."

Kace and I both unhooked our coil assault carbines from their body-mounted cradles, and slowly crawled back through undergrowth. I guided us farther south of the now scarred tree line that had been destroyed by droid cannon fire. As we neared the remaining pristine tree line, we lay face down on the ground—edging forward for a better view without being spotted by the echolocation emitters carried by the drones.

The towering figures of the Marine droids were visible through the trees. They had fanned out along the clearing, around fifteen meters apart, each surveilling a strip of tree line.

"What are they doing?" Kace whispered.

I glanced at him grimly. "What do you think?" He smiled back at me. "You take the two on the right? Quick shots, aim for the neck. The very instant we fire, they'll know. They have ballistic detection software. So if you miss, they'll have our position."

"No pressure then."

I heard Kace taking deep breaths next to me, as he activated his weapon and adjusted the sighting scope on his carbine. I could see from his technique that he really did know how to handle weapons.

I activated my own weapon to shoot live rounds, momentarily distracted by the green capacitor light booting on, the green LED line increasing along the length of the barrel as far-field charging came online. I lined up my two targets, the droids on the left, feeling the weight of the stock against my shoulder and the moist ground under my belly.

"Ready," Kace murmured, after a few moments.

"We fire on three, third beat is silent." Now my heart was pounding. I counted to two, before breathing out on the silent third beat. I had the first droid's neck centered in my scope. All I could do now was take care of my business, and hope that Kace did his part.

I gently squeezed the trigger, sensing the unseen coils switching on and off in a precisely timed sequence, causing the high-caliber projectile from the ammo clip to be accelerated rapidly along the barrel via magnetic forces.

A direct strike to the neck casing! The first droid in my sights dropped to its knees, before toppling forward, its head smashing into the damp ground of the clearing with a heavy thud. I swung my scope a few degrees, aiming at the second droid. I gently squeezed again and watched as the second droid keeled over.

I then glanced to my right. Kace had dispatched his first droid. But he'd snatched at his weapon as he pulled for the second— and missed. The remaining droid was not only still standing, but also now running at full tilt toward our position, just behind the tree line.

Before we could sit up, the droid was upon us. It reached into the underbrush and grabbed my arm, dragging me between two trees. I felt the sharp scrape of tree bark as I was jerked violently into the clearing. I was then thrown several meters forward, losing my carbine in the process. The drones were buzzing overhead, scanning me. The droid could see me now.

As I attempted to sit up, I watched in dread as the Marine droid scanned me. The large surveillance apparatus was wrapped around its head, underneath its black-domed titanium helmet, which shielded its head-mounted LS orb scanner. I expected imminent death. But to my surprise it hibernated its coil cannon in its torso cradle. The droid then activated a leg compartment, withdrawing a small packet of something I didn't recognize, before throwing it up into the air, toward me. The packet deployed midair, and transformed into a polymer webbing net, covering me where I sat. As the webbing net enveloped me, it automatically tightened around me. And as I struggled against the restraint, it tightened further, compressing my chest until I could barely breathe, forcing me to remain motionless. I watched through the webbing as the Black Condor helo dropped a few meters, a pulley lowering from beneath it. The droid moved toward me.

It doesn't want to kill me, it wants to capture me, I thought, as the realization struck me. And it was ignoring Kace. *Who the hell knows I'm here?*

I maneuvered one hand painstakingly, until I could brush it slowly against part of the interior of the webbing, channeling spirals of quintessence, releasing transposed energy into the seams of the webbing restraints, into its polymer adhesive. The corrupted compounds and stitching of the webbing fell away, allowing me to pull the restraint up over my head. I stood and unsheathed my coil pistol from my kydex holster.

"Gun activate," I shrieked, readying my aim at the droid's neck as it rapidly advanced. I fired, but the bullets bounced harmlessly off the droid's hydraulic neck casing. As the droid reached out to grab me again, I rolled forward on the ground, evading its grasp, my pistol spilling from my hand. My knee brushed against the broken webbing. Blood was now oozing out of my torn pants. The droid was unperturbed. In one stride, it reached my location. Its large graphene-coated open palm struck the side of my face.

As it made contact, the force flipped me over, so that I came to be lying on the damp soil of the forest clearing, landing face first. The droid continued pressing against the side of my face. It was ramming my cheek down into the dirt. *I guess that's also an effective way of capturing me*, I mused, as I began to pass out from the pressure being exerted by the droid, now kneeling above me.

Just then, I heard a sound from somewhere behind me. Through the droid's fingers, on my upward facing cheek, I glimpsed Kace, standing in front of the tree line. He was aiming his assault rifle past me, at the droid kneeling next to me. As the droid reacted, standing up sharply and drawing a hip blaster, I felt Kace fire. And this time, he didn't miss. The droid froze before toppling backward, its head thudding as it landed on the clearing floor, barely missing me.

The Black Condor helo above us immediately responded, rapidly ascending before beginning to circle. One door slid open, exposing a large coil machine gun from a side-mounted platform.

"It's going to open fire, a broadside," I called back at Kace as I picked myself up. "Toss me the blaster and aim your carbine at the rotors." Kace ran a few meters to cover the distance between us. I caught the blaster midair, just as the helo opened fire on us. Jets of soil from bullet fire flew up into the air, crisscrossing our position, as I fired back. But the speed and low-angle maneuvers of the helo made it a difficult target to hit. I ducked to the ground, as the intensity of the barrage made escape impossible.

The precision of the coil fire could only mean one thing. "It's not trying to eliminate us, just pin us down," I muttered. The gunfire from the helo abruptly ceased, as it continued to circle. "It definitely wants to capture us."

Just then, Kace flinched and yelped. Blood began streaming through the shoulder of his shirt.

"Just you," he replied, looking at me grimly. "I'm disposable collateral, apparently." With that, Kace sucked in his cheeks and crouched on one knee, adopting a low center of gravity. He aimed his weapon, steadying the sighting scope. I saw him switch to automatic fire. And after what felt like an eternity, he fired a continuous burst at the helo. One of the wing rotors began issuing smoke, and the vehicle jerked about fifteen meters up, before beginning a low dive, an uncontrolled trajectory into the trees behind us.

"Run," I screamed, as I dashed toward the hermetically sealed transit corridor. I was vaguely aware of Kace throwing down his weapon as he sprinted after me. And behind us came a huge explosion, throwing us both forward. As I lay on the ground, winded, I turned onto my back. There was a huge fireball about twenty meters from us, just inside the tree line. Kace was lying nearby. As I turned to him, I heard several thuds nearby. The six drones had all fallen out of the sky in an even pattern around us. The explosion had fried their telemetry systems.

I suddenly began laughing, almost hysterically. Kace twisted his head to look at me and smirked. I took some calming gulps of air, and gingerly attempted to stand. My blouse was ripped from where the droid had dragged me, striations of blood streaked the fabric, and my pants were shredded around the knees. I glanced at Kace as he stood. He pulled his shirt partially down to examine his shoulder.

"Just a flesh wound," he said, glancing at me. "I'll live."

"You just saved my life …" I muttered.

"Again," he replied.

"I got you down from that tree. So that's two saves apiece, all square," I said gruffly, as I pondered the next challenge.

* * *

Kace followed me toward the armor-reinforced transit corridor. We peered down through the semicircular glass dome covering the transit lanes. It was sunk deep into the ground.

"What do we do now?" he asked. "We can't get inside that."

"I'm thinking," I whispered back. "There," I said at last, pointing to a small aperture, an emergency exit, farther along the sealed glass structure.

Kace followed my gesture, looking toward the doorway.

"You can open it?" he asked. I raised an eyebrow at him. Kace smiled, shaking away the superfluous question.

Transport vehicles passed every few minutes on the other side of the glass, only a few meters from us. Right inside was a narrow gantry for service droids, running along the side of the transit corridor. The emergency doorway only opened from within. There was a lever inside, next to it, on a mounted console on the service gantry. I pressed my hand against the glass pane as I channeled quintessence, emitting radiant energy through the glass. I opened my Eye, guiding the electromagnetic energy on the other side of the glass. I used the invisible energy to pull the lever. I could feel Kace's breath on my face as he watched the lever inside the glass structure slowly depress. And as it slotted into open mode, the glass doorway slid wide open. We stepped inside onto the gantry above and alongside the transit corridor below.

"What now?" Kace asked.

"There," I said, pointing toward the security perimeter, a large metallic protective wall that encircled the base. An automated security system was in operation. "We'll need to board a transport to get through."

LiDAR-operated auto-transport vehicles were carrying operational staff and military personnel into the spaceport. As they approached the security turnstiles, the vehicles slowed for security clearance scanning.

"Board how?" Kace asked.

"Hitch a ride on the roof," I said, as I pointed to a squat glass vehicle moving toward us. "Just follow me and stay close. We're still cloaked. Remember what happened last time you wandered off ..." Kace nodded thoughtfully.

I jogged along the gantry, ahead of the vehicle. As it began slowing to pass through the security channel, it came alongside us. I quickly climbed up the guard rail on the side of the gantry and stepped deftly onto the vehicle's roof. I crouched down and grabbed hold of the plastic polymer bearing of the autogyro blades, neatly stowed into the roof sheath, to prevent myself from falling off. I gestured to Kace and he followed.

I nearly laughed as I watched his long, muddied body fly through the air as he almost misjudged his leap. But there he was, next to me, also holding fast as he too crouched on the vehicle's roof. I looked down beneath our feet, through the glass roof. The people below, riding the transport vehicle, were oblivious to our cloaked presence just a meter above them.

Once we'd cleared security, the vehicle moved inside the perimeter. The familiar control towers and transport hubs rose up around us. I spied the distant gleam of the sea. The sun was lower in the equatorial sky. After a few minutes, we reached a disembarkation hub. The vehicle came to a standstill, and an airbridge slid out to allow the passengers to disembark directly into the terminal. I gestured to Kace and we both slid down from the glass roof onto the modular plastic surface of the large apron on which the vehicle was parked.

"That way," I whispered. We would need to make our way across the spaceport apron to reach the perimeter hub. "We still have ten minutes. We should make it."

Kace glanced at me with a wry look. "Won't it look strange that a Europol scramjet arrived with two Europol contractors on board, but no one came out of the ship? And then the scramjet leaves four hours later?" he asked.

"Don't forget the contractors' itinerary got erased," I replied. "Europol will have some questions to answer in due time from the spaceport authorities. But at least we'll be safely back before then."

CHAPTER 36

On the flight back across the Atlantic, Kace went to the onboard WC to seal his shoulder wound with medical foam and change out of his wet things. This time he even managed to find a Europol top that fitted. Those were things I wouldn't be seen dead in, so instead, I remained in my bloodied blouse, zipping up my jacket over it. I'd change properly later, once we retrieved our bags from the hotel in Paris. First, we had to get back to The Hague, to drop off the scramjet.

As soon as we landed on the Europol communication tower, I knew something was very wrong—I could feel it. And as I looked out of the scramjet window, Lina de Bolle's bowed head, awaiting us at the disembarkation point, told me everything I needed to know. Only when I stepped out of the aircraft and set foot on Europol HQ's landing apron did Lina slowly raise her eyes. She looked into mine as I took in the scene—there were three armed Europol Challenger-class security droids standing behind her. Their weapons were raised, pointing at me.

"Sorry, Lilith," Lina began.

"Who?" I asked.

"Bastien Cardinale. He's threatening a lawsuit against the Union. Claims you destroyed SkyLink. And it seems he's surprisingly well-connected in the Imperium and Magisterium."

"It worked, then?" I asked, changing the subject.

"SkyLink's gone." She threw me a grim smile.

"I meant the insomnia pandemic."

"We're waiting to receive an update from the UN—but we think so. Although Director Fleischman is still insisting there's no evidence of a link with Phoenix."

Kace was now out of the scramjet, too. He moved down the air stairs unit and came to stand next to me, studying the scene. He looked around at the Europol Challenger-class droids standing in a semicircle around Lina de Bolle.

"No hero's welcome?" he asked, glancing at me.

"Apparently, Europol has a warrant out for your arrest," I said. I saw Lina glance at me in surprise, before smiling and nodding.

"At the request of the Proelium military command in Brussels," Lina added, addressing Kace apologetically. "You were identified at Kourou Spaceport."

"They wanted to put me on a NocioPerception Rack," Kace exclaimed.

That took Lina aback. "But that requires an executive order, director level," she said. "They wouldn't have been able to get that without high-level clearance from the Imperium or the Magisterium."

"And you've heard nothing about it?"

Lina shook her head, studying us both.

"And Interpol have issued an arrest warrant for me, haven't they?" I asked.

Lina eyed me thoughtfully. "It seems Director Fleischman wants your head," she said quietly.

"Does he have any evidence I was involved?" I asked, knowing that he didn't. I had been under the cover of my psychic cloak the entire trip.

"The Space Force captain who stole the spaceplane turned up in Latvia," Lina said. "Union Marine droids raided his house. LS and sec-cam data showed he hadn't in fact left the country. They concluded his identity had been stolen. Director Fleischman says you did it."

"But he can't prove it."

"Herr Fleischman seems to believe you were spotted at Phoenix HQ by a surveillance droid. He claims you have some tech that enables you to cloak your LS rebounds."

"Can I ask who authorized deployment of the Marines in Latvia?"

"A directive from the Imperium, obviously, but—"

"At the request of Fleischman?" I asked. Lina pursed her lips. "And do you happen to know anything about a Marine droid deployment earlier at Kourou Spaceport?"

Lina looked at me, bemused. "I've not heard of one."

I smiled at her. *So that's it.* I had my answer. Fleischman was in bed with Bastien Cardinale and Phoenix. I knew it.

Lina moved forward, out of earshot of the droids. "You and I know you were there, at Kourou. But that stays between us," Lina whispered. "Just out of curiosity, how did you do it? A voice print embedded in encrypted metadata when an individual speaks?"

"Nothing will happen to Captain Briedis, I hope, right?" I asked, ignoring Lina's question. I was concerned for the guy. He had done nothing wrong, after all.

"He has a watertight alibi."

"And now you're here to take Kace in?" I muttered.

"Afraid so. I can't let Dr. Westwood leave, you know that Lilith. I haven't received the formal memo of assistance from Interpol for you. So ..."

"I can go?"

"I will look the other way, but you don't have long. Then, well …"

"You'll have no choice."

"That's right," she muttered.

"You know I can't let you have Kace," I announced, slightly more menacingly than I had intended, staring directly at Lina.

"I understand how you feel, I really do. But you see, well, you're outnumbered." I looked past her, toward the coil weapons of the Challenger droids.

"It makes no difference. I can't give him up," I replied. Lina smiled. "So what do we do now?"

"They will escort Dr. Westwood down to the cells. There will be criminal articles brought. Trespass, illegal entry, vandalism, espionage." I glanced at Kace. His face was priceless. Poor guy. He looked mortified as Lina spoke. "But …" Lina paused, now speaking quietly again so that only Kace and I could hear. "… I can give you five minutes, if you request it." She glanced behind her at the armed droids, and then back at me with an expectant look.

Now I spoke loudly enough for the droids to hear. "Lina, can Kace and I go somewhere to debrief? I just need a few minutes with him."

Lina looked at me for a moment. "I can give you five minutes," she replied, also speaking loudly.

With that Lina turned, instructing the droids to let us through. They parted as we followed her; Kace glanced nervously at the coil weapons as we passed, and then once more over his shoulder as they followed us.

Lina led us below the flight deck on top of the Europol tower to a small room. She issued a voice command, opening the glass door. We followed her inside. There was a narrow window that looked out over the Scheveningen woods far below. A sec-cam in one corner of the room blinked at us. I glanced up at it. Lina was watching me intently. She gave me the slightest of nods, as if acknowledging that we were being monitored. We couldn't speak freely.

"Five minutes," Lina announced.

Before turning to leave, she held out her hand, offering it to me while looking into my eyes. I took it. I soaked up the rush as I saw into her, feeling the quickened beat of her heart, the gurgle of blood through her veins, the breath of her lungs. And there it was, an emotional halo—I saw myself with Lina, in a past I hadn't yet experienced. I withdrew my hand in startled surprise. But Lina reached forward and took my hand again. And this time, I grasped a second emotional halo—she was reciting a thought over and over. This was the emotional halo she had wanted me to see. As I released her hand for a second time, I gazed at her in wonder. Lina's face suddenly flickered with a knowing smile as I gaped at her. I was amazed anew by this small woman. As she left the room, the door securely locked with a loud click. We were now imprisoned. Lina turned and raised her hand slightly, a gentle farewell. But this was not adieu—I was now certain I would be seeing her again.

"What's going on, Lilith?" Kace asked nervously as I turned back to him. He was pacing up and down, now that we were alone. The waveform display on the LED smart wall panels slowly swirled with different shades of textured hessian.

"Come and sit, before you make me nervous too." As Kace sat, I used quintessence to block our sound waves from being heard by the mic attached to the sec-cam. "Lina de Bolle and I have met before ..."

"Before today?" Kace asked. "You said you'd never met her."

"We've met in her past, not in mine. I meet her in my future."

Kace scrunched up his eyes. "You're making no sense." I nodded and threw him a quick shrug. *Go figure*, I thought. "So what's the plan? You have one, right? To get us out of here. I saw your reaction, when you touched her. You saw something, didn't you?" I feigned surprise. "Look, I have eyes, and you definitely know I'm not dumb, all the stuff you can do …" he added in exasperation.

"Fair enough. In four minutes, there will be a power outage in this part of the Europol tower. That door there will no longer be locked. We'll be able to get out."

Kace let out a long breath of relief. "Good!"

"You believe me?"

"Of course," Kace replied. "I've seen you do things with my own eyes that are kinda freaky, supernatural. But you have to tell me, how do you do it, know things through touching someone?"

"A feeling, feelings. That's all."

Kace shook his head. "That's not all. We both know that."

"Okay. How shall I put this? We all have a Wi-Fi in our brains, a means of connecting with others. I'm just a bit farther along."

"Wi-Fi in the brain? What are you talking about?"

"I can use my brain's electrical signals not just to communicate with my own body, but with those of others. The brain is basically a battery, that sends out motor signals …"

"Right. That's my area of expertise, remember? Part of our brain's rotational motor is bacterial, known as V1. It functions as a pump that moves sodium ions across the membrane as part of normal cellular processes. But what you can do goes beyond anything a normal brain can do, at least a human brain. And I still don't see how what you're saying about brain function relates to Wi-Fi."

I thought again for a moment before replying. "I can consciously control my brain's rotational dynamics in my motor cortex, and reverse the process, creating kinetic energy, a signal. And I can express that, to create electromagnetic radiation. I can also harness it to connect with the bodies of other people. I can feel what they feel. I can sense what they sense. I can experience what they experience. Sometimes it's quite specific. What they're thinking. That's why I think of it as a Wi-Fi connection."

"You're talking about telepathy?" Kace asked, incredulous.

I shook my head. "No. What I can do is grounded in the physical laws of the universe, the same laws that constrain all of us. It's just that …"

"You're better able to exploit those laws."

"Yeah, right," I said. "I'm more evolved, I guess. I can exploit things in slightly different ways."

Kace shook his head. "What are you really, Lilith?"

I stared at him intently and held out my hands. I wasn't quite sure how to respond. "Look …" I began. Just then, there was a flicker as the LED panels glitched. The outage had struck. The door clicked open. I was relieved I didn't have to answer. That had sure felt like a long four minutes.

CHAPTER 37

As soon as the door opened, the three Challenger-class droids moved forward to secure the room. Their coil weapons were raised—the green line of the far-field charging capacitors flickered ominously on the sides of their barrels.

"Do not attempt to leave," commanded the leader in a metallic-sounding drawl—black shoulder markings beneath its neck-casing denoted the rank of lieutenant. Unlike consumer-facing androids and gynoids, which had gendered differentiation, the Union's security and miliary droids were designed without such niceties—the same gray integumentary face finishing. However, unlike the Marine-class droids we had encountered in French Guiana, Challenger-class droids featured a full-body gray skinsuit.

By the time I reached the door, the Challenger-class lieutenant was in my face, or rather its chest was, as it stared down at me from its height of two meters. The face had strangely-distorted humanoid features, yet without a mouth—the speaker system for verbal output when interacting with humans came from a small grille in the facial graphene display; droids used neural linking for communication with their own cohort. Its long eyeline aperture blinked as it scanned my facial expressions, gauging my emotional state and intent. Its head-mounted LS orb scanner was vibrating.

"Back into the room, High Commissioner King," the droid instructed, now prodding my midriff with the tip of its coil rifle.

Those were the last words it uttered. The droid stiffened in stationary inertness, its coil weapon falling back into hibernation mode in its torso cradle. I had shut down its Einstein chip, encased inside its head.

The two remaining droids moved forward, immediately aware that their lieutenant had been decommissioned. I closed my eyes as I attempted something new, channeling quintessence and projecting electromagnetic radiation at a distance. As I concentrated, I searched for the deactivation code in the droids' command-and-control Einstein chips. First, one was deactivated, and then the other came to a sudden standstill as its weapon auto-returned to its sheath casing. *I'm getting better at this*, I thought, as I opened my eyes.

"Come on, let's go," I called back, over my shoulder. I squeezed my body past the droid lieutenant partially blocking the open doorway. I heard Kace breathing heavily as he tried in vain to move the droid—he was too big to get through.

"These droids weigh a ton," Kace exclaimed. "I'm stuck."

I moved forward and placed my hand on its graphene-covered back. The coating was slippery to the touch, a flexible yet highly force-resistant layer of protection. I closed my eyes again as I concentrated. *Kace is right*, I thought. *This thing does weigh a ton.* I knew that wasn't due to the titanium core, which was forty-five percent lighter than steel, while being just as strong. It came from the heat-resistant tungsten compartments inside the droid's trunk and head that housed all its vital operating processors and memory database.

Using quintessence transposed into radiant energy, I created an adhesive force and dragged the standing droid across the floor, nearly half a meter, as if glued to my hand on its back. I stepped away and opened my eyes. Now there was enough space—Kace was through.

I led the way, running back up the incline to the rooftop vertipads of the Europol tower. Outside, I paused, as the wind flicked my hair against my face, scanning for engineering personnel or more droids. We were in luck for a change; the power outage had caused just the diversion we needed. No one was in sight.

"What now?" Kace asked, panting. I pointed to an unmanned Europol hover patrol vehicle on one of the vertipads.

"We'll borrow that."

"Borrow?" Kace asked, raising an eyebrow.

"We need to get back to Paris."

***

After appropriating the Europol patrol vehicle, we landed fifteen minutes later at a corner vertipad, a couple of blocks from our hotel. We abandoned the vehicle and hurried through the streets. I was getting tired and hadn't covered us in a psychic cloak. Europol would have tracked our flight path in any case.

As we made our way through pedestrian lanes, I experienced the familiar feeling of eyes watching me, being surveilled by unseen spies.

"We're being followed," I whispered. It was getting late. Back on Central Union Time, dusk had already set in. The pale arc of lights from e-scooters and e-bikes wobbled past in the adjacent lane, the jerky penumbra from the small headlights merging with the twilight.

Kace gave a furtive glance over his shoulder. "I can't see

anyone. How do you know?" I threw him a quick glance. "Forget I asked."

It was a warm evening in the French capital. We were approaching our hotel near the Place du Tertre.

"There are two of them," I continued.

"Europol?"

"I'm not sure. We won't be able to stay at the hotel."

"What about our things?" Kace asked.

"We'll collect our bags first. Then lose those guys." We turned right as we approached the Calvaire stairs along rue Poulbot.

A sec-cam's DigID system, on one street corner, instantly scanned and recorded our face data. We were in the open now. I knew I needed some rest. Somewhere up in space, the Union-DEF satellite servers were picking up the LS rebounds on my language chip. Every few seconds, my precise location was being pinpointed. Interpol knew where I was. Of course they did. I was a goddamn homing beacon. We both were.

"Mind mapping," I announced, as we walked.

"What?" Kace asked.

"Analysts, data scientists will be trying to figure out what we're up to, our plan, as I speak. Using an AI algorithm."

"I still don't get it," he replied. We were walking briskly now. The shadows lunged out at us, startling me. I disliked being visible, especially now that I was a wanted woman.

"That's what we call it, at Interpol."

"Mind mapping?" he asked.

"Cross-referencing LS records, sec-cam data, and social media activity, Interpol can identify every person you have ever interacted with, every location you have ever occupied across your entire lifespan. And using this rich array of data, the algorithm will infer your future actions and motives, even attempting to deconstruct your likely next thought. What you will do next. Even before you know it yourself. The ultimate crime-fighting tool."

"Sounds more like overreach," he replied.

We arrived at the hotel. I glanced around us. Two figures loitered in the pedestrian corridor farther down the street, behind us. We quickly retrieved our bags from the auto-storage lockers.

"Can't you cloak us?" Kace asked. I shook my head. I felt too weak. Kace glanced at me questioningly, but didn't say anything. Suddenly, he began to yawn.

"I'm so beat," he said.

"Do you think you can sleep?"

"I'd sure like to try." He grinned at me in the semidarkness.

We were now alone in the pedestrian corridor. The networked system of LED streetlights slowly dimmed behind us before slipping into darkness, while one ahead booted up. Another began flickering, as if glitching, before flicking on.

It was just then that I heard the click. And too late, I sensed the drone. It was a small stealth unit above us. It had stayed out of range, before dropping down quickly.

It deployed a flexible netted fabric sheet that dropped over us just as my Eye kicked in. It must have been the fatigue. As it enveloped us, the netting automatically tightened. I fell against Kace as we collapsed on the pavement. I felt his weight pressed against mine, his breath on my neck. And I glimpsed the look of fear in his eyes as he realized what was happening.

I struggled inside the netting, feeling for the polymer threads that my Eye could burn through, as I had done when caught by the Marine droid. But I quickly realized this was an altogether different proposition. We were enveloped by Faraday fabric—I sensed the copper and nickel composition in the weave. This was not standard

Interpol or Union military webbing restraint. It was only usually used by specialist forensics teams to block wireless signals. That had to mean that whoever was after us was adapting their strategy—to me. They knew something about what I could do.

As I lay with my head pressed against the pavement, I heard another click and saw shoes approaching. The flat soles of a woman's pumps. I managed to see at a slight upward angle as I strained my neck. The muzzle of a large-caliber coil pistol came into view.

"High Commissioner King," the voice said. It was a hard, sharp voice.

"They're secure," came a second voice, this one male, gruff. "This stuff seems to be actually working."

"We're here to take you in," said the female voice. "The Director sends his regards."

So they are Interpol, I thought. *The Monster is behind it.* I could feel Kace's thumping heart through his chest, awkwardly pressed against mine.

"Nice touch, this fabric," I croaked hoarsely at the woman's feet.

"We didn't want you vanishing into thin air again," she replied. "You're one difficult lady to track down."

With that, I heard the sound of a hydraulic system. The red beam of LiDAR sensors grazed the ground. They had a transport unit. A mechanized arm hauled us upright, suspending us slightly off the ground. The woman moved toward us—she was quite big, athletic, with short-cropped, military-style hair. I watched her dark eyes approach mine as, at last, I saw her face. She came so close that I could smell an admixture of evening perspiration and faint morning perfume. She eyed me coolly. She clearly disliked me, whatever I had done to her. Perhaps it was just what I represented. Who knew?

In the end, everyone makes a mistake. And hers was that she was overconfident of her webbing restraint. And hence too close. I managed to slip a finger through the netted fabric. Before she had time to move back, I touched her left wrist, dangling by her side. My Eye had her. I began burning. And from this point on, she was locked in, until I deigned to release her. Her eyes widened slightly. I felt the echo of her pulse, the blood flowing through her veins. And I saw her vindictiveness, her overweening pride. Her vicious laughter at the romantic failures and career missteps of her younger sister. I also now sensed her fear, at what I was doing to her. She was frozen under my touch, unable to escape—but I sensed she wanted to. Fear snared her. As I released her, she backed away, shaken, until she turned and ran as fast as she could, disappearing into the sultry Paris darkness. Her male colleague watched in surprise, his mouth opening and closing almost comically.

We were left suspended in midair, attached by a levered arm to an automotive wheeled flatbed unit. But the minute of time I had burned had rejuvenated me. I brushed my hand slowly over the interior of the netting's seams, looking for a weakness. And this netting had one—old-fashioned cotton stitching. I channeled quintessence, corrupting the stitching. The netting fell away—even this was no match for what I could now do. As we dropped onto the firm ground of Paris, I immediately threw a psychic cloak over us. The face of the remaining Interpol agent took on a stunned expression as if dazed, as he watched us disappear into thin air. He slowly backed away from the spot we had occupied just a moment before, then he too turned and fled.

"What now?" Kace asked.

I glanced down at my blouse and torn pants. "For starters, I need to clean up and grab some fresh clothes."

CHAPTER 38

We found a new hotel, somewhere almost virtually off the grid. It was exactly what I'd been looking for.

"It's a fleapit!" Kace exclaimed. "I didn't know such places still existed."

The twin beds each had dirty-looking throws over them. I made a face as I saw them before glancing at him.

Kace smiled at me and lowered his shoulders in relief. "I know, but I don't care. I could sure use some shuteye."

While Kace went into the bathroom for his turn to take a shower, I sat on one of the beds, taking the dirty-looking throw by one corner and placing it in a closet. The sheets smelled musty. The room's carpet was worn and curled at the edges, while the once white-painted walls were yellowed with age and neglect. There were no smart LED wall panels here. A cracked lamp provided an eldritch glow from an old wooden writing desk in the corner, riddled with tiny pinprick holes on one paneled side, the vestiges of a long-ago woodworm infestation.

We had paid at reception via simple electronic ledger transfer that I could disguise. Not even sec-code registration, which was illegal. The receptionist, an actual human who turned out to be the owner, had apologized, claiming it was being fixed in the morning, and said we'd need to do the formal city police registration then. I agreed, knowing we'd already be long gone.

The room itself was lock-operated using an old-fashioned key card system. There wasn't a VirDa in sight. No internet-of-things connectivity. Here I could uncloak us and we wouldn't be traced.

As my thoughts wandered, I lay back on my bed. Fatigue seeped back through me. I idly listened to the drum of water on porcelain through the paper-thin walls, as Kace washed in the bathroom. Yet, I knew my weariness would be nothing compared to his.

* * *

I awoke with a start. I adjusted my body slightly on the bed and realized I must have dozed off momentarily. The sound of gushing water through the bathroom wall had ceased. After a few minutes, the bathroom door opened wide and Kace re-entered the room, dressed.

He sat down on his bed, his back toward me. Then he turned to face me and smiled. "We did it, didn't we?"

"SkyLink?" I asked. He nodded. "You'll sleep tonight. But we're not finished yet."

"That's why we're back in Paris?"

I gazed at him without saying anything for a moment. "We should rest," I murmured finally. Kace lay down on his bed, a couple of meters from me. I looked at his long body and started laughing.

"What's funny?" he asked.

"Your feet reach over the end of the bed."

He frowned before issuing a retort of his own. "Do you go to bed in your shoes?" He was looking at my patent leather brogues.

"Of course not," I replied, disarmed and still laughing as I sat up to unlace them. As I did so, my pants raised slightly, revealing my ankles.

Kace made a strange, startled sound. "What's that?" he asked as he saw the burn scar on my lower right leg, just above the ankle. He paused. "Sorry. That was plain rude."

"Don't worry. It's an old burn wound."

"But I didn't think you could be hurt," he said, genuinely taken aback. "No, really. I saw what happened to you back in the rainforest. If that had been anyone else, well ..." His voice trailed off.

"Apparently, this is the one spot that never heals."

He sat up, on the side of his bed facing mine. He peered down at my ankle. "It looks like the shape of ... a hand!" he exclaimed.

"My father's hand," I whispered. Kace looked into my face, taken aback, eyebrows raised. "There was an incident when I was small. A fire in my childhood home, in the nursery in fact. My mother, she was suffering from long-term postpartum depression, it had become an ongoing depressive disorder—at least that's what the medics said. She claimed she heard voices, telling her I was a demon."

"That sounds like an extreme case of PPD," Kace interrupted.

"My father arrived home one evening to find our living room on fire. He found my mother unconscious from smoke inhalation, and me lying on the floor, wailing, surrounded by a wall of flames. Apparently, she had been sitting on the floor, holding me in her arms, encircled by rags she'd set on fire. My father stepped through, grabbed me by my ankle, pulling me toward him, before scooping me up into his arms and carrying me to safety. But then, three days later, this mark came, the shape of his handprint, from where he held me when he saved me. I've had it ever since. Sometimes it itches real bad."

Silence rose between us, while I lay back on my bed. I closed my eyes.

"What do we do tomorrow?" Kace asked finally.

I opened my eyes and studied his face, as he peered down at me. "Tomorrow we end this. Everything. We cut off the serpent's head."

"Good," Kace replied.

"And tonight you sleep."

* * *

When I awoke, for a split second I couldn't remember where I was in the dreary early morning light. I turned on one side and saw the long torso of Kace, sleeping on the single bed near mine. I had always longed for a sibling during my adolescent depths of despair, someone I could confide in. Kace increasingly felt like the younger brother I had never had.

As I studied his sleeping form, I wondered again what it meant that I didn't need to block when I touched him. There was somehow a balance between us that prevented me from burning him. *How is this possible? Is Kace my soul friend of ancient Celtic lore, my anamchara? Or something else?* For the first time since the age of seven, I had found someone I could touch without fear. For that I was grateful.

My eyes wandered from Kace, beyond him, to the windows. I could see from the edges of the grubby night shields that it was light out, although still early. After a few moments Kace began to stir. His eyes flickered open.

"Morning." I spoke the word quietly. He smiled and sat up. "You slept!"

"I feel much better."

Just then I received a memo alert in my ear implant. I activated my holotab and began reading, furrows spreading across my brow as I took in the news.

"What's up?" Kace asked.

"An Interpol memo. There's going to be a general strike, global, across most Tier One states—Start Apollo has been making waves."

"The Unskill leader? But the Unskills don't have jobs, how can they strike?" Kace asked, perplexed.

I shook my head. "Not the Unskills, the Semiskills. They're joining forces."

Now Kace frowned. "But I thought they hated the Unskills?"

"New state obs-jobs lists were published yesterday. A rare joint statement by the Union's High Representative and the Secretary of State. Semiskill jobs are being pared back. Looks like the Grand Union and the United Federation of America have both shot themselves in the foot."

"By provoking the Semiskills?"

"Looks like it. Start Apollo claims there's a Tier One global conspiracy. He's even claiming the insomnia pandemic has been initiated by the global elite to eradicate Unskills, that Semiskills are next." I grimaced as I continued reading. "The High Representative says the Union won't comment on ridiculous conspiracy theories. The Secretary of State has referred the press to the High Representative's remark. No one's saying anything."

"It's hardly a conspiracy theory," Kace muttered.

"At least that's one thing the Dark Court managed, apparently. To unite the two lower soc-ed classes. Now that is ironic!"

CHAPTER 39

Today was the day of reckoning. I could feel it was almost time. I sensed it in the streets of Paris. I could smell it in the air. Today the Dark Court would be meeting in their temple in the catacombs for their so-called crossing ceremony.

I was sitting outside a café, near the suburban railroad we would soon descend. Kace had disappeared inside in search of a service unit to place our order—the tabletop VirDa order system had a glitch. I breathed in the fading aroma of late-flowering clematis, carried by the warm morning breeze, as it wafted toward me. The heady scent of almonds dueled with the cloying, pungent smell of the sewer, rising up from a break in the modular plastic transit lane nearby, in need of repair. I closed my eyes and drifted into a reverie. What I experienced was a waking vision that felt so real it gave me goosebumps.

A bright figure was drawing closer in my mind's eye. It was without a clear outline at first, glowing orange, sketchy, as if approaching through mist. I peered through the haze, attempting to get a better view. As the figure approached, its form began to take shape, fiery, with wings of orange flame, the same color as my hair. The burning creature had six wings, a fiery angel, that was floating in the air before me. To my amazement, as the mist slowly cleared away, the apparition transformed into me.

I emerged out of the air, from the cloud of mist, that transformed into a mystical doorway. I stepped down onto the ground, the rocky terrain of a clifftop, the sea at my back, on a cold early morning. And before me, startled, was another woman, this one with the blackest of hair, coal-black eyes, a woman I instantly recognized. Hers was one of the most famous faces on the planet, even long after her disappearance. The woman was dressed in running attire and eyed me in amazement, her exercise interrupted by my unexpected arrival. And as I looked down, in my hand was a crystalline orb, containing a strange serpent-bird-like creature, spinning on itself, pulsating red before dissipating back into pale translucence. Each time the creature pulsated red, it spoke to me in a strange tongue that I was inexplicably able to understand. Yet, the orb felt of nothing, it weighed nothing, but I sensed the immense power contained within.

* * *

"Lilith?" Kace's voice was insistent. My eyes flickered open. He was peering into my face. "Boy, you were miles away." He was relieved to have me back. "You didn't hear me, before?" The robotic server was moving lazily among the tables out on the terrace, toward us.

"The strangest thing …" I muttered. "I just had a weird experience … an emotional halo …"

"Your brain's Wi-Fi?" Kace asked. "Strange how?"

"I saw myself with Ebba Black, before the Great Language Outage … or at least I think so."

"Ebba Black? But I thought you didn't know her, isn't that what you told the Broads?"

"I've never met her in my life. And the weird thing is, I only get emotional halos through touch, or at least usually …"

"A premonition, maybe?" Kace suggested. "Something to come?"

"I don't see how. There's been no sign of the woman since, what, early 2126 … and this felt earlier, the previous year maybe, it had to be. It was her estate in the Nordic Republic, the one that was in the news, that blew up. But in my vision, everything was still intact."

"Perhaps you did meet her five years ago, and …" Kace pursed his lips and raised an eyebrow as his words petered out. The silence felt accusatory.

"What, and I just forgot about it?" I exclaimed, shaking my head. Our coffee arrived. I took a cautious sip. The strange emotional halo was puzzling, disturbing even; I'd never had one like it before. I pondered for a moment, deliberately focusing on the present, the task at hand. "They're gathering there right now," I announced, changing the subject.

"The adjudicators?"

"I can feel the swell of something bad building. And those people. Poor people. They were the first ones, the guinea pigs."

Kace watched me, absorbed, his brow furrowed. "Can I ask you a question?"

"I wish you would," I replied. "There's clearly something on your mind."

He leaned forward slightly. "Why do you care so much? You know, about the Unskills?"

"Why wouldn't I care? Shouldn't I?"

"Of course you should. But I have my own reasons, my brother … but you, it's almost as if you care more for them than anyone else."

I looked past Kace, over his shoulder into the distance, as I contemplated how I should answer, what my answer even was.

I was proud of my case clearance rate, although I never spoke of it. I had been a bureau director in Singapore, and that had made me proud too. But most of all, I was proudest of solving cases that helped the lowest soc-ed class, the voiceless and marginalized.

I adjusted my gaze, looking directly at Kace. "I was once described as the patron saint of all worthless things. It was meant as a put-down. An attempt to put me in a box where all worthless things are shut away. But I guess I won't be shut away." I paused again. "I see virtue in the discarded because they have intrinsic value. They suffer, sometimes nobly, sometimes not. Sometimes they rage at the inequity of it all. But I understand their pain, their anger, their frustration. It speaks to me. I fight for them because I know what it feels like to be abandoned, uncared for and insignificant. But mainly I fight for them because no one else does. And I can."

Kace stared at me, breathlessly, without saying anything. Then, slowly, he smiled. This wasn't his flashy charm, the charm that drew you in. It was a gentle smile of acknowledgment, of recognition. And again, I felt a sense of connection, that we somehow shared something that joined us, in a greater purpose, maybe.

"We should head down," I muttered. We both drank up and left the café.

I led us to the polymer palisade security fence. It was an off-white color, with a scrolling, holographic warning banner running along it: *Danger. Ne pas entrer. Voies ferrées électrifiées.*

But my Eye located a way through—a concealed cut-out, most likely courtesy of a previous urban explorer, concealed behind a bush farther along. As we approached the opening, I cloaked us. Once through, we sat on the embankment, amid foliage, waiting while two autonomous overground city trains passed, taking the few commuters across the sprawling metropolis—the Professionals, Executives, and maybe one or two Superiors—to their high soc-ed classified jobs. These were the lucky classes, those who still had work.

Once the trains had passed, we dropped down onto the tracks. Everything looked different in daylight. I could feel the warmth from the sun, in the rails, through the soles of my brogues.

We reached the entrance to the catacombs, adjacent to the rail track. Inside, the catacombs were chilly, the drip of limestone-infused water making occasional splashes as we walked. The Melody—there it was. Almost deafening but menacing, my mind drug to keep me in line. I also sensed a preternatural foreclosure. This was to be the end, the closure of this chapter of things, at least. My career, maybe. But then again, a career could be overrated. I heard the celestial voices, the singing somehow even brighter than before.

This time, as we approached the temple of the Dark Court, something was different. I listened—there was scraping, metallic feet on the stone ground.

"They have sentries," I said. "Security droids." Just before the main chamber branched off toward the large metal door, I made out the menacing figures. "Kill the flashlight. They're packing sidearms," I whispered.

As we moved closer, I could see these were mean-looking private security units, with arm-mounted coil rifles, heavy-duty grenade launchers. Pistols were the least of our problems.

The drip of water from above punctuated the silence. We were in darkness, only a faint glow emanated from their eyeline slit apertures.

"The Dark Court is well funded," Kace whispered.

"They should be. Funded by financiers, wealthy senators, and big-tech CEOs. You're about to meet some of the world's most influential people."

"You know who they are?"

"Based on Interpol intel, we have reasons to believe the Dark Court comprises members of the world's elite." Kace looked startled. I smiled grimly. "Sounds far-fetched, doesn't it?"

Kace gave a quick, noncommittal shrug. "But why, what do they want?"

"I suspect we're about to find out."

I stood and walked slowly through the puddles of water toward the droids. They were in sentry mode. I glanced at the LS scanners on their head units, which were emitting stroboscopic pulses of light as they scanned their environs. We walked past undetected, hidden by my psychic cloak. I glanced back at Kace. He eyed them suspiciously. I gestured toward the metal door—it was wide open. The sound of a solemn dirge was echoing out of the underground chamber.

We moved toward the corridor that led to the large cavern we had visited twice before. This time, as we crossed the threshold, there was a pungent aroma in the air, a woody smell, floral notes with hints of spice. The dim glow of the LED lighting dappled the dank, chilly walls of the underground temple, mounted on metal struts in concentric semicircles running around the room.

Kace wrinkled his nose. "What's that?" he sniffed.

"Incense," I replied. The chanting and aroma made for a heady sensory combination.

"I feel strange."

"Giddy?" I asked. Kace dipped his head, pulling a face. I felt it too. The odor was intoxicating. I began to feel as if my energy were being sapped by the insistent sensory overload. The dirge-like chanting was now everywhere and was invading my mind, for a brief moment even overpowering the Melody inside my skull.

We reached the end of the corridor that connected the catacombs outside with the cavernous interior of the large chamber. The familiar seating lay below in a semicircle of descending stone banks; the chamber's high-domed stone ceiling loomed above us. As we stood, having paused in the uppermost aisle, I half expected to see a malign choir of death chanters. But the arena was empty save for some medical equipment adjacent to the stone altar at the bottom. And beside the altar was acoustic equipment—a large microphone on a stalked floor stand attached to a large metal box, on supporting legs, with switches and dials. The metal box included a battery power pack and a long cable, resembling an isolation booth ear-implant cord.

"That's new," Kace whispered, gesturing to the acoustic equipment.

And there in front of us, on the cave ceiling above the altar, was the same large motif—the lone sentinel on top of the watchtower, staring out. I now knew that this was not only the emblem for the Dark Court, but a representation of a Watcher. But this time, the figure's eyes were visibly brighter, as if the stone ceiling were burning, illuminated somehow from within. The sensation of the eyes following you seemed even stronger. I wondered who or what had created the engraving. What manner of strange sect?

"It looks like the stone in the eyes is on fire," Kace exclaimed. "How is that even possible?"

I closed my eyes and brushed my left hand against the damp wall. And there it was all at once, the rush of a new, strange emotional halo. I blinked my eyes open and peered through the dim lighting toward the motif of the Watcher engraved in the rocky ceiling. And yes, as my Eye had seen, I could make out a long, narrow fissure. I knew I'd found the crossing point Selaphiel had warned me would likely be here. I could feel it, even see thin beams of quintessence passing through, seeping out into our world from whatever lay through the fissure. I was certain this was the break in spacetime that connected this planet, in the Elyonim, with the parallel universe from whence the Watcher had come.

Behind us in the rocky wall, on the top aisle above the cavea, were the same large wooden double doors I had seen before. But now they were slightly ajar. And through the gap I made out a large room, with movement within.

"In here," I whispered to Kace. The doors were made of thick oak, with decorations and motifs on metal panels.

I peered through the narrow gap. This was the first time we had access to what lay behind the doors. I was taken aback by what I saw—it was a robing chamber. The room was lined with deep crimson couches encircling a large stone pillar that supported the ceiling. Inside were well over a dozen robed figures, faces occluded by dark cappa hoods of a velvet-like material dyed a deep malevolent indigo-black, attached to dark-colored habits, a few also draped with varying numbers of gold sashes.

The figures looked as if they were part of some arcane religious cult. Shadowed eyes peered out from the long hoods. Some of the robed figures sat on the cushioned seating in near stillness, as if in thrall to the strange, otherworldly chanting—save for the slightest inflected movements of their heads, hinting at the rhythm of the infectious aural reverb. Others were pacing in a circular motion, as if lost in the somber, primordial dirge, following in bizarre procession. These robed figures marched in slow circles around the stone pillar at the room's epicenter.

I realized that the chanting was coming from overhead

speakers dispersed throughout both the robing room and the larger chamber below us.

"A preponderance of chanting," I whispered.

"A superfluity," Kace replied.

I grimaced. "Dueling with collective nouns, are we?"

"A mass of chanting," he shot back.

"A lechery," I replied darkly.

As we looked in, the chant was increasing in intensity, becoming almost hypnotic. And the robed figures did appear to be in a quasi-trancelike state. Slowly, carefully, I pulled open the doors.

"Over there," I said, pointing to some unused robes hanging on a stone rail carved into one wall in the far corner of the room.

As the chant reached a crescendo, the seated robed figures began standing, as if a signal had been issued. They started assembling into a single-file procession, apparently in a prescribed order. I suspected, as the line formed, that the golden sashes denoted rank, their length and number seemingly indicating a hierarchy.

"I count eighteen," Kace whispered.

We moved toward the far end of the room and quickly donned robes of our own. The ceiling was low near the entrance but curved upward, forming a high, concave center illuminated by soft LED lighting, almost mesmerizing. I breathed in the cold underground air, now ripe with the incense that was seeping in through low-level vents dispersed at equal distances around the large circular room.

The eighteen robed figures were now aligned, looking ahead out of the oak-paneled doors, which had been opened by the robed leader of the procession, onto the temple below. I moved to the back of the line and Kace followed. I eased out of the psychic cloak, allowing our own figures, now disguised in robes, to become visible once more. I needed some respite. The cloying mix of chanting and incense was beginning to make me feel slightly drowsy, enervated.

The figures began filing out. The surreal procession began. The adjudicators descended the stone-banked arena, moving almost robotically into what were clearly preassigned seats. The ones with the gold sashes—the higher ranks, I assumed—sat low down, within touching distance of the stone altar. We followed at the back of the snake, as the procession broke off into lines of banked seating at different points down the descending chamber. We remained high up, sitting to the left-hand side at the top. I saw that three robed figures were already present, down in the arena, facing us all.

The first figure was sitting on the high wooden seat—which resembled a throne—behind and to the left of the stone altar as we looked on. That adjudicator was a large figure; male, from the outline. To the other side of the altar, to our right, stood another, smaller robed figure. And in a slightly more darkened area, immediately behind the lectern, stood the third robed figure. I could spy a large book resting on the lectern, open, with edges and binding decorated in a gold-colored material, glinting in the dim light.

To my horror, on the stone altar there now lay a person—one of the human Unskill test subjects from the underground medical center, beneath the chamber. A woman. She lay on the stone in the same white medical gown. A medical cap had been placed across her scalp. She was hooked up to a life-support system, tubes and a catheter dangling from the robotic diagnostic unit adjacent to her, connected to a valve into her heart underneath her medical shroud. She lay supine, exhibiting periodic convulsions, her twitches creating ripples in the fabric of her tunic.

It was then that I became aware of the genesis of the chanting—the robed figure on the seated throne down in the arena. That was the High Adjudicator—it had to be. He was the one chanting! And his amplified menace was penetrating the stone chamber, the reverb of the hypnotic sound promoted through an auditory system, picked up from an unseen microphone, creating a surreal echo.

"I bet that one, seated, is the mysterious Bastien Cardinale," I whispered to Kace.

The chanting subsided. The robed adjudicator standing to the right of the altar moved forward, facing out to address the seated throng.

"Welcome, adjudicators," a female voice called out.

I froze. That was a voice I knew, a pitchy voice. *Her* voice. I gasped. Kace looked at me, shaking his head in disbelief. He recognized the voice, too. It was the voice of Michèle Lejeune—UN Assistant Secretary-General Lejeune.

CHAPTER 40

Lejeune began addressing the congregation of adjudicators seated before her. "Throughout history, the Lateran and the Cancelleria Chapters, together governed by one High Adjudicator, have continuously served the command of the Grigori. Awaiting the revelation of transcendence, the destiny of the worthy. And the final cleansing, the destiny of the lost." Lejeune's voice echoed eerily around the large stone chamber now that the chanting had ceased.

I glanced at the surreal shapes of the robed and hooded figures as they genuflected in place, on the stone seats. These would all be members of the highest soc-ed class, all elite Superiors. And they counted an Assistant Secretary-General from the United Nations among them.

"And of all the brethren vessels that came before us, over the course of the long wait, the honor falls to us, the twenty adjudicators of the Lateran Chapter, to lead the worthy to a higher state. We are the elite of the elite. We are truly blessed, and truly worthy."

Lejeune paused. I glanced at Kace, seated beside me; his hands were trembling as he held them in the lap of his dark disguise.

Lejeune started speaking again. "The Social Cleansing program has been disrupted. But it matters not, for the Grigori have communicated to the High Adjudicator that the skeletal editing program is now ready in the other place, the dark place. And with it comes a new method of cleansing which we test today." The chamber was suddenly filled with echoing clapping as the seated figures applauded Lejeune's words. "You are here because the world is overpopulated," she continued. "You are here because your economies are creaking under the weight of paying for the useless eaters, those who do nothing. Can do nothing. You are here because you have the purest mental hygiene. Intelligence is fixed and inherited. We are the special ones. Our lines are special. And that gives us the right to decide—a moral responsibility. The world needs cleansing. And our place, as the worthiest, is to be pure vessels for the Grigori."

No sooner had she uttered the words than the throng of seated adjudicators stood as one. Kace and I sprang to our feet, too, to avoid detection. In unison, the hooded figures began reciting.

"Cleanse! Cleanse! Cleanse!"

The chanting increased in intensity and speed, developing into a crescendo, a wall of sound. Until finally, the man seated on the throne down at the front raised one hand. The adjudicators sat once more and fell silent, as Lejeune continued.

"But our main purpose, today, is the crossing ceremony," she cried out, glancing up at the glowing eyes of the Watcher's motif on the curved stone ceiling high above her. "And Adjudicator Five has the honor of crossing, to become an agent of the Grigori, a vessel through ensoulment." Lejeune glanced at the hooded figure standing behind the lectern, below to our left. "Five will achieve transcendence and return to cleanse, the first noble subject of the skeletal editing program."

Kace glanced at me, concerned. He gently touched my arm. I was concerned, too. Where was this going?

Lejeune continued ominously. "And the world will be forever changed, reborn. Free of lives not worthy of life."

"This really is meant to be a temple of death," I whispered.

With Lejeune's closing remarks, the adjudicators began a new chant.

"Cleanse the useless eaters! Cleanse the useless eaters! Cleanse the useless eaters!"

One by one, they stood. Kace and I stood, too. And there it was, a murder of adjudicators baying for death, for mass genocide on a scale that would surpass in horror the worst atrocities in human history.

Lejeune looked around the auditorium, glowing at the cacophony of approval, the baying chant of these self-appointed adjudicators. After a minute, she slowly raised one hand.

"Friends," she called out. "Fellow travelers." The chanting gradually ceased, while the robed figures sat. "I give you the High Adjudicator."

Cheering and the stamping of feet erupted around the cavea. This was an unholy sect. I felt only dread and rank evil.

The large, hooded man stood up slowly from the wooden throne. His silhouette, his gait, was strangely familiar. He walked past the altar toward Lejeune and gave her a brief, clumsy hug. His large shape towered over her. She moved back, while he glanced down at the supine figure of the woman on the stone altar. He then moved forward to the front of the arena, to address the auditorium.

"Friends, brethren," he began. A bolt seared through me as I heard the lisp of the man I hated more than anything in the world. This was him—the Monster. *The Monster is the High Adjudicator!* I sucked in my cheeks in involuntary shock. I felt Kace's gaze upon me. He was taken aback too. I glanced around at the other adjudicators. In that case, which one would be Bastien Cardinale? *Maybe the one standing behind the lectern below, near the Monster and Lejeune*, I thought.

"We are gathered here today because we are under threat. Our way of life is under threat," the Monster began. "Resources are increasingly scarce, and employment is largely a thing of the past. You—we—are uniquely placed to judge, to adjudicate upon who, in such circumstances, has the right to life." As the Monster paused, clapping erupted once again. He raised his hands. "And to reaffirm your right, our right, as the fittest and smartest, as Superiors, to make decisions in the collective global interest," he concluded. The chanting from the adjudicators began anew.

"Cleanse! Cleanse! Cleanse!"

And then it hit me. The Dark Court, the ancient cult of the Brethren of the Sacred Vessels of the Grigori, or whatever they called themselves, was a front. The whole sect, which I now knew comprised two chapters, was being manipulated by a Watcher, hosted by the High Adjudicator. And that realization led me to wonder whether all previous High Adjudicators had hosted Watchers. The whoops of delight of the hooded adjudicators in the audience were sickening—they believed in the *cause*, the cleansing of so-called "useless eaters," the Unskills. But did they know they were being deceived by a Watcher? They probably had no inkling what was in store. They thought they were performing some act of perverse good, social cleansing, eradicating the lowest soc-ed classes. And that they would be rewarded with some higher state, transcendence, whatever that was. But they would only be spared to serve as empty vessels, as hosts to gaseous beings from the Chaos, stripped of their very souls.

Fleischman looked around at the hooded figures gathered before him in the dim light. As he glanced up, his rheumy eyes and sagging jowls were unmistakable. His gaze briefly rested on me as I withdrew into the dark silhouette of my indigo-black hood. The High Adjudicator held up his hand.

"It begins with this woman, our test, the initiation of the new procedure for cleansing," the Monster continued, gesturing down at the altar. "These are beings unworthy of life," he said. "They repulse me. They should repulse us all."

The woman was young, maybe mid-twenties. She was bound by medical webbing. The dim light was amplified by her rhythmic twitching, the reflected horror of the occasion rippling out from where she was fastened.

A male medic moved out of the shadows near the steps of the vomitorium, leading down to the medical chamber beneath this one. He inserted a cable into the supine woman's ear implant transceiver. He then connected it to a socket in the strange-looking device with the large microphone that was mounted below us, to one side of the altar.

"An experiment in infrasound, a new way to cleanse, a merciful killing," the Monster boomed out. His words were received with loud cheers.

"Now, my friends, my brethren, I need your assistance. I need the sublime power of your speech, to perform this inauguration."

"What's going on?" Kace whispered, tugging at my robe. "Infrasound?"

"Sound waves with a frequency below the lower limit of human hearing," I muttered, watching the scene in front of me as the medic below used his holotab to power up the box. The microphone began humming. "Infrasound traveling through air is harmless. Although …"

"Although, what?" Kace whispered back.

"Vibrations at that frequency can cause anything mechanical

to erupt, explode."

"Like what?" Kace asked.

"The language chip … synced to the ear implant. If infrasound is channeled directly to the ear implant …"

Kace's eyes bored into me. "A neat trick, bypassing the language chip's protective casing. Her brain will be irradiated."

I looked back down at the scene below, grimly, before glancing back at Kace.

"They don't need to create an EMF anymore …" I was about to add that this explained why the Dark Court no longer needed SkyLink. But then it struck me—how would this method of so-called cleansing work on a mass scale, if infrasound had to be physically channeled, via a cable, into the ear transceiver? But before I could ponder this conundrum further, the Monster began speaking again, his booming words from below drowning out my whispers.

"With our killing words, this will be the next step in our social cleansing program." He was now in the middle of the arena, parading menace, the young woman on the stone slab just a couple of meters from him. This was the most tragic and horrific metaphor of all. *Always the women*, I thought.

"Killing words," I whispered, glancing back at Kace. "That device looks like a sonic weapon."

CHAPTER 41

The entire auditorium of adjudicators stood. They began their chanting again, their morbid recital bouncing off the stone walls and ceiling in a near-deafening climax. The Monster raised his hands to silence them. Then he raised his hand slightly, in the direction of the medic—a signal. The medic issued a blink-command at his holotab, and the large microphone buzzed for an instant, before a green capacitor on one side flickered. The device was live. And as if they had been awaiting this very sign, the standing audience of adjudicators began chanting anew.

"Cleanse her! Cleanse her! Cleanse her!"

I scanned the figures nearby and below us, spread out in their foul rows. I glimpsed the snarled lips partially hidden in darkened hoods, along the banks of the cavea, as the adjudicators let out their baying cry in unison. There was initial feedback from the large microphone below, a sharp boom of crackled reverb, before the device settled as it picked up the sound, directing it into the large box. I guessed this would convert the sound into a silent weapon, before channeling it into the prone woman's language chip via her ear implant.

The woman on the stone altar began to writhe, arching her back. I twitched; I felt I had to do something. As I was about to stand, to spring into action, Kace lightly touched me, shaking his head.

"There's nothing you can do for her now," he whispered. "And we can't give ourselves away."

I let out a growl of frustration, drowned out by the chanting around us. And with one final, hideous convulsion the woman slumped back onto the stone slab. Still, finally. The adjudicators fell silent, while the Monster looked expectantly at the medic. He pored over vital functioning diagnostics on the medical console attached to the woman. The medic gave the slightest of affirmative nods. With that, the Monster raised his arms aloft and let out a roar. I almost jumped out of my skin as the entire auditorium of adjudicators followed suit. It struck me that all the roars from the banked seating sounded male.

As the din died down, the Monster signaled for the adjudicators to retake their stone seats.

"But now, the most important part of our ceremony today. The crossing. Crossing ceremonies are rare. Most of you, our newer adjudicators, were not present at the last one, a crossing to this planet from the dark place, in the southern temple over forty years ago. Today, Adjudicator Five is honored at having been selected to serve as the living vessel to cross to the dark place from this temple, and will soon return during a new crossing at the southern temple. And thanks to the Grigori skeletal editing program, Five will have the biological means to deliver the killing words. To cleanse the entire planet."

"What's going on?" Kace asked.

I shrugged slowly. "Beats me."

The Monster stepped back, returning to his seat in the large throne-like chair at the rear of the stage area. The third of the three robed figures, facing us from below, moved forward slightly now standing immediately behind the lectern. *Adjudicator Five?*

I wondered. *Is this Bastien Cardinale, finally?* He was standing directly over the opened book resting on the lectern. *Are we about to finally hear what he sounds like?* The robed figure began reciting from the text:

"The multitude shall suffer death without redemption in the burning lake of fire, the destiny of the lost. The worthy shall be granted immortal life, with their sacred burden. And with the gift of everlasting life from the Mashiach, the host will smite the false prophet who manifests as the Sage." As the words were uttered, the seated congregation repeated the lines in a solemn chant, as if they represented some form of well-worn catechism.

But I jumped in my seat, and nearly fell to the ground. Kace turned toward me in surprise, grabbing my arm, to prevent me drawing attention to us.

"What is it?" Kace hissed in alarm. But I couldn't speak immediately. I could barely believe it. This new shock was overwhelming. The robed figure below us, reciting from the book, was someone I knew. The mellifluous baritone was unmistakable—it was Clyde.

I pulled myself together. "That's my therapist," I gasped.

Clyde turned some pages in the large, ornately decorated book on the lectern, and began reciting again:

"I offer my body to the Grigori, as a sacred vessel, to cross to the dark place beyond, and to return transcendent walking in flesh and blood. I give my solemn oath to serve my ensouled master."

And with that, the onlooking adjudicators threw back their hoods, roaring in unison:

"Serve! Serve! Serve!"

As all the hoods around us came down, I gasped. The Union's High Representative, the United Federation's majority leader of Congress, the President of the Unified Korean Republic, the

CEO of Tele3—even the UFA Secretary of State. Kace glanced at me, unsure what to do. I knew what he was thinking: *Should we remove our hoods too?* But then we would reveal ourselves. I threw him a slight shake of my head. We remained the sole hooded members of the audience.

The Monster stood, and he too threw back his hood, followed by Lejeune and finally Clyde. The Monster moved toward Clyde and hugged him, before turning to the audience.

"And now the oath is pledged, we come into the light …"

Just as he uttered these final words, Fleischman froze and gazed directly at Kace and me before holding up his hand again for silence.

"We have guests," he bellowed ominously. "Unwelcome guests." The others turned toward us, surprise and alarm spreading over their faces.

The Monster walked slowly, menacingly, up a stairway on the far side of the cavea, adjacent to us. He climbed the stone steps laboriously until he was next to Kace, who was sitting at the end of the aisle. As Fleischman looked down, Kace jumped up to face him, anger spreading over his features; anger at what he knew the Monster had done to me. Fleischman grabbed his arm. With his other hand, the Monster pulled back Kace's hood, revealing his face, while the entire auditorium looked on in amazed silence.

"A usurper. A medic, Kace Westwood," Fleischman shouted out. "I should have known. And that must mean that you are …"

With that, I too stood, flinging back my hood. I would not allow his clammy hands to be placed on me ever again.

"I am Lilith Errapel King," I bellowed directly toward his face as he looked at me, on the other side of Kace, before glancing round the room. "And this ends here and now."

As I surveyed the shock of the other adjudicators below us, I was jolted by a rumble of laughter, vicious laughter. It was Fleischman. His face was screwed up in tight, monstrous cackling. He opened his eyes wide and looked directly at me before addressing the entire chamber.

"A so-called famous detective. You've heard of her? Well, I can tell you, she gave herself to me. This one is nothing more than a whore." He spat out the final word with such malice that it nearly stopped my heart.

With that, Kace's look of anger turned to raw hatred. He pushed against the Monster's chest with his free arm while twisting his body, managing to escape Fleischman's grip. He then threw a sharp punch at the vile Monster, which glanced the side of Fleischman's face. The Monster stepped back momentarily, taken aback by the blow, before breaking into a smile.

"Is that the best you've got?" the Monster lisped. With that he grabbed both of Kace's arms this time, pinning them back against the sides of Kace's body—I was surprised at how strong the Monster was, perhaps aided by his inner occupant. Kace struggled anew, but the Monster held his arms fast.

Fleischman smirked at Kace before addressing me, his lips curling with the viciousness of his words as he spoke. "You are right about one thing. This does end here and now. For you. Your final lesson," the Monster roared, studying the spectrum of emotions flickering across my face as I stood motionless.

But the mistake the Monster made was in taking my seeming inaction as a signal of apparent impotence. In that moment, it felt as if a hundred thoughts, feelings, and impulses raced through my mind. But in the midst of it all, I was assessing each potential response to our predicament, calculating its merits, attempting to spot weaknesses as I determined what my move would be.

Amid the emotional maelstrom, in the eye of the mental storm, I felt stillness and calm.

Then, I acted, in a blur of motion. I stepped across and past Kace, laying my hand on the Monster. My Eye could see—I was strong, stronger than ever. There it was—the familiar rush, always the same but always so different; each individual's life choices, experiences.

And as the Monster felt my Eye penetrate him, I sensed the recoiling of the Monster's long-lived inhabitant. Fleischman himself spun around, glancing at the etched figure in the ceiling above us. I experienced the stab of a second emotional halo, not from the Monster, but from the Watcher itself, the dreadful pain of an ancient being.

Unlike years before, Fleischman was unable to block me; his body's secret dweller had been taken by surprise. My Eye penetrated its defenses. Now I was on top. I saw its pain, its fear, its raw hatred even. I felt the anguish of a threshing, a screaming, as a soul was stripped from its soma and exiled through a portal to a new place, to the Chaos, where everything burned, everything was being ripped apart into a million pieces by physical forces of unimaginable power.

But now I could burn him, the Monster—Fleischman. I twisted him back around and looked straight into his eyes. I saw his shock, suddenly, as the recoiling of the Watcher became a separation. A dark, misty presence evacuated the Monster's body, spiraling slowly out of his mouth, now wide open, finally vacating its long-time mortal chamber.

I heard gasps from around the chamber. Kace and the other adjudicators were watching in transfixed horror as a lithe stream of dark mist slithered up into the air above us, rippling under the high ceiling of the chamber.

And in that moment—as I rained down my fire, my inner scream of vengeance on Fleischman's body, my hand scorching him, purging his flesh of everything I hated—a second body of mist evacuated Fleischman. It followed the first through his still wide-open mouth. I paused, taken aback, stepping backward. This second dark presence was even larger, a greater gaseous expanse. It spiraled up, occupying a larger area beneath the domed ceiling, directly in front of the etched motif of the Watcher on the wall, eyes staring out at all it beheld. The Monster had been host to not one, but two Watchers.

As the two dark, misty shapes rippled, I realized they were moving toward the long, narrow fissure in the stone ceiling that I had seen earlier. The two bodies of darkness were shifting in degrees of blackness as the tendrils of dark mist that made up the gaseous beings eddied and flowed above me.

As I watched on, two dark, misty hands reached out from above, one from each form. The tendril-like hands stretched out and snatched Kace by his arms, holding him fast. And in that instant, the two gaseous forms began a surreal vibration. The original chant was back, growing in intensity as the mist-like shapes writhed, beginning to spin in perfect synchronicity, with Kace attached to and held by each. And as the centrifugal spinning gathered pace, it moved up into the fissure in the ceiling, beginning to fade from view. And Kace, he was also fading.

I moved away from Fleischman, releasing him—I had already burned at least a decade. I lunged toward Kace as he was being taken away from me, to grab him and pull him back. But as I reached out, my hand passed through him. His form was wispy. He glanced at me, a look of shocked surprise on his face, then down at his thinning body. And just like that, Kace vanished through the fissure into vaporous nothingness, along with the phantoms that clung to him.

As I gazed at the fissure in the ceiling, through which the Watchers and Kace had disappeared, there was an anguished cry from down below.

"No …" Clyde wailed. "That should have been me."

CHAPTER 42

As I stared up into the empty space that Kace had just occupied, and occupied no more, I felt numb shock at first. Which then turned to righteous anger. And then burning rage; the rage that would gut a volcano. As I turned to face the Monster, he retreated from me. He stumbled, suddenly unsure of his footing. He had aged. He had been aged by me. He now resembled a man well into his seventies. He wore the frightened look of someone suddenly presented with a newly emerged apparition.

There was a changed gauntness to his appearance; the pride and bombast had been peeled away, and he was now undefended. He knew it. I could, for the first time, see something akin to fear in his eyes. At least a prelude to fear. At what I had done to him. And swelling panic at what I could do. He backed away at the top of the banked seating, along the aisle toward the wooden doors of the robing room.

Panic also spread through the adjudicators. They began moving down the stone-banked aisles toward the arena, then down the steps of the vomitorium, away from me as I stood above, near the top. They sidled away slowly at first, before starting to run, fleeing past the stone altar and the hapless victim of their cruelty still strapped to it. Clyde and Lejeune turned and ran too, following the other adjudicators down. But that way led to a cul-de-sac. Down there lay only the subterranean store of half-alive Unskills, preserved on life support in their glass capsules.

Meanwhile, the Monster continued moving away from me with wary twitchiness at the top of the cavea, toward the corridor that led out into the catacombs. The aroma of incense had dissipated. The chamber slowly fell silent as the final few adjudicators fled down the stone stairs, going farther underground in what I knew to be a doomed retreat.

"Guards," the Monster called out. His voice was a croak, the weakness of an infirm old man.

The sound surprised even him. He glanced at me again. I heard the thud of the two sentinel droids' metallic footsteps moving into the corridor, summoned by his voice command. They came into view, emerging from the passageway connecting us to the exterior catacombs. The Monster continued to back away from me until he was safely behind them.

And now I had a decision to make. I longed to finish him off—once and for all. The revenge I ached for; a dish best served cold for all he had done to me. I was crippled inside by what he had made me. But I also wanted to save the innocents below, housed in the medical capsules, victims of a cruel experiment. I knew I still could. I was momentarily snared by indecision as I sensed I had reached an existential inflection point.

I wanted to lunge at Fleischman, to burn his life away from him, peeling it off his rotten body. But the Unskills! And Lejeune and the other adjudicators, cowering down the steps beneath me, now unseen—I needed to deal with them too.

As I paused, wracked by indecision, Fleischman moved out of view. I could still hear the heavy rasp of his breathing echoing eerily along the stone corridor that led out of the large chamber, the gasping rattle in his throat, the quasi-fear he now felt. I heard his echoing shuffling, stumbling, knocking against the heavy metal door. After I had lost sight of him, the droids followed, monitoring me as they too backed away in silent departure.

Finally, I acted. I turned and headed quickly down, toward the arena. I walked with fiery purpose down the stone steps and then along the corridor that led to what the Phoenix medics had branded the clinic. Rage was upon me, flames engulfing my heart. Once through the steel door under the temple chamber, I pressed it closed. I shut my eyes until I heard the click of the lock as I channeled quintessence, before using radiant energy to slide the bolt into the door's frame, locking it fast.

Lejeune was there, standing in front of me as I entered, her mouth agape. The other adjudicators were either cowering or hiding. I spotted Clyde, a diminished figure, partially hidden beyond the cone in the center of the concentric rows of capsules, farther back in the large chamber. Lejeune's eyes were struck with horror. She was either not that smart, or she really had no plan whatsoever. She had apparently made no attempt to hide.

As I marched toward Lejeune, she was framed by the hideous spectacle of the rows of glass capsules behind her, containing their inmates still hooked to enforced life support within, stripped of the last vestiges of humanity. My rage and loss rendered me, for a moment, blind to everything. No mercy or remorse; I was possessed by a red mist descending before my eyes. I wanted to wreak justice. Someone needed to pay. It felt as if death was in my pocket, death was at my back, death would soon be all around me.

"It's not what you think," Lejeune shrieked as I zeroed in on her.

"You were sworn to protect," I yelled. "To protect!"

"Life unworthy of life," she muttered.

Now my rage was all-consuming. The descent of crazed passion was overwhelming, rendering me giddy with my own power and hate, the hate that made me powerful. It obscured reason; it lent my fiery anger the clamor of dizzying madness. Somewhere amid the powerful sensations that ripped through me, I achieved a moment of transitory lucidity. I realized suddenly what a fine line lay between rage and insanity.

I grabbed Lejeune by her throat. But as my Eye saw her, the emotional halo surprised me even more. I released her in startled shock. The woman, now wretched and afraid, fell to the floor, tangled up in her ridiculous oversized robe.

"You're an Unskill?" I exclaimed, both perplexed and amazed.

She was half lying, half kneeling, peering up at me, her cappa and dark habit oddly skewed, the fabric twisted around her as, in her desperation, she flailed on the floor, attempting to flee. Her eyes widened in surprise, taken aback. Not at the revelation, I saw that. But that I knew.

"My parents," she cried out in a faltering voice. "They were rich, part of the Union elite in Brussels. It was too much shame to bear, my job certification."

"They bribed an official in the Magisterium," I whispered, incredulous at what my Eye had seen.

I wondered how she'd even managed, with her IQ level, to pretend all these years; I imagined the stress she must have felt trying to survive at this level, not even a higher soc-ed, a Professional or an Executive. But at the rarefied level, wholly out of her depth.

"The Union's database was amended. I was certified as Superior."

"Then why?" I asked. I heard a voice that sounded like a wild demon reverberating around the underground chamber, echoing off the fronts of the glass cells. I realized the voice was mine.

"Why did you do it? Why this?" I asked, gesturing around us, at the cells behind her, the physical manifestation of her crazed subscription to a slogan, life unworthy of life, when she was one of those very creatures that her slogan sought to rob of life.

"Why?" she whispered, shaking her head in incomprehension.

"You're one of them!" I continued, screaming in almost deranged accusation.

"I could have only risen so far. My parents had big plans and ambitions for me. My life has been a lie."

"So someone had to pay?" I asked. "You hate them, because they remind you of yourself, is that it?" I knew that was it, as any psychologist would confirm. People often despised others who had the same characteristics as them, if they loathed those characteristics in themselves. Lejeune was attempting to extinguish others, Unskills, who shared the same traits as her, so that she wouldn't be confronted with what she despised most about herself. Lejeune glared up at me, her thin lips puckered and cruel.

"They all had to pay." She spat the words, resentment and anger suddenly illuminating her face. The old, barbed steel was back. Now, as I watched her attempting to writhe away from me, I felt only disgust and pity.

"I am here to judge …" I began, before pausing. I was calmer now. *But who will judge me?* I wondered, with sudden lucidity. *Am I so pure in thought and deed that I really can be judge, jury, and executioner? Do I want the lives of Lejeune and the others here on my conscience? Do I really have that right?*

As the tumult of thoughts ricocheted around my mind, my conversation with Selaphiel came back to me. The creature had announced that matters of life and death, of killing, were akin to a category error, a constraint imposed by mortality, of human thinking. But I knew I was at least half human. And as I gazed with pity and contempt at Lejeune, I caught a glimpse of movement behind her, in the enclosed glass capsules. The Unksills—they were no longer catatonic! Kace and I had done it, destroying SkyLink. These Unskills had slept, and some at least had survived.

And with that I realized I was here to save, not to wreak further death. I would choose to be a savior, not an executioner. With that, I willed away the rage that was still there within me, banging around inside my head like a relentless, resounding drum of war. I mentally stepped back, in my mind's eye, out of the red mist, back into the light of righteous justice, unblemished by the heat of rage.

Lejeune, Clyde, and the others, they would remain locked in, prisoners in this chamber, until I could summon agents from Interpol to escort them away. They would answer for their crimes in a court presided over by their peers or, depending on their luck, by lower soc-ed classes. Meanwhile, I would attend to the Unskills, establish how many had survived.

I walked with purpose to the outer concentric row of glass medical capsules. The same green light from within surrounded each Unskill in a strange, unnatural halo. I began at one end of the row, from where I had spotted movement. Inside the first glass capsule was a man. He looked young, gaunt, a confused expression flickering across his face as he gazed out. As he saw me, he began banging feebly on the inside of the glass.

The console lights on the black frontage, beneath the glass door, blinked at me. There was a voice command port. But I didn't have the authorization to release the glass door. I pressed my hand on the glass surface and sensed the quiet puffing of the patient's ventilator from within, which had been sustaining the Unskill's life while he remained unconscious, now required no more. I refused to allow any of those remaining alive to die. They would all walk out of here.

I took a breath. This one, here—he would be the first I would save.

"To be repaid at the resurrection of the righteous," I said aloud, solemnly, unsure what had inspired me to utter the words. I channeled quintessence, releasing radiant energy into the VirDa display on the console. There was a soft click and the glass front popped open. I pressed my fingers under the lower part of the glass front and pulled on the edge that was now ajar. The front lifted up, until the glass door was raised above the top of the capsule, exposing the Unskill inside.

He blinked at me as I peered into his face. He was secured with webbing on a medical support raised to near vertical position. Tubes connected him, under his tunic, to a medical console inside the capsule, with sensors attached to his arms, chest and forehead. I carefully reached inside his tunic and slowly eased out the needles connected to his heart valve. I then transposed some burned time to create healing energy to seal the wound, as I withdrew the slender hollow silicon probes. Then I removed the webbing and the sensors.

"Can you walk?" I asked softly.

"I think so," he replied.

He stepped out gingerly, hooking his legs over the black base of the capsule as he stood on the rocky ground of the chamber. As he supported himself, upright, on the exterior of the capsule that had imprisoned him, I threw him a smile.

"Welcome back! Wait here, I'll free the others."

I glanced back as he slid into a sitting position, watching me with fatigued curiosity. I moved along the row of capsules. Inside were other Unskills, having emerged or emerging from their catatonic stupor. I released each in turn. They sat against their capsules as I continued my work.

Finally, I reached the epicenter. Clyde was crouching on his haunches against the cone, no longer vibrating, in the very center. His face was creased, his brows lined with worry.

He gulped as I approached. "I know what you must think … Lilith."

I raised my hand, demanding silence. "Don't you dare utter my name," I growled. "I'm not here for you. You will answer for what you have done." The game was up. At least, this iteration of whatever it was that the Dark Court was planning.

I moved with renewed purpose around the inner concentric row. But when I reached the last capsule, and had it open, the woman inside wasn't yet awake. Her DigID identifiers showed her name to be Eve Class DeBorne.

"Eve," I whispered. Her eyes remained closed fast. I touched her brow with my fingertips, attempting to see into her. I could feel the absence, the hollowness, the shell of life, consciousness almost evaporated. There was severe damage to the thalamus. She was beyond help—conventional help, at least. I knew I would have to concentrate. Repair the cells, feel my way in. I closed my eyes anew and opened my one channel of true vision, my Eye. And I set to work, expressing the energy I had burned from Fleischman, energy I had burned but not fully consumed. I targeted it, providing regrowth to the nerve cells that had died, that had been murdered, that rendered this so-called Unskill's life unworthy of life when, in my ministry, only the unblessed were truly blessed.

I spent nearly ten minutes rebuilding the dead and damaged cells. I expressed a lot of energy. But I had learned. I sat back and watched, gasping for air, suddenly numb with the effort of concentration. The woman's eyes flickered open.

"Eve?" I asked again. She looked at me for a split second without comprehension. Then she gasped too. She glanced around. "That's your name, right?"

She blinked at me. "Where am I?"

"Alive," I replied. "You will be weak, and very tired. When I come back, we will all leave together. Okay?"

She gazed around in wonder. "I could use some sleep," she replied.

"That's a good sign," I said quietly. "Tonight, you will sleep in a proper bed. You have my word."

When my work was done, I crouched on the floor in the middle of the strange underground clinic. I was surrounded by the occasional sobs of adjudicators, shrouded in robes, the reliquary of hubris.

The white-clad figures were now all outside their cells, all except Eve. I helped her out, calling two others to support her. I gestured that they should follow. The faces of the Unskills thronging around me looked confused. There was hushed, whispered chatter.

"I am Lilith," I called out. They fell silent. "You are safe now. I will take you out of here."

I led and the crowd of Unskills followed behind. I unlocked the heavy metal door and ushered the Unskills out into the corridor, before locking the adjudicators inside, behind us. I then walked to the head of the group, leading them up the steps toward the temple chamber. And there, on the altar, was the same young Unskill woman, dead. The Unskills moved up and flanked me as we walked toward her. I touched her gently as we passed, in valedictory tribute. They touched her, too. I wasn't able to save this one. Suddenly, sorrow overwhelmed me.

CHAPTER 43

Three weeks later, as the world began to turn the corner on the Fatal Insomnia pandemic, I was finally able to come up for air. I had given myself thirty-six hours off—I was back at my apartment in Manhattan.

Like everyone else at Interpol and the WHO, I had worked around the clock, putting order back into things, resolving the suffering that the pandemic had caused. That had at least spared me time to dwell on the pain I felt at Kace's absence. For the second time, I had lost a man who mattered, taken from me way too soon. I felt immense sorrow when I thought of him.

We had all the adjudicators in custody from the Dark Court's Lateran Chapter—all twenty of them. Although not Fleischman, of course. And we had rounded up all the cultists we could identify, mainly Semiskill and Skill punks and wannabe anarchists. The search was now on for the second Dark Court chapter—although we had little to go on, so far.

Phoenix had been shut down, while a UN team was investigating its management and financial structure. And one of my first acts as the newly promoted Interpol Director was to assign a team of investigators to go over the Phoenix sites in Paris and Lyon with a fine-tooth comb. We also had a team of quantum engineers, geologists, and astrophysicists surveying the temple under the catacombs, trying to figure out what kind of alien phenomenon we were dealing with. Kace was listed as a missing person, and I hoped there would be sufficient clues to help me figure out how to locate him.

Up-skilling had resumed, although one controversial development was that Up-skilling centers were being rolled out across all Tier Three states. The rationale from the powers-that-be was that, as the Tier Three world underwent its own version of the automation agenda, the same problems of poverty and hardship that befell the automated world should not be their fate too. The world's big tech CEOs welcomed it with open arms—they had been clamoring for exactly this. There was a business incentive, of course: as Up-skilling in those states came with language chipping, this opened up new markets to western big tech. The prospect of yet more individuals giving up on language, becoming slaves to Universal Grammar tech, made me sick with dread.

There had been deaths from the insomnia pandemic. That had been inevitable, the ones we couldn't save, those I couldn't save. But for the majority of the Unskill populations across the Tier One and Tier Two nations, the symptoms had resolved themselves after the destruction of SkyLink. And Avie had made a full recovery too, as had Park's daughter. At least that brought me some measure of relief. *The human brain is a wondrous thing,* I reflected. Sleep was nature's balm. And for the majority of those affected, recovery, without too many complications, had been achieved.

After some well-deserved sleep of my own, I headed down to see Kaye and Avie—to celebrate Avie's return to health. I had promised Kaye we would make merry.

On my way down in the transit capsule, I received an incoming facecall alert. It was Park. I activated my holotab and issued an eye-blink command to accept the call. His face jumped to life on my translucent screen. He was positively beaming.

"Ah, Lilith, I just wanted to say thank you. Choon-Hee arrived home today, now well enough to be released." I smiled. "My wife … she is so happy."

"And you are too, I can tell," I replied.

"I am," Park said. "Thank you again for all you have done."

As I reached Kaye Wilbur's door, I could hear laughter inside. I paused for a moment, before alerting Kaye and Avie of my arrival, suddenly wistful. It would be churlish not to celebrate with them, despite my own sense of loss. At least today would be a welcome distraction before the next phase of my quest.

* * *

Twenty-four hours later I was in a hover car, gazing down on the Alpine landscape. I was finally able to take my aim at the Monster—I was hunting Fleischman. He was hiding somewhere in the Swiss Alps. I knew that much. As I flew toward Mürren, I issued my voice command.

"Kalpana Ng." My facecall app lit up on my holographic screen.

"Yes, Lilith," the app replied. I heard in my ear implant the faint echo of the holotab, shrill, ghoulish, distant, as the signals rebounded in the deep alpine crevices over which I was passing, searching for Fleischman's hideout.

Kal's burnished complexion filtered in on my holotab. Her dark brown twinkling eyes were the same as ever, her shoulder-length hair framing her delicate features. Now she could talk to me freely again. I was no longer on anyone's advisory list.

"Hello Lilith. Can I still call you that?" Her tone was hushed.

"Or do I now address you as Madame Director?" she asked mischievously.

"It's only temporary," I replied, laughing, shaking my head. Kal shook hers back at me.

"Of course it's not. Everyone knows they will make you permanent. It's only 'Acting' for now. The first female Head in Interpol's history. Now, that's something."

I shook my head again. "No, Kal," I said, suddenly deadly serious. "It really is temporary."

"You don't want it?" she asked, confused.

"It's not for me. I have other things to do."

Kal threw me a puzzled look. "I see the new Head of the UN's Counter-Cyberterrorism Command has issued a statement, formally thanking the guys in Geneva for the pandemic being over," she said, smirking. "Who knew the World Health Organization had such power?"

I smiled back at her. "Failure is an orphan, but success has a hundred fathers."

Kal laughed. "Or mothers," she whispered.

"So true."

"But we know," Kal added, still quietly. The official story was that the Fatal Insomnia pandemic was caused by a coding error arising in the Phoenix gaming app, which resulted in a malfunction of language chips. The game had been taken off the market. The powers-that-be didn't want to cause global panic, didn't want to reveal that there had been a global conspiracy to euthanize a large chunk of the world's population by a shadowy Doomsday cult that was in some way connected to aliens. For now, the Tier One's military agencies were on red alert, and the three major Space Force agencies, attached to the Union, the United Federation, and the Chinese state were searching for signs of first contact, and an alien invasion.

I was silent for a moment. "The device we found in the Dark Court temple; it's confirmed. It *was* a sonic cannon."

"How does that work?" Kal asked.

"It converts human speech into inaudible low-frequency sound. A sophisticated subwoofer system, using a variable-frequency sine wave oscillator. Streaming high decibel volumes of infrasound to the ear implant. As soon as it's picked up by a language chip, well, it explodes. Instant death."

"Horrible," Kal muttered. "You know that the effects of infrasound are sometimes confused with the supernatural, right? My grandma used to claim that the organ pipes in her church gave her visions, caused by spiritual forces. She really believed that, bless."

"Talking of mysterious forces, you know, they want to run tests on me," I whispered, changing the subject. Kal's eyes widened.

"Who?"

"They claimed to be with a United Federation military agency. A clandestine astrobiology unit, from the Groom Lake research center in Nevada."

"What?" asked Kal. "The Federation's Space Force science guys?" I scowled. "What did they want?"

"What do you think? They want me to volunteer. They had their Chief Medical Officer interview me about three weeks ago, when I was still in Paris, following my annual eval. And she contacted me again yesterday, a bit too insistent."

"You refused?"

"Of course. I won't be anyone's lab rat. Besides, that would only be the beginning. They'd never let me out again!"

"You look tired," Kal said.

"But it's done. The one remaining UN treatment hub was closed yesterday. And I have just this final thing to do."

"You could have sent in a team, you know that. You don't need to do this yourself."

"No, Kal, this is the one thing I have to do myself. This one is personal. Then I'll be free."

Kal looked at me thoughtfully through the screen. "You never did explain your beef with Herr Fleischman. But whatever it is, you know, revenge never really sets us free. Even for someone as remarkable as you."

I sighed. Somehow, I sensed the truth in that.

"Speaking of, still no LS signal from him?" I asked.

Kal smiled. "Fleischman? So that's the only reason you called?" she asked, feigning hurt. I laughed again. It was good to talk to her. "You've already gotten all the data, all the locational stuff, LS rebound records. The mind-mapping is the best we could do. But his signal has vanished. Nothing for over two weeks."

"He'll have a Faraday cage rigged up."

"A what?" Kal asked.

I shook my head absently. "Isolation booth. Same thing. He's definitely here."

"In Switzerland?"

"Holed up above Mürren. I can feel it."

After ending the call, I gazed out through the hover car's window. After Interlaken, the vehicle passed over the glacial waters of Trümmelbach Falls, gushing through mountain crevices, and approached the Lauterbrunnen municipality R airspace. As the vehicle dropped down into the valley's airway, the three-hundred-meter-high Staubbach Falls came into view.

The vehicle began descending the municipality's visitor-designated VTOL corridor. Wisps of hazy mist drifted around the steep limestone precipices on each side of me. Water was pouring off the mountain edge, tipping into the valley below. As we dropped below the clouds of mist, I glimpsed other waterfalls stretching into the distance as the valley curved round out of sight. If there were a heaven, this would surely be it. Except I knew a devil dwelled here.

On the ground, a Lauterbrunnen tourist welcome unit greeted me. I had a room booked in a local hotel. It was late afternoon. The air was cooler here, in the valley. Just one night—that was all I needed.

After I checked in, I changed into warmer hiking gear. I packed a bag with ropes, pulleys, a harness, a climbing helmet, and boots that I would change into. I wouldn't need quintessence for this. As the afternoon sun began to wane, I set off for the high mountain village of Mürren.

There wasn't a VTOL corridor into Mürren. It could only be accessed by automated cable car across the Bernese alpine peaks. I walked through Lauterbrunnen as afternoon began to turn to early evening. It was an hour on foot to the end of the valley. At the cableway station, I clicked my wrist chip against the payment console and the metal entrance bars slid open. At this time of day, I was the only passenger. I rode the cableway to Grimmelwald. I gazed around at the stunning scenery on the second cableway that rose steeply toward the mountain village.

Behind, in the distance, I made out the snowy peaks of the Eiger and Jungfrau. Ahead, looming over Mürren, was Schilthorn mountain. At nearly three thousand meters high, it was the highest peak in the range, overlooking the Lauterbrunnen valley, now far below. The Monster had chosen a remarkable Swiss redoubt in which to hide from me.

I stepped out of the cableway station into the hover-car-free Mürren. It consisted of little more than three streets, and the whole village could be covered on foot in around fifteen minutes. The cableway station lay at one end of the village. There was a bench in the funicular station. I sat, opened my rucksack, and put on my mountain boots. I walked away from the hilltop restaurant and gift shop complex along a trail.

The view down into the Lauterbrunnen valley was breathtaking. The light was deep and rich; the early evening sun was beginning to cast long shadows across the limestone valley walls below. Shadowed silver clouds drifted above me, the consistency of threaded cotton wool. At this height, my breath was exhaled as white wisps.

When the summit complex had receded from view, I paused, crouching on the ground. I felt with my Eye that I was in the right place. I pulled out my ropes and pulleys. Ten meters below was a large grassy ledge that could only be accessed from above, just as I had anticipated—as I had foreseen. I took out metal rock pegs, a mallet, and the helmet. I secured the rope I had brought with an auto-locking pulley system to scale the steep overhang. Once everything was set, I rappelled down the rock face, swinging myself off as I jumped back and forth off the rock until I reached the grassy ledge.

The ledge jutted out about five meters from the rock face before plunging down toward Mürren below. As I touched down on the grass, I uncoupled the carabiner hooks and threw a psychic cloak over myself. I heard a familiar hum. Drones moved into view from below the ledge, before fanning out along the mountainside, scanning the terrain. But my presence was safely hidden from the Monster's surveillance detail.

I walked along the ledge. Partially occluded from view in a slight depression in the rock was a thick metal door. It was just where I had sensed it would be. Impossible to see from the ground below and highly inaccessible, this was the perfect hiding place. I closed my eyes and placed my hand against the door, feeling inside its metal interior with my Eye. It was made from galvanized steel. The locking system consisted of vertical deadbolts set into jambs drilled into the rock. I channeled spiraling beams of quintessence, emitting energy into the steel frame, unlocking it. I heard a soft click and opened my eyes. I pressed against the door, opening it slowly inward.

CHAPTER 44

Inside was a small, low-ceilinged vestibule, which opened into a large room adorned with indigo and purple rugs and a high rock ceiling. I was surprised by the luxurious nature of the place. A crystal chandelier cast a golden glow. The room boasted exquisite wooden furniture, a walnut desk, a large desk chair, a long cherry-wood dining table with high-backed chairs and a bench, and a low full-grain leather sofa. The walls were dressed with wooden paneling. On one side, there was a large bookcase filled with leather-bound books, physical books! I stood stationary, dumbfounded. This was one spectacular den. At the far end was a large corridor leading to further rooms.

Just then, I heard a noise. Someone was approaching—steps echoing on the stone floor of the connecting corridor. A shadow grew along one wall, before the shape of a man emerged. It was him—the Monster. He froze on the threshold as he saw me standing in the entry vestibule. In one hand he was carrying a tray holding a plate of sandwiches and a mug of something hot. In the other, he held a walking cane, which supported him. This wasn't the same man who had terrorized my waking dreams for the last twenty years.

His shocked visage slowly gave way to a look of grim acceptance. He continued walking into the room and hobbled to the table, where he set down the tray. He slowly shuffled away and dropped into an easy chair near the desk. I could hear his ragged, rasping breathing. He hooked the handle of the cane over the arm of the chair. Then the Monster sat back, as if catching his breath, his eyes averted. Slowly, he shifted his gaze, looking up at me.

"Hello, Lilith," the Monster whispered, his voice hoarse. "I wasn't sure who it would be."

Suddenly I felt strangely nervous, my head foggy. The moment I had waited for was finally upon me.

"But you were expecting someone?" I asked quietly.

"Eventually," he whispered. One of his eyes twitched closed and reopened. Not quite a wink, but irritating, nonetheless. His crude mouth leered at me. He had always tried to make me feel worthless. I felt like punching his face more than ever. I walked forward and peered down at him. "I thought I might have more time, though," he said with a resigned air.

"Quite a setup you have here," I whispered. My voice came out scratchy. "Secluded." I could feel my heart pounding.

"But you found me anyway," he replied.

"I did. You and I have unfinished business," I said, without expression.

Now he smirked as he watched me, despite his new-found decrepitude. "You know, there are more of us. You can't kill truth," he lisped at me, stroking his grubby chin, flecked with patchy gray stubble.

"Truth?" Now I was taken aback.

"The Brethren already has a new leader, in some ways apt, someone previously in the shadows. The High Adjudicator is dead and gone, long live the High Adjudicator. And glory to the Sacred Vessels of the Grigori."

"You're talking about the Dark Court?" I asked, staring at Fleischman. "That's finished." The Monster smirked, giving a quick shake of his head. I ignored him—he was still trying to rile me up. I wouldn't allow him to get under my skin any longer. "What happened to Kace? Where is he?" I demanded.

Fleischman stared at me grimly for a moment before replying. "He's a lucky one. He'll be a vessel now. The temple under Paris, that's how they leave us. Your pretty boy was the first one they've managed to take through. And he wasn't even an adjudicator. Must be special." My expression probably revealed my confusion; the Monster began chuckling.

"What do you mean, a vessel? Like you, with those things inside you?"

The Monster shook his head solemnly. "Not like that. Different. We have waited thousands of years for this, adjudicators before me, foretold in the Book of Destinies. Your precious Kace, he will return from the other way through—the southern temple. That's how they get here from the dark place. But he'll be transformed. He'll come to cleanse the world of all the worthless souls. And that, Lilith, is also the truth."

I blinked. "You're making no sense," I hissed.

"Skeletal editing. That's his fate, with some very special modifications. And then the Grigori will be coming for you. They know what you are, who you are."

"What are you talking about?"

The Monster leered at me. "You don't even know it yourself, do you? Your coming has been foretold. And once the Grigori have you, you will serve, the key to everlasting life."

I frowned. The Monster gave off a stale smell, a smell of being unwashed. He leaned back in his chair and puffed out his fleshy chest. I waited, but he didn't continue. Then I became angry. Yet more talk of me serving others, just like Selaphiel and the Sage.

"You're still making no sense," I spat at him.

He watched me from lowered eyes. I could see he was struggling for breath. "You know what your problem is?" he said, smirking.

I crossed my arms. "I'm sure you're about to tell me," I snapped back at him, defiantly.

"Your gender," he said, before chuckling quietly and then coughing. "You were born weak, inferior, despite the prophesy," he continued once the cough had subsided. I snorted in response; I couldn't help myself. "You don't believe me? Women's brains are about ten percent smaller than a man's, taking into account body size. Even your amygdala is smaller. You know what that is, right? The olive-sized bit of the temporal lobe which is responsible for emotion. Men are better at emotional-social behavior, despite the myth that women have all the empathy."

"Pseudo-science mumbo jumbo. Is that what you use to justify your actions, your behavior? You are somehow superior?"

The Monster's eyes suddenly widened. "Oh, but I am superior."

"I'm not talking about soc-ed classifications," I countered.

"Nor am I. It is the moral duty of those who are superior to make decisions on behalf of those who are inferior."

"You're kidding, right?" I asked contemptuously. "Is that really your justification for your attempt at mass genocide?"

The Monster rolled his eyes and looked up at me as if with pity. Then he sighed. "You have no imagination. You always lacked insight. It was an act of kindness," he said quietly.

"A plot to mass murder Unskills?" I was incredulous.

"Let me tell you a story," the Monster began. "When I was a boy—maybe seven, I don't remember now—I had a dog, a bitch. She had a litter of six pups." He held up one arm as if to inspect his hand. "But she wasn't producing enough milk." He paused, watching me. "And the litter, all the pups, they were getting weaker by the day. I knew they would all die. So I took action. I chose the smallest three pups and I placed them in a sack. Then I took them to a nearby stream, where I drowned them. Funny, how easily a creature renounces life. They didn't fight much. That surprised me." His voice petered out.

"What's your point?" I asked through gritted teeth.

The Monster stared at me for a moment before continuing. "The other three pups—well, they thrived. They had enough milk. The three that were sacrificed, that was a mercy killing, to ensure the survival of the fittest, the strongest."

I looked at the Monster, now with pity of my own. "There's nothing original about your story. Have you forgotten your criminal psychology 101? Or was that not taught back in your day? All psychopaths start out, as a rite of passage, with helpless animals, before moving on, most often to women. You think you are strong, a goddamn Superior. But you're nothing but a cliché." The Monster gaped at me before shaking his head. I don't think he knew how to respond. "I'm sure your parents were proud of you," I added sarcastically.

He tutted. "Not my mother. She was a weak woman, like you. No imagination, either. My father, he would educate her; he knew how to handle a woman for her own good. Spare the rod and spoil the woman, he would tell me. Sound advice. But she never learned. Women should know their place."

"He sounds like a charmer," I muttered sarcastically.

"I had the power to make the important decision."

"The power of life and death over other creatures? If that's what drives you, you're even more of a monster than I thought."

Fleischman looked at me, confused. "But it's my duty to make life-and-death decisions for others. It's my purpose. Perhaps even a form of love. I know what's best. I always have," he said quietly. His chest was wheezing. I glared at him, not knowing what to say. Tears of indignant rage began to trickle down my cheeks. "There, you see," he lisped. "I was right. You are weak."

I shook my head at him. "That pitiful amygdala you are so proud of, in your head—that's what makes *you* weak. Your lack of empathy. But this is my strength," I said fiercely, as I brushed away my tears.

The Monster studied me silently before he spoke again. "I'm glad."

"You're glad?" I asked, bemused.

"That the wait is over," he whispered in reply. "That was the hardest part. Waiting. Wondering when it would happen and who it would be."

"And if it had been someone else, what then?" I asked.

"They would have come to arrest me, take me in. But you— they sent you to end me."

"I sent myself." The Monster looked confused. "It may come as a shock, but you have been replaced by a woman. I head up Interpol now."

The Monster's eyes widened in surprise. "That can't be right," he whispered, tremors worrying at the corners of his mouth.

"I've been busy. But now you have my full attention."

The Monster glowered. He looked weary. He reached down by his side, opened a silver case on a small side table, and pulled out a cigar.

"Do you mind?" he asked, glancing at me.

"I will grant you that."

He cut the end and used the fire app on his holotab to light it. I watched the tendrils of smoke curl up and away from the end of the cigar. The smoke dissipated across the room. I coughed and turned my face away. Suddenly, I felt tired and world-weary. I had waited twenty years for this moment, to bring an end to the man now seated in front of me. I had spent years in therapy and endured dreams full of pitch blackness and sucked-backward traveling, drowning in water. Yet now, suddenly, I felt empty. It no longer seemed to matter—he was going to die anyway.

Kace's face floated before my mind's eye. Sorrow welled up in me again. The loss I felt, the pain at his absence, not knowing where he was, whether he was even still alive. I glanced back down at the Monster. Now I almost pitied him, sequestered away in fear, hiding in a windowless bunker in an alpine retreat, waiting for someone to come after him. But I had found him, nonetheless.

"You know, Lilith, history will understand what I did. Humanity has a divine spark within, available just to the few. Our cult has nurtured that, for thousands of years. Waiting for our final transformation. You cannot prevent it, it is inevitable."

"Nobody will remember you ever existed, I promise you that," I retorted with venom.

He smiled back at me, now with a mix of pity and disdain, as the tendrils of cigar smoke wafted around him. I had wanted him to repent as I crushed his skull, to beg for forgiveness as the realization hit him of his monstrous deeds, as I caused him paroxysms of agony, as he died. But now, I realized, I had been kidding myself. The Monster was mad, sick in the head. He believed what he had done was right. That we were all inferior. I had wondered whether it was being possessed by a Watcher that had led him to do what he did to me when I was twenty-three. But I now realized that was all him. He believed he could defile me because I really was unworthy, a woman, someone he could take and choose to do with as he pleased. I had wanted to exact revenge, my form of divine justice. But the man didn't get it. From his warped perspective of jinxed evil, he could do as he wished. And therefore had. The Monster had a god complex.

As the smoke dissipated, I could see that the Monster was holding a small pistol, pointing it at me. *Sneaky old bastard. Where had he gotten that from?*

"You don't really know much about me, do you?" the Monster said after studying me for a moment.

"What don't I know?"

"Even my alter ego is superior," he whispered. He watched my face.

I gasped. "You're Bastien Cardinale!"

"See, I can still surprise you." He began chuckling. I moved forward, now with menace. "One more step and you're dead," he said, sneering at me. "You can never win. I will always be too good for you."

I stopped and closed my eyes. My head bent as my heartbeat slowed. Now I could feel everything around me. I could once more feel the particles in the air; I could see inside the atoms that made up the furniture in the room and hear the pumping of the Monster's blood, diving down into the corpuscles that continued to give him life as the three major stress hormones, adrenaline, cortisol, and norepinephrine, washed through his bloodstream as his adrenal cortex attempted to create action—decisive action, as he made to pull the trigger.

But now, through conduction waves, I could transpose beams of quintessence into electromagnetic energy. And I could hurl it at a distance, across space, creating a psychic hand, invisible to the Monster. My psychic hand reached out across the space between us. And with a short, sharp snap, I wrenched the gun from his hand. As it flew into the air, I caught it. The Monster looked stunned.

"You were never better than me," I snarled at him through clenched teeth.

I looked at the pistol in my hand. It was an old-fashioned live-action weapon. It felt light, with a wooden handle and a silver barrel. I turned it over and inspected it. Embossed on the barrel were the words: *Ruger Made in USA*. No such country existed anymore. This was a collector's piece. But it still worked just fine. I could tell that much. Now I expressed energy into the weapon. It slowly began melting in my hand. The metal dripped onto the ground, while the wooden stock began to burn. I dropped that too onto the rug, where it lay in a pool of flickering flame before subsiding into a small pile of smoldering ashes.

"What are you?" the Monster whispered. Finally, he was truly afraid.

"Your worst nightmare," I replied coldly. "A woman who is not afraid of you. This is where your misogyny-meets-psychopathy ends."

"Are you going to kill me now?" the Monster asked quietly. A pool of yellow liquid slowly ebbed out from underneath his chair, widening in a circle on the stone floor before attaching itself to the edge of the rug. The Monster's new-found fear had skewered him.

I imagined moving forward and pressing my hand onto his chest. After all, I had come here to burn him, to take all his time. As I paused, still, having reached another inflection point, I imagined the Monster sensing his life being taken, drawn, sucked from him as nothingness beckoned. In my mind's eye, I watched as I burned the Monster, as the cigar rolled away from his swollen lips, down his slumped form, and onto the floor. It continued burning as it came to a stop in the pool of urine at his feet. I imagined the acrid odor of burnt fabric slowly drifting up into the air from the burnt handgun stock mingled with the acidic smell of a snuffed-out cigar.

I imagined moving my hand off the Monster's still chest and looking at the pale, puny fist that I held before my eyes. The hand of a small woman who could destroy with a single touch. I imagined the time I had burned from him, which would now be throbbing inside my skull. I imagined the way my heart would be beating—way too fast.

But in my mind's eye, I was still not at peace. Even after killing the Monster, there would be no resolution where I had expected it. No redemption where I had sought it. There could be no solace derived from following that path. And in that same moment, I knew as surely as I knew myself that this ultimate revenge would never slake the unquenchable anger that had made me, that I had to bear; my own cross, the anger that I had to find another way to control.

I looked at Fleischman—at Cardinale, whoever he was—now diminished, sitting in his own piss. I felt only disgust, even the pity had gone. The girl I had once been long ago, she longed for revenge, lusted after it. And even the woman she had become, she had come here to enact exactly this brutal form of justice. But it is the decisions we make that define us. Here and now, I was no longer the same person, no longer *that* person—I was changed somehow, not in terms of how I viewed Fleischman, but how I viewed myself. If I killed out of pure, unadulterated hatred, what would that make me? Nothing more than a monster myself. The same as Fleischman, *the* Monster. So instead, I resolved to do something else.

Fleischman's eyes were still upon me. He watched as I pulled on the elastic band that I wore under the cuff of my blouse.

Carefully, I rolled it off my wrist. I held it up, squeezing the malleable plastic between my fingers in silent remembrance. Then I dropped it, just like that. The reliquary of all my suffering. It fell silently onto his bloated chest, coming to rest in his lap. Fleischman's eyes stared at me in wonder.

"Now I'm free." That was it. The last thing I ever said to him.

I turned around, away from his wheezing, and walked back outside. I closed the metal door behind me, before using quintessence to seal it shut. Then I turned to face the steep alpine valley below me. The riot of green pasture from earlier was now, in the gloaming, an impression of outlines in motion, charcoal and dark silhouettes. I took a deep breath and felt my lungs fill with the crisp mountain air.

In the fading light, on a grassy ledge, high up above Mürren, I lay down and wept. Tears wracked me, cascading down my cheeks, pulling like sharp splinters in an explosion of relief, while my sobs fell in swirling, dissipating echoes down into the rising dark of the valley far below.

CHAPTER 45

The next day, I traveled to the French south, seeking another temple, the second crossing point that Fleischman had spoken of. The Monster had claimed this was the way back from the Chaos, a crossing through which Kace might return. And now that I focused on this idea, I sensed the influx of quintessence, drawing me here, to the place where my father was born. And so, I arrived in the foothills of the Massif Central, at Saint-Maximin-la-Sainte-Baume in Provence. A feeling! After all, that's what I did, feelings.

Saints, monarchs, pontiffs, clergy, even commoners, especially them. All had trodden the so-called *Chemin des Roys*—the Walk of Kings. The Order of Preachers, the Dominican monks, had been the guardians of the holy rock, the Sainte-Baume Grotto, for nearly a thousand years.

Today it was hot. July the twenty-second, Mary's feast day. Flutes, drums, old-fashioned live-action rifles, horses too, from the Camargue. Her skull and other relics were being paraded around the town. My grandmother. I followed.

As the afternoon wore on, I peeled away from the crowds, made up of seasoned partygoers and pilgrims alike, to head toward the mountainous Massif de la Sainte-Baume. Her writing spoke to me, the Gospel of Mary. Not one of the canonical gospels. Of course not. After all, it was written by a woman.

Before she was a saint, they spoke of a woman unworthy. She was a free-thinker, independently wealthy, a beautiful, sensual woman, and far more than a disciple. Of course, that was why Pope Gregory branded her a whore. I had been branded a whore too. There were worse insults. Men lacked imagination and variety. But Mary the muse, the confidante, the advisor. Mary the lover, the wife, the mother. There was no greater threat to the male hegemony. She rivalled Peter of Bethsaida, Peter the vacillator, Peter the Apostle. Peter who made the Church in his own image. Gender politics always resulted in subjugation through force and sex.

I took a hover cab from Saint-Maximin as far as the local airway went. I was deposited on a vertipad near a tacky-looking restaurant and hostelry managed by the Benedictine Sisters of the Sacred Heart of Montmartre. I laughed to myself, a hollow laugh. In her death, Mary had become a holy martyr to some trumped-up religious fantasy that none of my line would recognize. What a joke. My grandmother would be turning in her grave.

It was a ninety-minute hike through ancient forest. It was getting hotter as the afternoon wore on. I felt sweat trickling down my back and down my front, between my breasts. Mosquitos buzzed around my face as I attempted vainly to brush them away.

I paused and sat at a table outside the hostelry, ordering a soda. The Melody had been feeling increasingly strange, an uncanny weight that was pressing into me, a threat, a weapon even, one being used to coerce, to control me. Now it felt as unsettling as the Aura had once been. The singing was chant-like, rising and falling, alien motifs constructing weird and wonderful melodies, embroidering larger themes, sequenced, rearranged into an endless harmony of sound.

Refreshed by the drink, I felt better. As I stood to resume the journey to the grotto, I sensed I was being surveilled. Two men at a nearby table. One was listening to something, his head cocked slightly, the distinctive tell he was receiving an ear-implant call with instructions, maybe. Both sets of eyes had been fixed on me. And then both suddenly stiffened as they saw I had clocked them.

I tested my theory. I walked back into the woods in the wrong direction, away from the trail to the grotto. They stood too, and attempting to be casual, followed my new path—they *were* following me. And from their sharp suits, and the distinctive North American tailoring, they were most likely from a United Federation agency. Maybe they were even from the UFA Space Force.

I moved quickly through dense underwood, my heart rate elevated. I meandered, as casually as I could, off the beaten track until I sensed I had lost them. I wandered farther into dense forest and crouched down, waiting, listening just to be sure. Quite suddenly, I heard something—the snap of a branch underfoot. I started, upright, ready to move off quickly. Someone was nearby.

Just as I stood to full height, I felt a jolt in my torso, and a sharp stinging. I staggered momentarily. Coil weapons were always silent—no recoil and zero sound. I glanced down in disbelief at the large patch of crimson seeping through my blouse along my chest. *I've been shot!* I looked back up, scanning my surroundings—a dark-suited shape was visible through a gap in the trees around ten meters away.

I threw a psychic cloak over myself, running through the trees in momentary panic, until I sensed the shape was no longer following. By the time I paused to catch my breath, I was already feeling faint. I crouched down on the ground, leaning back against a tree trunk, unable to maintain the psychic camouflage any longer. Even breathing was becoming difficult.

I knew I should examine the wound, check how serious it was, attempt to heal myself. I began fumbling at the blouse buttons, attempting a better look. After a moment, I had managed to pull back a flap of now red-sodden material—a coil round had passed clean through my upper left chest, leaving behind a neat incision. Blood was gurgling out of the wound, streaming in rivulets between my breasts each time I moved. And I heard my own breath come in rasps—I knew I was suffering from pneumothorax; my left lung had collapsed. I sank fully down on the ground, trying not to make any further movements. I had already lost a fair amount of blood.

I tried to summon the will, the energy I knew I needed, to heal the wound. But I was almost too far gone, too faint—close to losing consciousness. I fell sideways, trying to hold onto the tree that had been supporting me, but my flailing arms missed. I was now lying on the forest floor, my breathing short and ragged, with my arms by my side. *Is this how I die?* I wondered. I chuckled quietly, bitterly, as I eased my body to the ground—I hadn't expected my end to come in a forest in the south of France.

Precisely at that moment, my peripheral vision was distracted by something. I blinked, struggling to keep my eyes open, scanning the length of my arm until I reached my right wrist— the numbers on my SwissSecure bracelet had stopped spinning. A series of green digits aligned, just like the previous time, that morning in the hotel room in Paris. The bracelet established a proximity sync, activating my holotab. I could hear his voice before I could see him, my father's voice again.

"Hello, my little seraph. This is not how you die." His words were startling in their prescience. I concentrated, managing to heave my left arm up a little, so that I could now also see the holotab. And at last, my father's image floated before me as I moved my wrist, finally, in front of me. "This message is activated as your vitals, adrenaline and hormone levels show you are suffering from serious physical injury, that you are facing an existential threat. There are those who will seek to capture you, something we've foreseen. By now various vested interests will suspect or know what you can do."

I bit my lip as a sharp, shooting pain ripped across my chest. I needed to somehow hold on.

"Father, I need your help …" My voice came out as a croak.

"These same vested interests may even suspect who you are. It is prophesied that the female offspring arising from the union between one of golden blood and a time seer will be the Mashiach. Your mother and I firmly believe that is you, Lily."

I scrunched up my eyes as my father's words came, in momentary incomprehension. He was talking about the mad woman I had last seen when I was seven. What was he saying? That this woman, my mother, was a time seer, whatever that was?

He continued speaking. "The Mashiach has the potential to end everything, to begin everything. To stop the evil of the Sage. But what you must learn, to reach your potential, you cannot achieve alone. You will need the help of another special one, noble of heart, who will save you. That is also the prophesy. One who is unencumbered by the Mind Chant of the Sage. And you will need something from your mother, to make things possible, a living artefact, a special orb. You must go to her, there's no time to lose. And to do so, you have to let go of the past, how you feel about her, how you felt. She will explain many things."

As the words came out of my father's mouth, despite knowing him to be long dead, his image looked so real, bright, buoyant, lifelike. *Another special one*, I mused. *Does my father mean Kace? He has golden blood too. But where the hell is he? And how can I get to him, get him back?* As the thoughts swirled around my head, my father's words continued.

"One more thing. You face great peril from the Watchers, just as you do from the Sage. But the Watchers are not what you may think. They were once a force for good, protectors. They were turned to evil by the Sage. You can restore them. And in so doing, save this planet from what they might otherwise do. All is not lost. You must lead them back to their own forms. Their somas are cryogenically stored by the Sage, within the Nunciature Evangelion. A forever symbol of his power and a warning to others who might attempt to end his cruel and authoritarian rule."

"You mean the Tower of Songs?" I whispered.

My father's image began fading again. But this time, as tears again fell down my cheeks, I no longer felt anger at him, nor despair. I sensed the injustices I had felt, the wrongs I had believed myself to have endured, as a child, growing up, and later as a young woman, were morphing into a new existential state, one which might even allow me to right all wrongs, everywhere.

And just before my father's face disappeared from my holographic screen, there came those words again. "I love you, Lily." As his face flickered into pellucid nothingness, there was a click from my SwissSecure bracelet. It had self-released, and with just the slightest shake of my wrist it fell onto the forest floor next to me. I turned my head slightly and gazed at it in momentary wonder as it lay still. I felt suddenly naked, yet strangely free, no longer sensing its clasp. My holotab had deactivated, and now I was left with the forest sounds, the buzzing of mosquitoes in the hot afternoon, as I lay motionless on the ground.

Could I really face my mother again? I wondered. I took a deep breath before puffing out my cheeks. I knew I couldn't do it, even for him—to visit her secured in the asylum in Kurilo, in the mountains north of Sofia. I shook the thought away. I had a more pressing problem to attend to.

I summoned my last vestiges of strength and moved my right hand onto my chest, covering the bloody wound. *Can I do it?* I wondered, as I closed my eyes, attempting to locate the reservoir of burned time I stored within me. This I could channel, converting it, through patterns of brain wave activation, into radiant energy that I could use to heal. I groaned again with the effort. I knew I was close to the end, to the nothingness from which there could be no return. And in that moment, Kace's face floated before me, smiling. I knew I still had to find him, I owed him that; after all, his life had been placed in danger because of me. And I sensed, more than ever, that our fates remained entwined. With one final effort, I began healing myself.

I remained where I lay for a quarter of an hour, allowing my body temporary respite, time to recover. I idly wondered whether my pursuers had really just attempted to kill me. Or was their intent just to incapacitate and capture me? I finally attempted to stand, shakily, managing to heave myself upright. I still felt lightheaded. But at least now I could walk. I stepped over the bracelet, leaving it untouched where it had fallen. Without a backward glance, I began moving once more in the direction of the Walk of Kings, and the trail that would lead me up the rocky path toward the cave where my father had been born, the Sainte-Baume Grotto.

Now my Eye was alert again. It directed me high up on the French alpine ridge, toward the brick façade built into the long rocky bar at the head of the Walk of Kings. It was a forty-five-minute hike up the mountainside. I took it slowly, still weak from the loss of blood. It was getting late in the day. Now more pilgrims were descending than ascending. They were wending their way back down to the hostelry for the night. But the feeling of being followed was back, stronger than ever. Despite being protected under my psychic cloak, I glanced behind me, nervously, and ahead, scanning the faces of the pilgrims.

As I approached the top, below the Massif which rose up before me, I paused on the path to scan the face of the sanctuary. The entire place was a designated site of religious protection. And a tourist magnet. A would-be monastery where the four guardian friars posed with tourists for holographic MyPlace upload clicks at twenty e-Continentals a pop. The cynicism of organized religion made me sick.

Near the top there was a holographic sign in Standard European French. It began transmitting to my ear implant through auto-sync. It demanded silence—this was a venerated venue. Pilgrims had walked this path since the fifth century.

Selaphiel tried to talk to me, summoning me, demanding to know what I was doing, what I suspected. But now, I greeted the alien creature with silence. Things, for the first time, both made sense and didn't. Always the paradox of knowledge that led to an understanding of just how little you actually knew. Knowledge made you humble, made me humble. And exasperated, and mad. That too!

I escaped the throng of pilgrims, led by a robed friar in a black cappa and a dirty white habit in a pious tour of the sacred rock, the rock of mercy. I loitered within the inner cave, the holy grotto. Once inside the deep of the chapel within the cliff, I was surprised at how cavernous it was, how it echoed. I touched the wall. Cold, damp. There was nothing left—no resonance nor feeling that my father had ever been here. Wooden pews lined up in rows, in front of an altar. And behind that sat a large shrine, made from white marble, with white stone steps reaching up either side of it, toward the rocky ceiling. I didn't know exactly what I was looking for. But I knew I would recognize it when I saw it.

And there it was. The large etched shape in the cold stone ceiling above the large white shrine; the eyes, partially hidden by a tacky holographic cross that had been placed across it, as if the pastel coloring beneath symbolized nothing. The faint yet unmistakable trace of a watchtower, and at the top, the familiar figure. But it was the eyes, following me, peering out from the ancient stone, that made me freeze. This was the mark of the cult of the Dark Court, the motif of a Watcher, staring out at me from the ceiling. And in the place between the outstretched hands and the high tower, there was a long, narrow crack.

The ceiling was high at this point. I activated my holotab and selected the flashlight app. I held it high above me in my outstretched arm, directing the beam of light at the crack in the ceiling in the center of the stone engraving of the Watcher. The crack was in fact a fissure, splintering along the ceiling. It looked deep, deeper than the one in the catacombs beneath the streets of Paris, proceeding far into the high stone ceiling. I had found it, I knew. My Eye had shown me. Another crossing! A place that connected this universe, the Elyonim, with the other place. This was a second point in spacetime where our universes were connected—where passage through was possible.

There were a few pilgrims still inside the chapel, kneeling before the altar. One glanced at the flashlight I was projecting across the ceiling in bemusement. I was still invisible within my psychic projection. I instantly switched it off to avoid drawing further attention to my location.

And just at that precise moment, the pastel eyes of the Watcher motif began glowing, just like last time, at the crossing ceremony in the temple in Paris. A few seconds later, a distant rumbling started, as if coming from above the ceiling, within the heart of the mountain. The rumbling quickly evolved into a distant banging, deliberate, a reverberating hum that grated. I scrunched up my face. The kneeling pilgrims jumped up in alarm as the distant banging morphed into moments of high-pitched screeching, as if there was a giant with a boring drill inside the Massif, bearing down on us. The sound was like an aural infection, beginning to make me twitchy, inducing a reverberating madness. The pilgrims turned and ran out of the chapel. I dropped my psychic cloak. I no longer needed it inside, and I wanted to better check out the fissure in the ceiling.

But I was distracted by a crashing sound from outside. I turned away from the strange scene within the cave, and headed out to investigate. As I approached the exit, moving back into the baked-in heat of late afternoon sun, I caught a glimpse of a Dominican friar moving across the courtyard outside, in seeming panic. I walked down the stone steps that led out from the grotto into the courtyard, catching sight of the fleeing pilgrims disappearing out of the stone gates in the façade that lined the long bar of rock.

There was another crash to my left. It was a tile, its ceramic remnants scattering in shards on the brick courtyard floor, just a few meters away. I glanced up and noticed that several tiles were now missing from the roof of the sanctuary. It was as if the entire Massif was shuddering in rhythmic explosions.

As I stood in the middle of the courtyard, with the sound of falling tiles bouncing off the brick floor, I felt a sting on one side of my neck. I instinctively touched the spot with my right hand. I felt a tiny dart, which I pulled out. As I examined it, I began to feel lightheaded, nauseous, unable to control my limbs which were turning to jelly. Within a few seconds I could no longer stand, and I slipped to the floor, collapsing on my side. I realized I was paralyzed, defenseless against the mountain above me that was exploding with booms from within, and the falling masonry of the sanctuary around me.

As I lay immobile, I heard the sound of a hover vehicle above me. After a few seconds, I saw its landing gear touch down on the brick of the courtyard a few meters from me. It looked to be a medical transport. But by now my vision was blurry. I tried to summon some quintessence to overcome whatever had done this to me, but the drug had been too fast, and my nervous system was shutting down. I sensed I was close to losing consciousness.

A small vehicle emerged down the ramp and out of the hover transport. It was a daemon, towing a strange-looking glass medical capsule, coffin-shaped, one I'd never seen before. Inside was a mask attached to tubes, a breathing filter, and a small cylinder of oxygen. The capsule was the length of a person, the length of me. And the glass was gold-tinted, which could only mean one thing. The glass coffin capsule was coated with an electromagnetic shield—a glass Faraday cage; I wouldn't be able to use quintessence once inside. I would be powerless!

Behind the daemon and capsule, I saw legs, human legs, following, moving toward me. Two looked male, from their gait and suit pants. Most likely the two agents I'd spotted before, searching for me on the Walk of Kings, and before that at the hostelry. And the third pair of legs was definitely female, tight sky-blue uniform pants.

As the three sets of legs stood in front of my failing eyeline, the woman spoke.

"Get her prepped and stowed. Safety first, you know what she can do. Next stop, Groom Lake, Nevada."

Just as I began lapsing into unconsciousness, I recognized that voice. It was unmistakable, with its hard staccato. It was the voice of the woman who had interviewed me by virtual link in Paris: Colonel Oda Quade, Chief Medical Officer at UFA's Space Force Astrobiology Institute.

EPILOGUE

Ebba Black didn't know how long she had been away, or even where she had been. It had felt like the timeless nothing of dreamless sleep. She couldn't be sure whether it had been moments, months, or even years. As her eyes flicked open, her first stabbing thought was of Emyr. He had taken a bullet for her—Ebba knew the injury was serious. Lilith King had appeared out of thin air again, through a misty doorway, taking his damaged body. Then Lilith and Emyr had vanished back through it, before it disappeared, just like that.

After all the indecision that she hadn't expected, the conflict Ebba hadn't foreseen, she had spared one name on her list of lists. *No good deed goes unpunished*, Ebba thought. She wondered whether she might live to regret it—it would depend on what happened to Emyr. But she had not hesitated with Marc Barron, the name at the very summit of her list—her desire for vengeance ensured he was not spared. Ebba took her shot—and with that she had completed her work, finally.

The very last thing Ebba remembered after pulling the trigger was the dark, misty ghoul lunging forward, about to attack her. That was when pallesthesia overcame her—vibratory sensations emanating from the orb, there once again in her palm, as it synced with her body's own fundamental frequency. And the orb had begun glowing bright red, before actually communicating, speaking to her in a strange tongue she had somehow understood, before the nothingness. Until now.

Ebba blinked as her eyes adjusted. She was in a musty-smelling room, facing a small window with bars on the outside. The small, slit-like window provided the narrowest of vistas. She focused her coal-black eyes, attempting to glean clues to her location from the landscape outside. She saw mountainous countryside in the far distance, dappled in bright sunlight. *This doesn't look like California in late winter*, she thought. And closer, nearer to whatever building she was in, she made out part of an arch of crumbling concrete, apparently an entrance to a dilapidated compound. Over the arch ran metal lettering: Психиатрична болница.

Ebba recognized the letters. They were from the Moesian Cyrillic alphabet, one of the three official scripts of the Grand Union. Her Moesian was patchy. But still, a shock jolted through her as she deciphered the meaning of the words: *Psychiatric hospital*. With a start, Ebba realized she had come out of her trance in a mental asylum. And how was it that she should suddenly find herself in the Union?

Ebba glanced down, touching her body lightly where she stood. She was still clothed in the same attire. She even had her Beretta pistol in her hand, now down by her side, the weapon still warm from being discharged. *So, the trance must have been only momentary*, she thought. Ebba holstered the weapon in her leather shoulder carry.

Just then, she heard a sound, a sniffling. She turned abruptly, unafraid, to face the interior of the darkened room—after all, Ebba Black was almost never afraid. With the light from the small window behind her, the interior was, at first, all shifting murk. Ebba focused, narrowing her eyes. She took in walls made from concrete blocks, flaking paint, a streak of algae growing near the ceiling, an old faded green metal door, rusted edges, with a small metal plated opening in the center. And along one wall, a narrow metal bed, with a thin, bare mattress, and a single sheet; less than enough for the dank chill of the cell.

As Ebba's eyes continued to adjust, she made out a shape sitting on the bed. A woman. She looked old and decrepit. Her hair was long, uncombed, and wispy. She wore a thin, dirty dress—once white. Her legs were bare, the sandals on her feet had broken buckles. As Ebba moved forward, she saw that the woman had wisps of hair on her chin, and vivid green eyes that burned out from her gaunt, creased face.

"Душата на древния инженер," the woman said quietly, looking down, before chuckling. Ebba stared at her, moving closer, shaking her head slightly, trying to understand. She caught the last part. Something about an engineer.

"My Moesian's a bit rusty," Ebba whispered, peering down at the woman. She now saw that the woman was looking at something she was holding in one hand. Ebba had almost missed it. In her open palm, the woman was holding a spherical orb that was spinning. It looked just like the one Lilith had given to Ebba, the very same orb that had materialized in her palm after she had pulled the trigger, as the misty ghoul came at her. Inside the orb was the familiar spiraling shape, glowing in the dim light of the cell; it rotated, part serpent, part bird, pulsating white, then briefly red, and then white once more, languidly transforming back between shapes in a swirl of limpid motion. But now Ebba could no longer hear it, the strange tongue that she had somehow been able to understand.

"The soul of an ancient linguistician, a language engineer, one of the twelve original sages, the vessels of the genesis linguemes," the woman said, now speaking in English with a strange accent. "This Chol is Voynich."

Ebba gasped. "And do you understand the language, Voynichese, too?" The woman glanced up at her, fixing Ebba with her bright green eyes without replying. Ebba glimpsed lettering stitched into the shoulders of what she now realized was a hospital garment. It read: Пламена. "Plamena," Ebba continuing, pronouncing the word carefully in English. "Is that your name?"

The woman smiled faintly. Then she glanced at her other hand, turning it over, as if examining it.

"I got old," the woman whispered in almost a whimper, a moue of wistful sadness flickering across her face. She choked back a half sob. "I only get the lucids when the Chol of Voynich comes … less and less these days. My curse, my undoing of the bond. I was warned …" she continued, glancing at the spinning orb, before back up at Ebba.

"Where am I?" Ebba asked.

That made Plamena laugh, a guttural laugh. "You don't look like one they'd lock up."

Ebba gave an involuntary, dismissive shrug at the woman's response. "Some people would definitely like to see me locked up," she replied snarkily.

Plamena tilted her head slightly. "This is Kurilo."

"Near Sofia?" Ebba asked, startled. *So I am in Moesia*, she thought. "I have no idea how I got here."

"The Chol," Plamena replied. "The ancient soul brought you," before gazing back down at the spinning orb. "You are special. It bound to you. My Chol. You must be its future time seer."

Ebba frowned. She had no idea what the old woman was talking about. "I was just in the Republic of California, a moment ago."

"When?" Plamena asked, now gazing at Ebba with curiosity.

Ebba's shoulders dropped slowly. She studied Plamena carefully—the question was unexpected, but probably astute. The woman might be disheveled, but not deranged as Ebba had first suspected.

"After the language outage …" Ebba began.

The woman stood and tilted her head as she peered into Ebba's eyes to get a better look. Ebba saw that Plamena was unwashed, unkempt. "Which one?" Plamena asked.

"The second one. End of February."

"Well, it isn't February now. It's summer outside. See?" Plamena gestured out of the window.

"Which year is it?" Ebba asked, suddenly startled.

Plamena's eyes glazed over, drifting away. *She probably doesn't know*, Ebba mused. The woman's eyes refocused after a moment, seemingly coming back to the present.

"Time as you understand it doesn't exist inside the void prism," Plamena whispered. "That's why it feels like a moment. When it's been, well …"

"Well, what?" Ebba snapped in irritation.

"Years."

"Years?" Ebba asked with incredulity. "And what do you mean, 'inside the void prism?'"

"The orb exists in different states simultaneously. But here the Chol is bound to me, a fixed point in time. I am the keeper of Voynich. When the orb arrived, a moment ago …" the woman waved with her hand vaguely, through the walls of the cell, "… there was a waveform collapse … your release." Ebba narrowed her eyes as she glanced at the spinning translucence of the orb in the woman's open palm. "I know what you're thinking …" Plamena continued. "How can such a small object be so vast on the inside?"

Ebba smiled, mainly to herself. For one thing, she now knew for certain the woman wasn't deranged. And for another, with the mention of a waveform collapse, Ebba also realized that Plamena was talking about quantum temporal superposition. After all, Ebba knew the theory, just as she knew what Plamena's assertion implied—she had traveled into the future, while somehow located inside the orb. Still, such a proposition seemed far-fetched to say the very least.

Ebba thought for a moment. "Are you seriously suggesting that I've, what, just traveled through time?"

"In this place and time, this Chol and I are twin flames, bound by the rites of the Holy Curia of Kairos," Plamena replied, opaquely.

Ebba could tell she wasn't going to get a straight answer. So, she asked a different question. "Have you seen anyone else here? A tall man, dark, handsome, athletic build?" Plamena shook her head. "What about a woman, bright orange-red hair, bright green eyes ..."

"Like mine?" Plamena asked. Ebba nodded suspiciously. "You must mean Lilith."

Ebba gasped. "You know Lilith?"

Plamena gazed at Ebba for a moment, with a strange look, before replying. "Lilith is my daughter."

Ebba felt her mouth gaping. It took her a moment to regain her composure; Ebba Black almost never lost her composure.

"Is she here? I need to find out where she's taken Emyr ..."

"The void prism brought you to this time for a reason. Released you here. The Chol always knows. Let me see ..."

The woman sat back down on the rickety bed. She closed her eyes and began breathing slowly. The creature inside the orb started pulsing red as it swirled, until it was a continuous red, just like when Ebba had felt the vibrating, when it had appeared in her own palm, as the dark ghoul came at her. After a few moments, the woman came out of her trance-like state. Her eyes flickered open.

"Lilith's life is in danger," she whispered in a cracked voice.

Ebba looked down at the woman thoughtfully. "Lilith told me before the first language outage that I would save her from a prison in Groom Lake, Nevada. But she said that would be in five years' time."

Plamena stroked her chin and grinned. "The first one, the Great Language Outage, *was* five years ago." Ebba blinked at the old woman. "You must go to her, free her, and bring Lilith to me. She needs to be tested. If the ancient soul chooses her, binds to her, then we can be certain she is the one. And without this, the Mashiach cannot begin the path to fulfilling their destiny." The old woman glanced down at the spinning orb in her palm.

As Ebba was wondering where to start with her questions, there was a clanging at the door. The door slowly creaked open, inward, revealing a large service droid standing on the threshold. It immediately began scanning Ebba. A second later, an alarm sounded somewhere out in the corridor. Ebba knew the unit wouldn't be able to identify her. She was a *ghost*, after all—Ebba sneered. She glanced back at Plamena, but the woman had slumped back on the bed; the orb had now disappeared. The woman convulsed slightly, saliva dribbling from one corner of her mouth. The appearance of lucidity, humanity had vanished with the disappearing orb. And now the woman resembled what she apparently was: a patient with a broken mind, confined to a run-down asylum for the insane.

ABOUT THE AUTHOR

Vyvyan Evans is a native of the ancient Roman cathedral city of Chester, in England. He holds a PhD in linguistics from Georgetown University, Washington, DC, and has lived and worked extensively in Asia, Europe, and North America as a Professor of Linguistics, and is a full member of the Science Fiction and Fantasy Writer's Association (SFWA). He has published numerous acclaimed popular science and technical books on language and linguistics. His popular science essays and articles have been featured in publications ranging from *The Guardian* to *Psychology Today*, from the *New York Post* to *New Scientist*, from *Newsweek* to *The New Republic*. His award-winning writing focuses, in one way or another, on the nature of language and mind, the impact of technology on language, and the future of communication. His science fiction work explores the status of language and digital communication technology as potential weapons of mass destruction. For further biographical details, visit his official website: **www.vyvevans.net**. For details of his science fiction writing, visit the Songs of the Sage book series website: **www.songs-of-the-sage.com**.

9 781739 996246